THE
GREATEST MASTERPIECES
OF
RUSSIAN LITERATURE

IVAN S. TURGENEV

THE HUNTING
SKETCHES

Translated from the Russian by
Bernard Guilbert Guerney
with an Introduction by A. B. McMillin

Original Frontispiece by Marek Rudnicki
Original Illustrations by Jocelyne Pache

Distributed by
HERON BOOKS

Published by arrangement with
The New English Library Ltd.

© *1962, Translation, Bernard Guilbert Guerney*
© *1969, Introduction, Edito-Service S.A., Geneva*
© *1969, Illustrations, Edito-Service S.A., Geneva*

marek Rudnicki

INTRODUCTION

Turgenev was born into a rich landowning family on the 28th of October 1818. The estate and household at Spasskoye-Lutovinovo in the Orel province were ruled by Varvara Petrovna Turgeneva, the writer's mother, for his father, a handsome but irresponsible ex-cavalry officer, was content to enjoy a comfortable and superficially cultured life, without the trouble of administration. Varvara Petrovna's rule was one of autocratic terror and despotism, and there can be no doubt that the writer's decision to fight serfdom was in part prompted by the abuses of it he witnessed during his upbringing at home. "Under that title," wrote Turgenev, "I gathered and concentrated everything against which I had resolved to fight until the end. It was my Hannibal's oath, and not I alone took it then. I could not breathe the same air or remain alongside that which I hated ... I had to distance myself from my enemy, the better to attack him from afar. In my eyes this enemy had a definite image and a familiar name : the enemy was serfdom." The Hunting Sketches, *almost all written between 1847 and 1849, during the writer's stay in western Europe, are not, however, a mere political or sociological pamphlet on the peasant problem, but an objective, restrained and beautifully finished picture of country life in all its aspects—a number of the stories have nothing to do with the relationship between serf and master (for example,* A Country Doctor *or* A Prince

Hamlet of the Shchigrov District), *although some of these were not originally intended for the collection, but included later as Turgenev's concept of the work's thematic range expanded. In their detailed and evocative depiction of the different moods of nature, in their stylistically subtle characterisation, and in their apparently inconsequential, but in reality highly skilful constructions, the* Hunting Sketches, *like the later novels, retain their charm and appeal long after the topical problems on which they originally pivoted have subsided. Indeed, in the words of Frank O'Connor, the* Hunting Sketches *"may well be the greatest book of short stories ever written."*

In his memoirs Turgenev recalls the following episode: "On my way to Moscow from the country I went out onto the platform at a small station. Suddenly two young men came up to me—townsmen or factory workers judging by their clothes and their manners. 'Permit me to ask,' said one of them, 'are you Ivan Sergeyevich Turgenev?' 'Yes.' 'The one that wrote Hunting Sketches? *' 'Yes, that is me.' Both doffed their caps, bowing from the waist. 'We bow to you,' said one, 'to betoken the respect and gratitude of all Russian people.' The other bowed silently." This scene underlines the principally social significance of the* Hunting Sketches *for the writer's contemporaries, a mere decade before the abolition of serfdom in 1865. Earlier writers had barely touched on the immense problems inherent in maintaining a medieval system of feudal servitude in the middle of the nineteenth century. Karamzin, writing at the turn of the century, had been moved to exclaim in* Poor Liza, *his sugary tale of stylised seduction, "Even a peasant is capable of love". Twenty years later, Pushkin in* Eugene Onegin *had been chiefly concerned with representatives of his own class, although at one point we gain a brief glimpse of the peasants' lot, when the fruit pickers on the Larins' estate are seen singing—by order, to prevent them from eating the master's fruit. In his story* The Stationmaster, *however, Pushkin departs further from the aristocratic milieu, to portray the existence of a member of the lowest rank of the civil service, and it is this theme, particularly in an urban setting, that was to assume such significance in the later 1830s and 40s with Gogol's* The Overcoat *and* Diary of a Madman *and the young Dostoyevsky's first novel,* Poor Folk. *Country life, on the other hand, had been receiving more attention in western Europe, from writers like Auerbach and George Sand, with whose work Turgener was well familiar, whilst in Russia the indefatigable radical critic Vissarion Belinsky strove to draw attention to the plight of peasants; thus soon after the* Hunting Sketches *had appeared a number of other writers like Herzen, Nekrasov, Grigorovich and Goncharov, began to describe the life of the countryside, with varying degrees of indignation and sympathy for its inhabitants.*

Despite Turgenev's characteristic objectivity and willingness to see positive and negative aspects of both peasants and landowners alike, the Hunting Sketches *when assembled for the first collected edition in 1852 produced a shattering cumulative effect, notwithstanding the emasculation and 'plucking' they had undergone at the censor's hands. The author was promptly given a month's imprisonment, exiled to his estate and placed under police supervision for a year (ostensibly for an inoffensive obituary of Gogol), thus crowning his literary success with political martyrdom and its concomitant fame and popularity; the censor who had passed the book for publication, on the other hand, was relieved of his post by decree of Nicholas I himself, "for carelessness in the execution of his duty." This followed the report of another censor submitted on the 5th of August 1852, at almost exactly the same time as the first copies of* Hunting Sketches *appeared in the shops. It throws interesting lihgt on the atmosphere in which the stories were written: "I feel," reported the censor to the Minister of Popular Enlightenment, "that Mr. Turgenev's book will do more harm than good ... and this is why: Is it useful, for example, to show our literate peasants (and one cannot deny that* Hunting Sketches *like any other book may be read by a literate peasant or other members of the lowest classes) that our freeholders and peasants, whom the author has poeticised to such an extent that he sees in them administrators, rationalists, romantics, idealists, enthusiastic and reflective people (God knows where he found them!), that these peasants are suffering oppression, and that the landowners, whom the author mocks so, representing them as vulgar boors and scatter-*

*brains, behave indecently and illegally, that the rural clergy
lick the landowners' boots, that the district police officers and
other officials accept bribes, or, finally, that a peasant can live
more easily and better in freedom? I do not think that this
can bring any benefit or even pleasure to a right-thinking
reader; on the contrary, such stories leave behind a certain
unpleasant feeling."*

On the other hand, the *Sketches, particularly those that
were distasteful to the authorities, were highly praised by
Belinsky, Herzen and other radical critics of the time. Abroad
too they were appreciated by, amongst others, Lamartine,
George Sand, Daudet, Flaubert, and later Henry James,
whilst in England Dickens published* The Bailiff, Peter
Petrovich Karataev, Lgov *and* The Singers *in his journal*
Household Words, *1855. Nor was their influence on later
writers insignificant: Saltykov-Shchedrin said that* Hunting
Sketches *"inaugurated a new literature devoted to the people
and its needs," whilst in technique the stories with their subtle,
telescoped constructions look forward to Chekhov's non-
narrative, static ' slices of life ' at the end of the century. In
England they were much appreciated by later writers like
Galsworthy and Arnold Bennett, whilst the Irish novelist
George Moore said that his* The Untilled Field *of 1903 owed
its entire inspiration to Turgenev's collection.*

The first story, Khor and Kalinych, *was written at a
time when the author, after some early flops in both poetry
and prose, had almost decided to give up his literary endeavours
entirely. On the eve of departure abroad in 1846 he was
approached by Panayev to provide a story for the newly revived*
Contemporary *journal of which he was editor; the work
he submitted,* Khor and Kalinych, *met with unexpectedly
high praise from both critics and general readers, and in
consequence was, between 1847 and 1851, followed on the pages
of* The Contemporary *by another twenty sketches related by
their common setting of the central Russian countryside and
its inhabitants. Looking back over the* Sketches *as a whole
Belinsky thought the first to have been one of the best, despite
the generalised nature of the ' types ' portrayed—or perhaps
because of it, for the critic, like other radicals of the day,*

always sought to establish general principles from individual phenomena. This story, like all those that followed it, is based on ' real life ' people and events. In this respect it is typical of the author's work as a whole for as he wrote in 1880, "I have endeavoured . . . conscientiously and impartially to depict and embody in suitable types . . . what Shakespeare calls the body and pressure of time." *Or again: "In the last resort a writer's skill consists in his ability to observe closely a phenomenon in life and then afterwards to be able to represent this phenomenon in an artistic form."* In Khor and Kalinych *he is not entirely true to his original models, however, for the prototype of the illiterate Khor could really read and indeed would proudly entertain all his guests by reading the copy of the story which Turgenev had sent him. The change probably stems from the difficulty the author experienced in believing that active, positive people could be literate and thoughtful, or vice versa. He believed men to be divisible into two main types, personified on the one hand by Don Quixote and on the other by Hamlet, and it is this relatively naive division that finds expression in* Khor and Kalinych.

The vast majority of the sketches were written when the author was living abroad, but even in the first story one can observe a tendency to make general and often unfavourable comments on various features of Russian life and the Russian people, rather in the manner of Gogol. In Khor and Kalinych *he says "a Russian is so sure of his strength and fortitude that he sometimes comes near to straining himself: he pays little attention to his past, but gazes fearlessly ahead," but elsewhere his comments, for example on Russian tailoring (in* Ovsyanikov the Freeholder*) or Russian eating habits, are more of a sniping nature, and this, together with his constant sojourning abroad, brought him some accusations of lack of patriotism, accusations that were renewed, notably by Dostoyevsky, after the appearance of his novel* Smoke *in 1867. Turgenev's stay in western Europe, after his initial period of study, was occasioned by a lifelong love for the well-known singer Pauline Viardot, but he was aware that remaining abroad for long periods was dangerous for a writer like himself whose art consisted in reflecting the various movements and trends in*

Russian social and political consciousness; he wrote to his friend the poet Polonsky in 1869; "I understand well that my constant sojourning abroad is harmful to my literary work; so harmful that it may even destroy it." Indeed many readers felt that this process was already completed by that date, but there is no question of this being true of the Hunting Sketches, any more than there is justification for the suggestion of a few critics that Turgenev plagiarised George Sand for these early stories. They are very clearly honest reflections of scenes and personalities fresh in the author's memory; specific both in time (brought out very clearly in many stories, for example Ovsyanikov the Freeholder) and place (the Orel region of central Russia).

In Ermolai and the Miller's Wife we are first introduced to Ermolai, Turgenev's constant hunting companion. As in Khor and Kalinych and, indeed, the majority of the early Sketches, the ' simple ' characters are shown to be more responsible than their masters: Mrs. Zverkova in some ways reflects the writer's mother, whilst Zverkov who accuses Russians of not knowing their own country is revealed as being completely out of touch with reality himself. As elsewhere, notably in Raspberry Spring and Lgov, the human agony attendant upon serfdom emerges from a maze of irrelevance, whilst the narrative elements, slight as they are, are telescoped, and the ending ' thrown away '. Ermolai is based on a real peasant, Afanasy Timofeyevich Alifanov, who accompanied Turgenev on his hunting trips. The writer later secured the serf's freedom for him and employed him as a private servant, after his death doing a great deal for the surviving family. His descendents live in the village of Spasskoye-Lutovinovo to this day.

The next story, A Country Doctor, was spurned by Belinsky who declared it fit only for women and said he could not understand a word of it. His criticism no doubt stems in part from the story's total lack of social comment; similarly, with a later sketch Lebedyan Belinsky criticised the fact that the censorship had found nothing to remove. It comes at a time of increased interest in psychological rather than social problems (as is witnessed by Dostoyevsky's development *from* Poor Folk *to* The Double *and* The Landlady*)*; *the influence of Dostoyevsky may also be found in its somewhat sentimental tone, slightly reminiscent of* Poor Folk, *but it is skilfully written, capturing the rather prosaic doctor's nervous manner and showing how his dull life is briefly illuminated by a single event, which, however, he hardly understands; the story has often been compared to Kafka's* Ein Landarzt *of 1918. Although far from signifying the end of the peasant theme in the cycle,* A Country Doctor *is in fact the first story to step outside this narrow thematic circle and in this respect looks forward to some of the later stories.*

Lgov, *written in Berlin, is more humorous than most of the sketches, with comedy of situation (in the sinking of the boat), gentle irony at the peasant's simplicity (as when the twig carries the punt pole over his head in imitation of the hunters with their guns), and with a mixture of comic and pathetic elements in the landowners' ridiculous demands on the twig, whom they regard as barely human; their utter sefishness is brought out by Turgenev's characteristic device of question and answer, as is their unlimited power, epitomised, perhaps, by the twig's name being changed from Kozma to Anton to suit a pretentious whim of his mistress. Turgenev's humour has been criticised as unmanly, and, indeed, it is true that it is quiet, and generally at someone else's expense (in this collection usually that of the landowners, although in* Lebedyan *it is the author himself who is made to look foolish) ; but if it is usually destructive, it can also be very funny, as in the story* Chertopkhanov and Nedopiuskin *(1849) where Vasilisa Vasilyevna reveals her ridiculous reactionary fears by telling of a dream in which she saw a white figure riding a bear with a sign marked ' Antichrist ' on his breast, or in* Two Landowners *where the Gogolian Chvalynsky reads the* Journal des Débats *only in the presence of visitors.*

Bezhin Mead, *1851, is far removed from the generalised types of* Khor and Kalinych, *portraying as it does individuals in a particular situation; as Henry James, one of the story's greatest admirers, put it, "the terror of human souls alone with Nature and the night." In this story, as in the completely different* Singers, *Turgenev's descriptive art is at its highest, with some excellent similes to depict the beauties of nature, revealing great sensitivity to its infinitely varied colours, sounds, and scents. But at the end, in his laconic announcement of Pavel's death (removed, incidentally, by the censor, as was Kostya's story about the Antichrist) we catch a glimpse of the writer's Hardy-like morbidity, that had taken him to a graveyard in* Lgov, *led him to devote one of the* Sketches *exclusively to the theme of death, and another to an incurable invalid, and which permeated and poisoned the last fruits of his old age, the* Poems in Prose. *In the great novels Rudin, Insarov (*On the Eve*) and Bazarov (*Fathers and Sons*) had all died swift and premature deaths; thus Pavel's end is typical.*

In The Singers *Turgenev shows us how art can enrich the life of all strata of society. His picture is objective, and with a wide range of different characters assembled like a mosaic he shows both the sensitive and responsive aspect of the peasant's character along with its animal, depraved side, revealed in the drunken scene following the competition. In Yakov the Turk's songs, according to Belinsky, there "sounded and breathed a Russian, truth-loving, ardent soul," and in this respect* The Singers, *one of the finest sketches in the collection, was seminal, for the "ardent Russian soul" was later to sing forth with renewed vigor in the works of Mamin-Sibiryak, Korolenko and, above all, Gorky, although nowhere is it so accurately or evocatively described as in Turgenev's sketch.*

In sharp contrast to the simple and natural response to beauty in The Singers, *Tatiana Borisovna and her Nephew satirizes those who hold false, pretentious and vulgar concepts of ' art '. This sketch, which is incidentally much more like an attack on the younger generation than the celebrated portrait of Bazarov in* Fathers and Sons, *is close in subject to his first prose story,* Andrey Kolosov, *of 1844.* A Prince Hamlet of the Shchigrov District, *also looks back to the writer's early work, but also forward to the novels and particularly* Rudin, *for Vasily Vasilyevich is a recognisable type (Turgenev emphasises that "every district contains many such Hamlets") ; he is that characteristically Russian figure the ' superfluous man ', and a cousin of earlier ineffectual and* *disorientated heroes like Onegin, Pechorin and Chatsky. Although much of his life is made to correspond to the writer's own (his study at the universities of Moscow and Berlin, his travels in Italy and membership of philosophical circles, for example) Vasily's moment of self-discovery at the elections links him to some of the most pathetic characters in Russian literature like Gogol's Akaky Akakyevich (*The Greatcoat*) and Poprishchin (*Diary of a Madman*) or Dostoyevsky's Golyadkin (*The Double*). The story, which was in some ways strongly influenced by Belinsky, contains an attack on the Moscow ' circles ' of the 30s and 40s, against which Belinsky, Herzen and Saltykov-Shchedrin had all rebelled by this time; in 1840 Belinsky wrote to Bakunin, "I am heartily glad that this circle no longer exists; the circle in which there was much that was fine, but little that was lasting; in which a handful of people both made each other happy and at the same time tormented each other." In another letter of the following year he developed the theme further: "What is worst of all is that members of these circles alienate themselves from all that is outside their circle." Thus we can see how the* Hunting Sketches *are concerned not only with the evils of serfdom, but also with other current problems;* Kasyan of Fair Springs, *for example, gives a glimpse of one of the many religious sects existing at the time, despite persecution from the Orthodox Church, and* My Neighbour Radilov *echoes an article by Herzen attacking heartless and artificial morality that had appeared in* The Contemporary *slightly earlier: Turgenev, as always, was closely in touch with the ideas of his time.*

Hunting Sketches *may by viewed from many aspects. If one regards it primarily as a cavalcade of characters, then its variety is extraordinarily great: amongst the peasants we see stock types like Khor and Kalinych, with others like the Lone Wolf or Kasyan fully characterised as individuals; some like Ermolai or Akula have retained their simplicity, whilst others like Victor or the inhabitants of the counting house have been corrupted through contact with the landowners' ' civilisation '. Of the landowners many are both stupid and cruel, the worst example being Penochkin in* The Steward; *on the other hand, Karataev and Chertopkhanov have noble although muddled hearts. Parallel to this range of characters runs the broad intellectual and artistic scope of the stories: the earliest of them written in 1847 and 1848 are mostly concerned with Belinsky-inspired ideas on morality and individual rights within the context of serfdom. In the following year, however, the stories are devoted far more to the problems of the gentry (as in* A Hamlet of the Shchigrov District) *and show the author's broadened concept of the nature of the collection as a whole. Three stories added as late as 1871-2 (*The End of Chertopkhanov, Living Relics *and* Rattling Wheels) *extend the thematic bounds still further, and in two cases, provide unaccustomed narrative interest to a series otherwise remarkable for its almost Chekhovian static simplicity. The Epilogue,* Forest and Steppe, *underlines the importance of nature in these stories. In many ways it is superfluous, although extremely beautiful in itself, for few of the stories are without detailed natural settings, sometimes harmonising with the moods and situations of the characters (as in* The Tryst) *and sometimes in direct contrast (as in* Lgov). *Turgenev's pictures of nature, with their acute sensitivity to all its changing moods and seasons, surpass even Pushkin and Tolstoy, and* Bezhin Mead *remains unequalled in the panoply of Russian literature.*

Thus those critics who, perhaps misled by Turgenev's modest manner, regarded the Hunting Sketches *as a mere notebook for later, more mature work were clearly mistaken. The work portrays with consummate artistry a way of life that is now, happily, past, in a setting that is eternal.*

A. B. McMILLIN

London, March, 1969.

CONTENTS

HOR AND KALINYCH

WHOEVER MAY have chanced to make his way from the district of Bolhov to that of Zhizdra has, most probably, been struck by the sharp contrast between the breed of men in the Orlovskaya province and that in the Kaluzhskaya. The Orlov muzhik is of no great stature, is squat, glum; he eyes you from under his brows, lives in wretched little huts of aspen wood, does compulsory labor for his masters, doesn't go in for trading, eats poorly, wears bast sandals. The Kaluzhsk muzhik pays quitrent to his masters, dwells in roomy huts of pine, is tall of stature, eyes you boldly and cheerfully, is clean-shaven and white of face, trades in butter and birch tar and, of Sundays, goes about in boots.

The Orlov village (we're speaking of the eastern part of the Orlovskaya province) is usually situated amid plowed fields, near some gully which has been haphazardly turned into a muddy pond. Outside of a few willows, which are always ready to oblige by growing almost anywhere, and two or three scraggly birches, you won't see as much as a sapling for miles around; hut clings to hut, their roofs strewn, rather than thatched, with fusty straw. The Kaluzhsk village, on the contrary, is in most cases surrounded by woods; the huts have more space around them and stand more uprightly; they are roofed with hewn timbers; the gates shut snugly; the wattle fences toward the back aren't all broken and crawling apart, aren't extending an invitation to

1

every passing swine to drop in and visit awhile. . . . And the hunter, too, is better off in the Kaluzhskaya province. In the Orlovskaya province the last woods and "squares" [1] will disappear in five years or so; as to marshes, there's not as much as a sign of them; in the Kaluzhskaya province, on the contrary, timber stands stretch along for hundreds, and marshes for scores, of miles, and that noble bird, the grouse, has not yet become extinct; the good-natured double snipe is still to be found, and that fussbudget, the hen partridge, delights and startles both hunter and dog by her impetuous take-off.

While visiting the Zhizdra district as a hunter, I met in the field and became acquainted with a certain small Kaluzhsk landowner, Polutykin, a passionate hunter and, consequently, an excellent fellow. True enough, he wasn't free of certain foibles; he courted all the well-to-do marriageable misses in the province, for instance, and, after his hand had been rejected and further entry into the house forbidden him, he would brokenheartedly confide his woes to all his friends and acquaintances; as to the parents of the marriageable misses, he kept on sending them gifts of sour apricots and other produce of his orchard; he was fond of repeating the same funny story which, despite all the high regard which its narrator had for its good points, never made anyone laugh; he praised the works of Akim Nahimov [2] and the novel *Pinna;* was a stutterer, called his dog Astronomer, used to say "how'msoever" instead of "however," and had introduced the French cuisine into his household, the secret of which cuisine, insofar as his cook understood it, consisted of a complete transmogrification of the natural taste of each viand: meat at the hands of this artificer smacked of fish, fish of mushrooms, macaroni of gunpowder; but, to make up for that, not the smallest carrot found its way into the soup without taking on the form of a rhomboid or a trapezium. With the exception of these few and insignificant shortcomings, however, Polutykin was, as we've already said, an excellent fellow.

---

[1] The name given in the Orlovskaya province to great tracts grown over with nothing but brushwood. The Orlov dialect is, in general, distinguished by a multiplicity of words and turns of speech peculiar unto itself, at times rather apt, at times quite hideous.—*Author.*

[2] Satirist, 1782–1815.—*Trans.*

On the very first day of my acquaintance with him he invited me to stay the night at his house.

"It's about three miles to my place," he added; "too far to walk. Let's drop in on Hor first." (With the reader's permission, I will omit his stuttering.)

"And who may Hor be?"

"Why, one of my muzhiks. He lives no distance at all from here."

We set out for Hor's. His lonely farmstead, consisting of several fenced-in buildings of rough-hewn pine logs, rose before us on a cleared and cultivated glade in the midst of the forest; an overhang, supported by the slenderest of posts, ran the whole length of the main hut, which we entered. We were met by a young fellow of about twenty, tall and good-looking.

"Ah, Fedya! Hor home?" Polutykin asked him.

"No. Hor's gone off to town," answered the lad, smiling and showing teeth as white as snow. "Did you want to order a cart readied for you?"

"Yes, brother; let's have a cart. And bring us some bread-cider."

There wasn't a single one of the usual crude woodcuts stuck on the clean log walls; in one corner, before a ponderous holy image framed and trimmed with silver, a lampad glowed warmly; the table of lindenwood had been recently scraped and washed; in the chinks between the logs and over the jambs of the windows there were no spirited cockroaches roaming, no pensive blackbeetles lurking. The lad reappeared shortly bearing an enormous slice of wheaten bread, a dozen dill-pickled cucumbers in a wooden bowl, and a big white mug brimming with excellent bread-cider. He put all this provender on the table, leaned against the door, and fell to observing us with a smile. We hadn't had time to finish our snack when we heard a cart clattering up to the front steps.

We went out. A boy of fifteen, curly-headed and red-cheeked, was in the driver's seat and having a hard time reining in a well-fed piebald stallion. A half-dozen young giants, looking very much like one another and like Fedya, were standing about the cart.

"Hor's children, all of them!" remarked Polutykin.

"Little polecats, all of them!" Fedya chimed in, punning on the family name, as he followed us out on the porch.

"But those aren't all of them, by any means: Potap is in the forest, and Sidor's gone off to town with the old man. Watch out, now, Vassya," he turned to the driver, "get there like greased lightning—it's the master you're driving. Only, when there's any bumps, you watch out and go easy; you'll both damage the cart and upset the master's stomach if you don't."

The other young Hors smiled slyly over Fedya's sally.

"Get Astronomer up here!" Polutykin called out solemnly. Fedya, not without pleasure, lifted up in the air the constrainedly grinning dog and placed it on the floorboards of the cart. Vassya loosed the reins as a signal to the horse. We rolled away.

"And there's my office," Polutykin said to me suddenly, indicating a squat little house. "Would you care to drop in?"

"If you like."

"It's done away with now," he remarked, getting off the cart, "but it's still worth a look."

The office consisted of two empty rooms. The watchman, a one-eyed old man, came running from the back yard.

"Greetings, Minyaich," Polutykin let drop. "Where's the water, though?"

The one-eyed old man vanished and immediately reappeared with a carafe of water and two tumblers.

"Try it," said Polutykin to me. "Very good water, from a spring of mine."

We drank off a tumbler each, the old man bowing low before us all the while.

"Well, I think we can go now," my new friend remarked. "I sold eleven acres of timber at a good price to Halleluiev the trader, right in this office."

We got into the cart, and no more than half an hour later we were driving into the courtyard of his manor house.

"Tell me, please," I asked Polutykin at supper, "why do you have Hor living apart from your other muzhiks?"

"Well, it's this way: that's an intelligent muzhik I've got. About twenty-five years ago his hut burned down, so he came to my late father and told him: 'Let me settle in your forest, now, Nicholai Kuzmich—out on the marsh. I'll be paying you a good quitrent.' — 'But why should you settle on that marsh?' — 'Well, there's no particular reason; the only thing is, Nicholai Kuzmich, father of mine, don't be setting me to any work any more, if it please you, but name

4

whatever quitrent you know is best.' — 'Fifty rubles a year!'
— 'By all means!' — 'Watch out, though—don't you ever fail
to pay me, and don't fall back in your payments.' — 'That's
understood—I won't fail.' And so he settled on that marsh.
And it was from then on that they nicknamed him Pole-
cat."

"Well, and did he grow rich?" I asked.

"He did. Now he pays me a hundred silver rubles yearly
as quitrent—and I may raise that, likely as not. I've already
told him, more than once: 'Buy your freedom, Hor—buy
your freedom, I'm telling you!' But, cunning animal that he
is, he assures me he hasn't the wherewithal; he hasn't any
money, now. A likely story, that!"

Next day, immediately after morning tea, we again set out
hunting. As we were passing through the village Polutykin
ordered the driver to stop at a squat little hut and called out
sonorously:

"Kalinych!"

"Right away, father of mine, right away!" a voice came
from the yard. "I'm just tying on a sandal."

We rode off at a walk; beyond the village a man of about
forty, tall, thin, with a small head tilted backward, caught
up with us. This was Kalinych. His good-natured, swarthy
face, pockmarked in spots, proved to my liking at first sight.
Kalinych (as I found out later) went out hunting with his
master every day, carrying the latter's gamebag and, at times,
his gun as well, noting where the birds alighted, procuring
water, gathering strawberries, putting up tepeelike shelters
of branches, trotting after the droshky—Polutykin could
not take a step without him. Kalinych was a man of the
merriest, the meekest nature; he hummed incessantly, kept
glancing on every side of him in a carefree way, spoke somewhat through his nose, puckered up his light-blue eyes when
he smiled, and frequently put his hand up to his scanty,
wedge-shaped beard. His walk was unhurried, but he took
big steps, leaning a trifle on a long and slender stick.

During the course of the day he got into talk with me
more than once, waiting on me without servility; when it
came to his master, however, he kept an eye on him as if
the latter were a baby. When the unbearable noonday sultriness compelled us to seek shelter he led us to his beehives,
in the very heart of the forest. He opened for us his tiny hut,
which was hung about with bundles of dry, fragrant herbs,

bedded us on fresh hay, and putting over his head a sort of
a bag with netting, took a knife, a pot, and a firebrand and
set out for his beehives, to cut a honeycomb for us. We ate
the transparent warm honey, chasing it down with water
out of a wellspring, and dozed off to the monotonous buzzing of the bees and the gossipy babble of the leaves.

The light gust of a breeze awakened me. I opened my
eyes and caught sight of Kalinych; he was sitting on the
threshold of the half-open door and whittling out a spoon
with his jackknife. For a long while I admired his face,
benign and serene as the sky at evening. Polutykin had also
awakened. We did not get up immediately. It is a pleasant
thing, after walking long and sleeping soundly, to lie motionless in the hay: the body luxuriates and lazes, the face
gives off a light heat, a delectable indolence closes one's
eyes. We did get up at last and went off rambling again
until evening.

At supper I once more spoke of Hor and Kalinych.

"Kalinych is a good muzhik," Polutykin told me. "A zealous muzhik and obliging; however, he can't attend to his
husbandry properly—I'm always dragging him away. He
goes hunting with me daily. Judge for yourself, then, what
husbandry there can be under those circumstances."

I agreed with him, and we went off to bed.

The next day Polutykin had to go to town, about a suit
against one Pichukov, a neighbor of his. Neighbor Pichukov had plowed some land that was rightly Polutykin's and,
on top of that, had, on this very land, given a flogging to
one of Polutykin's female serfs. I rode off to hunt by myself, and toward evening turned in at Hor's. I was met at
the threshold of the hut by an old man, bald-headed, of low
stature, broad-shouldered, and robust—it was Hor himself.
I regarded this Hor with curiosity. The mold of his face reminded one of Socrates': the same high knobby forehead, the
same tiny eyes, the same snub nose. We entered the hut
together. It was Fedya again who brought me milk and black
bread. Hor perched on a bench and, stroking his beard with
the utmost equanimity, entered into talk with me. He had a
sense of his own dignity, apparently, moving and speaking
slowly, smiling at rare intervals from under his long mustache.

We discussed the sowing, the crops, the peasant's way of
life. He seemed to agree with me in everything; however,

later on I grew ashamed of myself and I felt I wasn't saying the right thing. Hor at times expressed himself in a roundabout way, probably out of cautiousness. Here is a short specimen for you of our conversation:

"Listen, Hor," I told him, "why don't you buy your freedom from your master?"

"And why should I? Now I know who my master is, and I know what quitrent I have to pay over to him. We've got a good master."

"Still, things are better when a man is free."

He gave me a sidelong look: "Everybody knows that," he let drop.

"Well, then, why aren't you buying your freedom?"

Hor twisted his head a little: "What would you have me buy it with, father of mine?"

"Come, now, old-timer—"

"Let Hor find himself amongst free folk," he went on in a low voice, as though he were talking to himself, "and whoever goes about beardless will be lording it over Hor."

"Why, you just shave off your own beard."

"What does a beard amount to? A beard is the same as grass: you can mow it."

"Well, what is it, then?"

"Why, I guess Hor will land right amongst the merchants; merchants live well, now, and they, too, stick to beards."

"Come, now, you do a little trading yourself, I guess?"

"We do trade a little, now—a trifle in oil and a bit in pitch. What do you say, father of mine—do you want to order your cart?"

"You've got a tight grip on your tongue and are a man who knows his mind," I reflected. "No," I said aloud, "I don't need the cart; I'll be tramping around your homestead tomorrow and, if you'll let me, will stay the night here in your hay barn."

"You're right welcome. But will you find it restful in the barn? I'll order the womenfolk to spread a sheet and put down a pillow for you. Hey, there, you women!" he called out, getting up. "Come here, you! As for you, Fedya, you go along with them—for women, you know, are foolish folk."

A quarter of an hour later Fedya, carrying a lantern, conducted me to the barn. I threw myself on the fragrant hay;

the dog curled up at my feet; Fedya wished me good night; the door creaked and slammed to.

For a rather long time I couldn't fall asleep. A cow ambled up to the door and breathed noisily a couple of times, while my dog growled at it in a dignified sort of a way; a pig went by, grunting pensively; a horse somewhere nearby took to champing hay and snorting. . . . At last I dozed off.

At dawn Fedya awakened me. This cheerful, lively lad proved very much to my liking and, insofar as I could notice, he was a favorite of old Hor's as well. They made fun of each other quite amiably. The old man came out to greet me. It may have been because I had passed the night under his shelter or for some other reason, but Hor treated me considerably more cordially than he had the day before.

"Your samovar is ready," he told me with a smile. "Let's go in and have tea."

We seated ourselves at the table. A husky country wife, one of his daughters-in-law, brought in a jug of milk. One by one, all his sons were coming into the hut.

"What a well-grown tribe you've got!" I remarked to the old man.

"Yes," he let drop, biting a microscopic piece off a lump of sugar, "they got nothing to complain of as far as I and my old woman are concerned, it looks like."

"And are all of them living with you?"

"All of them. That's the way they want things, so they live here."

"And are all of them married?"

"There, that one scalawag over there doesn't want to get married," he answered, indicating Fedya who, after his wont, was leaning against the doorway. "Vasska, now, is still young; he can wait a while."

"What should I be getting married for?" countered Fedya. "I find life good enough as it is. What do I need a wife for? To be squabbling with her, or what?"

"Oh, you . . . oh, I'm on to you! You're wearing silver rings; all you're after is to be sniffing around the house wenches all the time. 'That'll do you, you shameless creatures!' " the old man went on, mimicking the chambermaids. "Oh, I'm on to you, you lily-handed good-for-nothing!"

"And what's so good about a woman, now?"

"A woman is a worker," Hor remarked pompously. "A woman is a man's servant."

"But what would I be needing a worker for?"

"That's just it—you like to have others pulling your chestnuts out of the fire. I'm on to you and your kind."

"Well, marry me off, if that's the case. Eh? What? Why aren't you saying anything?"

"There, that'll do, that'll do, you tomfool. See, you're disturbing the master. I'll marry you off, never fear. And as for you, father of mine, don't you be angry: he's just a little child, you see—hasn't got any sense into him yet."

Fedya shook his head.

"Is Hor home?" a familiar voice sounded beyond the door, and Kalinych entered the hut with a handful of wild strawberries which he had picked for his friend Hor. The old man greeted the visitor heartily. I glanced at Kalinych in astonishment: I confess I hadn't expected such "tendernesses" from a peasant.

That day I set out to hunt four hours later than usual, and I spent the next three days as well at Hor's place. My new acquaintances engrossed me. I didn't know whereby I had merited their confidence, but they conversed with me without constraint. I listened to and observed them with pleasure. The two friends did not resemble each other in the least. Hor was a sedate person, practical, with a head for administration, a rationalist; Kalinych, on the contrary, belonged to the category of idealists, romantics, and people who are exalted and enraptured. Hor had a grasp of reality —that is, he had built him a snug nest, had saved up a bit of capital, got along with his master and others in power; Kalinych walked about in bast sandals and lived from hand to mouth. Hor had brought forth a large family, submissive and unanimous; Kalinych, on a time, had had a wife, whom he had feared—as for children, he had never had any. Hor could see right through Polutykin; Kalinych was full of reverent awe before his master. Hor loved Kalinych and patronized him; Kalinych loved and respected Hor. Hor spoke but little, smiled slyly, and figured things out in his own head; Kalinych explained things with warmth, even though he hadn't the voice of a nightingale, like one of your lively factory hands. But Kalinych was endowed with pre-eminent advantages which Hor himself acknowledged—he could, for instance, cast spells to stop the flow of blood, or against fright, or against frenzy; he could drive out worms, he had a way with bees, his hand had a light touch. Hor, in my

9

presence, asked him to lead into the stable a newly bought horse, and Kalinych with conscientious gravity carried out the old skeptic's request.

Kalinych was closer to nature but Hor was closer to people, to society; Kalinych did not like to rationalize and believed everything blindly; Hor rose to an actually ironic point of view on life. He saw much, he knew much, and I learned much from him. For instance, I learned from his stories that every summer, before mowing time, a small cart of a peculiar variety makes its appearance in the villages. A man in a caftan sits in this cart and sells scythes. If he sells for cash he takes for each scythe a ruble and twenty-five kopecks in silver and a ruble and a half in paper money; if on credit, for three rubles in paper and one in silver. All the muzhiks buy from him on credit, naturally. In two or three weeks the stranger appears again and demands his money. The muzhik has just reaped his oats and, consequently, has the wherewithal to pay; he and the trader betake themselves to the pothouse and only there do they settle up. Certain landowners struck on the notion of buying the scythes themselves for cash and distributing them to the muzhiks on credit at the same price, but the muzhiks turned out to be dissatisfied and even fell into low spirits: they were being deprived of the pleasure of twanging the scythe blade, of listening to its ring, of turning it in their hands this way and that and asking the knavish city trader twenty times in a row: "Well, now, young feller, ain't this scythe much too much sort of that way, you know?"

The same sort of goings on take place at the buying of sickles as well, with the sole difference that here the womenfolk put their oar in too, and occasionally make it necessary for the trader himself to give them a drubbing—solely for their own good, of course.

But it is on an occasion such as the following that the womenfolk suffer most of all. The suppliers of material for paper mills entrust the buying up of rags to a peculiar breed of men who in certain districts are called "eagles." An eagle of that sort will receive two hundred rubles in paper money from a trader and then set out hunting. But, in contrast to the noble bird from which he has gotten his name, he doesn't attack openly and boldly; on the contrary, such an eagle resorts to subterfuge and cunning. He'll leave his small cart somewhere in the bushes near a village, while he himself sets out through the back yards and back lots, like some way-farer, or simply like some idle fellow at a loose end. The womenfolk sense his approach through instinct and steal out to meet him. The deal is consummated in a hurry. For a few coppers the country wife will give away to the eagle not only all sorts of unneeded rags but often even her husband's shirt and her own wraparound skirt. Latterly the womenfolk have found it profitable to steal from themselves and to get rid in this manner of hemp, and particularly beaten flax; an important branching out and perfecting of the eagles' enterprise! But then the muzhiks, in their turn, have become sharp and, at the least suspicion, at a mere remote rumor, of the appearance of an eagle, quickly and briskly undertake corrective and preventive measures. And, truly, isn't it rather humiliating? Selling hemp is their business, and sell it they do, sure enough—not in town, however (they would have to drag themselves there for that), but to traveling traders who, for lack of a steelyard, reckon thirty-six pounds at forty handfuls—and you know what a handful and what a palm a Russian has, especially when he really puts his heart into a thing!

Of such stories I, a man inexperienced and not truly "countrified" (as we say in Orel), had heard plenty. Hor, however, wasn't telling stories all the time; he himself questioned me concerning many things. He had found out that I had been abroad, and his curiosity flared up. Kalinych did not lag behind him, but Kalinych was for the most part touched by descriptions of waterfalls, unusual structures, great cities; Hor was concerned with problems of administration and government. He took everything in order. "Well, now, are things the same with them there as they are with us here, or are they different? Well, speak up, father of mine—just what's what?" — "So! Oh, Lord, Thy will be done!" Kalinych would exclaim during my story; Hor kept silent, knitting his bushy brows, and only at rare intervals would he remark: "That, now, wouldn't go so well with us; but that other thing is fine—that's the way it should be."

I can't transmit all his questionings to you, nor would there be any point in doing so; but from my talks with him I did derive one conviction which, probably, my readers will find utterly unexpected: the conviction that Peter the Great was, pre-eminently, a man of Russia, Russian in his reforms. The man of Russia is so certain of his strength and stal-

11

wartness that he isn't averse even to breaking himself: he is but little taken up with his past and boldly looks ahead. Whatever is good, that's what he likes; whatever is sensible, that's the very thing you may offer him, but whence it comes is all one to him. His horse-sense will twit with a relish the gaunt rationale of the German; but the Germans themselves are, to quote Hor, a curious little folk, and he is ready to learn a thing or two from them. Thanks to the exceptional nature of his position, his factual independence, Hor spoke with me of much that one wouldn't have been able to pry out of another with a crowbar nor grind out with a millstone, as the muzhiks put it.

He had a real understanding of his position. As he discussed things with Kalinych, I for the first time heard the simple, intelligent speech of a Russian peasant. His stores of knowledge were, in their way, sufficiently extensive, yet he could not read; Kalinych, however, could.

"Reading and writing came easily to that loafer," Hor remarked. "He's never had any bees dying on him, either, in all his born days."

"And have you taught your children how to read and write?"

Hor was silent a while. "Fedya knows how."

"But what about the others?"

"The others don't know."

"How come?"

The old man made no answer to that and changed the conversation.

However, for all his intelligence, he too had many prejudices and preconceptions in him. He despised women, for instance, from the bottom of his heart, and in a merry mood would find amusement in them and jeer at them. His wife, old and snarlingly quarrelsome, would not come down from her ledge atop the oven all day long and was incessantly grumbling and scolding; her sons paid no attention to her, but she had put the fear of God into her daughters-in-law. It's not for nothing that in a certain Russian song the mother-in-law sings: "What sort of a son are you to me—what sort of a family man? You don't beat your wife—you don't beat the young thing!"

On one occasion I got the notion of interceding for the daughters-in-law, making an attempt to arouse Hor's compassion, but he calmly retorted to me: "What fun do you find in bothering with such . . . trifles? Let the woman creatures quarrel. The more you try to separate them, the worse it is; it's not worthwhile soiling your hands, even."

Now and then the vile-tempered crone would clamber down from her ledge and call to the watchdog to come to her out of the entry, coaxing it with: "Come here, come here, little doggie!"—and then belabor its gaunt back with a poker; or she'd take her place under an overhang and "yap," as Hor put it, at all the passersby. She was afraid of her husband, though, and at his order would get back atop her oven ledge.

It was particularly odd, however, to listen to Kalinych disputing with Hor when matters came to Polutykin.

"There, now, Hor," Kalinych would say. "Don't you pick on him before me."

"But why don't he have a pair of boots made for you?" the other would retort.

"Oh, boots! What would I be needing boots for? I'm a muzhik—"

"Well, now, I'm a muzhik too, but just take a look at that—" and Hor would lift up his foot and show a boot that most probably had been sewn out of a mammoth's hide.

"Eh! But then, are you one of us?" Kalinych said by way of an answer.

"Well, he might at least give you enough for bast sandals, for you go hunting with him—you use up a pair a day, I guess."

"He does give me money for sandals."

"Yes, last year he broke his heart and gave you all of a ten-kopeck piece."

Kalinych would turn away in vexation, while Hor went off into peals of laughter, during which his tiny eyes vanished altogether.

Kalinych sang rather pleasantly and played the balalaika a little. Hor would listen and listen, then suddenly twist his head to one side and start chiming in in a piteous voice. He was especially fond of the song "Oh thou my lot, my lot!"

Fedya did not let the chance slip of twitting his father: "What makes you feel so blue, old man?"

But Hor would prop up his cheek with his hand, close his eyes, and keep right on complaining about his lot.

On the other hand, there were times when there wasn't a man more active than he: he was forever fussing over something—repairing a cart, propping up a fence, looking over harness. He did not, however, maintain any particular cleanliness, and on one occasion answered my criticism with:

"A hut, now, ought to smell like it was lived in."

"Just see," I contradicted him, "how clean Kalinych keeps his beehives."

"The bees wouldn't live in them otherwise, father of mine," answered he with a sigh.

"Well, now," he asked me another time, "have you got an estate of your own?"

"I have."

"Far from here?"

"Sixty-five miles or thereabouts."

"Well now, father of mine, do you live on your estate?"

"I do."

"But, for the most part, I guess, you fritter your time away with your gun?"

"That's so, I confess."

"And you're doing right, father of mine; shoot grouse to your heart's content, and change your stewards as often as you can."

Four days later, in the evening, Polutykin sent for me. I felt sorry about parting with old Hor. I took my seat in the cart with Kalinych.

"Well, goodbye, Hor—and good health to you," said I. "Goodbye, Fedya."

"Goodbye, father of mine, goodbye—don't forget us."

We started off; the dawn glow was just bursting into flame.

"It'll be glorious weather tomorrow," I remarked, gazing at the radiant sky.

"No, it's going to rain," Kalinych contradicted me. "The ducks are plashing about, now, and the grass smell is far too strong."

We rode in among the scrubwood. Kalinych launched into a low-voiced song, bouncing on the box, and kept gazing at the dawn glow, gazing at it all the time. . . .

The next day I left Polutykin's hospitable roof.

ERMOLAI AND THE MILLER'S WIFE

IN THE EVENING Ermolai the hunter and I set out for a "night stand". . . . It's quite possible, however, that not all my readers know what a night stand is. Therefore hearken, gentlemen.

A quarter of an hour before the setting of the sun, in the spring, you enter a grove with a gun but without a dog. You seek out a spot for yourself somewhere near the edge of the woods, look about you, examine the percussion cap of your gun, and exchange winks with your companion. The quarter of an hour has passed. The sun has set, but it's still light in the forest, the air is pure and clear, the birds are chattering away at a great rate, the young grass gleams with the joyous gleam of an emerald. You wait. The inner recesses of the forest grow darker by degrees; the ruby light of the evening glow glides slowly over the roots and trunks of the trees, rises higher, passes from the lower branches, as yet almost bare, to the motionless treetops that are now falling into slumber. See, the treetops themselves have grown dim; the rosy-cheeked sky is turning to indigo. The forest smell becomes stronger; there is a slight breath of warm dampness; the wind that had burst in so near to you dies away. The birds are falling asleep—not all of them at the same time, but each according to its kind: there, the chaf-finches have fallen quiet; a few moments later the hedge sparrows do so; the siskins follow suit. It is growing darker in the forest, ever darker. The trees blend into great, dark-ling masses; the first tiny stars emerge timorously in the indigo sky. All the birds are asleep. Only the redstarts and certain tiny woodpeckers keep whistling from time to time, drowsily. Finally they, too, have fallen quiet. One more time the sonorous voice of the pewit rang out overhead; a yellow thrush sadly sounded its call somewhere; a nightingale sent out its first choppy note.

Your heart is languishing in expectancy, and suddenly—but it is only hunters who will understand me—suddenly in the deep quiet there resounds a peculiar sort of cawing and hissing, you hear the measured upsweep of agile wings, and a woodcock, its long nose gracefully tilted downward, flies smoothly out from behind a dark birch to encounter your shot.

There, that's what a "night stand" means.

And so, Ermolai and myself set out for a night stand—but, gentlemen, I crave your indulgence: I must first acquaint you with Ermolai.

Imagine a man of five and forty, tall, gaunt, with a long and thin nose, a narrow forehead, small gray eyes, hair all rumpled, and wide, mocking lips. This fellow walked about both winter and summer in a yellowish nankeen overcoat of a German cut, yet girded himself with a coachman's broad belt of leather; he wore blue Ukrainian trousers, so wide that they ballooned above his boot tops, and a karakul cap that had been presented to him in a lighthearted moment by a ruined landowner. He usually had two bags tied onto his belt: one in front, artfully twisted into two parts, one for gunpowder, the other for bird shot; the second bag, hanging behind, was for game; as for wadding, Ermolai always took it out of his seemingly inexhaustible cap. He could have easily bought himself a cartridge case and a gamebag for the money he made selling game, but the idea of making any such purchase did not once enter his head; and he went on loading his gun as he had always done, arousing amazement in all beholders by the art with which he avoided the risk of spilling shot and powder, or mixing the two. His gun was single-barreled, with a flintlock, endowed, furthermore, with an execrable habit of kicking, because of which Ermolai's right cheek was always plumper than his left. How he ever hit anything with that gun of his was something to stump even the cleverest man, yet hit the mark he did. He also had a setter by the name of Valetka—a most astonishing creature. Ermolai never fed it.

"I'm not going to bother feeding no hound," he argued. "Besides, a hound is a smart animal; it'll find what to eat for itself."

And, actually, although Valetka's exceeding gauntness struck even the indifferent passerby, he went on living just the same, and that for a long time and, despite his miserable situation, he never disappeared and evinced no desire to forsake his master. Only once, in the days of his youth, infatuated by love, had the hound happened to absent himself for a day or two, but this foolishness had soon left him.

Valetka's most remarkable peculiarity was his inconceivable indifference to everything in the world (if I were not talking about a dog, I would use the word "disillusionment"). He usually squatted with his stub of a tail tucked in under him, frowning, shuddering from time to time, and never smiled. (It's a known fact that dogs are capable of smiling, and even of smiling most charmingly.) He was extremely hideous, and there was never an idle house serf who let slip the chance of jeering venomously at Valetka's looks; all these jeers, however, and even blows, he bore with amazing *sang-froid*. He afforded special satisfaction to cooks, who would instantly drop their work and, shouting and cursing, go for him whenever he, through a frailty not confined solely to dogs, thrust his starving snout within the half-open door of the kitchen, temptingly warm and full of heavenly smells.

When it came to hunting he was distinguished for his indefatigability and had a passable scent; however, if he chanced to catch up with a wounded rabbit he lost no time in devouring it with gusto, down to the smallest bone, somewhere in the cool shade under a green bush, at a respectable distance from Ermolai, who would be cursing him in all dialects, both known and unknown.

Ermolai belonged to one of my neighbors, a landowner of the old school. Landowners of the old school aren't fond of snipe and stick to domestic fowl. Only on extraordinary occasions, such as births, birthdays, and elections, will the cooks of the landowners of the old school tackle the preparation of these long-beaked birds and, becoming imbued with that fervor peculiar to the Russian when he hasn't the foggiest notion of what he's about, they think up such complicated fixings for the birds that the guests for the most part scrutinize the proffered viands with curiosity and great interest but can't, somehow, bring themselves to partake thereof.

Ermolai was under orders to supply his master's kitchen monthly with two brace each of grouse and partridge but, on the whole, he was permitted to live where and how he liked. He had been rejected as a man unfit for any work, as "no account." Naturally, they didn't issue any gunpowder or bird shot to him, in keeping with the same principles on the strength of which he himself didn't feed his dog. Ermolai was a fellow of the oddest sort: as carefree as a bird, rather talkative, with an air of absent-mindedness and awkwardness, very fond of the bottle; he couldn't live too long in any one spot; he shuffled and waddled as he walked—and, shuffling and waddling, would put five and thirty miles behind him in a day. He went through the most diverse adventures: sleeping in swamps, up in the trees, on roofs, under bridges; more than once had he been locked up in attics, cellars, and barns, deprived of his gun, his dog, his most necessary garments; on occasion he had been beaten up, severely and protractedly—and, notwithstanding, after a time he'd come back home fully clothed, with his gun and his dog.

You couldn't call him a merry fellow, although he was almost always in fairly good spirits; on the whole he looked like a queer stick. Ermolai was fond of chinning a while with any good fellow, especially over a noggin—but not even that for long; he'd get up and be off.

"But where are you going, you devil? It's night out!"

"Why, I'm bound for Chaplino."

"And what would you be dragging yourself to Chaplino for? It's all of seven mile away—"

"Oh, I'm going to spend the night at a certain muzhik's place—Saphron, they call him."

"Come, spend the night here."

"No, I just can't."

And Ermolai was off with his Valetka, going out into the dark night, through bushes and washouts, yet, like as not, that little muzhik Saphron won't let him on to his place, even, and all the chances were he'd let Ermolai have it right in the neck: "Don't go 'round bothering honest folks, now!"

But then, no one could compare with Ermolai in the art of catching fish in the springtime, when the waters are at their highest, of getting crayfish out with his bare hands, of scenting out game, of luring quail, of training hawks, of snaring nightingales gifted with the "wood-sprite pipe," with the "cuckoo flight." [1] There was only one thing he didn't know how to do: train dogs. He hadn't patience enough for that.

He had a wife, too. He visited her once a week. She lived in a wretched, half-ruined little hut, getting along from hand to mouth, never knowing at night whether she would find food on the morrow and, in general, had to put up with a bitter lot. Ermolai, that carefree and good-natured man, treated her cruelly and roughly, assuming an awesome and harsh air in his house, and his poor wife knew not how she might please him, trembling at his mere look, buying liquor for him with her last coppers, and fawningly covering him with her own sheepskin coat when he, majestically sprawled out on the ledge atop the oven, would fall into titanic slumber. I myself had occasion to note, more than once, involuntary manifestations of a certain grim ferocity in him: I did not at all like the expression on his face whenever he finished off a wounded bird by biting through its throat.

However, Ermolai never remained home for more than a day, and when away from it he again became transformed into Ermolka, so nicknamed for threescore miles around, and as he at times called himself. The lowliest of house serfs felt himself superior to this vagabond—and for that very reason, perhaps, treated him amiably; as for the muzhiks, they at first took pleasure in cornering and catching him like a rabbit in a field, but later on they'd let him go with God's blessing and, having once learned what a queer stick he was, no longer harried him, even giving him bread and entering into conversation with him.

It was this very fellow whom I had taken on as my hunter, and it was with him that I set out for the night stand in the big grove of birches on the bank of the Ista.

Many Russian rivers have a resemblance to the Volga, in that they have one bank mountainous and the other meadowy; the Ista is like that, too. This small river winds along with exceeding whimsicality; it coils along like a snake, it

[1] Admirers of the nightingale are familiar with these designations: they denote the best passages in the bird's song.—*Author.*

won't flow straight for even a third of a mile, and there are spots, such as the top of a steep knoll, from which one can see a seven-mile stretch of this river with its dams, mill-ponds, mills, truck patches surrounded by clumps of willows and luxuriant gardens. There's no end of fish in the Ista, especially bullheads (when the heat is at its worst, the mu-zhiks take them with their bare hands from around the underwater roots of the bushes). The tiny sandpipers whistle as they flit along the stony banks that are streaked with chill and crystal-clear springs; wild ducks swim out into the middle of the ponds and look all about them warily; herons stand like sticks-in-the-mud in the shade, among the coves, under the cliffs.

The night stand lasted about an hour; we took two brace of woodcock and, wishing to try our luck again (for one can make a stand early in the morning as well) decided to sleep that night at the nearest mill. We left the grove, going down the knoll. The waves on the river rolled along, dark blue; the air was growing denser, weighed down with night moisture.

We knocked at the gate of the mill. The dogs in the yard broke into ecstatic barking.

"Who's there?" asked a hoarse and sleep-laden voice.

"A couple of hunters; let us in for the night."

There was no answer.

"We'll pay you."

"I'll go and tell the master. Stop your barking, damn your hides! There's no getting rid of you!"

We heard the hired man go into the hut; he came back to the gate shortly.

"No," said he, "the master's orders is not to let you in."

"Why not?"

"Well, he's afraid; you're hunters—first thing you know you'll set the mill on fire; just see what firearms you've got there!"

"Come, what sort of nonsense is that?"

"As it was, we had our mill burn down last year; we had some commission merchants stopping the night here, and I guess they must have set it on fire somehow."

"Come, now, brother—are we to pass the night out in the open, then?"

"Do as you know best," and he went off, his boots clumping.

Ermolai wished him all sorts of unpleasant things.

"Let's go to the village," he suggested, at last, with a sigh. But it was well over a mile to the village.

"We're staying here for the night," I told him. "It's a warm night out; the miller will send some straw out to us if we pay him."

Ermolai agreed without demur; we fell to knocking on the gate again.

"Well, what are you after?" we heard the hired man's voice anew. "You were told you can't stay here."

We made clear to him what we wanted. He went to consult his master and came back with him. The wicket in the gate creaked, revealing the miller, a tall man with a fat face, the nape of his neck like a bull's, his belly round and big. He agreed to my suggestion. There was a small shed, open on all sides, a hundred paces from the mill. Straw was brought out there; the hired man set a samovar for us on the grass near the river and, squatting on his heels, began blowing zealously into its chimney. The charcoal embers, flaring up, cast a bright light on his young face. The miller hurried off to wake up his wife; he finally suggested that I myself might stay the night in his hut, but I preferred to remain in the open air.

The miller's wife brought us milk, eggs, potatoes, bread. In a short while the samovar came to a boil and we settled to our tea drinking. Vapors were rising from the river; there was no wind; corn crakes were calling all about us; faint sounds, caused by drops falling from the paddles of a water wheel, by water seeping through the uprights of the dam, came from around the mill wheels. We made a small fire. While Ermolai was roasting potatoes in the hot ashes I managed to have a nap. A low, restrained whispering awoke me. I raised my head: the miller's wife was sitting before the fire on an upturned tub and talking with my hunter. I had recognized her even before, by her dress, movements, and speech, as neither a country wife nor city dweller but a house serf. She looked about thirty; her gaunt and pale face still bore traces of a remarkable beauty—her eyes, great and sorrowing, had proved especially to my liking. She had propped her elbows on her knees and cupped her chin in her hands. Ermolai was sitting with his back to me and adding chips to the fire.

"There's a murrain in Zheltuhino again," the miller's wife

was saying. "Both of Father Ivan's cows dropped from it. Lord have mercy upon us!"

"But what about your pigs?" Ermolai asked after a pause.

"Oh, they're alive!"

"You might make me a present of a little suckling pig, at least."

The miller's wife was silent for a while, then heaved a sigh: "Who's that with you?" she asked.

"One of the gentry—from Kostomarovsk." Ermolai tossed several fir branches on the fire; they at once began to crackle heartily; the thick white smoke billowed right into his face. "Why wouldn't your husband let us into the hut?"

"He's afraid."

"What a fat potbelly. . . . Arina Timotheievna, my dearest dear, bring me out a noggin of something to drink!"

The miller's wife got up and vanished in the murk. Ermolai began to hum:

> "When I went to see my sweet
> I wore the boots right off my feet—"

Arina returned with a small decanter and a tumbler. Ermolai raised himself a little, made the sign of the cross, and drank off a glass at one breath.

"I love the stuff!" he added. The miller's wife again seated herself on the tub. "Well now, Arina Timotheievna, you're still ailing, I guess?"

"I am that."

"How come?"

"My cough's killing me of nights."

"The master's fallen asleep, it looks like," Ermolai let drop after a short silence. "Don't you go to no doctor, Arina; it'll be worse for you if you do."

"I don't go to him, anyway."

"But you might drop in on me and stay a while."

Arina let her head drop.

"I'll chase my woman out—my wife, that is—in case you come," Ermolai went on. "I will, for sure."

"You'd better wake up the master, Ermolai Petrovich; see, the potatoes are baked."

"Aw, let him snooze," my loyal servant answered apathetically. "He's tuckered out from running around, so he's sleeping."

22

I began to turn in the hay. Ermolai got up and walked over to me.

"The potatoes are done, sir; come and eat, please."

I left the shed; the miller's wife got up from the tub and was about to leave; I spoke to her.

"Have you been renting this mill long?"

"The second year, beginning with Trinity."

"And where is your husband from?"

Arina failed to catch my question.

"Where does your husband hail from?" Ermolai repeated, raising his voice.

"From Belev. He's a Belev burgher."

"And are you from Belev too?"

"No; I'm a serf—or was, at least."

"Whose?"

"Squire Zverkov's. Now I'm free."

"What Zverkov is that?"

"Alexander Silych."

"Weren't you his wife's maid?"

"Why, how do you know? I was."

I looked at Arina with redoubled interest and sympathy.

"I know your master," I went on.

"You do?" she responded in a low voice—and stopped short.

I must inform the reader why I had looked at Arina with such sympathy. During my stay in Petersburg I had chanced to make the acquaintance of Zverkov. He held a rather important post and enjoyed the reputation of a well-informed and businesslike person. He had a wife—plump, touchy, lachrymose, and malevolent, a most ordinary and depressing creature; he had a darling son as well, a real young master, spoiled and foolish. The appearance of Zverkov himself predisposed one but little in his favor; out of his broad, almost quadrangular face, mouse eyes peeped slyly and a nose, big and sharp and with distended nostrils, jutted forth; closely cropped gray hair bristled up over a wrinkled forehead; his thin lips were incessantly in motion and smiling mawkishly. Zverkov usually stood with his little feet wide apart and his chubby little hands thrust into his pockets.

One day he and I somehow chanced to share a carriage for a ride to the suburbs. We got into conversation. As a man of business and experience, Zverkov began to "set me right."

"Permit me to point out to you," he squeaked out at last, "that all you young people judge and explain all things off-hand; you have but little knowledge of your fatherland; you are unfamiliar with Russia, gentlemen—that's what! All you ever do is read German books. There, for instance, you're now telling me this and that about . . . well, now, ahem . . . about house serfs. Very well, I'm not arguing; all that is very well, but you don't know them, you don't know what sort of people they are." Zverkov blew his nose loudly and took snuff. "Let me tell you, by the way, just one story, ever so brief—you may find it of interest." Zverkov cleared his throat. "I'm sure you know what my wife is; you'll agree it would be hard to find a kindlier woman. Her maids don't just live well, but simply have heaven on earth.

"However, my wife has laid down one rule for herself: not to keep any maids who are married. And really, that would never do; there are bound to be offspring and one thing or another—well, in that case, how is a maid to look after her mistress properly, to follow her mistress' habits? The maid is no longer interested in that; she's got other things on her mind. You must take human nature into consideration in judging such things.

"Well, sir, we were once passing through our village about . . . I wouldn't want to err in telling you how many years ago that was—about fifteen years, say. And what do we see at the village elder's house but a little girl, his daughter, the prettiest little thing; there was something so ingratiating about her manners, actually. And so my wife says to me: 'Kokó,'—that's what she calls me, you understand—'let's take this little girl to Petersburg; I like her, Kokó.' — 'Why, with pleasure,' I told her.

"The elder, naturally, bowed to our very feet; he could never have even expected such good fortune, you understand. Well, the little girl, being foolish, had a good cry. It actually was frightening at first, to be leaving her parental home—in general, there's nothing to wonder at about that. However, she soon became used to us; at first we placed her with the maids, training her, of course. Well, what do you think? The girl made astonishing progress; my wife grew simply mad about her, was gracious to her; finally, passing all the

Jocelyne Pache.

other girls by, she appointed her to be her personal maid, if you please!

"And one must give the girl her due; my wife had never yet had such a maid—absolutely not; she was obliging, modest, obedient, simply everything you could ask for. But then, it must be confessed, my wife did pamper her far too much: she dressed her excellently, gave her food from our own table, let her drink tea—oh, she indulged her in every imaginable way!

"And so she served my wife for ten years, or thereabouts. Suddenly, one fine morning—just imagine!—Arina (that's what they called her: Arina) entered my study unannounced and plumped down at my feet! That, I'll tell you frankly, is something I can't abide. A human being should never forget his or her dignity. 'What do you want?' — 'Alexander Silych, my father, I'm asking a favor.' — 'What favor?' — 'Allow me to marry.'

"I confess to you I was amazed. 'Why, don't you know, you fool, that your mistress has no other maid?' — 'I will go on serving my mistress as before.' — 'Nonsense! Nonsense! Your mistress won't keep any married maids.' — 'Melania can take my place.' — 'I'll ask you not to argue!' — 'Just as you will, master.'

"I confess I was simply bowled over. Nothing offends me as much—nothing offends me so powerfully, I venture to say—as ingratitude; that, I must inform you, is the sort of person I am. For I don't have to tell you what my wife is— you know that yourself: she's an angel incarnate, kind beyond words. You might think even the worst of villains would take pity on her.

"I chased Arina out. 'Guess she'll come to her senses,' I thought; one doesn't want to believe evil of human beings, to believe in their black ingratitude, you know.

"Well, what do you think? Half a year later she was pleased to come to me again with the same petition. At this, I confess, I chased her out with heartfelt anger, and threatened her, and promised to tell my wife. But, just imagine my amazement when, some time later, my wife came to me in tears, so agitated that I was actually frightened. 'What's happened?' — 'Arina . . . You understand? I'm ashamed to say it.' — 'It can't be! Who is it, then?' — 'Petrushka the flunky!' I blew up. I don't like half measures—that's the sort of person I am! Petrushka wasn't to blame. One could punish him but, in my opinion, he wasn't to blame. Arina, though—well! Well, now . . . well, now, what's the use of saying anything more?

"Naturally, I immediately ordered her hair to be cropped, to dress her in coarse ticking, and to pack her off to the country. My wife was deprived of an excellent maid, but there was no help for it: one cannot, under any circumstances, tolerate irregularity in a household. It's best to lop off a diseased limb at once. There, there—judge for yourself; why, you know my wife—she's . . . she's . . . she's a downright angel! Why, she'd become attached to Arina, and Arina knew this and hadn't felt the least compunction. Eh? No, what do you say to that, eh? Oh, what's the use of arguing about this! In any case, there was nothing to be done. As for myself—for myself, personally—I was for a long time grieved, offended by the ingratitude of this girl. No matter what you may say, you should never look for any heart, for any sensibility among these people. Feed a wolf as you will, he will eye the forest still. It'll be a lesson to me in the future. However, I merely wished to prove to you—"

And Zverkov, without finishing what he had wanted to say, turned his head away and muffled himself more closely in his cape, manfully downing his involuntary agitation.

The reader by now probably understands why I had looked with such sympathy at Arina.

"Are you married to the miller long?" I asked her at last.

"Two years."

"Why, did your master give you permission to marry?"

"I was bought off."

"By whom?"

"Savelii Alexeievich."

"Who's that?"

"My husband. [Ermolai smiled to himself.] Why, did my master speak to you about me?" Arina added after a short silence.

I didn't know what answer to make to her question.

"Arina!" the miller began shouting in the distance. She got up and left.

"Is her husband a good man?" I asked Ermolai.

"So-so."

"And have they any children?"

"They had one child, but it died."

26

"Well, now, did she prove to the miller's liking—was that it? Did he pay a high price to buy her freedom?"

"That I couldn't say. She knows how to read and write; in their business, now, that comes in handy. So she must have proven to his liking."

"And have you known her a long time?"

"Yes, a long time. I used to go to her master's before. Their estate is no great ways from here."

"And do you know Petrushka the flunky?"

"Peter Vassilievich? Sure, I knew him."

"Where is he now?"

"Why, he was took a soldier."

We were silent for a while.

"She doesn't seem to be in good health. What's the matter with her?" I finally asked Ermolai.

"No, you couldn't call her healthy! . . . Well, I guess we'll have a good stand tomorrow. It wouldn't be a bad idea if you were to get some sleep now."

A flock of wild ducks swept by over our heads, whistling, and we heard them settling on the river not far from us. By now it had grown altogether dark and the air was becoming chill; a nightingale was sonorously trilling in a grove. We burrowed down in the hay and dozed off.

RASPBERRY SPRING

AT THE BEGINNING of August the persisting hot spells are often unbearable. At a time like that the most resolute and purposeful man is, from noon to three, in no condition to hunt, and the most faithful dog begins to "polish" the hunter's heels, i.e., it heels him at a slow walk, with its eyes puckered up as if they are aching and its tongue lolling exaggeratedly, while in answer to its master's chidings it wags its tail in humility and its face expresses embarrassment, yet mend its pace the animal will not.

It was on precisely such a day that I happened to be out hunting. I had long been resisting the temptation to lie down somewhere in the shade, if but for a moment; my indefatigable bitch for a long while kept beating about the bushes, even though she herself evidently expected nothing worthwhile from her feverish activity. The stifling sultriness at last compelled me to think of conserving the last of our strength and faculties. Somehow or other I managed to drag myself to the river Ista (which my condescending readers are already familiar with), descended the steep bank, and went on along the yellow and damp sand in the direction of a spring known throughout that district as Raspberry Water. It gushes out of a cleft in the bank, which had little by little been turned into a small but deep ravine and, some twenty paces farther, tumbles with merry and chattering noisiness into the river. Scrub oaks grow thickly over the sloping sides of the ravine; short, velvety grass shows green near the wellspring; the rays of the sun hardly ever reach its chill, silvery waters.

I dragged myself to the spring somehow; lying on the grass was a dipper of birch bark, left by some passing muzhik for the general good. I drank my fill, lay down in the shade, and looked about me. Near the cove formed by the spring falling into the river and thereby covering its surface at that point with perpetual small ripples, two old men were sitting, with their backs to me. One of them, tall and quite stout, in a neat dark caftan and a brimmed cap of beaver felt, was fishing with a pole; the other, ever so spare and ever so small, in a patched little jacket of mouse gray and minus any head covering, was holding a pannikin of worms on his knees and every now and then passed his hand over his small gray head, as though he wished to guard it against the sun. I looked at him more fixedly and recognized him: he was Stepushka, the property of the Shumihins. I ask the reader's permission to introduce this man.

The big settlement of Shumihino, with a stone church reared to honor the names of those most worthy saints, Kozma and Damian, is situated a few miles from my village. Rising up in all its beauty before this church there was at one time a spacious, many-roomed manor house, surrounded by all sorts of outbuildings, offices, workshops, barns, toolsheds, carriage stables, bathhouses, and temporary kitchens, wings for guests and administrative workers, hothouses, swings for the common folk, and other structures of varying degrees of usefulness. Rich landowners had for a time lived in these spacious quarters, and everything had been going along smoothly when suddenly, one fine morning, all this wealth had burned down to fine ashes. The masters had made their way to another nest; this estate had become deserted. The extensive site of the fire became a truck garden, cluttered here and there with heaps of brick rubble, all that remained of what had been the foundations. Out of the lumber that had escaped the flames a small hut had been slapped together and roofed over with barge strakes which had been bought a decade or so before to build a pavilion in the Gothic manner, and Mitrophan the gardener with his wife Axenia and their seven children had been installed therein. Mitrophan was ordered to supply the masters' table (though the masters were living a hundred miles away) with potherbs and vegetables; Axenia was entrusted with the care of a Tyrolean cow, bought in Moscow for a great sum but, regrettably, altogether incapable of reproducing her kind and which for that reason had not yielded any milk from the day she had been acquired; it was also in Axenia's hands that they had placed a tufted, smoke-hued drake, the only "lordly" fowl; the children, because of their tender years, had not been assigned any definite duties—this, however, did not hinder them in the least from becoming thoroughly shiftless.

It was at this gardener's that I had chanced to stay for the night on a couple of occasions; I would, in passing, get cucumbers from him—which, God knows why, were remarkable even in the summertime because of their great size, execrable watery taste, and thick yellow skin. And it was precisely at his house that I had first laid eyes on Stepushka. Outside of Mitrophan and his family, and Gherassim, an old, deaf churchwarden who was living on Christ's charity in a cubbyhole in the house of a soldier's wife, lopsided and one-eyed, there wasn't a single domestic person left in Shumihino, inasmuch as Stepushka (with whom I intend to make the reader acquainted) could not be considered either as a person in general or as a domestic in particular.

Every human being has some sort of status in the social structure, has some sort of connections; every domestic is issued, if he gets no wages, at least a flour allotment, so called. Stepushka received no subsistence aids whatsoever, was not related to anybody; nobody was aware of his existence. This being hadn't even a past; people did not speak of him; it was doubtful if he was actually listed in the government's census of serfs. There were vague rumors current that he had been a valet to somebody at some time; but just who he was, whence he had come, whose son he was, how he had come to be of the number of those subject to the Shumihins, in what manner he had acquired the mouse-gray garment he had been wearing time out of mind, where he lived, what he lived on—of these things absolutely no one had the least notion, and besides, truth to tell, these questions did not arouse anybody's interest. Grandpa Trophimych, who knew the genealogy of all the house serfs for four generations back—well, even he said only once that, now, far as he could recall, Stepan was of kin to a

Turkish woman whom the late master, Brigadier Alexei
Romanych, had deigned to bring captive in a baggage cart
on his return from a campaign. Even on gala days, days of
good will and being treated to bread and salt, symbolic of
hospitality, to pastries stuffed with buckwheat grits, and to
green wine, according to the olden Russian custom—even on
such days as these Stepushka did not put in an appearance
at the food-laden tables and the barrels of spirits, all set
out in the open, did not bow low before his masters, did
not approach to kiss the master's hand, did not scoff off,
at one breath, under the eye of the master and to the master's health, the glass filled by the pudgy hand of an overseer; he got nothing, unless some kind soul, passing by,
bestowed a half-eaten piece of pie upon the poor fellow.
People did exchange Easter greetings with him; he did not,
however, roll up his greasy sleeve and reach in his back
pocket for the traditional red-dyed egg, did not proffer it,
panting and blinking, to the young masters, or even to the
mistress herself.

In the summer he lived in a cubbyhole back of the hen-
house, and in the winter in the entry to the bathhouse;
during hard frosts he slept in the hayloft. People were used
to the sight of him; every now and then they would even
bestow a kick upon him, but no one got into talk with him,
while he himself, apparently, had never opened his mouth
from the day he was born. After the fire this neglected
being had found shelter with (or, as the Orlov folk put it,
"leaned up against") Mitrophan, the gardener. The gardener
hadn't molested him; he hadn't told him "Live with me,"
but he hadn't driven him off, either. And Stepushka, if it
comes to that, did not actually live at the gardener's: he
abode in, he hovered about the truck garden. He walked
and moved without any noise whatsoever; he sneezed and
coughed into his fist, and even then not without appre-
hension; he was eternally taken up with cares and fossicking about ever so quietly, unobtrusively, like an ant—
and all for the sake of something to eat, solely for the
sake of something to eat. And, sure enough, were he not
taken up from morn till night with concern over his sustenance, my Stepushka would have died from hunger. Things
are in a bad way when a body doesn't know in the morning
what he'll fill his belly with toward nightfall! Stepushka
would be squatting close to the fence and gnawing away at

a radish, or sucking a carrot, or mincing up a dirt-covered cabbage head, screening it with his body; now he would be lugging a bucket of water somewhere, grunting hard; now making a bit of a fire under a little pot and, taking chunks of something black from the bosom of his shirt, would toss them into the pot; then you would find him in his cubbyhole, tapping away at a scrap of lumber, driving in a nail, putting up a little shelf to place a crust of bread on. And all this he did with nary a chirp out of him, as though he were eyeing you from around a corner: you'd look, and he'd already hidden himself. Or, all of a sudden, he would absent himself for a couple of days or so—of course, nobody noticed his absence; then you might look up, and there he was again, again somewhere close to the fence, shoving tiny chips into the bit of a fire under his little pot of cast iron.

His face is tiny, his little eyes are sort of yellow, his hair straggles down to his very eyebrows, his snip of a nose is ever so sharp, his ears are ever so big, translucent, like a bat's, his beard looks just as if it had been shaved off a fortnight ago, and never gets smaller or bigger. And it was this very Stepushka whom I came upon on the bank of the Ista, in the company of another gaffer.

I walked up, exchanged greetings, and sat down alongside them. In Stepushka's companion I had recognized another acquaintance—he was Michailo Savelich, known under the sobriquet of Fog, a liberated serf of Count Peter Ilyich ————. He was staying with a consumptive burgher of Bolhov, who kept an inn at which I put up quite frequently.

Travelers along the main Orlov highway, young government clerks and other folk who aren't any too busy (merchants, sunk deep in their featherbeds of striped ticking, have other things on their minds) can observe, even to this day, at no great distance from the large settlement of Troitsk, an enormous two-storied house jutting out to the very road, a house utterly neglected, with its roof fallen in and its windows tightly boarded up. At noontide, when the weather is clear and sunny, one can imagine nothing more woeful than this ruin. It was here that Count Peter Ilyich, well known as a hospitable host, as a rich grandee of a time gone by, had once lived. The whole province used to gather at his place, dancing and making merry most gloriously to the deafening music of home-talent musicians, to the crackling of rockets and sputter of Roman candles, and probably more than one little crone, as she now drives by the deserted seignioral mansion, will sigh and recall the times past and past youth. For a long spell did the count feast; for a long spell did he keep promenading, amiably smiling, amid his thronging, fawning guests; unfortunately, however, his estate did not last out his lifetime. Utterly ruined, he set out for Petersburg to find a post for himself, and died in a hotel room after waiting in vain for something definite to turn up.

Fog had served him as a major-domo and had been granted his freedom even during the count's lifetime. He was a man of about seventy, his face pleasant and with regular features. He smiled almost constantly, as only the people of the era of Catherine the Great smile nowadays—good-naturedly and imposingly; when he spoke he would slowly thrust out and compress his lips, pucker up his eyes in a kindly way, and pronounce his words somewhat through his nose. He was likewise deliberate about blowing his nose and taking his snuff, as though he were engaged in a task of some importance.

"Well, now, Michailo Savelich," I began, "have you caught plenty of fish?"

"Why, just take a look in the creel, if you please; I've made sure of two perch and five bullheads. Show them to the gentleman, Stepka."

Stepushka held out the crudely plaited creel to me.

"How are you getting along, Stepan?" I asked.

"Why . . . why . . . why, not . . . not so bad, now, father of mine, in my small way," Stepan answered haltingly, as though he were turning thirty-pound weights with his tongue.

"And Mitrophan—is he in good health?"

"He is, to be . . . to be sure, father of mine." The poor fellow turned away.

"But they're biting rather poorly, somehow," Fog began. "It's mortal hot; the fish, now, are all hiding beneath the underwater roots of the bushes, asleep. Put a worm on the hook, now, Stepa." Stepushka got out a worm, placed it on his palm, smacked it a couple of times, put it on the hook, spat on it, and handed the line to Fog. "Thanks, Stepa. And you, father of mine," he went on, turning to me, "are you after a little hunting?"

"As you see."

"So-o. And what sort of a hound might you have there —English, or some sort of Fourland [1] breed?" The old man loved, when the opportunity offered, to show his mettle, as if to say: "There, now, we too have lived a bit in this world!"

"I don't know the breed, but it's a good dog."

"So-o. And do you like to ride to hounds?"

"I keep two packs."

Fog smiled and shook his head. "That's the way of it, for sure: one man will be wild about dogs, whilst another wouldn't have them for free. To my simple way of thinking, dogs ought to be kept mostly for the grand looks of the thing, so to say. And everything that goes with them should also be fit and proper; the horses, too, ought to be right, and the whippers-in ought to be right, as is fitting, and everything else as well. The late count—may the Kingdom of Heaven be his!—wasn't a hunter born and bred, it must be confessed; yet he did keep hounds, and twice a year was pleased to ride after them. The lads would gather in the yard, in red caftans with gold braid, and blow the horn; His Excellency would deign to come out, and a steed would be led up for His Excellency, whilst the chief huntsman would put His Excellency's dainty feet in the stirrups, doff his cap, and then hand up the reins nested in that cap. His Excellency would snap his long whip—so!—and the whippers-in would begin hallooing and start out from the yard. The chief groom rode off behind the count, meanwhile holding two of the master's favorite little hounds on a silken leash and sort of keeping an eye on everything, you know. And he sat high in his Cossack saddle, this chief groom did; such a rosy-cheeked fellow, now, and rolling his huge eyes. Well, there were guests too, naturally, on an occasion like that. It was a diversion, and at the same time all due honor was observed. Ah, he got away, the low-down creature!" he added suddenly, jerking his line.

"Well, now, is it true what they say—about the count's having lived a full life in his day?" I asked.

The old man spat on the worm and cast his line.

"He was a right noble person, to be sure, sir. The foremost people from Petersburg, you might say, used to come

---

[1] Probably meant for Newfoundland.—*Trans.*

for a stay with him. All rigged out in the blue ribbons of their decorations, they were, as they sat and ate at his table. And, naturally, he was a great hand for treating them. Used to summon me into his presence: 'Fog,' he'd say, 'I must have some live sterlet sturgeons by tomorrow; give orders to get some.' — 'Right, Your Excellency!' There were embroidered long coats, wigs, canes, perfumes, *ladecologne* of the first sort, snuffboxes, all those big paintings—he used to write away for them all the way to Paris itself, he did. When he'd get set to give a banquet—O Lord, Sovereign of my life!—the fireworks would begin, and the pleasure jaunts. They used to shoot off cannon, even. Of musicians alone there was an active staff of forty. He used to keep a maestro, a German fellow, but that heinie got some high and mighty notions into his head—got to hankering to eat at the same table with the masters, so His Excellency gave orders to send him packing with God's blessings: 'My musicians,' said His Excellency, 'understand their trade even as it is.' You know the way of things: the will of the masters must be obeyed.

"They'd start in to dance and keep dancing till dawn— *lacossaise, matradura,* mostly. Eh, eh, eh—I got you, brother!" The old man pulled a small perch out of the water. "Here you are, Stepa. A master, he was, a right proper master," the old man went on, casting in his line again, "and a right kind soul he had too. He'd give you a beating, now and then, but, first thing you know, he'd forgotten all about it. There was one thing, though: he used to keep mistresses. Oh, those mistresses, the Lord forgive us! It was just them that ruined him. And, mind you, it was from a low class he picked them, for the most part. What more could they want, a body might think? But no—you had to serve them with whatever stuff was most expensive in all of Yurrup. And why not live for one's own pleasure, you might say—that's what masters are for; still, there's no sense in ruining yourself. There was one in particular—Akulina, they called her; she's no longer amongst the living, may the Kingdom of Heaven be hers! A simple wench, she was, the daughter of the constable at Sitov, but what a vile temper she had! Used to slap the count's cheeks for him. She'd bewitched him entirely. Had a nephew of mine cropped for a soldier—he'd overturned some choc'lit on a new dress of hers. Yes. . . . But, after all, them was the good old days!" the old man added with a deep sigh and, casting his eyes down, fell silent.

"But your master was a strict sort, I can see," I began, after a short pause.

"That was all the go then, father of mine," the old man retorted with a shake of his head.

"They no longer do such things nowadays," I remarked without taking my eyes off him.

He gave me a sidelong look: "Things are better nowadays, everybody knows that," he muttered—and cast his line far out.

We were sitting in the shade, but even in the shade it was stifling. The oppressive, sultry air seemed to be holding its breath; one's heated face longingly sought a breeze, yet a breeze was the one thing missing. The sun was simply beating down out of the blue, now darkened sky; straight ahead of us, on the opposite bank, a field of oats showed yellow, with patches of wormwood breaking through here and there—and if but one stalk would stir! On a somewhat lower plane a peasant's horse was standing knee-deep in the river and lazily swishing itself with its wet tail; now and then, but only at long intervals, some large fish would come to the surface under an overhanging bush, let out a few bubbles, and quietly sink to the bottom, leaving light ripples behind. The grasshoppers were whirring away in the grass, now turned to a rusty hue; the quail were calling—halfheartedly, somehow; sparrow hawks were soaring smoothly over the fields and often hovered in one spot, beating their wings fast and fanning out their tails. We sat without moving, crushed by the heat.

There was a sudden noise behind us, in the ravine—someone was making his way down to the spring. I looked over my shoulder and saw a muzhik of fifty, all dusty, in blouse and bast sandals, with a knapsack of plaited birch bark and a rough overcoat slung over his shoulders. He walked up to the spring, drank his fill avidly, and stood up again.

"That you, Vlass?" Fog cried out after a good look at him. "Greetings, brother. Whence has God brought you?"

"Greetings, Michaila Savelich," said the muzhik, walking up to us. "I've come a long way."

"Where have you been keeping yourself so long?" Fog asked him.

"Why, I went to Moscow, to see my master."

"What for?"

"I went to petition him."

"To petition him about what?"

"Why, to lower my quitrent, or to hire me out, or to resettle me, or something like that. My son died, so I can't manage things all by myself now."

"Your son died?"

"He did that. He's no longer amongst the living," the muzhik added after a pause. "He was living in Moscow, driving a cab; to tell you the truth, it was him that paid my quitrent for me."

"Come, are you under a quitrent now?"

"I am that."

"Well, what did your master do?"

"Well, what do you expect of a master? He drove me out! 'How dare you come straight to me!' says he. 'That's what stewards are for—you must make a report to the steward first,' he says. 'And besides, where am I to resettle you? You pay your quitrent arrears first,' he says. Got real riled, he did."

"Well, what did you do then? Start back for home?"

"That's just what I did. I wanted to find out if my dead son had left anything behind him, but nothing came of that. I told the man he was working for: 'I'm Philip's father, now.' But he says to me: 'How am I supposed to know that? And besides, your son didn't leave anything. As a matter of fact he was in debt to me.' And so I started out for home."

The muzhik was telling all this with a mocking smile, as though it were somebody else he was talking about, but tears were welling up in his little half-closed eyes; his lips were twitching.

"Well, are you heading for home now?"

"Why, where else? I'm heading home, naturally. My wife must be perishing from hunger right now, I guess."

"You might . . . now. . . ." Stepushka spoke up unexpectedly, then became confused, fell silent, and began fussing with the worms in the pannikin.

"And are you going to the steward?" Fog went on, not without a surprised look at Stepa.

"What would I be going to him for! I'm in arrears as it is. My son was ailing for a year before he died, so he didn't pay in even his own quitrent. Not that I'm grieving over

37

the arrears too much—they can't get anything out of me. Yes, brother, no matter how you twist and turn, you're wasting your time—you can't hold me to anything!" The muzhik broke into laughter. "No matter how he schemes and connives, this Quintilian Semënych, now, it won't get him nowheres, nohow!" Vlass laughed again.

"Well, now. That's bad, brother Vlass," Fog uttered thoughtfully.

"Why, what way is it bad? No. . . ." Here Vlass's voice broke. "What a hot spell we're having," he went on, mopping his face on his sleeve.

"Who's your master?" I asked.

"Valerian Petrovich, Count ———."

"Son of Peter Ilyich?"

"Peter Ilyich's son," Fog answered. "The late Peter Ilyich, whilst he was still alive, gave his son the village Vlass belongs to."

"How is your master—well?"

"He's well, glory be to God," Vlass retorted. "He's grown all red; his face is all bloated, like."

"There, father of mine," Fog went on, turning to me. "Things wouldn't be so bad if he were around Moscow, but he's been put under quitrent here."

"And how much is that for each household?"

"Ninety-five rubles for each house," Vlass muttered in answer.

"There, you see—yet of land there's ever so little; all there is to it is the master's woods."

"And even that has been sold," the muzhik put in.

"There, you see. . . . Let's have a worm, Stepa. Eh, Stepa? Have you fallen asleep, or what?"

Stepushka came to with a start. The muzhik sat down next to us. We again fell silent. Someone on the other side of the river started a long-drawn-out song—and such a dismal song, at that. My poor Vlass slumped over in his misery.

Half an hour later we all went our different ways.

A COUNTRY DOCTOR

ONCE, IN AUTUMN, on my way back from a remote field, I caught a cold and had to take to my bed. Fortunately, the fever came upon me in the district capital, at a hotel; I sent for a doctor. Half an hour later the general practitioner for the district appeared, a man of no great height, rather thin and with black hair. He prescribed the usual sudorific, ordered a mustard plaster to be applied, quite deftly thrust the five-ruble note into the cuff of his coat sleeve—during which, however, he gave a dry little cough and looked aside —and was just about to go on about his affairs, but somehow got to talking and stayed. My high temperature was tormenting me; I foresaw a sleepless night and was glad to have a chance of chatting with a kindhearted person. Tea was served. My doctor launched into talk. He was far from being a foolish fellow, expressing himself briskly and quite amusingly. Strange things befall in this world: you may live a long time with some man and be on terms of friendship with him, yet not even once get to talking with him frankly, from the very soul; with some other, however, you have barely had time to become acquainted when, first thing you know, you have either spilled your innermost secrets to him or he has spilled his to you, as if at confessional. I don't know how I had earned the confidence of my new friend, but the fact remains that he "upped" (as they say) and, for no particular reason, told me a rather remarkable incident,

39

and so I now bring his story to the attention of the well-disposed reader. I will try to express myself in the doctor's own words.

"You haven't the pleasure of knowing—" he began in a strained and quavering voice (such is the effect of straight Berezovsky tobacco), "you haven't the pleasure of knowing Mylov, Paul Lukich—our local judge? You haven't that pleasure. . . . However, it doesn't matter." He coughed to clear his throat and wiped his eyes. "Well, you see, this affair took place about—when shall I say? I wouldn't want to give you a wrong date—it was during Lent, at the height of the thaw. I was sitting at his house—the judge's house, that is—and playing preference whist. Our judge is a fine man, and he's a great hand for playing preference. Suddenly"—my medical friend used the word "suddenly" often—"they tell me: 'There's a man asking for you.' I asked them what he wanted. 'He's brought a note,' they told me, 'must be from someone who's sick.' — 'Let's have the note,' said I. Sure enough: it was about someone who was sick. Well and good: that sort of thing is, you understand, our bread and butter. Here's the thing in a nutshell: a certain landed proprietress, a widow, wrote me that her daughter was dying, now: 'Come, for the sake of Our Lord God Himself; I have even sent the horses to fetch you!' Well, that part of it wasn't so bad—but she lived fifteen miles out of town, and it was night, and the state of the roads was simply unspeakable! Then, too, she herself was struggling with poverty: you couldn't expect more than a couple of silver rubles from her, mind you, and even that was doubtful, for all the chances were you'd have to do the best you could with a piece of homespun linen and whatever crumbs might come your way. However, duty comes first of all, you understand: there was a human being dying. I suddenly handed my cards over to Kalliopin, the permanent councilman, and set out for home.

"I look, and there's a wretched little cart before my entrance; it's drawn by plow horses, with bellies on them ever so big, and the wool on them like downright felt, while the driver, to show his respect, is bareheaded up on his box. 'Well,' I thought, 'I can see, brother, that your masters aren't exactly rolling in wealth!' It pleases you to laugh, and yet I'll tell you this—those of our fraternity are usually poor: they have to take everything into consideration. If the driver

40

is sitting up there like a lord, and doesn't doff his cap, and on top of that sort of sneers through his beard and keeps flicking his dainty whip—it's a safe bet to count on two lovely bank notes of the higher denominations. But here, I saw, things weren't shaping up that way. 'However,' I reflected, 'there's no help for it: duty comes first of all.' I picked up the most necessary medicines and set out. Would you believe it, it was all we could do to drag ourselves there. The road was hellish: swollen streams, snow, mire, washouts, or, all of a sudden, a dam breaking up—what trouble!

"However, get there I did. The house was ever so small, straw-thatched. There was light in the windows, which meant they were waiting for me. A little old woman came out to meet me—most venerable, she was, in a headdress. 'Save her!' said she. 'She's dying!' — 'Please don't upset yourself,' I told her. 'Where's the patient?' — 'Come right this way, please.'

"I looked about me: a neat little room, a holy lamp in a corner, a girl in bed—about twenty, unconscious. You could feel she was simply burning up with high temperature; she was breathing heavily: obviously in a fever. There were two other girls right there—her sisters—thoroughly frightened, all in tears. 'There,' they told me, 'yesterday she was perfectly well and eating with appetite; this morning she complained about her head, while toward evening, all of a sudden—there, you see the state she's in.'

"I told them once more: 'Please don't upset yourselves'—a doctor's duty that, you know—and began attending to her. I let her blood, ordered mustard plasters to be applied, prescribed a mixture. In the meanwhile I kept looking and looking at her, don't you know: well, by God, never yet had I seen such a face—a beauty, and that's all there was to it! Pity was simply rending me apart. The features so pleasing, and such eyes. . . . Well, glory be to God, she quieted down at last; perspiration appeared, she seemed to regain her senses, looked about her, smiled, passed her hand over her face. 'Well,' I told them, 'now we ought to let the patient rest.' And so we all tiptoed out; only a maid remained, against any contingency.

"And in the parlor a samovar was already standing on the table, and a bottle of Jamaica rum as well: in our work you can't get around things like that. They gave me tea, begging me to stay for the night; I agreed—how could one travel then! The little old lady kept oh'ing all the time. 'Why do you act like that?' I told her. 'She'll live; please don't upset yourself; it would be better if you were to get a little rest yourself—it's going on two in the morning.' — 'But you'll leave orders to wake me up if anything happens?' — 'I will, I will.' The little old woman retired, and the girls also went to their room; a bed was made up for me in the parlor. Well, I lay down; the only thing was, I couldn't sleep—and that was something to wonder at! There, one might think, I'd had enough to tucker me out. Just couldn't get my patient off my mind. Finally I wasn't able to hold out any longer, and got up, all of a sudden: 'There,' I thought, 'I'll go and have a look how my patient is doing.' And, as it happened, her bedroom was right next to the parlor. Well, I got up, opened her door, ever so quietly—but my heart was simply pounding.

"I looked: the maid was asleep, her mouth open and actually snoring, the low-down animal, while the sick woman was lying with her face toward me and had flung out her arms, the poor thing! I approached . . . when all of a sudden she opened her eyes and stared at me! 'Who is it? Who is it?' I became embarrassed. 'Don't be frightened, ma'am,' I told her, 'I'm the doctor; I've dropped in to see how you're feeling.' — 'You're the doctor?' — 'I am, I am. Your mother sent to town after me; we have let your blood, ma'am; now go to sleep, if you please, and in a couple of days or so, God willing, we'll have you up on your feet.' — 'Ah, yes, yes, Doctor—don't let me die . . . please, please!' — 'Whatever are you saying? God be with you!'

" 'And yet she's running a high temperature again,' I said to myself; I felt her pulse: she had high temperature, sure enough. She gave me a look, and then just gripped my arm, all of a sudden: 'I'll tell you why I don't want to die—I'll tell you, I'll tell you . . . we're all by ourselves now—only, please, don't tell anybody . . . listen—' I leaned toward her; she put her lips to my very ear, her hair touching my cheek —I confess my own head started spinning—and fell to whispering. I couldn't understand a thing. Ah, yes, she was raving! She kept whispering and whispering, and so fast, at that, and just as if in some foreign language; when she had done she shuddered, dropped her head on the pillow, and shook her finger at me. 'Watch out, now, Doctor—not a word to anybody. . . .' Somehow or other I calmed her down, gave her a drink, woke up the maid, and went out."

At this point the doctor again took a pinch of snuff like a hardened addict, and for a moment seemed to be in a catalepsy.

"However," he went on, "the next day, contrary to my expectations, my patient felt no relief. I considered, considered, and suddenly decided to stay on, even though I had other patients expecting me. And, as you know, one can't afford to neglect such things: the practice suffers thereby. But, in the first place, the sick woman really was in a desperate state and, in the second, I must tell you the truth: I myself felt powerfully disposed toward her. Besides that, I had taken a liking to the whole family. Even though they were folks who hadn't much, they were nevertheless cultured—to a rare degree, one may say. The father, now, had been a man of learning, a writer; he had died in poverty, of course, but he had succeeded in imparting an excellent education to his children; he had also left them a lot of books. Whether it was because I attended with such zeal to the sick woman, or for some other reasons, still, I will venture to say, they had come to love me in that household as if I were one of the family.

"Meanwhile, the roads had become frightful—all communications had been cut off, so to speak; even the medicines could be brought back from town only with difficulty. The sick woman wasn't getting any better—day after day, day after day. But now, sir . . . at this point, sir. . . ." The doctor was silent for a while. "Really, I don't know how to put the matter to you." He took snuff anew, grunted, and had a sip of tea. "I'll tell you without beating about the bush— my patient . . . how am I to put it? Well, she fell in love with me, sort of. Or no; it wasn't that she fell in love with me, exactly . . . well, anyway . . . really, now, how can I put it, sir—"

The doctor cast down his eyes and turned red.

"No," he went on with animation, "how can one call it falling in love? After all, one should know one's worth. She was an educated young lady, clever, well read, whereas I'd forgotten even my Latin—forgotten it altogether, I may say. As far as my physique is concerned"—the doctor looked at himself with a smile—"I've nothing to brag about, either. But the Lord God hadn't put me on this earth as a fool, at that;

I wouldn't call black white—even I know a thing or two. I had, for instance, grasped thoroughly that it wasn't love which Alexandra Andreievna—they called her Alexandra Andreievna—had come to feel for me, but a friendly inclination, so to say, an esteem, or something of that sort. Even though she herself was mistaken in that respect—but then, judge for yourself what her situation was. However," added the doctor, who had uttered all these impetuous speeches without pausing for breath and with evident embarrassment, "I think I've strayed a little too far in my explanations. That way you won't understand anything. But now, if you'll permit me, I'll tell you everything in order."

He finished his glass of tea and began speaking in a calmer voice:

"Very well, then; very well, sir. My patient was getting worse—ever worse. You aren't a medico, my dear sir; you cannot understand what goes on in the soul of one of our fraternity, especially at first, when one begins to surmise that it is the ailment which is getting the upper hand over him. Wherever does one's self-confidence go to, then? You suddenly become so timid that you can't even put it in words. It seems to you that you've simply forgotten not only everything you ever knew, but that the patient, now, has no confidence in you, and that by this time all the others as well are beginning to notice that you've lost your head—and they tell you the symptoms unwillingly, they look at you from under their brows, they whisper; eh, but things are in a bad way! For there is a remedy against this ailment, you keep thinking—all you have to do is find it. There, isn't this it, by chance? You try it out—no, that's not it! You don't give the medicine time to work as it should—you clutch now at this straw, now at that. You'd pick up your pharmaceutical handbook—surely, you think, the remedy is here; it's bound to be here! Upon my word, now and then you'd open the book at random: Maybe fate will decide, you think to yourself. Yet in the meanwhile there's a human being dying—and yet another doctor might save him. 'It will be necessary to have a consultation,' you say. 'I do not take any responsibility upon myself.' And what a fool you look on such occasions!

"Well, in time, you get hardened—it wasn't your fault: you acted according to the rules. But here's something else that's still more agonizing: you see a blind confidence in you, yet you yourself feel that you're unable to help. There, it was precisely such confidence which Alexandra Andreievna's whole family had acquired—they even forgot to think that one of the daughters was in danger. I, too, assured them for my part that, now, it really was nothing—yet at the same time my heart was in my boots.

"To crown the misfortune, the condition of the roads became such that the coachman had to take all of a day to get the medicine. But I didn't set foot out of the sickroom, couldn't tear myself away, kept on telling her all sorts of funny little stories, don't you know, and playing cards with her. I sat there whole nights through. The little old woman thanked me with tears, but I was saying to myself all the time: 'I don't deserve your gratitude.'

"I confess to you frankly—there's no use in concealing anything now—I'd fallen in love with my patient. And Alexandra Andreievna had become attached to me: there were times when she wouldn't let anybody into her room but me. She would start talking with me, questioning me as to where I had studied, how I was getting along, who my kin were, whom I called upon socially. And I felt it wasn't right for her to talk, yet to forbid her—forbid her, in such a positive manner, you know—was something I couldn't do.

"There were times when I'd clutch my head: 'What are you up to, you cutthroat?' Or else she'd take my hand and hold it, looking at me for a long while—then she'd turn away, sigh, and say: 'What a kind man you are!' Her hands were so hot; her eyes huge, languishing. 'Yes,' she would say, 'you're a kind, a fine man; you aren't at all like our neighbors. No, you aren't like that. How is it I hadn't known you up to now!' — 'Alexandra Andreievna,' I'd say, 'do calm down. Believe me, I sympathize; I don't know how I have merited this—but do calm down; calm down, for God's sake; everything will come out right, you will be well.' Yet at the same time, I must tell you," added the doctor, bending forward and raising his eyebrows, "that the reason they had so little to do with their neighbors was because the lesser ones didn't come up to them, whereas pride forbade them to mingle with those who were rich. It was an extraordinarily cultured family, I tell you, and therefore I felt flattered, you know. She would take the medicine only from my hands: she'd raise herself a little with my help, the poor thing, take the medicine, and give me a look—and my heart

45

would simply sink. For at the same time she was getting worse, ever worse. 'She's going to die,' I reflected, 'she's bound to die.' Would you believe it: I felt like lying down in a coffin myself—but there were her mother, her sisters observing me, looking into my eyes—and their confidence was passing. 'Well, how is she?' — 'It's nothing, ma'am, nothing!'—and yet that 'nothing' was of such a nature that it was enough to drive you out of your mind.

"Well, sir, one night I was sitting there, again all by myself, near the sick woman. The maid was sitting right there too, and snoring her fool head off. Well, there was no use calling the wretched wench to account—she, too, had become all tuckered out. As for Alexandra Andreievna, she had felt quite bad all evening; her high temperature had exhausted her. She kept on tossing all the time, right up to midnight; at last she seemed to have fallen asleep—at least she didn't as much as stir as she lay there. There was a holy lamp burning before the images. I was sitting there, you know, my eyes fixed on the floor; I, too, was dozing. All of a sudden, just as though someone had nudged me in the ribs, I turned around. Oh Lord, my God! Alexandra Andreievna was staring at me with all her might—her lips were open, her cheeks simply flaming.

" 'What is the matter with you?' — 'Doctor, I'm going to die, am I not?' — 'God forbid!' — 'No, Doctor, no, please don't tell me I'm going to live—don't! If you but knew— listen, for God's sake: don't conceal my condition from me!' —and at the same time she's breathing ever so fast. 'If I knew with certainty that I must die . . . I'd tell you everything, then—everything!' — 'Alexandra Andreievna, do be reasonable!' — 'Look—why, I wasn't sleeping at all; I've been watching you a long while. For God's sake . . . I have faith in you, you're a kindhearted man, you're a man of honesty: I appeal to you, in the name of everything that is most sacred in this world—tell me the truth! If you but knew of what importance this is to me. . . . Tell me, Doctor, for God's sake: am I in danger?' — 'What am I to tell you, Alexandra Andreievna? Do be reasonable!' — 'For God's sake—I implore you!' — 'I can't conceal it from you, Alexandra Andreievna—you are, it's true, in danger, but God is merciful.' — 'I'm going to die, I'm going to die—' and it seemed as if she were actually rejoicing, so blithe had her face become: I was frightened. 'Oh, don't be afraid, don't

Evelyne Pack.

be afraid; death does not terrify me in the least.' She suddenly raised herself and leaned on her elbow. 'Now . . . well, now I can tell you that I am grateful to you with all my soul, that you're a kind, a fine man, that I love you—'

"I was staring at her as if I'd gone daft; I felt eerie, you know. 'Do you hear me? I love you. . . .' — 'Alexandra Andreievna, how have I merited this!' — 'No, no, you don't understand me—' and then, speaking to me as to an intimate: 'You don't understand me.' And suddenly she held out her arms, seized my head, and kissed me. Would you believe it, I all but cried out; I threw myself on my knees and buried my head in the pillows. She was silent; her fingers, plunged in my hair, were trembling; I heard her weeping.

"I began to comfort her, to reassure her—really, now, I don't know just what it was I told her. 'Wake up the wench, Alexandra Andreievna,' I told her. 'I thank you . . . believe me, I do . . . calm yourself.' — 'Oh, that will do, now—that will do,' she kept repeating. 'God be with them all; well, they'll wake up, and they'll come—what does it matter? For I'm going to die, after all. Yes, and why are you losing heart—what are you afraid of? Lift up your head. Or, perhaps, you do not love me; I have deceived myself . . . in that case, excuse me.' — 'Alexandra Andreievna, whatever are you saying? I love you, Alexandra Andreievna.' She looked straight into my eyes and opened her arms: 'Take me around, then—'

"I'll be frank with you: I can't understand how I did not lose my mind that night. I felt that my patient was killing herself; I saw that she wasn't quite in her senses; I also grasped that, if she hadn't considered herself at death's door, she would never have thought of me; for, surely, no matter what they say, it's dreadful to be dying at twenty-five, without having loved anyone: for that was what was torturing her, that was why she had, in despair, clutched even at me —do you understand now? But still she wouldn't release me from her arms.

" 'Spare me, Alexandra Andreievna—and spare yourself, too,' I told her. 'What for?' she said. 'What's the sense in pity? For, after all, I am bound to die—' She kept repeating that, without cease. 'There, if I knew I'd live on, and again be one of those respectable young ladies, I'd be ashamed . . . ashamed, true enough . . . but the way things are, what

47

does it matter?' — 'But whoever told you that you would die?' — 'Oh, no, that'll do—you won't deceive me, you don't know how to lie—just look at yourself!' — 'You're going to live, Alexandra Andreievna; I'm going to make you well; we'll ask your mother's blessing . . . we'll be joined in wedlock, we'll be happy—' — 'No, no, I have your word—I must die—you promised me . . . you told me.' I felt bitter —bitter on many accounts. Why, just judge for yourself— here's the sort of odd things which befall you sometimes: they would seem to be nothing, and yet they hurt. It came into her head to ask me what my name was—not my family name, that is, but my given name. And it would have to be such a miserable one—it so happens that they call me Triphon. Yes sir, yes sir, they call me Triphon—Triphon Ivanovich. In my house, now, they all addressed me as Doctor. There was no help for it: 'It's Triphon, ma'am,' I told her. She narrowed her eyes, shook her head, and whispered something in French—oh, but it was something not at all complimentary—and then started in laughing, and that laugh, too, wasn't anything good.

"Well, that's how I passed almost the whole night with her. Toward morning I went out, just as though I were in a daze from charcoal fumes; when I came into her room again it was in the daytime, when tea was already over. My God, my God! You couldn't recognize her—a corpse laid out in a coffin couldn't have looked worse. I swear to you upon my honor, I can't understand now—I absolutely can't—how I stood up under that torture.

"For three days more, and three nights, did my patient linger on . . . and what nights they were! The things she said to me! And on the last night, now—just imagine this to yourself—I was sitting near her, and by that time there was just one thing I was begging God for: 'Take her now, as quickly as possible—and me with her!' Suddenly her old mother dashed into the room. For I'd already told her the evening before that, now, there was but little hope, and it mightn't be amiss to send for the priest. Soon as the sick woman saw her mother, she said: 'Well, now, it's a good thing you've come . . . look at us: we love each other, we have exchanged vows.' — 'What's she saying, Doctor— what's she saying?' I was stunned. 'She's in delirium, ma'am,' said I. 'Running a high temperature.' But the sick woman spoke up: 'That'll do, that'll do—you were telling me something altogether different just now, and accepted a betrothal ring from me. Why are you pretending? My mother is a kindhearted woman; she'll forgive us, she'll understand. As for me, I'm dying—there's no reason for me to lie; give me your hand—' I jumped up and dashed out of the room. The little old woman surmised everything, naturally.

"However, I'm not going to depress you with this any longer—and besides, I confess, I myself find it painful to recall all this. My patient died the very next day. May the Kingdom of Heaven be hers!" The doctor added this in a patter and with a sigh. "Before her death she asked all her folks to go out of the room and leave me alone with her. 'Forgive me,' said she, 'perhaps I am at fault before you— it's due to my illness. But believe me . . . I have never loved anyone more than you. Don't forget me—take care of my ring—' "

The doctor turned away; I took his hand.

"Eh," said he, "let's talk of something else—or would you like to have a go at preference, for small stakes? Those of our fraternity oughtn't, don't you know, to yield to such exalted sentimentalizings. Those of our fraternity ought to have but one thing in mind: to keep the little ones from squalling and the wife from scolding. For since then I've managed to enter into what they call lawful matrimony. How else . . . I took a merchant's daughter: with a dowry of seven thousand. They call her Akulina: just the very thing for a Triphon. A female, I must tell you, with a vile temper —she sleeps all day, though, and that's a blessing. . . . Well, what about preference?"

We sat down to preference for kopeck stakes. Triphon Ivanych won two rubles and a half from me—and left late, quite satisfied with his victory.

MY NEIGHBOR RADILOV

DURING THE AUTUMN snipe often linger in ancient linden parks. Of such parks we have quite a large number in the province of Orlov. Our grandsires, whenever they chose a site for a dwelling, inevitably set aside five acres or so of good land for an orchard with linden-bordered paths. After fifty years—or seventy, at the most—these country estates, these "nests of gentlefolk," disappeared little by little off the face of the earth; the houses decayed or were sold for whatever the building materials would fetch, the stone outbuildings became transformed into cairnlike ruins, the apple trees died out and were chopped down for firewood, the fences and wattles were done away with. The lindens alone kept growing as gloriously as of yore, and now, surrounded by cultivated fields, proclaim to our flighty generation concerning "our sires and brethren who have gone before us." A splendidly beautiful tree is an old linden of that sort. Even the merciless ax of the Russian peasant spares it. The leaves upon it are small; its mighty branches spread far out in all directions—there is eternal shade beneath them.

One day, while ranging the fields with Ermolai after partridges, I caught sight of a neglected park off to one side and headed toward it. No sooner had I set foot within it than a snipe whirred up out of a bush; I fired, and at that same instant I heard a cry a few paces away from me— the startled face of a young girl peeped out from behind the trees and immediately disappeared. Ermolai ran up to me: "Why are you shooting here? This is where the landowner lives."

I hadn't had time to answer him, my dog hadn't had time to bring over to me, with noble dignity, the bird I had shot, when I caught the sound of brisk steps and a tall, mustachioed man emerged from the grove and with a displeased mien took a stance before me. I apologized as best I could, gave him my name, and offered him the bird I had brought down on his property.

"I'll accept your game bird, if you like," he told me with a smile, "but only on the condition that you stay with us for dinner."

I was not, I confess, overjoyed at his suggestion, yet it was impossible to decline.

"I am Radilov, the landowner here and a neighbor of yours—you may have heard of me," my new acquaintance went on. "It's Sunday, and the dinner at my place will probably be a decent one, for otherwise I would not have invited you."

I made the answer which is usually made on such occasions and set out after him. A recently cleared path shortly led us out of the linden grove; we came into a truck garden. Between the old apple trees and the luxuriantly growing gooseberry bushes was a motley show of round, pale-green cabbage heads; hopvines wound in corkscrew coils about tall poles; dark-brown rods, closely spaced and tangled over with dried up peapods, stuck up out of plat beds; big flat squashes sprawled along the ground just as if they had been thrown there; cucumbers showed yellowly from under dusty, angular leaves; tall nettles swayed along a wattle fence; in two or three spots, growing in clumps, were honeysuckle, Queen Anne's lace, sweetbrier—all that was left of erstwhile "flower beds." Near a small pond flooded with rusty-hued and slimy water one could see a well with puddles all around it. Ducks were fussily plashing and waddling in these puddles; a dog, its body all aquiver and its eyes narrowed, was gnawing a bone out on a meadow; there, too, a dappled cow was lazily nibbling the grass, every now and then switching her tail over her gaunt back.

The path turned aside; an ancient, gray little house with a roof of hewn timbers and a small lopsided porch peeped out at us from behind stout-trunked willows and birches. Radilov stopped.

"On the other hand," said he after a good-natured and direct look at my face, "I've thought things over by now— perhaps you're not at all inclined to drop in on me, in which case—"

I did not give him a chance to finish what he was saying and assured him that, on the contrary, it would be a very great pleasure for me to dine with him.

"Well, do as you know best."

We entered the house. A young fellow in a long caftan of blue broadcloth had met us on the porch; Radilov had immediately bidden him to bring some vodka to Ermolai: my huntsman had made obeisance to the back of our magnanimous host. From the entry, with all sorts of brightly tinted pictures pasted on its walls and its many hanging cages, we came into a small room—Radilov's study. I took off my hunting accouterments, putting my gun in a corner; a lad in a long-skirted coat fussily brushed off my clothes.

"Well, now, let's go into the drawing room," Radilov said amiably. "I'll introduce you to my mother."

I followed him. A short little old woman in a brown dress and white cap, her small face rather kind and gaunt, her gaze timid and sad, was seated on a divan in the middle of the room.

"Here, Mother, let me present our neighbor—" and he gave my name. The little old woman rose a trifle and bowed to me, without letting out of her hands a stout beaded reticule shaped like a sack.

"Have you been in our parts long?" she asked in a weak and soft voice, blinking the while.

"No, not long, ma'am."

"Do you intend to remain here any length of time?"

"Until winter, I think."

The little old woman fell silent.

"And this," Radilov broke in quickly, pointing out for my benefit a tall and thin man whom I had failed to notice on my entrance into the drawing room, "this is Fedor Miheich. . . . Well, now, Fedya—show your artistry to our guest. Why are you huddling in that corner, now?"

Fedor Miheich immediately got up from his chair, reached for a wretched little fiddle lying on the windowsill, took up a violin bow—not by the end, which is the proper way, but by the middle—propped the fiddle against his chest, closed his eyes, and went into a dance, humming some ditty and scraping away at the strings. He looked seventy or so; a long nankeen surtout flapped dismally about his withered and bony limbs. He danced: now tossing his small, bald head in a dashing sort of way, then, as though swooning, moved it from side to side; he craned his scraggy neck as he stomped on one spot; every now and then, with noticeable difficulty, he would bend his knees. His toothless mouth emitted a senile voice. Radilov must have surmised from the expression on my face that Fedya's "artistry" was not giving me great pleasure.

"There, that's fine, old fellow—that'll do," he remarked. "You can go and help yourself to your reward."

Fedor Miheich immediately replaced his fiddle on the windowsill, bowed to me first (since I was a guest), then to the little old woman, and lastly to Radilov and left the room.

"He, too, was a landowner," my new friend went on, "and a rich one, at that, but he went through all his wealth and so now he's living with me. Yet in his time he was considered a very devil of a fellow, the foremost in all the province—he got two wives away from their husbands, kept a choir of his own, used to sing himself, and danced superbly. . . . But won't you have some vodka? For dinner is already on the table."

A young girl, the same one I had caught a glimpse of in the garden, entered the room.

"Ah, here is Olga!" remarked Radilov, averting his head a little. "I hope you will like and favor her. There, let's go in to dinner."

We headed for the dining room and took our seats. On our way from the drawing room, and while we were seating ourselves, Fedor Miheich, whose little eyes had taken on a glow and whose nose had turned a shade redder from his "reward," had been singing "Let the Peals of Victory Resound!" A separate small table had been set for him in a corner, but no napkin had been provided. The poor old man could hardly have boasted of cleanliness, and for that reason they constantly kept him at a certain distance from company. He crossed himself, sighed, and attacked his food like a shark.

The dinner really was not at all bad and, since it was

a Sunday dinner, its desserts were inevitable: a palpitating jelly and a pastry called Spanish Breezes. At table Radilov, who had served for ten years in a regiment of infantry and had campaigned in Turkey, launched into stories of his army life. I listened to him attentively yet at the same time kept observing Olga on the sly. She was not particularly good-looking, but the resolute and serene look on her face, her broad white forehead, her luxuriant hair, and, in particular, her hazel eyes, not large yet intelligent, clear and animated, would have struck anybody else in my place. She seemed to be hanging on Radilov's every word; it was not sympathy, however, which her face expressed but rather a passionate interest. As far as age went, Radilov might have been her father; he addressed her familiarly, yet I immediately surmised that she was not his daughter.

During the conversation he mentioned his late wife. "Her sister," he added, indicating Olga. She instantly blushed and lowered her eyes. Radilov was silent for a space and then changed the subject. The little old woman had not uttered as much as a word throughout the dinner; she ate almost nothing herself and did not press anything on me. There was about her features some sort of timorous and hopeless expectancy, that sadness of old age which makes the heart of the beholder contract so excruciatingly. Toward the end of the meal Fedor Miheich launched into the traditional glorification of the hosts and their guest, but Radilov, after a glance at me, asked him to desist; the old man ran his hand over his lips, took to blinking, made a bow, and sat down again, but this time on the very edge of his seat. The dinner over, Radilov and I repaired to his study.

One can perceive about persons who are deeply and constantly taken up with a single idea or a single passion a something which they have in common, a certain outward similarity in their conduct, no matter how different, in general, their traits and abilities, or their position in society and their upbringing. The more I observed Radilov the more did it seem to me that he belonged to this category. He spoke about managing the estate, about crops, about the rumors going the rounds of the district, and the approaching elections—he spoke without constraint, even with sympathy, but then he would suddenly sigh and sink into an armchair like a man tired out by crushing work, running a hand over his face. All his soul, kindly and warm, was, it seemed, transpierced, was saturated by but one emotion. I was struck, if by nothing else, by my inability to detect in him any passionate devotion to food, or wine, or hunting, or nightingales of the Kursk region, or tumblers (those pigeons which are afflicted with epilepsy), or Russian literature, or pacing horses, or Hungarian women, or cards, or billiards, or balls, or trips to capital cities (either provincial or national), or paper factories and beet-sugar refineries, or brightly painted arbors, or tea, or carriage horses, so pampered that they became depraved, or even to obese coachmen, whose sashes come up to their very armpits—those magnificent coachmen whose eyes, God knows why, become crossed and goggling every time they move their necks.

"What sort of landed proprietor have we here, then?" I reflected. Yet at the same time he wasn't at all pretending to be a gloomy fellow and one dissatisfied with his lot; on the contrary, there was actually an aura of indiscriminate good will, of geniality about him, and of an almost offensive readiness to become intimate with every Tom, Dick, and Harry he came across. True, you felt at the same time that he was incapable of forming any close friendship, of becoming genuinely intimate with anyone, and that he was incapable of these things not because he had, in general, no need of other people but because his whole life had for a time become withdrawn. As I regarded Radilov more closely I simply could not picture him to myself as a happy man, either at present or at any other time. He was no Adonis, either, but there lurked in his gaze, in his smile, in all his being something that was exceedingly attractive— lurking, precisely. There, it seemed, one would simply love to get to know him better, get to love him. Of course, the landed proprietor and the steppe squire in him would emerge every now and then, but nonetheless he was a fine person.

We had just begun to discuss the next district leader when Olga's voice came from the doorway: "Tea is ready." We went to the dining room. Fedor Miheich, just as before, was sitting in his nook between a small window and the door, his feet meekly tucked in to be out of the way. Radilov's mother was knitting a stocking. Autumnal freshness and the fragrance of apples was wafted through the windows from the garden. Olga was busied with pouring the tea. I regarded her now with greater attention than at dinner. She said very little, as all provincial young ladies do as a rule, but in her case, at least, I did not observe their desire to say something witty coupled with an excruciating sense of vacuity and impotence; she did not keep sighing, as though from an excess of inexplicable emotions, did not roll up her eyes under her very forehead, did not indulge in pensive and vague smiles. Her look was calm and indifferent, like that of one relaxing after a great happiness or a great disturbance. Her walk, her movements, were resolute and unconstrained. She was very much to my liking.

Radilov and I again got into talk. I no longer remember in just what way we came to the well-known observation: how frequently the most insignificant things will create a greater impression than those of the utmost importance.

"Yes," Radilov remarked, "I've experienced that in my own case. As you know, I was married. Not for long—three years; my wife died in giving birth. I thought I would not survive her; I was dreadfully grief-stricken, mortally hurt, yet weep I could not—I walked about as if in a daze. They dressed her fittingly, laid her out on a table—here, in this room. The priest came, so did the sacristans; they started chanting, praying, censing with labdanum; I bowed down to the very ground—and if I could but have shed a single tear! As if my heart had turned to stone, and my head with it—and all of me had become dead weight, for the matter of that. That's how the first day passed. That night —would you believe it?—I actually fell asleep. Next morning I came in to see my wife. It was summertime, the sun lit her from head to foot, and that very vividly. Suddenly I saw"—at this point Radilov could not help shuddering—"what do you think? One of her eyes wasn't completely closed, and a fly was walking over that eye. . . . I collapsed like a sheaf of wheat and, when I came to, I started weeping and weeping—I couldn't make myself stop."

Radilov fell silent. I looked at him, then at Olga. Were I to live forever I would not forget her expression. The little old woman put down the stocking she had been knitting, got a handkerchief out of her reticule, and stealthily wiped away a tear. Fedor Miheich suddenly stood up, grabbed his fiddle, and launched into a little song in a hoarse and wild voice. He probably wished to put us in a merry mood,

but we were all startled by the first sound and Radilov requested him to calm down.

"However, what's over is over; there's no bringing back the past and, finally . . . everything is for the best in this world—as Voltaire, I believe, said it," he hastily added.

"Yes," I contributed, "of course. Besides, one can bear up under any misfortune, and there's no situation so wretched that one can't find a way out of it."

"Do you think so?" Radilov commented. "Oh, well, perhaps you're right. I remember the time I was in Turkey, lying half dead in a hospital. I had putrid fever. Well, the accommodations weren't anything we could have boasted about: there was a war on, and glory be to God for whatever we did have! Suddenly a new batch of patients was brought to our place—and where were the beds for them? The chief medical officer went this way and that way. There just wasn't any room for them. Well, he walked up to my bed and asked an assistant: 'Is he still living?' — 'He was, this morning.' So then the medical officer leaned over and heard me breathing. He couldn't restrain himself, this friend of mine. 'There,' said he, 'what a fool thing nature is! Why, now, the man is going to die. There, he's going to die without fail, yet he's still creaking along, dragging things out; all he's doing is taking up room and making things hard for others.' — 'Well,' said I to myself, 'you're in a bad way, Michailo Michailych. . . .' And yet, get well I did, and am living to this day, as you can see. Consequently, you're right."

"I would be right in any case," I answered. "Even if you had died you still would have been out of your wretched situation."

"Naturally, naturally," he added, thumping his hand hard on the table. "All one has to do is to find the resolution. Where's the sense in being in a wretched situation? Why shilly-shally, why drag the thing out—"

Olga quickly stood up and went out into the garden.

"Well, now, Fedya, strike up a dance tune!"

Fedya bounded up and started through the room in that dandified peculiar step with which the "she-goat" in the well-known folk dance struts around a trained bear, and began singing "It all happened at our gates."

The sounds of a racing sulky came from the front entrance, and a few moments later a tall old man, broad-shouldered and stout, a petty squire by the name of Ovsianikov, entered the room. However, Ovsianikov is a personage so remarkable and original that, with the reader's permission, we will have more to say of him in another fragmentary sketch.

And now, for my part, I will add only that the very next day, as soon as it was light, Ermolai and I set out hunting and, after hunting, headed for home; that a week later I again dropped in at Radilov's but found neither him nor Olga at home, while a fortnight later I learned that he had suddenly vanished, had forsaken his mother, and had gone off somewhere with his sister-in-law. The whole district was stirred up and took to talking about this affair, and it was only then that I at last came to understand the expression on Olga's face at the time Radilov was telling his story. It was not compassion alone that it had evinced then: it had been ablaze with jealousy as well.

Before my departure from the country I paid a visit to the little old woman, Radilova. I found her in the drawing room, playing cards with Fedor Miheich—the game was "booby."

"Have you any word from your son?" I asked her at last.

The little old woman burst into tears. I did not question her any further about Radilov.

OVSIANIKOV, THE FREEHOLDER

JUST PICTURE to yourselves, my amiable readers, a man stout, tall, about seventy, whose face reminds you somewhat of the fabulist Krylov, with a clear and intelligent gaze from under beetling brows, with dignified bearing, measured speech, and a deliberate walk: there you have Ovsianikov. He was wearing a roomy, long-sleeved blue surtout buttoned to the very top, a kerchief of lilac silk about his neck, brightly polished boots with tassels, and in general, his appearance resembled that of a well-to-do merchant. His hands were beautiful—soft and white; frequently, in the course of conversation, he would take hold of the buttons of his surtout. Ovsianikov, in his dignity and immobility, his horse sense and indolence, his forthrightness and stubbornness, reminded me of the Russian nobles of the times before Peter the Great. Their tall, ornate headgear would have looked right on him. He was one of the last men of the old era.

All his neighbors held him in exceedingly high esteem and deemed it an honor to know him. His brother squireens all but prayed to him; they doffed their hats to him from afar, they took pride in him. Generally speaking, it is difficult in our society, right up to the present, to distinguish a petty squire from a muzhik: his estate is hardly much better than that of a muzhik, his calves are never out of the buckwheat fields, his horses are barely breathing and their harness is of rope. Ovsianikov was an exception to the prevail-

59

ing rule, even though he did not have the reputation of being a rich man. He and his wife lived by themselves in a snug, neat little house, he did not maintain many servants, he dressed his serfs in the Russian manner and called them farmhands. And they did plow his land well for him. He did not proclaim himself as one of the gentry, or pretend to be a landed proprietor; he never "forgot his place," as the saying goes; he would not sit down at the first invitation and, whenever a new guest entered, would never fail to rise, yet would do so with such dignity, with such stately cordiality that the guest would involuntarily make him a rather deep bow.

Ovsianikov kept to the olden customs not out of superstition (his was quite a free soul) but through habit. He had no liking for spring carriages, for instance, because he did not find them comfortable, but drove about either in a racing droshky or in a small handsome leather-cushioned cart, and drove his good bay trotter himself. (He kept nothing but bays.) His coachman, a young, rosy-cheeked lad whose hair was cut badger and who wore a low hat of ram's wool and a short overcoat of bluish cloth with a belt of leather, sat respectfully alongside.

Ovsianikov always took a nap after dinner, went to the baths on Saturdays, read spiritual books exclusively (during which reading he would with an important air saddle his nose with round, silver-rimmed spectacles), arose and went to bed early. However, he was clean-shaven and wore his hair trimmed after the German fashion. He received his guests kindly and heartily but did not bow to them from the waist, did not bustle about or regale them with all sorts of dried and salted delicacies. "Wife!" he would say slowly, without getting up from his place and turning his head slightly toward her. "Bring the company a bite of something good."

He deemed it a sin to sell grain—God's gift!—and in '40, during the prevalence of famine and frightfully high prices, distributed all his store of it among the landowners and muzhiks in the vicinity; the following year they gratefully repaid him in kind. Ovsianikov's neighbors often resorted to him with requests to judge between them, to reconcile them, and almost always submitted to his decisions, heeding his counsel. Many of them had, through his good offices, settled definitely the boundaries of their adjoining lands. But, after coming two or three croppers with landed proprietresses, he let it be known that he refused to act as mediator between persons of the female sex. He could not abide haste, disquieting hurry, womanish chatter, and "fuss." One day his house somehow caught on fire. One of the hands came running to him, all flustered and shouting "Fire! Fire!" — "Well, what are you shouting about?" Ovsianikov asked him calmly. "Hand me my cap and walking stick."

He liked to break in his horses himself. On one occasion a fiery Bitiuk [1] stallion ran away with him downhill, heading for a ravine. "There, that'll do, that'll do, you're not fully grown yet, you little stallion—you'll hurt yourself," Ovsianikov kept admonishing his steed good-naturedly—and a moment later went flying into the ravine together with the racing droshky, the boy sitting in back, and the horse. Fortunately, there were mounds of sand at the bottom of the ravine. No one got hurt—the Bitiuk alone dislocated a leg. "There, now, you see," Ovsianikov went on in a calm voice as he picked himself up off the ground, "that's what I was telling you."

And the wife he had sought out for himself also suited him perfectly. Tatiana Ilyinichna Ovsianikova was tall, sedate, and taciturn; she always went about in a headkerchief of brown silk. There was a chill wafted from her, yet not only was there never a complaint against her sternness but, on the contrary, many of the poor folk called her mother and benefactress. The regular features of her face, her big dark eyes, her fine lips—all bore witness to the beauty she had once been celebrated for. The Ovsianikovs were childless.

I had made his acquaintance at Radilov's, as the reader already knows, and a couple of days afterward took a ride to his place. I found him at home. He was seated in a roomy leather easy chair and was reading *The Lives of the Saints*. A gray cat was curled up on his shoulder, purring. He received me, after his wont, in kindly and stately fashion. We fell into talk.

"But truthfully speaking, Luka Petrovich," I said inci-

---

[1] The term "Bitiuk" (or "Bitiuk-bred") is applied to a special breed of horses developed in the province of Voronezh in the vicinity of Hrenov (the well-known stud farm which at one time had belonged to Countess Orlova).—*Author*.

The Bitiuk earth-shaker is the Russian counterpart of the Percheron or the Clydesdale—the most magnificent creatures, after woman and the Piedmontese white ox, on the face of the earth.—*Trans*.

dentally, "surely things used to be better before—in your times, that is?"

"Some things used to be better, true enough," Ovsianikov replied, "I can tell you that. We lived at an easier pace, true enough. But just the same things are better now—and as for your little ones, things will be still better for them, God willing."

"Why, I was expecting you to start praising the old times to me."

"No, I have no reason to be praising the old times particularly. There, take even you for example, let's say—you're a landowner now, the same sort of landowner as your late grandfather was, yet you'll never have such power as was his! And besides, you yourself aren't that kind of a man. Even now there are others of the gentry who are squeezing us against the wall but, the way things look, that's something that can't be avoided. The grain will be ground, and then there'll be flour—I guess. No, I certainly won't see nowadays that which I have seen so much of in my youth."

"Well, just what was it, for instance?"

"Well, just for instance, I'll again tell you about your grandfather. A domineering man, he was! Took advantage of us freeholders. There, now, you may know—for how can you help knowing the land you own?—you know the wedge of land stretching from Cheplyghin to Malinin. You've got it under oats now. But then it's ours. All of it is ours, just the way it lies. Your grandfather took it away from us. He came riding on his horse, pointed out the land with a wave of his hand, said 'That's my property,' and take possession of that property he did. My father, he's dead now—may the Kingdom of Heaven be his!—was a just man, but he was a hot-tempered man, too—and besides, who wants to lose what belongs to him?—and so he petitioned the court. But he was the only one to do so; the others wouldn't go along—they were afraid. Well, they informed your grandfather that 'Peter Ovsianikov has lodged a complaint against you, saying you have willfully taken his land away from him, see.'

"So, right off, your grandfather sent over Baush, his master of kennels, and a band of men with him. And so they seized my father and hauled him off to your ancestral estate. I was only a snip of a boy then; I ran after him, barefooted. Well, what was the upshot? They hauled him up to your manor house and gave him a flogging under its very windows. And

your grandfather was standing there on the balcony and looking on, while your grandmother was sitting right by a window
and also watching. My father kept calling out 'Maria Vassilievna, mother of mine, speak up for me—you, at least,
might spare me!' But all she did was to sit up a little better
and keep right on watching. And so they got my father's
word that he would give up his land, and on top of that bade
him give thanks for having been let off alive. And that's how
the land was left as yours. Just go and ask your muzhiks:
'What do they call this land, now?' They give it the name of
Oakland—because it was taken away by oaken cudgels. And
so that's why we little people have no call to feel any too
sorry about the passing of the old ways."

I didn't know what answer to make to Ovsianikov and
hadn't the courage to look him in the face.

"And then there was another neighbor come amongst us
at that time—Komov, Stepan Niktopolionych. He did my
father in altogether—if it weren't one thing, it was another.
He was a hard-drinking man and loved giving folks a good
time, and when he'd get one or two under his belt and say
'C'est bon!'—just like that, in French—and lick his lips, there
was the Devil and all to pay! He'd send around for all the
neighbors to call on him. Why, he had troikas all ready and
standing, and if you didn't start off to see him he'd come
down on you himself like a clap of thunder. And what an odd
man he was! When he was cold sober he didn't go in for
lying, but let him get a little drink in him and he'd be off
telling stories: that he had three houses in Peter's town, and
all three of them on Fontanka itself—one red, with a single
chimney, another yellow, with two chimneys, and a third
blue, without any chimneys. And he had three sons (and
yet he'd never been married, mind you): one in the infantry,
another in the cavalry, and the third all on his own. And he'd
say that he had a son living in each house, and that the oldest
had admirals calling on him, the second generals, and the
youngest Englishmen only!

"And so he'd get up on his feet and propose: 'Here's to the
health of my eldest son: he respects me the most!'—and with
that he would burst into tears. And if anyone got the notion
of refusing to drink to that there'd be trouble aplenty. 'I'll
shoot you down,' he'd say, 'and I won't let anybody bury
you!' Or else he'd jump up and start yelling: 'Dance, you
God's own folk, for your own diversion and for to pleasure

me!' Well, you had to start dancing; it might be the death of you, yet dance you must.

"As for his serf wenches, he'd simply tucker them out. There were times they'd be singing in a chorus all night through, actually—until the very morning—and whichever wench sang the highest, why, she would win the prize. But should they begin to tire he would put his head down on his arms and start grieving: 'Ah, poor orphan that I am and all forlorn! They're forsaking poor me!' So then the ostlers would put new life into those wenches right then and there.

"Well, now, the way things fell out he grew really fond of my father—and what could one do about it? Why, he all but drove my father into his grave, and he sure would have done that, too, if it hadn't been for his dying himself, glory be: he fell off a dovecote in a drunken state. There, now, that's the sort of good neighbors we had!"

"How times have changed, though!" I remarked.

"Yes, yes," Ovsianikov concurred. "And one must also admit that in the old days the nobility used to live on a more magnificent scale, and that goes without saying as far as the grand lords are concerned: I've seen more than enough of them in Moscow. But there's talk of their having died out even there by now."

"You've been in Moscow?"

"Yes, long ago—very long ago. I'm in my seventy-third year now, and it was in eighteen-sixteen that I made a trip to Moscow." Ovsianikov sighed.

"And whom did you see there?"

"Why, I saw many of the grand nobles—and everybody saw them, for that matter: they lived right out in the open, in glory and to the wonder of all. Only there wasn't a one that could come up to the late Count Alexei Grigorievich Orlov-Chesmensky. Alexei Grigorievich, now, I used to see often— an uncle of mine worked for him as a major-domo. The Count deigned to live near the Kaluzhiskiya Gates, on Shabalovka. Now there was a grandee for you! Such a bearing, such a gracious address as one couldn't imagine or tell about. Take his height alone—his strength, his gaze! As long as you didn't know him, hadn't the entry to him, you'd be afraid, sure enough, you'd feel timid; but as soon as you entered the room he was in it was just as though the dear sun had warmed you and you felt all blithe. He'd let any man into his presence and had a great liking for everything. In

racing he took the reins himself and would race against anybody, and he'd never get ahead of anybody at the very start,
wouldn't hurt anybody's feelings or take any advantage, but
would rather win in the homestretch. And he was ever so
kind: he would cheer up the loser and praise his horse.

"He kept tumbling pigeons of the very first sort. He used
to come out into the courtyard, seat himself in an easy chair,
and order the pigeons to be released, and all around there
were men with guns posted on the roofs, to keep the hawks
off. A huge silver basin filled with water was placed at the
feet of the count, and he'd watch the pigeons as they were
reflected in the water. The lowly, the poverty-stricken lived
in their hundreds on bread provided by him—and how much
money he handed out! But if he got angry it was like a roll
of thunder—a great fright yet nothing to cry over: first
thing you know there he was, actually smiling. If he gave a
feast he made all of Moscow drunk! And what a clever fellow
he was—for it was he who really beat the Turk. He was fond
of wrestling, too; they brought strong men to him from Tula,
from Harkov, from Tambov—from all over Russia: if he
won the match he would reward the loser, but if he lost, why,
he would simply shower the winner with gifts and kiss him
right on the lips. And then there was the time—this was
during my stay in Moscow—when he staged a hunt the like
of which had never been in Russia. He invited all the sports-
men, absolutely all, from every part of the empire to be his
guests, setting a date and giving them three months' time.
And so all of them gathered. They brought plenty of dogs
and huntsmen along—why, a whole army arrived, a downright army! First they had themselves a feast, all proper and
fitting, and after that they set out for the stand. The folks
came running—there was just no end to them. And what do
you think happened? Why, it was your father's dog that out-
ran all the others."

"Was it Prettyface, by any chance?"

"Prettyface—Prettyface it was. So then the count fell to
imploring your grandfather: 'Sell me your dog, now. Take
whatever you want for it.' — 'No, Count,' the other told him,
'I'm no shopkeeper. I wouldn't sell as much as an old rag
that I have no use for; if my honor were involved, however,
I would yield my wife—but never Prettyface. I'd liefer yield
myself to servitude.' As to Alexei Grigorievich, he praised
him: 'I love you,' he told him. Your grandfather, now,

brought Prettyface back in his carriage, and when she died he buried her in his garden with a band playing; he buried that bitch, and over the grave of that bitch he put up a gravestone with an epitaph."

"There, you see, Alexei Grigorievich never hurt anybody," I remarked.

"Yes, it's always that way: whoever doesn't draw much water himself is always making others back water."

"But what sort of a man was this Baush?" I asked after a certain silence.

"How is it, now, that you've heard about Prettyface but not about Baush? He was the chief huntsman and whipper-in for your grandfather. Your grandfather, now, loved him no less than he did Prettyface. A daredevil, he was, and no matter what your grandfather might order him to do he would carry out in an instant, even though it meant being run through with a knife. And whenever he hallooed, why, the woods would simply resound with his voice. Or else he would turn mulish, all of a sudden, get down off his horse, and lie flat on the ground. And as soon as the dogs ceased hearing his voice it was all over! They would abandon the freshest scent, wouldn't run in pursuit, no matter how you urged them on. M-my, and would your grandfather get angry! 'I won't want to go on living if I don't hang that good-for-nothing! I'll turn that Antichrist inside out! I'll draw that murderer's heels through his throat!' But the thing would wind up with his sending someone to find out what the other wanted, why he wasn't hallooing. And on such occasions Baush would usually demand liquor, drink it down, pick himself up off the ground, and again start in ho-hoing in all his glory."

"Apparently you too like hunting, Luka Petrovich?"

"I would like to hunt, true enough, but not now: now my time for that is gone, but in my younger days . . . but then you know, it's sort of awkward, on account of my station. There's no call for our sort to go tagging after the gentry. True enough, now and then there might actually have been one of our class, a hard drinker and not of much use, who would get next to the squires—but what joy would he get out of that! All it meant was disgracing himself. They'd give him some wretched nag that stumbled all along, they would knock his hat off to the ground, time and again, or make believe to put the whip to a horse but would flick him

66

instead, yet he would have to laugh all the while—and be making the others laugh. No, I'll tell you this much: the lesser your station the more straitly you have to behave, or else you will besmirch yourself, sure as sure.

"Yes," Ovsianikov went on with a sigh, "a lot of water has flowed over the dam the while I've been on earth; different times are upon us. It is among the noblemen in particular that I perceive a great change. Those with small estates have all either spent time working for the government or just can't stay put in one place; as for those of the bigger sort, there's no recognizing them, actually. I had plenty of opportunities to observe them—these big fellows, that is—at the time the land boundaries were being settled. And I must tell you this: it gladdens one's heart to see them. They're considerate, courteous. Only there's one thing which makes me wonder: they have learned all there is to learn, they speak so well that your soul is touched, yet when it comes to something real they can't get the hang of it. They don't sense even what's for their own good. One of their own serfs who's clerking for them can bend them to his will, just as wood is bent into a yoke.

"There, now, perhaps you know Korolev, Alexander Vladimirovich—is there any shortcoming in him as a nobleman? Handsome of person, rich, has studied at universities and has been abroad, it seems; he speaks agreeably, modestly, and shakes hands with all of us. You do know him? Well, just listen to this. Last week we all gathered in Berezovka, at the invitation of Nikiphor Ilyich, the mediator. And Nikiphor Ilyich, the mediator, he told us: 'Gentlemen, we must settle the boundaries of our estates; it's a shame—our district has fallen behind all the others in this respect; let's get down to business.' Well, get down to business we did. Arguments sprang up and disputes, the way they usually do; our attorney began showing off. But the first one to get on his high horse was Ovchinikov—Porphyry Ovchinikov. And what was making the fellow raise such a rumpus? He doesn't own an inch of land himself—he was acting on his brother's behalf. 'No!' he kept shouting. 'You're not going to take me in! No, you've run into a different sort of fellow here! Let's have those maps! Let me get my hands on that surveyor—bring that Judas-soul here!' — 'But just what is your demand, after all?' — 'There, you sure have found a fool! Do you think I'm going to make my demand known to you right off, just like that? No, let's have those maps here, that's what!' And all the while he's got those selfsame maps under his fist and is pounding them. He insulted Martha Dmitrievna in such fashion that the insult could be avenged only in blood. 'How dare you malign my reputation?' she screamed. 'Your reputation,' he told her, 'is something I wouldn't wish on my chestnut mare.'

"Well, it was all we could do to bring her to with Madeira. We calmed him down at last—so then the others started getting rough. Korolev, now, the dear little fellow, was sitting there in a corner, nibbling away at the head of his walking stick, but could only keep on shaking his head. I felt ashamed of myself; just couldn't stand it; wanted to run out of the room: what would the man think of us? Then I saw my Alexander Vladimirych getting up on his feet—it looked as if he wanted to speak. The mediator perked up: 'Gentlemen, gentlemen—Alexander Vladimirych would like to have the floor!'

"And you can't help praising the gentry: there was immediate silence. And so Alexander Vladimirych began, and he said: 'We have apparently forgotten what we have come together for; although the settling of estate boundaries is indisputably to the advantage of landowners, why has it really been initiated? So that it may afford relief to the peasant, so that he might work with less trouble, so that he might carry out his obligations. For the way things are now he himself does not know which land is allotted to him and not infrequently has to ride two miles to do the plowing—and you can't hold him responsible.' Then Alexander Vladimirych said it was a sin to pay no heed to the welfare of the peasants; that, finally, if one were to use one's common sense, their interests and our interests were all one: if they were well off, we were well off, too; if they were in a bad way, so were we— and that consequently it was sinful and senseless not to come to an agreement because of trifles. And he was off to a good start—and really, how he did talk! He just took hold of your soul. The gentry, now, they let their noses droop; I myself was on the very verge of shedding a tear or two. I give you my word you wouldn't find any speeches like that in the old books. And yet, what was the upshot? He himself wouldn't yield a ten-acre lot of mossy bog and didn't want to sell it. 'I'll have my own people drain that bog,' said he, 'and build me a woolen mill on it, with improvements. I have already chosen that site,' he said, 'I have my own considerations on that score.' And it wouldn't have been so bad if only there had been some justification for his stand, but it was simply a matter of Karassikov's—Anton Karassikov, a neighbor of Alexander Vladimirych's—having been too niggardly to come across with a hundred rubles in depreciated government notes to Korolev's clerk. And that's how we broke up and went our ways, without having concluded our business. And yet Alexander Vladimirych considers himself in the right to this day and still keeps talking about the woolen mill, only he never gets around to draining that bog."

"And how does he manage his estate?"

"He's introducing new ways all the time. The muzhiks aren't singing his praises, but then it's no use listening to them. Alexander Vladimirych is doing the right thing."

"But how is that, Luka Petrovich? I thought you were an adherent to the old order of things."

"It's different with me. For I'm no nobleman and no landed proprietor. What does my estate amount to? And besides, I actually don't know how to do things any differently. I try to act according to justice and according to law—and glory be to God even for that! The young gentry have no liking for the old ways: I praise them for that. It's time we came to our senses. The only trouble is that the young gentry are far too clever. They treat the muzhik like a moppet: they'll twist him and turn him, wear him out, and then cast him aside. And the clerk, who is himself a serf, or an estate manager who is a German by birth, will get the peasant into his paws again. And if but one of the young squires, now, would set us an example, would show us: 'There, that's the way to run things!' How will all this end, then? Can it be that I will simply die without ever seeing the new ways? What sort of comeuppance is this? That which is old has died out, yet that which is young is not coming to birth!"

I did not know what answer to make to Ovsianikov. He glanced over his shoulder, moved a little closer to me, and went on in a lowered voice: "But have you heard about Vassilii Nicholaich Liubozvonov?"

"No, I haven't."

"Do explain to me, please, what sort of wonders these may be? I just can't get them through my head. His own muzhiks told me the story, but I can't get the hang of the things they say. He's a young man, as you know, and came into his inheritance recently, after his mother's death. Well, then, he arrived at his patrimonial estate. All the little muzhiks gathered to have a look-see at their master. Vassilii Nicholaich came out to greet them. The muzhiks gaped: what kind of a raree-show was this? Their master was rigged out in plush trousers, just like a coachman, and he had put on boots with fancy tops; he had donned a red shirt, and his caftan, too, was like a coachman's; he'd let his beard grow, and he was wearing such a queer dinky hat, while his face, too, was ever so queer You couldn't say the man was drunk, exactly, but he didn't seem to be in his right mind, either.

" 'Greetings, lads!' said he. 'May God come to your aid!' The muzhiks bowed to him from the waist—but they weren't saying a thing: they had turned timid, you know. And he himself seemed to be turning timid. He started delivering a speech to them: 'I am a Russian,' said he, 'and you are Russians; I love everything that's Russian; my soul, now, is Russian and my blood, too, is Russian.' And then, all of a sudden, he fires a command at them: 'And now, dear children, sing me a Russian song, a folk song!' The muzhiks felt the backs of their knees quivering; they became altogether dazed. There was one brave fellow who did strike up a song, but then he immediately squatted to the ground, hiding himself behind the others.

"And here's the thing to wonder at: we've had landowners of that sort, too—reckless fellows, arrant rakes—that's true enough; they dressed in such fashion you couldn't tell them apart from the coachmen; they went in for dancing and prancing, they strummed the guitar and hummed to it, they sang and drank with the lowest of their house serfs and caroused with their peasants. But you take this Vassilii Nicholaievich, now. He's just like some fair maiden: he's reading his books all the time, or writing, or else reciting away at those poems; he won't get into talk with anybody, he shies away from everybody; all he knows is to stroll about the garden all by his lonesome, as though he is bored or downhearted.

"The clerk who had been in power before had a thorough scare thrown into him at first; just before Vassilii Nicholaievich's coming he had hastily made the rounds of the peasants' households—evidently the cat was aware whose cream she had lapped up! And the muzhiks had their hopes aroused.

Jacelyne Pache.

'No you don't, brother!' they were thinking. 'You sure will be brought up to answer for everything, dear man; there, you'll have to dance aplenty, slave-driving skinflint that you are!' But instead of that things turned out in such a way that—how could I put it to you?—the Lord Himself couldn't make head or tail of the way things turned out! Vassilii Nicholaich summoned the clerk to him and told him—while he himself turned all red and was breathing fast, you know—'I want you to be fair; don't go oppressing anybody. Do you hear?' And from then on he hasn't even once summoned the clerk into his presence! He lives on his own hereditary lands as if he were a stranger there. So that clerk has had a breathing spell, and as to the muzhiks, why, they durst not come nigh Vassilii Nicholaich. They're afraid. And here's still another thing that breeds wonder: the master bows to them and the master regards them amiably, yet they simply get cramps in their bellies from fright. What sort of wonders be these? Tell me that, father of mine. Either I've fallen into my dotage or something, but I can't understand it."

For answer I told Ovsianikov that Liubozvonov was probably unwell.

"Unwell nothing! He's greater in girth than he is in height, and the face on him, God be with him, is such a full one, for all that he is so young. Still and all, the Lord knows what's what." And Ovsianikov heaved a profound sigh.

"Well, leaving the noblemen to one side," I resumed, "what can you tell me about the freeholders, Luka Petrovich?"

"No, that is something you must really excuse me from," he hastened to say. "Truly, I actually could tell you a thing or two—but what's the use!" He made a gesture of futility. "We'll be doing better by setting down to a dish of tea. We're muzhiks, sure enough muzhiks; but then, truth to tell, how are we to be anything else?"

He fell silent. Tea was served. Tatiana Ilyinichna changed her seat for one much closer to us. In the course of the evening she had noiselessly left the room several times and had returned just as quietly. Silence reigned in the room. Ovsianikov kept draining cup after cup, gravely and leisurely.

"Mitya was here today," Tatiana Ilyinichna remarked in a low voice.

Ovsianikov frowned. "What did he want?"

"He came to ask for forgiveness."

71

Ovsianikov shook his head. "There, now," he turned to
me, "what would you have one do with one's relatives? For
it's out of the question to repudiate them. There, God has
rewarded me, too, with a dear little nephew. He's a lad with
a head on his shoulders, a mettlesome lad, there's no arguing
about that; he did well in his studies—only I'll never see any
good from him no matter how long I live. He was working
for the government—and left: there was no advancement for
him, you see. But then, is he one of the nobility? Even noblemen aren't promoted to generals right off. And so now he's
living without anything to do. Even that wouldn't be so bad—
but he had to go and turn pettifogger! He makes up petitions
for the peasants, writes reports, admonishes village constables,
smokes the surveyors out into the open, traipses around the
pothouses, hobnobs with the town's burghers and with the
porters of wayside inns. Will it be long before all that leads to
trouble? Both the police commissioners and the rural police
have already threatened him more than once. But then, it's
a good thing he knows how to play the tomfool: he'll set
them to laughing, only to land them in a fine kettle of fish
afterward. But come, isn't he sitting in your little room
right now?" he added, turning to his wife. "For I know you,
you're so tenderhearted, you're protecting him."

Tatiana Ilyinichna cast down her eyes, smiled, and turned
red.

"There, it's just as I said," Ovsianikov went on. "Oh, you
pamperer! Well, bid him come in; so be it. For the sake of a
dear guest I'll forgive the foolish lad. There, bid him come
in, do!"

Tatiana Ilyinichna went over to the door and called out:
"Mitya!"

Mitya, a lad of twenty-eight, tall, well built, came into the
room and, on catching sight of me, halted at the threshold.
His clothes were after the German mode, but the unnaturally
big shoulder pads alone served as obvious proof that they
had been cut by a tailor who was not merely Russian but a
bred-in-the-bone Russian.

"There, draw nearer, nearer," the old man began. "What
are you ashamed of? Thank your aunt: you are forgiven.
There, father of mine, let me introduce you," he went on,
indicating Mitya. "Even though he is my own nephew I just
can't get along with him. The last days of the world are upon
us!" Mitya and I exchanged bows. "Well, speak up, what sort

72

of a mess have you gotten into now? What's the complaint against you now? Go on and tell us."

Mitya evidently did not feel like giving an explanation and justifying himself in my presence. "Later on, Uncle," he muttered.

"No, not later on but now," the old man continued. "I know you're embarrassed before this gentleman: so much the better, do penance. If you please, go ahead and talk—now, if it pleases you. We'll listen."

"I've nothing to be ashamed of," Mitya began in animation and with a toss of his head. "Judge for yourself, Uncle, if you'll be so kind. The freeholders of Reshetilov came to me and said: 'Intercede for us, brother.' — 'What is it?' — 'Why, this is the way of it: our grain storages are in good order, they couldn't possibly be any better; suddenly an official arrived among us—he had orders to inspect our grain storages, now. He inspected them and then told us: "Your storages are all in disorder; there are serious violations. I am compelled to inform my superiors." — "But just what do the violations consist of?" — "Why, I know just what they are," said he. So we held a meeting and decided to show our gratitude to the official in the appropriate manner, but old man Prohorych stood in our way: "That way," said he, "you'll only work up their appetites. What is all this, really? Come, is there no redress for us whatsoever?" So we listened to the old man, but that official got his dander up and handed in a complaint, lodged information against us in writing, that is. Well, so they're summoning us now to answer the charges.' 'Come, are your storages actually in good order?' I asked them. 'As God is our witness they are that, and the legal quantity of grain is all there.' — 'Well,' I told them, 'there's nothing for you to be scared about,' and I drew up a paper for them. And nobody knows yet in whose favor the matter will be decided. But as for anybody complaining to you about me on this score, that's an understandable thing: it's each man for himself."

"Each man—except yourself, it looks like," said the old man in a low voice. "And what sort of shenanigans have you been up to with the peasants at Shutolomov?"

"Why, how do you know?"

"I know, right enough."

"And there, too, I'm in the right—if you will again be kind enough to judge for yourself. Their neighbor

Bespandin plowed up ten acres or so of land that belonged
to them. 'It's my land,' said he. The Shutolomov muzhiks
are paying quitrent, mind you; their landowner has gone
abroad. Who's to intercede for them? Judge for yourself.
And the land is theirs, beyond any dispute, the deed for
it going back to times out of mind. Well, then, they came
to me and said: 'Write a petition for us.' And write it I did.
But Bespandin found out and took to making threats: 'I'll
tear this Mitka's shoulder blades out of their sockets, or else
I'll knock his head clean off his shoulders.' We'll see how he'll
do that; it's still all there."

"Don't you go bragging, now; it won't come to any good
end, that head of yours," the old man let drop. "You're altogether a madman, for a fact!"

"Well, now, Uncle, wasn't it you yourself who were pleased
to tell me—"

"I know what you're going to say to me," Ovsianikov cut
him short. "Right: a man must live in accordance with what
is right and is obligated to help his fellow man. There are
times when he must not spare even himself. But then, are
your actions always of that nature? Do people take you to some
tavern, or don't they? Do they ply you with drink, do they
bow down before you, or don't they? 'Dmitrii Alexeich, our
father, help us, now, and as for our gratitude, be sure we'll
show it'—and a ruble note, or even a greater, passes from
under the skirt of some coat and into your hand. Eh? Isn't
that what happens? Tell me, isn't it?"

"I am guilty of that, true enough," Mitya answered, his
eyes cast down. "But I don't take anything from the poor,
and I don't pervert my soul!"

"You may not be taking anything now, but if you should
find yourself in a tight spot you will. You don't pervert your
soul? Oh, you! I guess it's saints only you're always sticking
up for! But what about Borka Perehodov—have you forgotten about him? Who busied himself about his affairs?
Who acted as his protector? Eh?"

"Perehodov suffered through his own fault, true enough."

"He embezzled government funds. No joke, that!"

"But do consider things, Uncle. He was in poverty, he had
a family—"

"Poverty, poverty. . . . He's a drinking man and given to
gambling—that's what!"

"It was from grief that he took to drink," Mitya remarked, lowering his voice.

"From grief, was it! Well, you might have helped him, seeing you have so eager a heart, instead of sitting around in pothouses yourself with the drunkard. Suppose he does have the gift of eloquence—my, what a rare wonder that is!"

"But he is the kindliest of men."

"Everybody is kind, according to you. . . . By the way," Ovsianikov went on, turning to his wife, "was something sent to that fellow—well, you know where—"

Tatiana Ilyinichna nodded.

"Where did you disappear to these last few days?" the old man resumed.

"I was in town."

"Playing billiards all the time, never fear, and lapping tea; strumming a guitar and humming, hurrying and scurrying in and out of government offices, cooking up petitions in back rooms, showing off and chumming with the precious sons of merchants? Wasn't that so? Speak up!"

"That's so, if you like," Mitya spoke with a smile. "Ah, yes—I'd almost forgot: Funtikov, Anton Partenych, is asking you over to his place for a bite on Sunday."

"I'm not going to that potbelly. He'll serve a seventy-five-pound fish, but the butter he'll cook it with will be rancid. God be with him, altogether!"

"And I also ran across Theodosia Michailovna."

"What Theodosia may that be?"

"The one that belongs to Harpenchenko the landowner, the same who bought up the Mikulino estate at auction. This Theodosia, now, hails from Mikulino. She was living in Moscow as a seamstress and paid her quitrent regularly, a hundred and eighty-two rubles and a half each year. And she knows her work—used to get good orders in Moscow. But now Harpenchenko has recalled her from Moscow and keeps her hanging around just so, without assigning her to any definite work. She would be glad to buy her freedom, at that, and she told her master so, but he doesn't make his decision known, one way or the other. You are acquainted with this Harpenchenko, Uncle—so couldn't you put in a good word for her? And Theodosia would pay a goodly ransom."

"Would it be with your money, by any chance? Eh? There, there, so be it; I'll tell him, I'll tell him. The only thing is, I don't know what will come of it," the old man went on, his face evincing dissatisfaction. "This Harpenchenko, the Lord forgive me, is an extortioner: he buys up promissory notes, puts out money at usury, acquires estates that are sold under the hammer. What ill wind has blown him into our region? Oh, the way I feel about these come-latelies! You can't come to a sensible agreement with a fellow like that so quickly; however, we'll see."

"Do take care of it, Uncle dear!"

"Very well, I shall. Only you watch out—I'll have you watch out! There, there, don't justify yourself. God be with you, God be with you! Only in the future watch out, or else, by God, Mitya, you won't come to any good end—you'll perish, by God. For I'm not going to be carrying you out of tight corners on my shoulders forever. Besides, I myself am not so influential a man. There, go now, and God go with you."

Mitya left the room. Tatiana Ilyinichna followed him. "Give him tea, you pamperer," Ovsianikov called out after her. "Not a foolish lad, and he's got a kind heart; only thing is, I have apprehensions about him. However, do excuse me for having taken up so much of your time with trifles."

The door from the anteroom opened. A short little, gray little man in a bobtailed little jacket of velvet entered.

"Ah, Franz Ivanych!" Ovsianikov cried out. "Greetings, how is God treating you?"

Permit me, amiable reader, to acquaint you with this gentleman as well.

Franz Ivanych Lejeune, my neighbor and an Orlovian landowner, had attained the honorable status of a Russian nobleman in a manner not altogether ordinary. He had been born in Orléans, of French parents and, as a drummer boy, had set out with Napoleon to conquer Russia. At first everything went like clockwork and our Frenchman entered Moscow with his head up in the air. But on the way back poor Monsieur Lejeune, half frozen and minus his drum, fell into the hands of some darling muzhiks from Smolensk. The said darling muzhiks of Smolensk locked him up for the night in a vacant fulling mill, while the next morning they led him up to a hole in the ice near a milldam and fell to begging the drummer *de la Grrrrande Armée* to pleasure them, i.e., to dive in under the ice; Monsieur Lejeune could not accede to their request and, in his turn, fell to persuading the darling

76

muzhiks of Smolensk, in his patois, to let him go back to Orléans. "I have a mother living there, Messieurs," he told them, "*une tendre mère.*"

But the darling little muzhiks, probably owing to their ignorance of the geographical location of the city of Orléans, persisted in urging upon him the underwater journey down the current of the sinuous small river of Gniloterka [Rottengrater], and had already taken to encouraging him by light taps on the vertebrae of neck and spine, when suddenly, to the indescribable joy of Monsieur Lejeune, there came the sound of jingle bells and an enormous sleigh came dashing onto the dam, a sleigh with the gayest of rugs on an exaggeratedly elevated back seat and drawn by a troika of monstrous roans. A stout and rosy-cheeked landowner in a wolfskin overcoat was enthroned on the sleigh.

"Whatever are you doing there?" he asked the muzhiks.

"Why, we're just drowning a Frenchy, Your Honor."

"Ah!" the landowner commented indifferently and turned away.

"Monsieur! Monsieur!" the poor fellow called out.

"Ah, ah!" the wolfskin coat spoke up reproachfully. "Speaking twelve tongues, you came to invade Russia, you burned down Moscow, accursed that you are, you stole the cross off the Ivan the Great Tower, and now it's 'M'sieu'! M'sieu'!' And now it's you that's got your tail tucked in betwixt your legs! The thief has it coming to him. Get going, Philka-a!" he commanded the coachman.

The horses started off.

"Hold on, though!" the landowner commanded as an afterthought. "Hey, there, you M'sieu'! Do you know music?"

"*Sauvez-moi, sauvez-moi, mon bon Monsieur!*" Lejeune kept pleading to be saved.

"Look at them, now—what a miserable little folk! Why, there isn't a one of them knows how to talk Russian. *Musique, musique—savvy musique, vous? Savvy?* Well, do speak up! *Comprenez? Savvy musique vous?* Do you know music? On the pianoforte—*jouer savvy?*"

Lejeune at last grasped what the landowner was trying to get at and started in nodding: "*Oui, Monsieur, oui, oui, je suis musicien, je joue tous les instruments possibles! Oui, Monsieur—sauvez-moi, Monsieur!*" The poor man assured him of being a musician who could play all possible instruments.

"Well, you sure have a lucky God!" the landowner retorted. "Let him go, lads; here's twenty kopecks for you to buy vodka."

"Thanks, our father, thanks. Take him, please do!"

They seated Lejeune in the sleigh. He was gasping for joy, weeping, shivering, bowing, thanking the landowner, the coachman, the muzhiks. All he had on was a thin shirt of tricot, green and trimmed with pink ribbons, and yet the frost was a gloriously crackling one. The landowner took one look at his legs, blue and stiff from the cold, and without a word wrapped the unfortunate fellow in his own fur coat and brought him home. The house serfs gathered on the run. It wasn't long before the Frenchman was warmed, fed, clothed. The landowner led him off to his daughters.

"There, children," he told them, "I've found a teacher for you. You were pestering me all the time: 'Teach us music, now, and how to parleyvoo'; so here's somebody for you who's not only a Frenchman but can play the piano. Well, M'sieu'," he went on, indicating a wretched little pianoforte which he had bought five years before from a Jew—who, however, dealt primarily in Eau de Cologne—"show us your art. *Jouer!*"

Lejeune, his heart sinking within him, sat down on the stool: he hadn't as much as touched a piano in all his born days.

"*Jouer,* now! *Jouer,* now!" the landowner kept at him. The poor fellow attacked the keys in his despair as if they were a drum and began to play utterly at random. "I thought for sure," he told the story afterward, "that the man who had saved me would grab me by the scruff of my neck and throw me out of the house."

But, to the extreme amazement of the involuntary improviser, the landowner after a brief wait patted him on the shoulder approvingly. "Fine, fine," he let drop. "I can see you have the hang of it; now go and rest."

A fortnight or so later Lejeune went from this landowner to another who was a man of wealth and culture, who came to like him because of his cheerful and mild disposition; he married this landowner's ward, entered government service, worked his way up into the rolls of the nobility, married his daughter off to Lobyzaniev, a landowner of Orlov, a retired dragoon and a versifier, while he himself resettled in Orel and took up permanent residence there.

It was that very Lejeune, then, or Franz Ivanych as they call him now, who, while I was there, entered the dining room of Ovsianikov, with whom he was on friendly terms.

But perhaps the reader has by now wearied of sitting with me at freeholder Ovsianikov's place, and I therefore lapse into an eloquent silence.

LGOV

"Let's go to Lgov," Ermolai (whom my readers are already familiar with) said to me one day. "We can shoot all the ducks we want there."

To a real hunter the wild duck does not represent anything particularly fascinating, but owing to the absence for the time being of other game (this was at the beginning of September: woodcock had not yet arrived, and I'd become fed up with running over the fields after partridges), I heeded my hunter and set out for Lgov.

Lgov is a large settlement out in the steppes, with a church that is quite ancient, built of stone and with but one cupola; there are also two mills on the swampy little river Rossota. This river turns, about three miles from Lgov, into a broad pond, with thickly growing reeds (*maier,* they call such growths in the Orlov dialect) along its banks, as well as here and there right in the middle of it. It was on this very pond, in among the river's creeks or stagnant stretches between these clumps of reeds, that one came upon the breeding places and favorite haunts of a countless host of all possible species: mallards, half-mallards, pintails, teal, divers, and so on. Small flocks were forever winging across or darting over the water, and a shot would raise such clouds of them that the hunter could not help grabbing his cap with one hand and drawing out a "Whew!" of astonishment.

We started off, Ermolai and I, along this pond but, in the

first place, the duck is a wary bird and doesn't keep close to the very bank; in the second place, even if some lagging and inexperienced teal did subject itself to our shots and was deprived of its life, our dogs were unable to retrieve it out of the dense *maier:* despite their most noble self-abnegation they could neither swim nor walk along the bottom, but merely gashed their precious noses all in vain against the sharp-edged reeds.

"No," Ermolai decided at last, "things aren't so good; we got to get hold of a boat. Let's go back to Lgov."

We started off. Hardly had we taken a few steps when a rather wretched setter came running out from behind a thick willow toward us, followed by a man of middle height, in a blue, exceedingly threadbare jacket, yellowish vest, trousers of a *gris-de-laine* or *bleu-d'amour* hue, thrust without much care into boots that were full of holes, with a red kerchief about his neck and a single-barreled gun over his shoulder. While our dogs, with that Chinese ceremonial peculiar to their nature, were sniffing up an acquaintance with this new canine personality, and that personality was being patently poltroonish, tucking its tail in between its legs, throwing its ears back and quickly turning its body with unbending knees and at the same time baring its teeth—while all this was going on the stranger walked up to us and bowed with exceeding politeness. To judge by his looks, he was five and twenty; his long, flaxen hair, slicked down with generously applied bread-cider, stuck out in rigid little wisps; his small brown eyes were cordially blinking; his whole face, bound up in a black kerchief as though he had a toothache, was cloyingly smiling.

"Allow me to introduce myself," he began in a soft and ingratiating voice. "I am Vladimir, a local hunter. Having heard of your arrival, and learned that you were pleased to set out for the banks of our pond, I have ventured to place my services at your disposal, if you have no objections."

Vladimir the hunter spoke for all the world like a beginning provincial actor doing leading juveniles. I agreed to his proposal and, even before I had reached Lgov, succeeded in learning his history. He was a liberated house serf; in his tender youth he had studied music, had served as a valet, knew his letters, had, as far as I could make out, dipped into books of one sort or another from time to time, and now, living as many in Russia do live nowadays, without a copper in cash, without any steady occupation, had, to all intents and purposes, to depend upon manna from heaven for his sustenance. He expressed himself with unusual elegance and, obviously, was showing off his manners; he must have been a desperate Lothario, too, and in all probability had met with success: Russian girls love eloquence.

Among other things he let me perceive that he occasionally called on the squires in the neighborhood, and that he stayed with friends whenever he went to town, and that he knew how to play preference, and was on friendly terms with people from both capitals. He knew well how to smile, and that in the most diversified ways: especially becoming to him was a modest, restrained smile which played on his lips as he listened attentively to the speeches of others. He heard you out, he agreed with you utterly, yet just the same never lost the sense of his own dignity, and apparently gave you to understand that he, too, could on occasion make his own opinion known. Ermolai, being a man none too well educated, and surely none too "subtle," had attempted to "thou" him. It was a sight to see with what a mocking smile Vladimir used not only "you" but "sir" in addressing him.

"Why is your face tied up in that kerchief?" I asked him. "Have you a toothache?"

"No, sir," he responded. "It is all due to something far more serious—a ruinous consequence of carelessness. I had a friend, a good fellow, sir, but not at all a hunter—no uncommon case, sir. And so, sir, one day he says to me: 'My dear friend, take me hunting; I'm curious to know what that diversion consists of.' Naturally, I did not want to refuse a comrade; for my part I obtained a gun for him and took him hunting. And so, sir, we had our proper fill of hunting; finally we thought it would be a good idea to rest. I sat down under a tree; but he, for his part, started going through the manual of arms, during which he took aim at me. I begged him to stop but, owing to his inexperience, he would not listen to me. A shot rang out—and I was deprived of my chin and the index finger of my right hand."

We reached Lgov on foot. Both Vladimir and Ermolai had decided that it was impossible to hunt without a boat.

"Suchok has a flat-bottomed boat made out of the strakes of an old barge," Vladimir observed, "but I don't know where he has hidden it. We ought to run over to him."

"Whom do you mean?"

"Why, there's a man living here, nicknamed Suchok." [1]

Vladimir went off with Ermolai to Suchok. I told them I'd wait for them near the church. As I examined the graves in the churchyard, I came upon a blackened, quadrangular urn with the following inscriptions: on one side, in French characters, *Ci-git Théophile Henri, vicomte de Blangy;* on another, *Under this Stone Lies Interr'd the Body of a French Subject, Count Blangy; Born* 1737—*Died* 1799; *the Whole Span of His Life was* 62 *Years;* on the third side: *Peace unto His Ashes;* and, on the fourth:

A Son of France, an Emigrant, lies 'neath
   this Stone and Earth,
A Man of Talent, he; likewise of Noble Birth.
His slain Spouse and Family he dutifully
   Mourn'd,
And left his Native Land, that was by Tyrants
   Spurn'd;
When he at last far Russia's shores Attain'd,
In his declining Years he welcome Shelter gained;
He taught the Young, their Parents did console—
Here the All-Highest gave Peace unto his Soul.

The arrival of Ermolai, Vladimir, and the man with the odd nickname of Pine Knot cut short my meditations. Barefooted, tattered, and disheveled Suchok, to judge by his looks, was a superannuated house serf of sixty.

"Have you a boat?" I asked him.

"I have that," he answered in a muffled and broken voice, "but it's in mighty poor shape."

"Why, what's wrong with it?"

"It's all coming apart, and the calking is all fallen out of the holes."

"Things aren't so bad!" Ermolai chimed in. "We can stuff them up with oakum."

"Of course we could," Suchok concurred.

"And who may you be?"

"I'm the owner's fisherman."

"How does it happen, then, that you're a fisherman and yet your boat is in such disrepair?"

"Well, if it comes to that, there's no fish in our river, either."

---

[1] "Pine Knot."—*Trans.*

"Fish don't like swamp scum," my hunter remarked with an authoritative air.

"Very well," I told Ermolai, "go and get some oakum and fix up the boat for us—and do it as quickly as you can." Ermolai went off. "But if things are as bad as all that, aren't we likely to go down to the bottom?" I turned to Vladimir.

"God is gracious," he answered. "In any case, we must suppose that the pond is not deep."

"Ay, that it isn't," remarked Suchok, who spoke somehow oddly, as if he were half asleep. "Besides, there's silt and grass on the bottom—the whole pond is grown over with water grass, for that matter. However, there's also deep holes there."

"But if the grass is so thick," Vladimir remarked, "perhaps we may not even be able to row."

"Why, whoever rows a flat-bottom boat? You got to shove it with a pole. I'll go along with you; I've got a pole—or you could use a shovel, even."

"It might be sort of clumsy to use a shovel. You might not reach bottom in some spots, likely as not," said Vladimir.

"It *is* clumsy, true enough."

I sat down on a grave while waiting for Ermolai. Vladimir withdrew a few paces to one side, out of politeness, and sat down in his turn. Suchok continued standing where he was, his head cast down and his hands, through an old habit, clasped behind him.

"Tell me, please," I began, "have you been a fisherman here long?"

"Going on seven years," he answered, livening up a little.

"And what did you work at before?"

"I was a coachman before that."

"And who discharged you as a coachman?"

"Why, the new mistress."

"What mistress?"

"Why, the one that bought us, now. You wouldn't know her—Alena Timotheievna, her name is; sort of stout, no longer young."

"How did she ever get the idea of making you her fisherman?"

"Why, God knows what she had in mind. She came to us from her family estate, from Tambov, gave orders to call all the domestics together, and came out on the steps to us. First off we go to kiss her hand, and she don't mind—she weren't displeased at all. But then she started questioning us, one after the other: 'What work have you been doin', what was your duties?' Then it came my turn, and so she asked me: 'What were you?' — 'A coachman,' I told her. — 'A coachman? Come, now, what sort of coachman are you? Just take a look at yourself! It isn't fitten for you to be no coachman; you catch fish for me, and shave off your beard. Supply fish for my table, to mark my coming. Do you hear?' And so, ever since then, I'm listed as a fisherman. 'And mind you, you keep my pond in good order.' But then, how is one to keep it in good order?"

"Whom did you belong to before, in that case?"

"Why, to Serghei Sergheich Pehterev. We came to him by inheritance. However, he didn't own us long—six years in all. It was for him, now, that I worked as a coachman. Not in the city, though—he had other servants there—but in the country."

"And were you a coachman all the time, from your youth on?"

"By no manner of means! It was during Serghei Sergheich's time that I got to be a coachman, but before that I was a cook—not a citified cook, though, but just a plain country one."

"Whom did you cook for, then?"

"Why, for my master before that: Athanassii Nethedych, uncle to Serghei Sergheich. It was him that bought Lgov, Athanassii Nethedych did; Serghei Sergheich, though, he got the estate by inheritance, now."

"Whom did Athanassii Nethedych buy it from?"

"Why, from Tatiana Vassilievna."

"What Tatiana Vassilievna?"

"Why, the one that died last year, near Bolhov—or Karachev, rather. A spinstress, she were. Never did get married. You don't happen to know her? We came to her from her father, from Vassillii Semenych. She owned us for a longish while—twenty years, or thereabouts."

"Well, now, were you her cook?"

"That's right; I was her cook—at first, that is; but then I became a *coffeeshenk*."

"A what?"

"A *coffeeshenk*." [2]

---

[2] *Kaffeeschenk,* one who pours, or serves, coffee.—*Trans.*

"What sort of duty may that be?"

"Why, I don't know, father of mine. I worked at the sideboard, and they called me Anton and not Kuzma. Them was the orders the mistress was pleased to give."

"Your real name is Kuzma?"

"Kuzma it is."

"And you were a *coffeeshenk* all the while?"

"No, not all the while. I was a play actor, too."

"You don't say!"

"Oh, sure, I was—played in a thee-ayter. Our mistress started up a thee-ayter of her own."

"What roles did you play, then?"

"What was that, sir?"

"What did you do in the theater?"

"Why, don't you know? There, they'd take me and dress me all up, and I'd walk around like that, all dressed up, or I'd stand about, or sit, whichever it happened to be. They'd tell me: 'Here's what you say,' and I'd say it. One time I played a blind man. They put a pea under each of my eyelids. Oh, sure!"

"And what were you after that?"

"Well, then I became a cook again."

"But why did they discharge you as a cook?"

"Well, it so happened that my brother run off."

"So. But what work did you do for the father of the first lady who owned you?"

"I did all sorts of things, now: I was a page at first; then an outrider, and a gardener after that, and a whipper-in, likewise."

"A whipper-in? And did you ride to the hounds?"

"I did that same, too, but hurt myself bad; fell with the horse, and hurt it bad, likewise. Our old master, now, was strict as strict can be; he ordered me to be flogged and to be apprenticed in Moscow, to a shoemaker."

"Apprenticed, did you say? For you were no child, I guess, when you became a whipper-in?"

"Why, I was twenty and a bit over."

"What sort of apprenticeship can there be at twenty, then?"

"Guess that don't matter, and one can go through with it, if such be the master's orders. But it were a good thing he died soon, and so they sent me back to the village."

"And when did you ever learn cooking, now?"

Suchok lifted his gaunt, yellowish little face and smiled wryly:

"Why, does a body have to learn that? Even the women-folk know how to cook!"

"Well," I spoke up, "you've certainly seen a thing or two in your time, Kuzma! And what may you be doing now as a fisherman, seeing you have no fish hereabouts?"

"Oh, I'm not complaining, father of mine. Glory be to God they made me even a fisherman. For there's another fellow, Andrew Pupyr, an old man just like me. Well, the mistress ordered him to be put in the paper mill, as a dipper. 'It's sinful,' says she, 'to be eating bread for nothing.' And Pupyr, now, he was hoping to gain her favor—his cousin's son was a clerk in the main office, and had promised to put in a word for him with the mistress, to remind her about him. There, he sure did remind her! And yet Pupyr had bowed down to that fellow's very feet, right before my eyes."

"Have you a family? Were you ever married?"

"No, I never was, father of mine. The late Tatiana Vassilievna—may the Kingdom of Heaven be hers—would never allow any of her people to marry. God save you from saying a word to her about marriage! 'There,' she used to say, 'after all, I'm living as a spinster—what's the idea of pampering them? What do they want?' "

"Well, what are you living on now? Do you get a salary?"

"What salary, father of mine! They issue provisions to me. Well, thank God even for that! May God prolong the life of our mistress!"

Ermolai came back.

"The boat's fixed," he announced morosely. "Go get the pole, you!"

Suchok ran off after the pole.

Throughout my conversation with the poor old man Valdimir had been glancing at me with a disdainful smile.

"A foolish fellow, sir," he declared when the other had gone. "An altogether uneducated fellow, a peasant, sir—nothing more. You couldn't call him a house serf, sir, and yet he kept boasting all the time. How would he ever come to be an actor. Judge for yourself, sir! You were pleased to trouble yourself and to converse with him all for nothing, sir!"

A quarter of an hour later we were already seated in Suchok's flat-bottom boat. (The dogs we had left in a hut, under the eye of Jehudiel, the coachman.) We weren't any too comfortable, but then hunters aren't a finicky folk. Suchok stood at the blunt stern and poled; Vladimir and I were sitting on a thwart; Ermolai had found a place forward, at the very nose. Despite the oakum, the water appeared at our feet very shortly. Fortunately, the weather was calm, and the pond seemed to have fallen asleep.

We floated along rather leisurely. The old man had difficulty in drawing his pole, all entangled with the green cords of underwater grasses, out of the clinging slime; the thickly growing round pads of the water lilies also hindered the progress of our boat. Finally we managed to reach the thick reeds, and the fun began. The ducks rose noisily, impetuously from the pond, frightened by our unexpected appearance in their domains; our shots followed them in unison; it was exciting to see how these bobtailed birds tumbled through the air, smacking heavily against the water. Of course, we didn't get all the ducks we hit; those but slightly injured dived; others, killed outright, fell into such thick clumps of reeds that even the lynx eyes of Ermolai could not search them out; but, just the same, toward dinner-time our boat was filled to the gunwales with game.

Vladimir, to the great satisfaction of Ermolai, was by no means an excellent marksman, and after every unsuccessful shot was astonished, inspected his gun and blew down its barrel, evinced perplexity, and at last would elucidate for our benefit why he had missed. Ermolai shot as he always did, like a conquering hero; I, after my wont, rather poorly. Suchok kept glancing at us from time to time with the eyes of a man who from his youth up had been in the service of masters, calling out now and then: "There's another bird, there!" and was forever scratching his back, not with his hands, however, but by putting his shoulders into play. The weather was splendid: white, round clouds, clearly reflected in the water, were gently speeding high overhead; the reeds were whispering all around us; the pond, here and there, glittered like steel in the sun. We were about to go back to the settlement when a quite unpleasant accident befell us.

We had long since been able to notice that the water was little by little but steadily accumulating in our flat-bottom boat. Vladimir had been entrusted with the task of bailing out the boat by means of a dipper which my farsighted hunter had, against any contingency, filched from a country wife who had not been sufficiently wide awake. Everything had been going along well while Vladimir had not been forgetful of his duty. But toward the end of the hunt, as though in farewell, the ducks had begun to rise in such flocks that we barely had time to load our guns. During the heat of the skirmishing we paid no attention to the state of our scow—when suddenly, from a powerful move of Ermolai's (he was trying to reach a dead bird and had leaned with all his body against the gunwale), our frail and ancient craft careened, took on water, and went in solemn grandeur to the bottom—fortunately, however, not at a deep spot. We let out a yell, but it was already too late: a moment later we were standing in the water up to our necks, surrounded by the bodies of the dead birds which had bobbed up. Now I can't recall without loud laughter the frightened and pale faces of my companions (probably my face, too, was not particularly ruddy just then); but at that moment, I confess, it did not even occur to me to laugh. Each one of us was holding his gun over his head, and Suchok (probably from his habit of aping gentlefolk) had raised his pole aloft.

Ermolai was the first to break the silence:

"Hell and the bottomless pit!" he muttered, spitting on the water in disgust. "What a fix! And it's all your fault, you old devil!" he added with heartfelt vexation, turning on Suchok. "What sort of a boat have you got?"

"Sorry," babbled the old man.

"And you're all right, too!" my hunter went on, turning his head in the direction of Vladimir. "Where was your eyes? Why wasn't you bailing? You . . . you . . . you—"

But by now Vladimir wasn't up to answering back; he was shaking like a leaf, his teeth were hopelessly chattering, and his smile was utterly inane. Whither had his eloquence gone, his sense of refined decorum and of his own dignity?

The accursed scow was swaying under our feet. At the moment our craft had foundered the water had seemed exceedingly cold to us, but we soon got used to it. When our first fright had passed I looked about me; all around us, some ten paces away, grew the thick reeds; in the distance, above their tips, one could see the bank.

"Things are bad," I reflected. "What are we to do now?" I asked Ermolai.

"Why, we'll see; after all, there's no sense in passing the night here," he answered. "Here, you—hold my gun," said he to Vladimir. The latter submitted without a word of objection. "I'm going to find the ford," Ermolai went on with assurance, as if every pond was inevitably bound to have a ford; he took Suchok's pole and set out in the direction of the bank, carefully exploring the bottom.

"Come, do you know how to swim?" I asked him.

"No, I don't," his voice came from behind a clump of reeds.

"Well, if that's the case, he'll drown," apathetically remarked Suchok, who even before had been frightened not at the danger but at our wrath and now, utterly reassured, merely drew a long breath every now and then and apparently felt no need whatsoever of changing the situation he was in.

"And he will perish without any good at all, sir," Vladimir added plaintively.

Ermolai did not return for more than an hour. That hour seemed eternity to us. At first we had called to him most diligently and he had called back; then his answering calls had come to us at ever greater intervals; finally he did not answer at all. The bells in the settlement began ringing for vespers. We did not talk much among ourselves; we even tried to avoid looking at one another. The ducks were darting over our heads; some were preparing to settle in the water near us, but would suddenly rise in a "wedge," as they say, and fly off with noisy calls. We were beginning to grow numb. Suchok was blinking hard, as if he were about to fall asleep.

Finally, to our indescribable joy, Ermolai came back.

"Well, what's what?"

"I was ashore; I've found the ford. Come on."

We were all set to start off immediately, but he first fished underwater and got a cord out of his pocket, tied the dead ducks together by their feet, took both ends of the cord in his teeth and waded ahead; Vladimir followed him, I followed Vladimir, Suchok brought up the procession. It was about two hundred paces to shore. Ermolai strode along boldly and without pausing (so well had he studied the way), merely calling out at rare intervals: "More to the left—there's a deep hole to the right!" or: "More to the right—you'll get bogged down if you go to the left."

At times the water reached to our necks, and twice poor Suchok, being the shortest of all of us, gulped water and sent up bubbles. "There, there, there!" Ermolai would shout at him threateningly, and Suchok would flounder, splash with his legs, hop about, and in the end manage somehow to clamber out on some shallow spot—yet even in his extremity he could not find the resolution to catch hold of the skirt of my jacket.

All worn out, filthy, sopping wet, we reached the bank at last.

Two hours later we were all sitting in a big hayloft, as dry as we could get in that time, and getting ready for supper. Jehudiel, the coachman, an exceedingly slow fellow and heavy on his feet, who liked to reason everything out and looked sleepy, was standing near the gates and cordially treating Suchok to snuff. (I have noticed that it takes very little time for Russian coachmen to become close friends.) Suchok took snuff in a veritable frenzy, until it made him queasy; he spat, he coughed and, evidently, derived great pleasure from it. Vladimir was assuming a languishing air, his head inclined to one side, and said but little. Ermolai was drying and polishing our guns. The dogs were wagging their tails with exaggerated rapidity as they waited for their oaten porridge; the horses were stamping and neighing under an overhang.

The sun was setting, its last rays scattering in broad bands of purple; small clouds spread along the sky and grew smaller and smaller, just as if they were a cleanly washed, thoroughly groomed wave. . . . Songs came floating to us from the direction of the settlement.

BEZHIN MEADOW

IT WAS A splendid day in July, one of those days which occur
only during a long spell of good weather. Since earliest
morning the sky is clear; the dawn glow does not flare like a
conflagration—it diffuses itself like a gentle blush. The sun is
not fire, is not incandescent, as it is during a sultry drought,
nor is it a dull purple, as before a storm, but bright and
affably radiant; it floats upward peacefully from under a
narrow and lengthy cloud, sends its fresh radiance through it,
and then plunges into its lilac haze. The thin upper rim of
the distended cloudlet begins to coruscate with little snakes
of light: their gleam is like the gleam of wrought silver.
But now the playful beams have again gushed forth—and
blithely and majestically, as if it were winging upward, the
mighty luminary comes up.

About noontime a host of round, lofty clouds appears,
aureately gray, rimmed with soft whiteness. Like islands
scattered over a river in infinite flood that runs around them
in deeply transparent channels, they hardly budge; farther
on, toward the sky's rim, they move near to one another,
they huddle; there is no longer any blue to be seen between
them, but they themselves are of the same azure as the
sky; all of them are shot through and through with light
and warmth. The hue of the horizon, ethereal, pale lilac,
does not change throughout the day and is uniform all
around; nowhere is there a thunderstorm darkling, gathering,

92

save that here and there streaks of pale blue may extend downward: a barely noticeable drizzle, this, being sown upon the earth. Toward evening these clouds vanish; the last of them, rather black and of indeterminate form, like smoke, lie down in roseate swirls against the setting sun; at the spot where it has set, as calmly as it had risen in the sky, a ruby-red aura lingers for a brief while over the darkened earth and, gently flickering, like a candle solicitously borne along, the evening star will come to a soft glow against it.

On such days all pigments are softened, they are bright yet not vivid; an impress of some touching mildness lies upon all things. On such days the heat can, at times, be quite intense—occasionally it even steams along the slopes of the fields; but the wind scatters, sunders the accumulated sultriness, and whirlwinds (an indubitable sign of a long spell of good weather) wander in towering white pillars on their rounds over the roads, across plowed land. The dry and pure air is filled with the odors of wormwood, of reaped rye, of buckwheat; even at the hour before nightfall you feel no dampness. It is weather such as this that the husbandman longs for to gather in his grain.

It was on just such a day that I happened to be hunting grouse in the Chernov district of the Tula province. I had come across and had shot quite a lot of game; the full game-bag was cutting into my shoulder mercilessly; but it was only when the evening glow had already died out and the chill shadows were already beginning to grow denser and to spread through the air, which was still full of light although no longer lit by the rays of the set sun, that I at last decided to turn homeward. With long strides I traversed an extensive stretch of brushwood, clambered up on a knoll—and, instead of the familiar plain I expected, with a small oak grove to the right and a squat little church in the distance, beheld an altogether different locality which was unknown to me. A narrow dale stretched away at my feet; directly opposite me a thick copse of aspens rose in a steep wall. I halted in perplexity and looked about me.

"Eh!" I reflected. "I haven't hit on the right spot at all—I've gone too far to the right." And, wondering at my own mistake, I quickly descended the knoll. An unpleasant, stagnant dampness enveloped me at once, just as though I had stepped into a cellar; wet grass, thick and high, looked as white and even as a tablecloth at the bottom of the dale; one

93

felt somehow creepy walking on it. I clambered out as quickly as I could on the other side and went on, heading to the left along the copse of aspens. Bats, mysteriously circling and quivering against the dimly clear sky, were already flitting over the slumbering treetops; a young hawk, belated, flew past, hastening to its nest.

"There," I kept thinking, "as soon as I come out at that end I'll hit on the road at once. But, just the same, I must have gone almost a mile out of my way!"

I finally managed to reach the end of the woods, but there was no road of any sort there: some kind of untouched low bushes spread far and wide before me, while beyond them, ever so far off, one could glimpse a desertlike field. I stopped again.

"What is all this! Come, where am I, after all?"

I started in recalling which way I had been going and where I had been during the course of the day.

"Why, this is the Parahin stretch of brushwood!" I exclaimed at last. "Sure enough—that must be the Sindeiev copse over there. Yes, but how did I ever get here, as far as all this? That's odd! Now I'll have to turn to the right."

I started off toward the right, through the bushes. In the meanwhile the night was nearing and spreading, like a thundercloud; darkness seemed to be rising everywhere with the evening vapors, and even pouring down from on high. I came across a little-used, grass-grown path; I set out along it, peering ahead. Everything around me was darkling fast and quieting down; the quail alone were calling out at infrequent intervals. Some small night bird, darting low and without a sound of its soft wings, almost flew against me and then swooped to one side in fright. I came out on the edge of the brushwood and walked along the boundary line between two fields. By now I could make out objects in the distance only with difficulty: the field was glimmering whitely all around; beyond it, advancing with every moment in enormous swirls, somber murk was rising fast. My steps echoed dully in the congealing air. The sky, which had grown wan, had again begun to turn blue—but now it was the blue of night. The little stars had started twinkling, had started stirring in it.

That which I had taken for a copse turned out to be a dark and rounded mound. "Come, where am I, after all?" I repeated aloud, stopped for the third time, and looked questioningly at my yellow-spotted bitch Dianka, who was of an English breed, absolutely the cleverest of all four-legged creatures. But the cleverest of all four-legged creatures merely kept wagging her bit of a tail, blinked her tired little eyes dismally, and offered me no sound advice whatsoever. I became ashamed before her and desperately hastened onward, as though I had suddenly conjectured which way I ought to go, skirted the mound, and discovered I was in a shallow valley that had been plowed everywhere. At once a strange feeling took possession of me. This valley looked almost like a regular caldron with sloping sides; at its bottom several huge white stones were standing up on end—it seemed as if they had crept together there for a secret council—and so voiceless and forsaken was everything in that valley, and so flat, and so despondently did the sky hang over it, that my heart shrank within me. Some tiny beast emitted a faint and plaintive squeak among the stones. I lost no time in clambering back up on the mound. Up to now I still hadn't abandoned hope of finding the way home, but at this point I became definitely convinced that I had gone completely astray and, no longer making the least attempt to recognize my surroundings, by now almost sunk in gloom, I went straight ahead, following the stars—and trusting to luck.

For something like half an hour did I walk thus, shifting my feet with difficulty. It seemed to me as if I had never been in such a deserted locality in all my born days: not a light, no matter how small, glimmered anywhere, nor was there a sound of any sort to be heard. One sloping knoll succeeded another, field stretched endlessly after field, the bushes seemed to spring up unexpectedly out of the ground before my very nose. I kept on walking, and was just about to lie down somewhere until morning when I suddenly found myself above a frightful chasm.

I quickly drew my lifted foot back and, through the barely transparent dusk of night, saw an enormous plain far below me. A broad river curved around it, receding from me in a semicircle; steely reflections on the water, glimmering indistinctly and intermittently, marked its current. The knoll on which I found myself went down in an abrupt, almost perpendicular precipice; its enormous outlines stood out darkly from the bluish ethereal void and, directly beneath me, in the angle formed by that precipice and the plain, near the river which at that spot, under the steepest part of the knoll, was an unmoving dark mirror, two small fires were flaming

95

redly and smoking close to each other. People were bustling and shadows were swaying around them; now and then the forepart of some small curly head would become vividly lit.

I recognized, at last, the place I had come to. This meadow is celebrated throughout our parts under the name of Bezhin Meadow. However, there was no possibility whatsoever of turning homeward then, especially in the nighttime; my legs were caving in under me from fatigue. I decided to walk over to the fires and to bide the coming of the dawn in the company of those people, whom I took to be drovers. I came down safely, but hardly had I let go of the last branch I had seized when two great, white shaggy dogs suddenly threw themselves upon me with vicious barking. Children's voices were raised around the fires; two or three boys quickly got up from the ground. I answered their hails. They ran up, immediately called off their dogs, who had been particularly overcome when my Dianka had put in her appearance, and I came over to them.

I had erred in taking those sitting around the fires for drovers. They were simply peasant urchins from a village close by, tending a drove of horses. During the hot spells of summer the horses in our parts are driven out to graze at night; in the daytime the flies and gadflies would give them no rest. To bring out the drove toward evening and to bring it back at morning glow is a great and festal affair for peasant boys. Bareheaded, in old sheepskin jackets, astride the live-liest of the little nags, they race along with gay whoops and shouts, their arms and legs threshing about, their laughter ringing as they bounce high. The light dust rises and races along the road in a yellow pillar; the beat of hoofs pounding in unison spreads far and wide; the horses run with their ears cocked; at their very head, with his tail straight up and constantly changing stride, gallops some russet-colored shaggy stallion with cockleburs in his tangled mane.

I told the boys that I had lost my way and sat down near them. They asked me where I had come from, were silent for a while, and made room for me. We talked a little. I lay down under a small bush that had been nibbled clean and began looking about me. The picture was a wondrous one: a round, reddish reflection quivered near the fires and seemed to poise in midair, leaning against the darkness; the flames, flaring up, would cast occasional fleeting glints beyond the limits of that ringed reflection; a slender tongue of light would lick the bare boughs of the willow bushes and momentarily vanish; long, pointed shadows, impetuously intruding for an instant, in their turn darted up to the very embers: murk contending with light.

Now and then, when the flame burned fainter, and the ring of light contracted, out of the advancing darkness a horse's head would emerge suddenly—a sorrel head, with a winding scar, or one all white; it would regard you attentively and stolidly, champing the high grass in an expert fashion and, lowering itself again, would promptly disappear. All one could hear was its continued champing and its snorts. When one sits where it is light, it is hard to make out what is going on in the dark, and therefore everything near at hand seemed to have an almost black curtain drawn over it; but farther on, toward the horizon, one could glimpse the knolls and woods dimly, lying in long blotches. The dark clear sky in all its mysterious splendor was austere and unencompassably high above us. One's chest felt a delectable pressure as it breathed in that unique, stirring, and fresh fragrance—the fragrance of a Russian night in summer. All around us there was hardly a noise of any sort to be heard. Only at infrequent intervals, in the river close by, some large fish would plash with abrupt loudness, and the bankside reeds, barely stirred by some suddenly risen wave, would break into faint soughing. . . . All was quiet, save for the crackling, ever so low, of the small campfires.

The boys were sitting around them; here, too, squatted those dogs who had been so eager to devour me. For a long time they could not become reconciled to my presence and, drowsily puckering up their eyes against the fire and watching it askance, kept growling every so often with an extraordinary sense of their own dignity; they would growl at first, and then whine a little, as though regretting the impossibility of fulfilling their desire. There were five boys in all: Fedya, Pavlusha, Iliusha, Kostya, and Vanya. (I picked up their names from their conversations, and it is my intention to acquaint the reader with these boys right now.)

Fedya, the first and the oldest among them, one would judge to be fourteen. A well-built boy, this, with handsome and fine features, somewhat small, hair flaxen and curly, clear eyes and a steady smile, half merry, half absent-minded. By all the signs he belonged to a well-to-do family and had ridden out into the field not out of any necessity but just so, for the fun of the thing. He had on a shirt of brightly patterned calico, hemmed with yellow; his small, new overcoat, thrown over his narrow little shoulders, perched there precariously; a comb dangled from his belt of pale-blue leather. His boots, with low tops, were his own sure enough, and no hand-me-downs from his father.

Pavlusha, the second boy, had black tousled hair, gray eyes, broad cheekbones, a face pale, pockmarked, a mouth wide yet regular; his whole head was huge, big as a beer vat, as they say; his body was squat, unwieldy. None too good-looking a youngster—what's the use of talking!—but just the same I took a liking to him; his looks were very intelligent and forthright, and in his voice, too, there was the ring of strength. He could hardly have shown off with his clothes: they consisted, all in all, of a common linen shirt and much-patched breeches.

The face of the third, Iliusha, was rather insignificant: hump-nosed, long-drawn, purblind, it bore an expression of some dull, sickly care; his pursed lips did not move, his knit eyebrows did not relax—he seemed to be puckering his eyes from the firelight all the time. His yellow, almost white hair stuck out in pointed tufts like little pigtails from under his rather low, small felt cap, which he was forever shoving down over his ears with both hands. He had on new bast sandals and foot clouts; a stout rope, wound thrice about his waist, snugly girded his neat, black, short overcoat. Both he and Pavlusha looked no more than twelve.

The fourth, Kostya, a boy of ten, aroused my curiosity by his stare of melancholy and deep thought. His whole face was none too big; it was thin, sprinkled with freckles, sharply pointed toward the chin, like a squirrel's; one could barely make out his lips; but it was his eyes—big, dark, gleaming with a fluid gleam—which created a strange impression: they wanted to say something, it seemed, something for which language (his language, at least) had no words. He was short, of a puny build, and was dressed rather poorly.

The last, Vanya, I had at first actually failed to notice: he was lying on the ground, curled up ever so peacefully under stiff matting, and only at rare intervals did he thrust out his flaxen, curly head from under it. This boy was no more than seven.

And so, I was lying off to one side under a small bush and

looking at the boys from time to time. A small kettle was hanging over one of the fires, with "spuds" cooking therein. Pavlusha was keeping an eye on them, standing on his knees and thrusting a piece of kindling wood into the water, which was coming to a boil. Fedya was lying propped up on one elbow and with the skirts of his overcoat spread out. Iliusha was sitting alongside of Kostya and puckering his eyes as intently as before. Kostya had let his head droop a little and was looking somewhere off into the distance. Vanya did not stir under his matting. I pretended to be asleep. Little by little the boys got to talking again.

At first they chatted a bit about this and that, about the work they would have to face on the morrow, about horses—when Fedya suddenly turned to Iliusha and, as though he were resuming an interrupted conversation, asked him:

"Well, now, and did you see the hobgoblin for fair?"

"No, see him I didn't, and besides you can't see him," Iliusha answered in a hoarse and weak voice, the sound of which could not possibly have been more in keeping with the expression on his face. "But I did hear him. And I weren't the only one that did."

"And whereabouts in your place does he keep himself?" asked Pavlusha.

"In the old rolling room." [1]

"Why, do you people go to the paper mill?"

"Sure, why not? My brother Avdiushka and me work there as glossers." [2]

"So that's how. You're factory hands!"

"Well, how come you to hear him?" asked Fedya.

"Why, this is how. It so happened that my brother Avdiushka and me, and Fedor Mihievsky, and Ivashka Kossoi, and also another Ivashka, the one from Red Knolls, and still another Ivashka, by the name of Suhorukii, and there was other lads there, too—there must have been ten boys of us altogether—the whole shift, for the matter of that—well, it so happened we had to pass the night in that rolling room; that is, we didn't really have to, only Nazarov, the overseer, forbade us to go home: 'What's the use of you boys traipsing

[1] The building where the paper is dipped up from the vats in a paper mill is called the rolling or dipping room. It is located near the very dam, under the wheel.—*Author.*

[2] The glossers calendar and pare the paper.—*Author.*

home,' says he, 'there's a lot of work tomorrow, so don't you go home, lads.' So we stayed on there, and we was lying together, all of us, and Avdiushka he gets to talking: 'Well, now, lads, what if the hobgoblin was to come?' And hardly had he done saying this—Avdei, I mean—when all of a sudden somebody starts walking around over our heads; we was lying down below, see, but he starts walking around up there, near the wheel. We hear him walking around, the boards simply bending, simply cracking under him; there, he'd passed right over our heads—when all of a sudden the water starts making a noise, and what a noise! going over the wheel; the wheel begins knocking, knocking, and turning— and yet the gates to the castle,[3] now, was all lowered. So we wondered who could ever have raised them, so that the water had started flowing. However, that wheel turned and turned a while, and then stopped.

"Then he began walking about again, making for the door upstairs, and then he started down the stairs, and he was coming down them stairs like he weren't in no hurry at all; the steps was just simply groaning under him. Well, he walked right up to our door, hung around and hung around there for a bit—and then all of a sudden that door pops right open. All startled, we was; then we look—and there's nothing there. Suddenly, when we give another look, there was the form [4] at one of the vats moving, rising, dipping; it kept going like that for a while through the air, as if someone was rinsing it, and then got back to its place again. Then at another vat the hook took off of its nail and fell back on the nail again; after that it seemed like somebody had walked over toward the door, and all of a sudden he got such a coughing spell, such a sneezing fit, like a sheep or something, and that so loud and all. We just tumbled down in a heap, all of us, trying to crawl under one another. Lord, but we was plenty scared that time!"

"So that's how it was!" Pavel commented. "But what made him go off in a coughing spell like that?"

"Don't know; maybe it was the damp."

They were all silent for a space.

"Well, now, is them spuds cooked yet?" asked Fedya.

[3] A local name for the sluiceway bringing the water to the mill wheel.—*Author.*

[4] The wire cloth or apron for dipping up the paper.—*Author.*

Pavlusha prodded them:

"No; they're still hard. Listen to that splash!" he added, turning his face toward the river. "Must be a pike. And look at that little star rolling down the sky—"

"Well, now, fellows, here's something I'm going to tell you," Kostya began in a piping voice. "You just listen to what my dad was telling us the other day, whilst I happened to be there—"

"All right, we're listening," said Fedya with a patronizing air.

"Guess you know Gavrila, the carpenter in that big village near town?"

"Well, yes, we know him."

"But do you know why he's always down in the mouth like that, never saying anything? Do you know why? Here's why he's such a glum fellow; he once went, says my dad—he once went, brothers of mine, into the forest, after nuts. Well, so he went into the forest, after nuts, and he ups and loses his way; he went ever so far out of his way—God knows how far out of his way he went.. And he walked, and he walked, brothers of mine—but he couldn't find the right path, nohow! And it was already night out. So then he sat him down under a tree: 'There, now, let's wait for morning here'; he sat him down and dozed off. There, he'd dozed off, and all of a sudden he heard someone calling him. He looked—there was no one around. He dozed off again, and again he heard someone calling him. He looked and he looked—and right before him there was a nixie, perched on a bough; she was swinging there and calling him to come to her, whilst she herself was laughing, laughing fit to kill. And the moon, now —the moon was shining ever so bright, plain as plain; you could see everything, brothers of mine. There, she was calling him to come to her, and she herself, this water creature, was such a shining little thing, for all the world like she were some small dace, or a minnow—there's also a carp like that, all sort of white, silverlike. Gavrila the carpenter, he were plumb scared to death, brothers of mine; but all she knew was to laugh out loud, and all the time she kept beckoning to him with her hand to come over to her—like this. Gavrila, he'd already gotten up on his feet, actually; he was all set by then to heed that water fairy, brothers of mine, but I guess the Lord Himself must have sent him some sense: he did contrive to make the sign of the cross over himself.

And how hard it was for him by then to be making that sign, brothers of mine! 'My hand,' said he later, 'was like stone, for fair; couldn't even turn it. Ah, hang it all!'

"Well, soon as he'd made that sign, brothers of mine, that there little nixie she plumb stopped laughing—and all of a sudden started in to weep! My! She was weeping, brothers of mine, wiping her eyes with her hair—and her hair was all green, now, green as hemp. So Gavrila he looked and looked at her, and he started in for to question her: 'What are you weeping about, you evil forest creature?' But the nixie, she spoke up to him: 'You oughtn't to be crossing yourself,' said she, 'you that was born of woman, but ought to be living with me in blitheness to the end of your days; and the reason I'm weeping, killing myself for grief, is because you made the sign of the cross over yourself; however, I won't be the only one killing myself for grief: kill yourself with grief also, to the end of your days.' And right then and there, brothers of mine, she vanished; and as for Gavrila, everything at once became clear to him—how he was to get out of the forest, that is. Only thing is, since that time he walks about the way you see him, always down at the mouth."

"There!" Fedya got out after a brief silence. "But could such a foul forest creature ever spoil a human soul—after all, he had paid her no heed."

"And yet, there it is!" said Kostya. "And Gavrila was also telling us that her voice, now, was ever so high, ever so pitiful, like a toad's."

"Was it your old man himself who told this story?" Fedya persisted.

"He himself. I was lying on the ledge atop the oven; I heard everything."

"It sure is a queer business! Still, why should he be down at the mouth? Well, I guess he must have been to her liking, seeing as how she was calling him."

"Yes, was he to her liking?" Iliusha chimed in quickly.

"Guess again! She was after tickling him to death, that's what she was after. That's what they do, those nixies, now."

"Why, I guess there must be nixies right around here, too," Fedya remarked.

"No," answered Kostya, "this place is clean, right out in the open. The only thing is, the river is close by."

They all fell silent. Suddenly, somewhere in the distance, a long-drawn, ringing, almost moaning sound arose, one of

jocelyn Pade.

those incomprehensible night sounds which sometimes spring up amid profound silence; they soar, linger in the air, and at last spread slowly, as if dying away. Hearken closely—and it is as though there were no sound, and yet there is a ringing in the air. It sounded as if someone had emitted a long, long cry, under the very rim of the sky, as if some other had responded in the forest with high-pitched, piercing laughter, and a faint, sibilant whistle had then sped over the river. The boys exchanged looks, shuddered. . . .

"The power of the Cross be with us!" Ilya got out in a whisper.

"Oh, you crows!" Pavel called out. "What did you get all up in the air about? Look, now, them spuds is all cooked." They all moved up to the small kettle and began eating the steaming potatoes; Vanya alone did not stir. "Say, what about you?" Pavel asked him, but Vanya did not crawl out from under his matting. It was not long before the kettle was empty.

"But have you heard, fellows," Iliusha spoke up, "about what happened the other day in our Varnavitzy?"

"On the dam, now?" Fedya wanted to know.

"Yes, yes, on the dam—the one that the water broke through. Now *there's* an unclean place that's really unclean, and ever so forsaken. There's all them ravines and gullies roundabout, and the gullies is all full of snakes."

"Well, what happened there? Go ahead and tell us."

"Why, here's what happened. Maybe you don't know it, Fedya, but we've got a drowned man buried there, and he drowned himself ever so long ago, when the millpond was still deep; however, you can still see his small grave, although you can hardly make it out, at that—it's just a little mound. Well, a few days ago our clerk calls Ermila, the kennel keeper: 'You go and fetch the mail, now, Ermil,' he tells him. Our Ermil always goes after the mail, for he'd done all his hounds to death—they don't live under his care, somehow, and they never did, if it comes to that, yet he's a good man with dogs, in all ways. So this Ermil, now, he started off on a horse for the mail, but he hung around a little too long in town, and when he was driving back he was already tipsy. And it was night by then, a light night—the moon was shining. Well, so there was Ermil, riding across the dam. That was the road he'd happened to take. So there he was, riding along like that, this Ermil the kennel keeper, and what does he see but a little woolly lamb on the drowned man's grave—a white little thing, its wool all curly—a pretty little thing, ambling about. So Ermil, he thought to himself: 'Might as well take it along—what's the use of it getting lost, all for nothing,' and he got off of his horse and took that little lamb in his arms. And the lamb, now, it don't mind at all. So then Ermil he goes toward his horse—but the horse backs away from him, breathing hard, tossing its head; just the same, he quieted it down, got up on it together with the lamb, and rode on, holding the lamb in front of him. He looks at it, and the lamb just stares him right in the eye. He felt uncanny, did this Ermil the kennel keeper. 'I disremember,' he kept thinking, 'about any rams staring anyone in the eye like that.' However, it weren't so bad; he fell to stroking its wool, like that, and talking to it: 'There, little lamby, there!' But that there little ram, it bares its teeth, all of a sudden, and comes right back at him: 'There, little lamb, there!' "

Hardly had the narrator uttered the last word when both dogs suddenly rose up as one, dashed away from the fire with convulsive barking, and vanished in the dark. All the boys were thoroughly frightened. Vanya jumped out from under his matting. Pavlusha, shouting, rushed off after the dogs. Their barking was rapidly receding. One could hear the uneasy trampling of the startled drove. "Here, Gray! Here, Beetle!" Pavlusha was loudly calling. In a few moments the barking quieted down; by now Pavel's voice was coming from afar. A little more time passed; the boys were looking at one another in perplexity, as though waiting for what would happen next. Suddenly there came the hoofbeats of a galloping horse; it stopped short near the fire, and holding tight to its mane, Pavlusha sprang down nimbly from its back. Both dogs in their turn leaped within the ring of light and immediately squatted on their haunches, letting their red tongues loll.

"What happened there? What's up?" asked the boys.

"Nothing," answered Pavel, taking a swipe at the horse. "The dogs must have scented something, that's all. I thought it might be a wolf," he added in an indifferent voice, breathing quickly with all his chest heaving.

I involuntarily took an admiring look at Pavlusha. He was very fine at that moment. His homely face, animated from the fast ride, glowed with derring-do and firm resolve. Without as much as a dry twig in his hand, at night, he had without the least hesitation dashed off against a wolf all by himself. "What a splendid boy!" I reflected as I looked at him.

"But has anybody seen them, now—the wolves, I mean?" asked Kostya, the little poltroon.

"There's always plenty of them around here," Pavel answered. "But it's only in winter that they're troublesome."

He again snuggled down before the fire. As he had been about to sit down on the ground he let his hand drop on the shaggy neck of one of the dogs, and the animal, thus gladdened, would not turn its head for a long time, glancing out of the corner of its eye at Pavlusha with appreciative pride.

Vanya again burrowed deep under his matting.

"My, Iliushka, what dreadful things you were telling us," began Fedya, upon whom, as the son of a well-to-do peasant, it devolved to start the talk going. (He himself spoke little, as though wary of lowering his dignity.) "Then, too, the Restless One had to egg on the dogs to start barking. But it's true enough—I've heard tell your place is haunted."

"The Varnavitzy? I should say so! And how! They've seen our old master there more than once. He walks about in a long-skirted coat, they say, and all the time he keeps oh'ing, like this, looking for something on the ground. Grandpa Trophimych met up with him once. 'What, now, may it be your pleasure to be seeking for on the ground, Ivan Ivanych, father of mine?' "

"He asked him that?" the astonished Fedya interrupted him.

"Yes, he did."

"Well, I must say Trophimych is a brave fellow after that. Well, and what did the other have to say?"

" 'It's loose-all grass I'm looking for,' said he. And he said it in such a stifled voice, ever so stifled. 'And what would you be wanting loose-all grass for, Ivan Ivanych, father of mine?' — 'My grave is crushing me,' said the other, 'it's crushing me, Trophimych; I want to get out of it, I want to get out—' "

"So that's the sort he is!" remarked Fedya. "Guess he hadn't lived long enough."

"That sure is a great wonder!" Kostya commented. "I thought you can see the departed only on a Parental Sabbath." [5]

[5] A day of prayers for the departed on their graves. There were three such Sabbaths on the Greek-Catholic calendar: Tuesday after Quasimodo, Whitsun Sabbath, and during the Feast of the Inter-

"You can see the departed at any time," Iliusha chimed in with assurance—he, as far as I could observe, knew all the local superstitions better than the others. "But then, on a Parental Sabbath you can see even the living departed—those whose turn has come to die that year, I mean. All you've got to do is to sit down on the church porch at night, and keep watching the road. And those people will start marching past you along the road—those, that is, who are to die that year. There was Uliana, now, one of our womenfolk—she went to the church porch at night last year."

"Well, and did she see anybody?" Kostya asked with curiosity.

"I should say so! First off, she sat there a long, long while, without seeing or hearing anybody—only all the time it sounded like there was a little dog starting in to bark, sort of, starting in to bark somewheres. All of a sudden she gives a look, and there's a little boy walking along the road, in nothing but a little shift. She looked more closely: it was Ivashka Theodosiev walking along—"

"The one that died this spring?" Fedya cut in.

"The very same. He was walking along, and didn't even raise his little head, but Uliana recognized him. And then she looked again, and there was a countrywoman coming along. Uliana, she looked more closely and—the Lord be with us!—if it weren't her own self walking along that road . . . Uliana, her own self."

"Her own self, for sure?" asked Fedya.

"Her own self, by God!"

"Well, what of it? For she hasn't died yet, has she?"

"Yes, but the year ain't over yet. Just the same, you take a look at her: it's a wonder how she keeps body and soul together."

They all fell silent again. Pavel threw a handful of dry branches into the fire. They showed sharply black against the instantaneous flare-up of the flames, began to crackle, to smoke, and then to buckle, lifting up their charred ends. The reflection of the light, fitfully quivering, spurted in all directions, especially upward. Suddenly, coming from none knows where, a white pigeon flew straight against this reflection, timorously circled a while in one spot, all bathed in the warm glow, and vanished, beating its wings resoundingly.

---

cession of the Most Holy Virgin, which began October 1st (Old Style).—*Trans.*

"Guess it's lost its way home," Pavel remarked. "Now it'll keep on flying until it strikes against something, and wherever it strikes, that's where it'll stay through the night until dawn."

"Well, now, Pavlusha," Kostya spoke up, "weren't that some righteous soul winging its way to heaven, eh?"

Pavel threw another handful of dead branches into the fire.

"Could be," he let drop at last.

"But tell me, Pavlusha, do," Fedya began, "were you Shalamovo folks, too, able to see the heavenly prevision?" That is what our muzhiks call a solar eclipse.

"You mean when you couldn't see the sun any more? I should say so!"

"Guess your folks got plenty scared, too?"

"Why, we wasn't the only ones. Our master, now, even though he made it clear to us beforehand, telling us: 'You're going to have a prevision,' got scared himself as pretty as you please, they say, soon as it turned dark. And in the servants' quarters, I heard tell, the old woman that does the cooking, soon as it started turning dark in the middle of the day, why, she took and smashed all the pots with an oven fork: 'Who'd be eating now,' said she, 'when the Day of Judgment is upon us!' There was rivers of cabbage soup all over the place. And, brother, what rumors there were going around in our village! That there would be white wolves, now, running over the land, that they would be devouring folks, that there would be flights of birds of prey, and that folks might even behold Trishka [6] himself."

"What Trishka is that?" asked Kostya.

"Why, don't you know?" Iliusha chimed in ardently. "Why, brother, where do you come from that you don't know about Trishka? They sure must be a lot of sticks-in-the-mud in your village, that's what, just sticks-in-the-mud! Trishka, he's a certain amazing man who will come, and he'll come, this amazing man, in such a way that you won't be able as much as to lay hands on him, and there's nary a thing you'll be able to do to him; that's the sort of amazing man he will be. Suppose, for instance, the peasants want to take him; they'll come out against him with oaken staves, and will throw a ring around him, but he'll just pull the wool over their eyes, in such a way that they themselves will beat up one another.

[6] The belief concerning Trishka is, probably, an echo of the tradition concerning Antichrist.—*Author*.

They may put him in prison, for instance, so he'll beg for a drink of water out of a dipper; they'll bring him the dipper, but he'll dive right into it—and that's the last they'll ever see of him. They'll put him in chains, but he'll just clasp his hands together, and those chains will fall right off of him. Well, then, this Trishka will be going about through the hamlets and the towns, and this Trishka will be tempting Christian folks—and yet there'll be nary a thing you can do to him. For that's the sort of amazing, crafty man he will be."

"Well, yes," Pavel resumed after this interruption, "that's what he's like. The old folks was saying, now, that as soon as the heavenly prevision would begin, why, Trishka would come. And so the prevision began. All the folks poured out of doors, into the fields, waiting for what would come. And, as you know, our place is such that you can see everything—there's plenty of room. There they were, watching, when all of a sudden, coming down the hill from the big village near town, there's some sort of a man walking along, queer as can be, the head on him so amazing—they all just let out one yell: 'Oh, Trishka's coming! Oh, Trishka's coming!' and each one lit out for himself, every which way. Our elder, he crawled into a ditch; the elder's wife, she got stuck under a gate, screaming for all she was worth, scaring her own yard dog so that it tore loose off of its chain, and over the wattle fence it went, and kept on into the woods, whilst Dorotheich —Kuzka's father, that is—dived into a field of oats, squatted there, and started calling like a quail, figuring that, who knows, maybe the Enemy, the Destroyer of Souls, might spare a bird, at least. That's how upset they all was! But the man that was walking along, now, was none other than our own cooper, Vavila; he'd bought himself a new tub with handles, and had put that tub on his head, so's to carry it the better."

All the boys broke into laughter and again fell silent for a moment, as is so often the case when people are talking out of doors. I looked around me: night was all about us, silent and majestic; the damp freshness of late evening had been replaced by the crisp warmth of midnight, and for a long while yet was it to lie in a soft pall upon the fields that had fallen into slumber; still a long time remained to the first bird song, to the first dewdrops of dawn. There was no moon in the sky—at that period it rose late. The innumerable golden stars were trying to outtwinkle one another, were flowing along, it seemed, in the same direction as the Milky Way; and, watching them, you yourself seemed to feel vaguely the impetuous, never-ceasing course of the earth. . . . A strange, grating, pained scream broke out over the river, twice in succession, and a few seconds later was repeated, this time farther off.

Kostya shuddered: "What was that?"

"That's a crane calling," Pavel replied calmly.

"A crane, " Kostya repeated. "But there was something I heard yesterday," he added after a short silence. "Maybe you know—"

"What was it you heard?"

"Well, here's what. I was walking from Stony Ridge to Shashkino, and at first I kept close to our hazel bushes, then started going along a little meadow—you know, there where it comes out at a sharp turn from the gully, there's a deep water hole left after the spring freshets, you must know it, why, it's even all grown over with reeds—well, then, I started going past this water hole, brothers of mine, when all of a sudden somebody in that there water hole starts in to moan—and that so pitifully, so pitifully: *Oo-oo . . . oo-oo . . . oo-oo!* What a scare come over me then, brothers of mine! The time was so late, and the voice was full of such pain. Why, you felt you'd be starting in to cry yourself right then and there. What might that have been? Eh?"

"Last year some thieves drowned Akim the forester in that water hole," Pavlusha remarked, "so maybe it were his soul, complaining, like."

"Well, come to think of it, brothers of mine, that may be the very thing," Kostya spoke up, opening wide his eyes, which were enormous enough even without that. "And I didn't even know that they'd drowned Akim in that water hole—if I had, I'd have been scared still worse!"

"Then, too, they say there's a kind of tiny frogs," Pavel went on, "that have a way of croaking so pitifully."

"Frogs? Well, no, that weren't no frogs; how could it have been—" At this point the crane again sent forth its call over the river. "Eh, damn her!" Kostya said involuntarily. "Screeching like a forest fiend!"

"A forest fiend don't screech—he's mute," Iliusha caught him up. "All he does is clap his hands and cackle—"

"Why, did you ever lay eyes on him, by any chance—on a forest fiend, that is?" Fedya cut him short mockingly.

"No, I never did, and may God save me from seeing him, but there's others as has. There, just the other day he got around one of our muzhiks; he led him about and about, through the woods, and kept him going in circles over a certain meadow. It was all he could do to reach home just as it was getting light."

"Well, and did he see the forest fiend?"

"He did that. Ever so big, he was, big as big, says he, all dark, muffled up, just like he was behind a tree or something—no making him out well, like he were hiding from the moon, and he stares and stares at you with those huge eyes of his, now, and he keeps on blinking them, and blinking them—"

"Oh, my!" Fedya cried out, with a slight shudder and his shoulders jerking, and spat in disgust.

"And why have these foul things come upon this world in such numbers?" Pavel remarked. "Really, now!"

"Stop calling names," Ilya remarked in his turn. "Watch out, he may hear you."

There was another silence.

"Just look, lads, just look!" Vanya's childish voice suddenly broke the silence. "Just look at God's little stars; they're swarming like bees!"

He thrust out his fresh little face from under the matting, propped his head on one tiny fist, and slowly raised his big, gentle eyes. The eyes of all the boys were raised toward the heavens, and it was some time before they lowered them again.

"Well, Vanya," Fedya began kindly, "how is your sister Aniutka? Is she all right?"

"She is," Vanya answered, lisping a little.

"You ask her, why don't she come to us?"

"I don't know."

"You tell her to come."

"I will."

"You tell her I'll give her a present."

"And will you give me one, too?"

"And you, too."

Vanya sighed. "Well, no, I don't need it. Better give it to her; our Aniutka is such a kind little thing."

And Vanya again laid his head on the ground. Pavel got up and picked up the small kettle, now empty.

"Where you going?" Fedya asked him.

"To the river, to dip up some water; I feel like having a drink."

The dogs got up and followed him.

"Watch out; don't fall into the river," Iliusha called after him.

"Why should he fall in?" asked Fedya. "He'll be careful."

"Yes, he'll be careful. But there's all sorts of things can happen. There, he may lean over, start dipping up the water —and the water fiend will grab a holt of his hand and begin pulling him in. Later on they'll be saying: 'The little boy tumbled into the water, now.' Tumbled, me eye! The-ere, he's climbed in amongst the reeds," he added, listening intently.

Sure enough: the reeds, as they parted, were rustling.

"But is it true," Kostya asked, "that Akulina has been a little innocent ever since that time she'd been under water?"

"From that very time. And what she looks like now! And yet they say she used to be a beauty. The water fiend ruined her. Guess he weren't expecting they would pull her out so soon. Well, it was he that ruined her there, in his place at the bottom of the river."

(I myself had more than once come across this Akulina. Covered with tatters, frightful, gaunt, with a face black as coal, with a bewildered gaze and her teeth perpetually bared, she would stomp for hours on the same spot, somewhere on the road, with her bony hands pressed hard to her breast, and slowly shifting from foot to foot, just like some wild beast in its cage. She understood nothing, no matter what you said to her, and merely laughed loudly and spasmodically every now and then.)

"Still, they do be saying," Kostya went on, "that Akulina threw herself into the river for no other reason than that her lover deceived her."

"That's the very reason."

"And do you remember Vassya?" Kostya added sadly.

"What Vassya is that?" asked Fedya.

"Why, the one that drowned in this very river," answered Kostya. "What a fine lad he was, what a lad! His mother, Theklista, now—oh, how she loved him, how she loved this Vassya! And it was as though she felt, this Theklista, now, that he would come to his end because of water. Whenever that same Vassya would go with us in the summertime to swim in the river—why, she'd get all in a fluster. The other womenfolk, going by with their washtubs, waddling along, why, they don't pay no mind to their children; but Theklista, she'd put down her tub on the ground and start calling him: 'Come back, now, my little sun! Oh, come back, my young falcon!' And the Lord only knows how he come to drown! He was playing on the bank, and his mother was right there, raking the hay, when all of a sudden she hears a sound like someone was letting bubbles in the water. She looks, and there's nothing there but Vassya's little cap floating on the water. And it's from that very time that Theklista ain't in her right mind; she'll come and lie down at the spot where he drowned; she'll lie down, brothers of mine, and start singing a long-drawn little song—you remember, Vassya, now, always used to sing a song like that; well, that's the very song she'll start singing, and she'll cry, and cry, complaining bitterly to God—"

"There, Pavlusha is coming," Fedya remarked.

Pavel walked up to the fire, lugging the filled kettle.

"Well, lads," he began after a short silence, "it's a bad business."

"Why, what's up?" Kostya asked hastily.

"I heard Vassya's voice."

All of them plainly shuddered.

"What are you saying, what are you saying?" babbled Kostya.

"I did hear it, by God! No sooner did I start bending over the water when all of a sudden I heard someone calling me, like it was in Vassya's little voice, and just as if it was coming from under the water: 'Pavlusha, oh, Pavlusha—come here.' I walked a little ways off. I did draw some water, though."

"Oh, Lordy! Oh, Lordy!" the boys managed to say, crossing themselves.

"Why, that was a water fiend calling you, Pavel," Fedya added. "And we was just talking about him—about Vassya, that is—"

"Ah, that is a bad sign," Iliusha uttered, stopping at every word.

"Well, it don't matter—let come what may!" Pavel declared resolutely and resumed his seat. "No man can get around his fate."

The boys quieted down. It was evident that Pavel's words had made a deep impression on them. They began bedding down before the fire, as if preparing for sleep.

112

"What's that?" Kostya asked abruptly, raising his head. Pavel listened attentively. "Those are snipe, calling as they fly."

"But where are they flying to?"

"Why, to the place where there's no winter, they say."

"And is there such a land?"

"There is."

"Far away?"

"Far, far away, beyond the warm seas."

Kostya sighed and closed his eyes.

More than three hours had passed since I had joined the boys. The crescent moon rose at last; I did not notice it at once, so small was it and so slender. This practically moonless night was, it seemed, still as magnificent as before. But many stars that only a short while ago had been high in heaven had already inclined to the earth's dark rim; all about us everything had become perfectly stilled, as it usually does only toward morning; everything was sleeping the unbroken, motionless sleep that comes before dawn. The air was no longer so fraught with night odors; dampness seemed to be spreading through it anew. Not long do the nights of summer last! The talk of the boys was dying down together with the fires. Even the dogs were dozing; the horses, as far as I could make out in the barely glimmering, faintly flowing light of the stars, were also lying down, with their heads drooping. A slight drowsiness overcame me; it passed into dozing.

A stream of fresh air sped across my face. I opened my eyes: morning was being engendered. As yet the flush of the dawn glow was nowhere to be seen, but already something was showing white in the east. Everything had become visible, even though only dimly visible, all about me. The pale-gray sky was growing light, chill, blue; the stars now twinkled with a faint light, now vanished; the earth had had its fill of dampness, the leaves had broken into a sweat, living sounds began to spring up here and there, and voices, and the tenuous early breeze was already wandering and fluttering over the earth. My body responded to it by a light, joyous shiver. I got up quickly enough and went over toward the boys. They were all sleeping as if they had been slain; Pavel alone raised himself halfway and looked at me intently. I nodded to him and went my way along the river, now smoky with mist.

I had hardly gone a little over a mile when torrents of young, hot light came pouring down all around me—over the far-spreading wet meadow, and ahead of me, over the now newly green knolls, from forest to forest, and behind me, over the long, dusty road, over the sparkling, encrimsoned bushes, and over the river, diffidently showing its blue from under its now thinning mist—torrents of light, at first ruby-red, then red, and golden. . . . Everything began to stir, everything awoke, broke into song, into sound. Everywhere, in rayey gems, great drops of dew burst into glow; pure and clear, as though they too had been laved by the morning coolness, the peals of bells came floating toward me, and suddenly, urged on by the boys whom I now knew, the rested drove of horses raced by. . . .

I must add, to my regret, that in the same year Pavel was no longer among the living. He did not drown; he was killed in a fall off a horse. A pity; he was a fine lad!

KASSIAN OF FAIR STRATH

I WAS ON my way back from hunting; the small cart was jouncing and, crushed by the stifling sultriness of an overcast summer day (as everybody knows, the heat on such days is even more unbearable than on cloudless ones, especially when there is no wind), I was yielding, with grim fortitude, to the corrosive action of the fine white dust of the beaten road rising from under the heat-warped and jarring wheels— when suddenly my attention was aroused by the unusual restlessness and uneasy bodily movements of the young driver, who up to then had been even drowsier than I. He took to jerking at the reins, started fidgeting on the box, and began shouting at the horses, constantly looking somewhere off to one side.

I looked about me. We were driving over a spreading, thoroughly plowed plain; rather low but exceedingly sloped knolls, likewise thoroughly plowed, ran down into it like rolling billows; the eye took in no more than two miles or so of unobstructed distance; far-off copses of birch with their roundedly crenelated tops were all that broke up the almost straight line of the sky's rim. Narrow paths stretched away over the fields, becoming lost in the small hollows, coiling over the hillocks, and upon one of these paths, which happened to cross our road some five hundred paces away, I made out some sort of procession. This was precisely what my driver had been eyeing.

115

It was a funeral. At the head, in a cart drawn by just one little nag going at a walk, a priest was riding; a sacristan was sitting by his side and driving; behind the cart four muzhiks, their heads bared, were carrying a coffin draped with a white pall; two peasant women were trudging behind the coffin. The high-pitched piteous voice of one of them suddenly came to my ears; I listened closely: she was keening. Dismally did this trilling, monotonous, hopelessly sorrowing chant sound amid the empty fields. My driver put the whip to his horses: he wanted to head off the procession: meeting a corpse on a road is a bad omen. He actually did succeed in galloping ahead of the intersection before the corpse had time to reach it, but we had not driven as much as a hundred paces farther when our cart was suddenly jolted hard: it listed, all but turning over. The driver stopped the horses in full career, gestured hopelessly, and spat in disgust.

"What's up now?" I asked.

My driver climbed down in silence and taking his time about it.

"Come, what's up?"

"Axle broke—burned through," he answered somberly, and adjusted the collar of the off horse with such indignation and abruptness that the animal all but fell on its side; however, it kept on its feet, snorted, shook itself and, as calmly as you please, fell to scratching a fetlock joint with its teeth.

I got out and stood for some time in the road, yielding uneasily to a feeling of unpleasant perplexity. The right wheel was almost completely turned under the cart and seemed to be holding up its hub in mute despair.

"What we we to do now?" I asked at last.

"That's who's to blame!" said my driver, pointing with his whip at the funeral procession, which by now had had time to turn into the road and was approaching us. "For I've always noticed," he went on, "that it's a bad omen to meet a corpse. That's for sure!" And he again turned on the off horse, which, perceiving his disagreeable mood and harshness, decided to stand still where it was and merely gave an occasional and discreet switch to its tail. I walked to and fro for a little while and again stopped before the collapsed wheel.

In the meanwhile the corpse caught up with us. Having quietly turned off the road into the grass, the sad train began to creep past us. The driver and I took off our hats, bowed to the priest, exchanged glances with the pallbearers. They walked with difficulty; their broad chests were heaving. Of the two peasant women walking after the coffin one was very aged and pale; her set features, cruelly distorted by grief, maintained an expression of stern, solemn dignity. She walked in silence, every now and then bringing a gaunt hand up to her thin, sunken lips. The other, a young woman of twenty-five, had eyes reddened and tear-stained, while her whole face had become swollen from weeping; on coming abreast of us she desisted from keening and covered her face with her sleeve. But at last the corpse went past us, regaining the road, and her piteous, heart-rending dirge broke out again.

Having followed the even sway of the coffin with his eyes, the driver again turned to me. "It's Martin the carpenter they're burying," he said. "The one from Ryabovo."

"Why, how do you know?"

"I recognized the womenfolk. The old one, now, is his mother, and the young one is his wife."

"Was he sick, or what?"

"Yes, fever it was. Three days ago the manager of the estate sent for the doctor, but they didn't find the doctor at home. A good carpenter he was, now; he took a drop too much now and then, yet he was a good carpenter for all that. Just see how his woman is killing herself for grief. Oh, well, you know how it is: womenfolk don't have to lay out any money for their tears. Women's tears are the same as water—that's for sure!"

And he bent down, crawled under the off horse's rein, and seized the shaft bow with both hands.

"But, just the same," I remarked, "what are we to do?"

The first thing my driver did was to put his knee against the shoulder of the shaft horse, then he shook the shaft bow a couple of times, adjusted the pad, then again crawled through under the off horse's rein and, having poked it in the muzzle while he was at it, walked up to the wheel; he walked up to it and, without taking his eyes off it, slowly took out from under the skirt of his caftan a birch-bark snuffbox, slowly drew up the lid by a little leather tab, slowly thrust thick thumb and forefinger into the snuffbox (even the two digits hardly found room therein), kept rubbing and rubbing the pinch of snuff, screwed up his nose in anticipation, took the snuff deliberately, accompanying each application with prolonged snorting and then, painfully puckering and blinking his tear-filled eyes, plunged into deep reflection.

"Well, what's what?" I asked at last.

My driver painstakingly put the birch-bark snuffbox back in his pocket, shoved his hat down over his forehead without the aid of his hands, merely with a single motion of his head, and thoughtfully started clambering up on his box.

"Where are you going?" I asked him, not without astonishment.

"Please get in," he replied imperturbably and picked up the reins.

"But how can we drive?"

"We'll drive right enough, sir."

"But the axle—"

"Do get in."

"But the axle is broken—"

"Break it did, sure enough, but we'll manage to get to the new settlements—at a walk, that is. Right over that way, to the right, beyond the grove, there are some new settlements. Iudiny, they call them."

"And you think we can reach them in this cart?" My driver did not deign to answer me. "I'd better walk, then," said I.

"Please yourself, sir," and he brandished his whip. The horses started off.

We actually did manage to reach the new settlements, even though the right front wheel was barely hanging on and turning in an extraordinarily odd way. On one hillock it all but flew off, but my driver started shouting in an enraged voice and we came downhill without any mishap.

The Iudiny settlements consisted of six huts, low and tiny, which had already found the time to become lopsided even though they had been put up probably not so long ago; not all the huts had wattle fences about their barnyards. As we were driving into these settlements we failed to come across a single living soul; one couldn't see as much as a hen in the street, nor even any dogs, save for one black cur with a bobbed tail; on sighting us the creature hastened to jump out of a bone-dry trough into which it must have been driven by thirst and immediately, without as much as a bark, dived headlong under a gate.

I stepped into the first hut and called out for the owners: no one answered me. I called out once more: a hungry

miaowing came from behind another door. I kicked it open
—a gaunt cat darted past me, its green eyes glinting in the
dark. I put my head into the room and took a look; it was
dark, reeking of smoke, and deserted; I went out into the
yard, and there was nobody there, either. A calf pent up in
an enclosure lowed; a lamed gray goose hobbled off a little
to one side. I passed on to a second hut—and there wasn't
a soul in the second hut, either. Out into the yard I
stepped. . . .

In the very middle of this yard, glaring with the sunlight,
in the very sunbake, as they say, was lying someone whom
I took for a boy, his face to the ground and his peasant overcoat pulled over his head. A few paces from him, near a
miserable little cart, a bare-bones nag in torn harness was
standing under a straw-thatched overhang. The sunlight,
streaming in through narrow gaps in the thatching, mottled
its shaggy reddish-gray coat with small splotches of light.
Right close, in a birdhouse atop a tall pole, starlings were
chattering, looking down with calm curiosity from their tiny
aerie. I walked over to the sleeper and started waking him.

He raised his head, saw me, and at once sprang to his
feet. "What . . . what do you want? What is it?" he began
to mutter, still half asleep.

I did not answer him immediately, so struck was I by his
appearance. Imagine a dwarf of fifty, with a tiny swarthy
and wrinkled face, a sharp little nose, hazel-hued, barely distinguishable eyes, and curly, thick black hair which, like the
cap of a mushroom, squatted and spread out upon his diminutive head. His whole body was exceedingly puny and
thin, and it would be utterly impossible to convey in words to
what an extent his gaze was extraordinary and odd.

"What do you want?" he questioned me again.

I explained to him what the matter was; he listened to me
without taking his slowly blinking eyes off me.

"So can't we get a new axle?" I concluded. "I'd pay for it
with pleasure."

"But who might you be? Hunter, or what?" he asked, his
eyes taking me in from head to foot.

"That's right."

"You shoot the innocent little birds of God, never fear?
The beasts of the forest? And isn't it a sin for you to be slay-
ing the little birds of God, to be spilling innocent blood?"

The queer little old man spoke very drawlingly. The sound

of his voice also amazed me. One did not merely fail to catch in it any note of senility; it was astonishingly sweet, young, and almost femininely tender.

"I have no axle," he added after a short silence. "That one"—he indicated his small cart—"won't do. You must have a big cart, I guess."

"But could I find one in the village?"

"Call this a village? Nobody's got an axle here; they're all out working. Be on your way!" he said suddenly, and again lay down on the ground. I had not at all expected such a termination.

"Listen, old man," I spoke up, touching his shoulder, "do oblige me—help me out."

"Go your ways, and God go with you! I'm all tuckered out after my ride to town," he told me, and started pulling the overcoat over his head.

"But do oblige me," I went on. "I'll . . . I'll pay."

"I've no need of your payment."

"Come, old man, please!"

He raised himself halfway and sat up, crossing his thin little legs.

"I might guide you to the clearings. There's some merchants bought up our grove; God be their judge, they're ruining that grove and they've put up an office, God be their judge! And there you might order an axle from them, or buy one ready-made."

"Why, that's fine!" I cried out joyfully. "Fine! Let's go."

"An axle of oak, a good axle," he continued without getting up from his spot.

"And is it far to the clearings?"

"A couple of miles."

"Well, what of that? We can get there in your little cart."

"Oh, no—"

"Come on, now, old man," said I. "Come on, old man! My driver is waiting out there."

The old man got up reluctantly and followed me out into the street. My driver was in a state of irritation: he had been about to drench his horses, but there turned out to be mighty little water in the well, and what little there was had a bad taste—and water, as drivers put it, is something that comes ahead of all else. However, on catching sight of the old man, he bared his teeth in a grin and called out: "Ah, Kassianushka! Greetings!"

120

"Greetings, Erothei, thou just man!" Kassian responded in a dejected voice.

I immediately informed my driver of the old man's proposition; Erothei declared his readiness and drove into the yard. While he was unharnessing his horses with deliberate alacrity the old man stood with one shoulder leaning against the gate and kept eyeing him and me by turns, far from cheerfully. He seemed to be perplexed: he was not, as far as I could perceive, overjoyed by our unexpected coming.

"Why, have they resettled you too?" Erothei, as he was taking off the shaft bow, asked him suddenly.

"Me, too."

"Think of that!" my driver got out through clenched teeth. "You know Martin the carpenter, now—you do know Martin of Ryabovo, don't you?"

"I do."

"Well, he died. We met his coffin on the way just now."

A shudder ran through Kassian. "He died?" he managed to say, and fixed his eyes on the ground.

"Yes, he died. How come you didn't cure him, eh? For they say that you cure folks, that you're a healer." My driver was, evidently, having a bit of fun, jeering at the old man. "And what about that cart—is it yours, or what?"

"It's mine."

"Well, it's a cart that's a cart!" Erothei commented and, taking it by the shafts, all but turned it bottom up. "What a cart! But what will you use for horseflesh to drive to the clearings with? There's no harnessing one of our horses between those shafts—our horses are big—but what sort of a contraption do you call this?"

"Why, I don't know what you could drive," Kassian answered. "Unless you take that bit of livestock," he added with a sigh.

"This thing here, you mean?" Erothei caught him up and, walking up to Kassian's wretched little nag, contemptuously prodded its neck with the ring finger of his right hand. "Look at that!" he added reproachfully. "It's fallen asleep, the crowbait!"

I requested Erothei to harness it as quickly as possible, having become eager myself to go with Kassian to the clearings: in such places one can frequently come upon grouse. But when the little cart was all ready and I, together with

121

my dog, had somehow contrived to find room on its warped bottom of bast, and Kassian in his turn was seated on the front boards, all of him squeezed into a ball and with his expression still that of unchanged despondency, Erothei walked up to me and with a mysterious air whispered: "You did well, father of mine, in going along with him. Why, he's such a fellow, such an innocent—why, they've even given him the nickname of Flea. I don't know how you were able to make out what he said."

I was about to remark to Erothei that, up to now, Kassian had struck me as quite a sensible person, but my driver immediately resumed in the same tone:

"The only thing is, watch out that he brings you to the right place. And, if you please, do pick out the axle your own self. Well now, Flea," he added loudly, "is there any chance of getting a bit of bread among you folks?"

"Look around, maybe you'll find some," Kassian answered; he tugged at the reins and we were off.

His nag, to my genuine wonder, ran along very far from poorly. Kassian maintained a stubborn silence all the way and gave curt and unwilling answers to my questions. We reached the clearings shortly and there found our way to the office itself: a tall hut standing solitary at the edge of a gully which had been dammed up in a makeshift way and turned into a pond. In this office I found two young men who were clerking for the merchants, with teeth as white as snow, with sweet eyes, sweet and lively of speech, and with sweetly knavish smirks; I bargained with them for an axle and set out for the site where the felling was going on. I thought that Kassian would stay behind with the horse, that he would wait for my return, but he suddenly walked up to me.

"Well, now, are you off to shoot down the dear birds?" he began. "Eh?"

"Yes, if I find any."

"I'm going with you. May I?"

"You may, you may."

And off we went. The cleared space was actually less than a square mile in extent. I watched Kassian more closely than I did my dog, I confess. It was not in vain that he had been nicknamed Flea. His black, small head without covering of any sort (however, his hair could take the place of any cap) simply flitted among the bushes. He was extraordinarily spry and seemed to be constantly hopping when on the go, incessantly bending down, plucking some herbs or other, thrusting them into the bosom of his shirt, muttering something to himself under his breath and forever glancing at me and my dog, and doing so with such a searching, odd look. Low bushes, scrubwood, and clearings are often the haunts of certain gray little birds which never stop exchanging one sapling for another and keep up an intermittent whistling, dipping unexpectedly in their flight. Kassian mimicked them, kept calling to them, while they called right back to him; a young quail flew off, *chik-chillik*'ing, from under his feet—Kassian sent his own *chik-chillik* after the bird. A skylark began its descent high overhead, fluttering its wings and in full resounding song—Kassian chimed in with it. But with me he would not enter into talk at all.

The weather was splendid, still more splendid than hitherto, yet the heat would not abate. Lofty and tenuous clouds, yellowly white like snow in late spring, flat and elongated like sagging sails, were barely, barely drifting across the clear sky. Their figured edges, downy and light as cotton, underwent a slow yet perceptible transformation at every moment; they melted away, did these clouds, and they cast no shadow.

For a long while Kassian and I roamed through the clearings. Young shoots, which had not yet had time to stretch upward for more than three feet or so, surrounded with their slender smooth stems the low, blackened tree stumps; round spongy growths, bordered with gray—those same growths from which tinder is extracted by boiling—clung to these stumps; strawberry plants sent their rosy tendrils over them; mushrooms also squatted there in closely knit family groups. One's feet were incessantly getting caught and entangled in the tall grass, saturated with the heat of the sun; everywhere the eyes were dazzled by the cutting metallic glitter of the reddish young leaves of the saplings, by the motley of the light-blue clusters of vetch, the aureate little calices of the large celandine, the half-lilac, half-yellow flowers of cow wheat; here and there, bordering the abandoned paths, the wheel ruts upon which were defined by rows of stubby red grass, rose stacks of firewood darkened by wind and rain, something like three cords to each stack; they cast faint rhombs of shade: of other shade there was none, anywhere. A light breeze would awaken, only to quiet down;

it would instantly start blowing straight in your face and seem to be playfully increasing; everything would become joyfully noisy, take to nodding; the pliant tips of the ferns would start swaying gracefully; one would rejoice at its coming . . . but there, it again died away and everything quieted down again. Only those little smiths, the grasshoppers, persisted in rattling away in unison as if they were infuriated, and tiresome was this unceasing, crisp sour-note sound. It was in keeping with the unremitting noonday heat, as though it were born thereof, as though it had been evoked thereby out of the incandescent earth.

We at last reached some new clearings, without stumbling on a single covey. There the recently felled aspens were despondently stretched out on the ground, having crushed both the grass and the underbrush beneath their weight; on some the leaves, still green but already dead, drooped listlessly on the unstirring branches; upon others the leaves had already turned dry and become mummified. From fresh, aureately white chips lying in mounds near the stumps glistening with moisture there was wafted a peculiar, exceedingly pleasant, acrid odor. Farther off, closer to the grove, one could hear the dull blows of axes, and, at times, solemnly and gently, as though it were bowing and flinging wide its arms, a curly-topped tree would sink to the ground.

For a long time I had not come upon game of any sort —at last, from behind a spreading oak bush thickly interlaced with wormwood, a corn crake took wing. I fired: it turned over in the air and fell. On hearing the shot Kassian quickly put his hand over his eyes and would not stir until I had reloaded my gun and picked up the corn crake. But after I had moved on he walked up to the spot where the slain bird had fallen, bent over the grass on which several drops of blood had spattered, shook his head, and glanced at me timorously. Afterward I heard him as he whispered: "It's a sin! Ah, but that is a sin!"

The heat compelled us at last to enter the grove. I flung myself down under a tall hazelnut bush, over which a young straight maple had gracefully spread its light branches. Kassian perched on the butt end of a felled birch. I was watching him. The leaves were faintly stirring high above us, and their tenuously green shadows kept gliding over his tiny face, over his puny body, haphazardly wrapped in his peasant's overcoat of dark cloth. He would not raise his head.

Growing tired of his speechlessness, I lay down flat on my back and began admiring the peaceful play of the tangled leaves against the far-off radiant sky. An amazingly pleasant occupation, this lying on your back in a forest and gazing upward! It seems to you that you are looking into a bottomless sea which is spreading wide *beneath* you, that the trees are rising not out of the earth but, just as if they were the roots of enormous plants, are going down, are plunging straight down into those glassily limpid waters; the leaves upon these trees are now shot through with emerald tints, now thicken into aureate, almost black greenery. Somewhere, far off, serving as the termination of some slender branch, a small leaf stands out all by itself against a light-blue scrap of sky; swaying alongside this leaf is another, its motion reminding one of a reach of water teeming with fish, as if that motion were self-willed and not brought about by the wind.

Round white clouds that look like underwater islands come floating forward gently and gently float past, and lo, instantly all this sea, this refulgent air, these sun-drenched branches and leaves—all these begin to stream, to quiver with a fleeting glitter, and there springs up a fresh, tremulous babbling, resembling the never-ending, choppy plash of surging waves. You do not move—you gaze: and there is no expressing in words how joyous and gentle and delectable is the mood that enters your heart. You gaze: and that profound pure azure brings to your lips a smile as innocent as itself, as innocent as the clouds against the sky, and it seems as if together with them, in a lingering file, happy recollections pass over your soul, and all the time it seems to you that your gaze is receding farther and farther into that tranquil, shining abyss and is drawing you after it, and it is impossible to tear yourself away from that height, from that depth. . . .

"Master—oh, master!" Kassian uttered suddenly in his sonorous voice.

I raised myself in surprise: hitherto he had hardly replied to my questions, and now he had suddenly spoken up of his own accord.

"What do you want?" I asked.

"Well, now, what did you go and kill that bird for?" he began, looking me straight in the face.

"What do you mean, what for? A corn crake is a game bird: it's all right to eat it."

"That's not what you killed it for, master—as if you would ever eat it! It's for your sport you killed it."

"Well, now, I guess you yourself eat geese or chickens, for instance?"

"Such fowl are provided by God for man, but a corn crake is a free bird, a bird of the forest. And not the corn crake alone: there's lots of others, all creatures of the forest, and of the field, and there's river creatures, and those of the swamp and the meadow, of highland and lowland, and it's a sin to be killing any such creature—just let it live upon the earth until its time comes. As for man, there's other food set aside for him, other food and other drink: bread, God's own good gift, and the waters of heaven, and tame creatures that have come down from our fathers of old."

I looked at Kassian in wonder. His words flowed freely; he did not grope for them, he spoke with quiet animation and meek solemnity, closing his eyes from time to time.

"So, according to you, it's a sin to kill fish as well?" I asked.

"A fish is cold-blooded," he retorted with assurance, "a fish is a dumb creature. It has no fears, no joys—a fish is a voiceless creature. A fish has no feelings—even its blood has no life in it. Blood," he went on after a silence, "blood is a sacred thing! Blood sees not the dear little sun of God, blood hides from the light—it's a great sin to bring blood out into the open, a great sin and something to dread . . . oh, a great sin!"

He sighed and fixed his eyes on the ground. I looked at the strange old man with, I confess, utter amazement. His speech had not in it the ring of peasant speech: the common folk did not talk thus nor did the fine speakers. A language meditatively solemn and strange, this. Never had I heard anything like it.

"Tell me please, Kassian," I began without taking my eyes off his face, which had turned a trifle red, "what trade do you follow?"

He did not respond to my question at once. His eyes, for an instant, darted about uneasily.

"I live as God wills," he uttered at last, "and as for following a trade, now—no, I don't follow any. I am very far from having any sense, ever since I was little: I work, as long as my strength lasts; I'm a poor worker—how could I be a good

126

one! There's no health in me, and my hands have no cunning. Well, now, comes spring, I snare nightingales."

"You snare nightingales? But how is it you were saying that one oughtn't to harm any creature of the forest, the field, and so on?"

"You mustn't kill it, true enough; death will get its own, even without that. There, you take Martin the carpenter, just for an instance: there was Martin the carpenter, living his life, and it weren't long he lived, and he died; his wife is killing herself now for grief over her husband, over her little children. There's no man, no creature can outwit death. Even though death runs not, yet there's no running away from it, either; but just the same one oughtn't help it along. But as for the little nightingales, I don't kill them—the Lord keep me from that! I don't snare them for to torture them, or to put an end to their life, but for to pleasure man, to solace and cheer him."

"Do you go to Kursk to snare them?"

"Yes, I go to Kursk, too, and even farther, as things may fall out. In the swamps do I pass the night, and in the woods; I pass the night all by myself out in the field, in the wilderness: that's where the snipe whistle the loudest, where the rabbits squeak, where the drakes chatter. Of evenings I mark down the nightingales; of mornings I listen to them; as dawn glows I cast my net over the bushes. Now and then you come upon some little nightingale that will sing so piteously, so sweetly . . . it's pitiful, so it is."

"And you sell them?"

"I give them away to good folks."

"But what else do you do?"

"How do you mean, what do I do?"

"What's your occupation?"

The old man was silent for a space. "I've no occupation in particular. I'm not much of a worker. I know how to read and write, though."

"You do?"

"I know how to read and write. The Lord helped me, and so did some kind folks."

"Are you a family man, or what?"

"Things didn't fall out that way; I have no family."

"How come? Did they die off, or what?"

"No; things just worked out so; no luck befell me in my life. But all that is under God's will—all of us are under

God's will in our comings and goings, yet man must live righteously, that's what! He must find favor with God, that is."

"And you have no kin either?"

"I have . . . that is . . . sort of—" the old man became flustered.

"Tell me, please," I began, "I thought I heard my driver asking you why you hadn't cured Martin, now. Why, do you know how to make people well?"

"Your driver is a fair man," Kassian answered me thoughtfully, "yet he, too, is not without sin. A healer, they call me. What sort of healer am I! And who can heal? All that is at the bestowal of God. There are certain things, though. There are herbs; flowers there are that can help, that's true enough. There, you take bud marigold, for instance, a herb that's good for man; there's buckthorn, too; there's nothing blameworthy in talking about them, now—they're pure herbs, they're God's own. But then there's others, they're not that sort: they may help, even, yet it's a sin to use them—and it's a sin even to speak of them. Unless, of course, one adds a prayer. Well, to be sure, there are also certain words. . . . However, he that hath faith shall be saved," he added, lowering his voice.

"You didn't administer anything to Martin?" I asked.

"I found out about him too late," answered the old man. "But what does it matter! Each man meets the fate written down for him at birth. He weren't meant to live long, this Martin the carpenter—he weren't long for this world, that's the way of it for sure. No, if any man is not fated to be long for this world, that man will be neither warmed by the dear sun, as another would, nor will the blessed bread do him any good—as though something were calling him to come away . . . yes! May God rest his soul!"

"Is it long since they resettled you in our region?" I asked after a brief silence.

Kassian perked up: "No, it's not been long; four years or thereabouts. When our old master was alive we were all living in our former localities, but the board of guardians resettled us. Our old master was a meek soul and a resigned one—may the Kingdom of Heaven be his! Well, the guardians decided the matter justly, of course: that's the way things had to be, it looks like."

"And where were you living before?"

128

"We hail from Fair Strath."

"Is that far from here?"

"Over sixty miles."

"Well, and were things better there?"

"They were, they were! There it's open country every-where, plenty of rivers; it was our nest. But here it's all cramped, dried out; here we've become orphaned. There, in our Fair Strath, you'd climb up on a knoll; you'd climb up, and you'd say 'Lord my God, what is this? Eh?' There'd be a river, and meadows, and a forest, and over that way a church, and then there would be meadows again, stretching away into the distance. You could see far, far off. Why, you could see *that* far—you'd look, you'd look, and it was enough to make you cry out, for sure! Well, over here the land is bet-ter, true enough: clayey soil, good clayey soil, the peasants say; but then, there'll always be a crop of grain to do me, anywhere."

"Well, now, old man, tell the truth: I guess you'd like to visit your native region, wouldn't you?"

"Yes, I'd take me a good look at it. However, any place is good. I'm a man without a family; I can't stay put. Yes, and what does that matter! Will a man get a lot, now, by sitting at home? But then, soon as you get going, going on and on," he warmed up, raising his voice, "things ease up, sure as sure. There's the dear little sun shining on you, and God can get a better look at you, and you sing more in tune, too. Here you look to see what grass is growing—so you make a note of it and pluck a few blades; there you find running water, let's say: spring water, out of a well-spring—holy water, that is; so you drink your fill of it, and likewise make a note of it. The birds of heaven are in song. Or else, beyond Kursk, the steppes begin—steppe reg-ions, you know; there's something to make a man wonder, something to pleasure man, there's spaciousness itself, there's God's own good gift! These steppes go on, folks say, to the warm seas themselves, where the sweet-voiced bird Gamaiun has its being and no tree sheds leaf nor in winter nor in fall, and apples of gold grow on branches of silver, and each man dwells in content and righteousness. And that's the very place I'd like to go to. For where haven't I gone to! I've gone to Romen, and to Sinbirsk, the city of glory, and to Moscow itself, of the golden domes; I've gone to Oka, the bread giver, and to Tzna, the dove, and to the

Volga, our mother, and many men have I seen, good Christen folk, and in cities of honor have I been. Well, then, that's where I'd go. And so . . . and sure enough. . . . And not only I, sinner that I am. There's many other Christen folk in bast slippers wander the wide world over, hither and yonder, seeking for truth. Yes! But as for what's at home, now—what do you find there? There's no righteousness in man, that's what—"

Kassian delivered the last words in a patter, almost indistinctly; after that he said something else, which I could not even hear clearly, while his face took on such a strange expression that the appellation of *innocent* came involuntarily to my mind. He cast down his eyes, coughed to clear his throat, and apparently recovered his self-possession.

"What a dear sun!" he uttered in a low voice. "What a blessed thing it is, Lord! What warmth there is in these woods!"

His shoulders twitched; he was silent for a while, glanced about him, and began to sing, ever so quietly. I could not catch all the words of his long-drawn-out little song; I thought I heard the following words:

> "For Kassian is the name I go by,
> And my nickname is The Flea—"

"So!" I reflected. "He's creating his own song!"

Suddenly he shuddered and fell silent, peering into the denser part of the woods. I turned around and saw a little peasant girl of eight in a sleeveless coat, long and blue, with a checkered kerchief on her head and a small, squarish woven basket over her bared, sunburned little arm. Probably she had not at all expected to encounter us; she had run into us, as they say, and was standing motionlessly in a green thicket of hazel bushes on a small shady glade, timorously glancing at me from time to time with her dark eyes. I hardly had time for a good look at her: she immediately dived behind a tree.

"Annie! Annie! Come here—don't be afraid," the old man called her caressingly.

"I'm afraid," came her piping little voice.

"Don't be afraid; come to me."

Annie silently forsook her lurking place, came quietly in a roundabout way (the child's tiny feet barely swished through the thick grass), and emerged from the thicket at a point very close to the old man. But this was no girl of eight, as she had seemed to me at first glance because of her short stature: she was thirteen or fourteen. Her whole body was small and slim, yet most graceful and agile, while her pretty little face bore a striking resemblance to the face of Kassian himself, even though Kassian was no raving beauty. The very same sharp features, the very same strange gaze, sly and trusting, pensive and penetrating—and the movements were the very same. Kassian ran his eyes over her: she was standing sideways to him.

"Well, were you gathering mushrooms?" he asked.

"Yes, mushrooms," she answered with a shy smile.

"Find a lot?"

"A lot!" She glanced at him quickly and again smiled.

"Get any white ones, too?"

"White ones, too. I've got them."

"Show them, now. Show them." She slid the basket off her arm and half-raised a broad burdock leaf that covered the mushrooms. "Eh!" said Kassian, bending over the basket. "Why, what glorious mushrooms they are! Good girl, Annie!"

"That's your daughter, Kassian, isn't she?" I asked. A faint flush came over Annie's face.

"No, just a relative, sort of," Kassian let drop with assumed nonchalance. "Well, Annie, be off with you," he immediately added. "Be off, and God go with you. And watch out, now—"

"But why should she walk?" I interrupted him. "We could take her in the cart wherever she wants to go—"

Annie's face flared up as red as a poppy; she clutched the rope handle of her basket with both hands and looked in alarm at the old man.

"No, she'll get there on foot," he retorted in the same apathetically languid voice. "What does it mean to her? She'll get there on her own. Be off with you!"

Annie nimbly went off into the forest. Kassian followed her with his eyes for a while, then looked down and smiled a little. About this prolonged smile, about the few words he had said to Annie, about the very sound of his voice while he had been talking to her, there had been inexplicable, passionate love and tenderness. He again looked in the direction in which she had gone, again smiled and, rubbing his face, shook his head several times.

"Why did you send her away so soon?" I asked him. "I would have bought the mushrooms from her."

"Why, you'll buy them at home anyway, whenever you like," he answered, and for the first time his speech became a little more formal.

"You've got a very pretty little girl there."

"No, not at all . . . just so-so," he answered as though unwillingly and, at that same instant, lapsed into his former taciturnity.

Perceiving that all my exertions to make him loosen his tongue would again remain useless, I went off toward the clearings. Then, too, the heat had abated a little; however, my lack of luck—or my "poor luck," as they say among us— persisted, and I returned to the settlements with nothing but one corn crake and a new axle. It was only as we were approaching his barnyard that Kassian abruptly turned around to me:

"Master, oh, master!" he began. "Why, I am at fault before you—why, it was me that made all the game keep clear of you, now."

"How so?"

"Why, that's something I know for sure. There, your hound is both trained and good, yet he couldn't do a thing. Just think of it, what are human beings? What are they, eh? And there you have an animal—yet what have they made of it?"

It would have been in vain for me to try convincing Kassian of the impossibility of "casting a spell" over game, and therefore I did not answer him. Besides that, we very shortly turned in at his gate.

Annie was not in the hut; she had already managed to get there and leave the basket with the mushrooms. Erothei fitted the axle, after first subjecting it to a thorough and unfair appraisal, and an hour later I rode away, after leaving Kassian a little money, which at first he did not accept, but, after deliberating and holding it a while on his palm, he thrust it within the bosom of his shirt. During the course of this hour he had uttered hardly a word; he had stood as before, leaning against the gate, would not respond to the reproaches of my driver, and parted with me quite coldly.

I had not failed to notice, immediately upon my return,

that my Erothei's spirits were again in a somber state. And, truly, he hadn't found a thing to eat in the village; the water for the horses had been bad. With displeasure that found expression even on the nape of his neck he sat on his box, and was simply itching to get into talk with me, but, while awaiting my opening question, he confined himself to grousing under his breath and delivering admonitory—and at times caustic—speeches directed at his horses. "Some village!" he muttered. "My, what a village! I asked for some bread-cider, at least—and there weren't even any bread-cider to be had! Oh, Lordy! And the water—why, it's enough to make a body spit!" And spit he did, noisily. "No cucumbers, no bread-cider—nothing. Hey, you," he added loudly, addressing the off horse on the right, "I'm on to you, you conniving she-creature, you! You're fond of conniving to make things easier for yourself, never fear!" And he gave her a taste of his whip. "That horse has gotten much too sly, and yet it was a willing enough animal before. There, there, keep looking back!"

"Tell me, Erothei, please," I opened the conversation, "what sort of man is this Kassian?"

Erothei did not answer me for some time; he was, in general, a man who reflected and took his time, but I could surmise at once that my question had cheered him up and calmed him.

"The Flea, now?" he spoke up at last after a tug at his reins. "A queer fellow—an innocent, for a fact; such another queer fellow would take some finding. Well, for instance . . . well, now, he's for all the world like that there roan of ours: he, too, has gotten all out of hand—gotten out of the habit of working, that is. Well, to be sure, what kind of a worker is he—it's a wonder he keeps body and soul together; but still, after all. . . . Why, he's been that way ever since he was little. At first he used to go carting with his uncles—he had three of them; well, later on he got tired of that, I guess—and he dropped it. Took to staying home, but he couldn't stay put even there, he's that restless, like a sure-enough flea. Happened he got a kind master, glory be, that didn't force him to do anything. And that's the way he's been knocking about ever since that time, the same as a stray sheep. And he's such a puzzling fellow, God knows what he's up to: either he'll keep mum as a tree stump, or all of a sudden he'll start talking away, but what he's talking about

God alone knows. Is that any way to be? It's no way at all. A muddled fellow, that's what he is. Sings well, though. Sort of solemn; not bad, not bad at all."

"And what about his being a healer? Is that true?"

"Healing? What healing? There, where does he come to that! He's not that sort. However, he did cure me of scrofula. . . . Where does he come to being a healer! A foolish fellow, that's what," he added after a brief silence.

"Have you known him a long time?"

"A long time. Him and me used to be neighbors in Sychovka, which same was in Fair Strath."

"And who was that girl we came upon in the forest—the one they call Annie—is she related to him?"

Erothei looked at me over his shoulder, and his grin was of the broadest. "Hmm! Yes, they're related. She's an orphan —has no mother, and besides, nobody knows just who her mother was. But then, she must be a relative of his; she favors him in looks much too much. At any rate, she's living at his place. A keen wench, no gainsaying that—a good wench; as for the old man, she's his heart and soul: she's a good wench. And—there, you won't believe it, yet like as not he'll strike on the notion of teaching her to read and write. By God, that would be just like him: that's the sort of unlikely fellow he is. He's such a weathercock; he's past figuring out, even. . . . Hey, hey, hey!" my driver suddenly broke off his own monologue and, bringing the horses to a stop, leaned over the side and took to sniffing the air. "Isn't there a smell of something burning? Just as I thought! Oh, what these new axles do to me! And yet it seems that I greased it plenty enough. I'd better go and fetch some water. There, it so happens there's a small pond right over there."

And Erothei, taking his time about it, clambered down off his box, untied a bucket, went to the pond, and, upon returning, listened not without satisfaction to the hissing of the wheel box under the dousing. Six times in seven miles or so did he have to slosh water over the heated axle, and it was definitely evening by the time we got back home.

THE STEWARD

THERE IS A certain person of my acquaintance living about ten miles from my estate, a young landowner, an officer of the Guards (retired)—Arcadii Pavlych Penochkin. His place abounds in game, his house was built according to the plans of a French architect, his house serfs are togged out after the British style, he stages excellent dinners, he receives his guests amiably, but just the same one visits him not without reluctance. He is a reasonable and responsible man; his education has been an excellent one, of the accepted sort; he has been in government service, has been around in higher society, and now keeps himself busy in running his estate with great success. Arcadii Pavlych is, to use his own words, strict and just, takes thought for those subject to him, and when he punishes them he likewise does so for their own good.

"One must treat them like children," he will say on such an occasion. "It's ignorance, *mon cher; il faut prendre cela en considération.* One must take that into consideration, my dear fellow."

But he himself, on the occasion of what is called a deplorable necessity, avoided any brusque and impulsive gestures and did not like to raise his voice, but for the most part kept pointing his hand straight in front of him, adding calmly as he did so: "Why, I requested you to do so, my good man"; or, "What's wrong with you, my friend? Come to your senses," during which he clenches his teeth and twists his mouth, but only slightly.

He is of no great height, has the build of a dandy, is not at all bad-looking, is very neat about his hands and nails; his rosy lips and cheeks simply glow with health. His laughter is sonorous and insouciant, his clear hazel eyes pucker affably. He dresses excellently and with complete taste. He imports French books, prints, and newspapers, yet has no great love for reading: it was all he could manage to get the best of *The Wandering Jew.* He plays cards like a master. Arcadii Pavlych is, on the whole, considered one of our most cultured aristocrats and most to be envied among the marriageable bachelors in our province; the ladies are simply mad over him, and it is his manners they particularly praise. He does conduct himself amazingly well, is as wary as a cat, and not once in all his born days has he been mixed up in any affair, although, on occasion, he does love to throw his weight around and to nonplus some timid soul and bring him up short.

He has a positive aversion for low company; he is afraid of compromising himself. On the other hand, in a jovial hour, he declares himself a devotee of Epicurus, although he has but a poor opinion of philosophy in general, styling it a misty pabulum for Germanic minds and, at times, as simply bosh. Music, too, he loves: while sitting at cards he hums through his teeth, but with feeling; he also remembers snatches from *Lucia* and *Les Somnambules,* but always hits too high a key, somehow. During the winters he takes trips to Petersburg.

His house is kept in extraordinarily good order: even his coachmen have yielded to his influence, and not only do they polish the horse collars and brush their tentlike overcoats every day, but actually go to the extent of washing their own faces. Arcadii Pavlych's house serfs do, true enough, have a hangdog look about them, somehow—but then, in our Russia, there's no telling a morose fellow from a sleepyhead.

Arcadii Pavlych speaks in a voice soft and pleasing, lingering over each word and with apparent relish letting each word strain through his splendidly beautiful, perfumed mustache; he also uses many French expressions, such as *"Mais c'est impayable*—but that is priceless! . . . *Mais comment donc*—but that goes without saying!" and the like. But with

all that I, at least, visit him none too willingly and, were it
not for the grouse and partridges, I would probably drop
my acquaintance with him altogether. Some sort of queer
disquietude takes possession of you in his house; even its
comforts do not gladden you, and every time that, toward
evening, a becurled valet appears before you in his blue
livery with armorial buttons and fawningly gets down to
drawing your boots off, you feel that if, instead of his wan
and spare figure, there were to spring up before you the
amazingly broad cheekbones and unbelievably blunt nose of
a young, well-grown country lad just taken from the plow
by his master, yet who had already managed to split at the
seams in half a score places the nankeen caftan recently
bestowed on him, you feel you would rejoice beyond all telling and would willingly subject yourself to the peril of being
deprived, together with the boot, of your leg as well, right
up to the kneecap. . . .

Despite my lack of enthusiasm for Arcadii Pavlych I did
have occasion to pass a night at his place. Next morning,
early, I ordered my carriage to be ready, but my host would
not let me leave without breakfast—a breakfast after the
British manner—and led me off to his study. Together with
the tea we were served with chops, soft-boiled eggs, butter,
honey, cheese, and so forth. Two flunkies in immaculate
white gloves anticipated our least wishes. We were seated on
a Persian divan. Arcadii Pavlych was sporting ballooning
Ukrainian trousers of silk, a jacket of black velvet, a fez
with a blue tassel (on him it looked well), and yellow, heel-
less Chinese slippers. He drank tea, laughed, examined his
nails, smoked, kept shoving cushions under his side and, in
general, was in excellent spirits. Having put away a solid
breakfast, and that with obvious gusto, Arcadii Pavlych
poured himself a glass of red wine, brought it up to his lips
—and suddenly his brow became overcast.

"Why wasn't the chill taken off this wine?" he asked one
of the flunkies in a rather sharp voice. The flunky became
confused, halted as if he were rooted to the spot, and turned
pale.

"Come, it's you I am asking, my good man—am I not?"
Arcadii Pavlych went on in a calm voice without taking his
eyes off the other.

The unfortunate flunky shifted from foot to foot without
moving from the spot, gave his napkin a twist, and did not

utter a word. Arcadii Pavlych lowered his head and gave the other a thoughtful look from under his brows.

"Pardon, mon cher," he uttered with a pleasant smile, amiably patting my knee, and fixed his eyes anew upon the flunky. "There, be off with you," he added after a brief silence, raised his eyebrows, and rang a bell.

The man who entered was stout, swarthy, black-haired, with a low brow and eyes that were absolutely sunk in fat.

"About Fedor . . . attend to him," Arcadii Pavlych let drop in an undertone and with perfect composure.

"Right, sir!" answered the stout man and left the room.

"Voilà, mon cher, les désagréments de la campagne— there, my friend, you have the unpleasantnesses of country life," Arcadii Pavlych commented gaily. "But where are you off to? Do stay; sit here a little longer."

"No," I answered. "It's time I went."

"Always this hunting! Oh, what these hunters make me feel like! But where are you driving to now?"

"About twenty-five miles from here—to Ryabovo."

"Ryabovo? Ah, my God, in that case I'll take a ride with you. Ryabovo is only a little over three miles from my Shipilovka and, after all, I haven't been to Shipilovka in quite a long while—never could find the time for it. There, how very opportune this is: you'll put in some hunting in Ryabovo today, and in the evening you'll come to my village. *Ce sera charmant*—that'll be charming. We'll have supper together, we'll take a chef along, and you'll pass the night at my place. Splendid, splendid!" he added without waiting for my reply. "*C'est arrangé.* Hey, who's out there? Order a carriage ready for us, and be lively about it! You've never been to Shipilovka? I might feel embarrassed about suggesting that you pass the night in my steward's hut, but then I know that you are not exacting and that in Ryabovo you're likely to sleep in some hay barn. We're off, we're off!" —and Arcadii Pavlych launched into some sentimental French ditty.

"Probably you may not know it," he resumed, rocking on his heels, "but I own some muzhiks in Shipilovka who are paying me quitrent. That's the constitutional law—what can one do? However, they do pay me the quitrent regularly. I would, I confess, have put them back to working for me, but there's so little land. I wonder how they manage to make ends meet, even as it is. However, *c'est leur affaire—*

that's their business. My steward there is a handy fellow, *une forte tête;* he has a head on his shoulders, he's a statesman! You'll see. Really, how very fortunately this has turned up!"

There was no help for it. Instead of nine in the morning we started out at two in the afternoon. Hunters will understand my impatience. Arcadii Pavlych loved to indulge himself on occasion, as he put it, and he took along such a world of linen, victuals, potables, perfumery, pillows, and all sorts of *nécessaires* or traveling cases that all this blessed stuff would have sufficed some thrifty and self-controlled Teuton for a year. At every downhill stage Arcadii Pavlych delivered a brief but forceful speech to the coachman, from which I concluded that my acquaintance was quite a coward. However, the journey was, on the whole, consummated without mishap, save that on a certain recently repaired bridge the cart carrying the chef collapsed, and one of its hind wheels had crushed his belly.

Arcadii Pavlych, on witnessing the fall of his home-bred Carême,[1] became quite alarmed and at once sent someone to inquire: Were the chef's hands uninjured? On receiving an affirmative answer to this he immediately calmed down. What with one thing or another our ride was quite a long one; I was sharing the same carriage with Arcadii Pavlych, and toward the end of the journey had come to feel deathly boredom, all the more so since during the course of several hours my acquaintance had turned altogether flat, and was already beginning to play the liberal.

We did arrive, at last—not at Ryabovo, however, but right in Shipilovka: that's the way things had worked out, somehow. At any rate, I wouldn't have been able to put in any hunting that day and therefore, possessing my soul in patience, I submitted to my lot.

The chef had come a few minutes before us and, evidently, had already managed to see to things and to alert the proper people, inasmuch as at our very entry into the village limits we were met by its headman, the steward's son, a well-grown and red-headed muzhik a good seven feet in height; he was on horseback and bareheaded, in a new peasant overcoat which he wore unbuttoned.

[1] Carême, Marie-Antoine (1784–1833), Paris-born master *cuisinier;* author of sundry works on the culinary art.—*Trans.*

"But where is Sophron?" Arcadii Pavlych questioned him.

The headman, having first jumped spryly off his horse and salaamed before the master from the waist, delivered himself of: "Greetings, Arcadii Pavlych, our own father!" and then raised his head, shook himself, and reported that Sophron had set out for Perov, but that word had already been sent to him to come back.

"Well, fall in behind us," said Arcadii Pavlych.

The headman, out of decorum, led his horse off to one side, piled up on top of it, and started off after the carriage at a trot, clutching his hat but not putting it on. We drove through the village, coming across several muzhiks in empty carts; they were on their way back from the threshing floor and singing songs, bouncing bodily and with their legs dangling in the air, but on catching sight of our carriage and the headman instantaneously fell silent, doffed their winter caps (although it happened to be summer) and raised themselves up as though awaiting orders. Arcadii Pavlych bestowed a gracious bow upon them. An uneasy excitement was evidently spreading through the village. Country wives in checkered wraparound skirts were shying chips at dogs that were either slow-witted or overzealous; a gimp-legged codger with a beard that started right under his eyes yanked his horse away from the well before it had done drinking, thumped it in the ribs, nobody knows why, and only then did he salaam before the master. Urchins in overlong shirts ran screaming toward the huts: they belly whopped on the high thresholds, brought their heads low, threw their legs up, and in this manner rolled quite nimbly through the doors into the dark entries, from which they did not show themselves again. Even the hens made tracks on the double-quick under the gates; one enterprising rooster with a black breast that looked like a satin vest and a red tail that curled up to his very comb did make a stab at sticking in the middle of the road and had got all set to crow, but suddenly became abashed and likewise started running.

The steward's hut stood apart from the others, in the middle of a field of thickly growing green hemp. We came to a stop before the gate. Penochkin, Esq., stood up, picturesquely shed his cape and got out of the carriage, looking about him genially. The steward's wife met him with low curtsies and approached to kiss the master's little hand. Arcadii Pavlych let her kiss it to her heart's content and then ascended to the porch. The headman's wife was standing in the entry, in a dark corner, and she too curtsied, but to approach the master and kiss his hand she durst not. Two other country wives were already fussing in the so-called cold room to the right of the entry; they were carrying out of it all sorts of rubbish: empty vats, sheepskin coats as stiff as boards, butter crocks, a cradle holding a heap of rags and a raddled baby; they were sweeping up the dirt with birch-leaf besoms, the kind used to beat yourself with in a steam bath. Arcadii Pavlych sent them packing out of the room and installed himself on the bench under the holy images. The coachmen began carrying in trunks, coffers, and other appurtenances of comfort, trying their utmost to subdue the stomping of their heavy boots.

In the meanwhile Arcadii Pavlych was questioning the headman about the crops, the sowing, and other topics having to do with the estate. The headman answered satisfactorily but somehow listlessly and awkwardly, just as if he were trying to button a coat with frozen fingers. He was standing near the door and was constantly on the alert and glancing over his shoulder to make way for a spry flunky. From behind the headman's mighty shoulders I succeeded in catching a peep of his wife giving a drubbing, ever so quietly, to some other country wife out in the entry. Suddenly a cart came clattering and drew up at the porch: the steward entered.

This statesman, as Arcadii Pavlych had described him, was of no great height, broad-shouldered, gray and corpulent, with a red nose, small pale-blue eyes, and a fan-shaped beard. We will remark, by the bye, that ever since Holy Russia has been in existence, it has never yet known an instance of a man who has put on flesh and gained wealth who did not have a full, bushy beard; a man may have been wearing a skimpy little beard all his days, and a wedge-shaped one at that; suddenly, look and behold ye, he has rimmed himself in with a beard as if with a nimbus: wherever does all that hair come from! The steward must have put one or two under his belt at Perov: the face on him had become quite bloated and, besides, one could catch a whiff of spirits coming from his direction.

"Ah, there, our father, our gracious benefactor!" he launched into singsong, and with such emotion on his face that it looked as if, at any moment now, the tears would come spurting. "You did deign to put yourself out at last and pay us a visit! Let's have your little hand, father of mine, let's have your little hand!" he added, his lips already snouted in anticipation.

Arcadii Pavlych gratified his wish. "Well, now, brother Sophron, how are things going with you?" he asked in a kindly voice.

"Ah, there, our father!" Sophron cried out. "How should they go badly—things in general, that is! Why, you are our father, our gracious benefactor, and you have deigned to shed light upon our little village by your coming, you have made us happy till our dying days! Glory be to Thee, Lord! Arcadii Pavlych! Glory be to Thee, Lord! Everything is in good stead, through your gracious favor."

At this point Sophron fell silent for a space, eyed his master, and as though carried away anew by a rush of emotion (besides that, his tipsiness was coming into its own), once more asked to kiss his hand and then began chanting more ardently than ever. "Ah, there, our father, our gracious benefactor . . . and . . . well, now! By God, I've grown altogether foolish for joy! By God, I'm looking at you, but I just can't believe my eyes! Ah, there, our father!"

Arcadii Pavlych glanced at me, smiled slightly, and asked: "*N'est-ce pas que c'est touchant*—touching, isn't it?"

"Yes, Arcadii Pavlych, father of mine," the irrepressible steward kept right on, "but how could you do such a thing? You make me grieve entirely, father of mine—you did not deign to send me word of your coming. Where will you pass the night, then? Why, this place is dirty, filthy—"

"It doesn't matter, Sophron, it doesn't matter," Arcadii Pavlych answered him with a smile. "This is fine."

"Yes, our father, but fine for whom? Fine for us muzhiks, but then you are . . . ah there, my father, my gracious benefactor . . . ah, there, my father! Forgive me, fool that I am —I've gone clean out of my head; by God, I've turned plain foolish."

In the meanwhile supper had been served; Arcadii Pavlych started eating. The old man chased his son out: he was spoiling the air, you see.

"Well, now, have you settled your field boundaries, old-timer?" Penochkin, Esq., asked him, obviously wanting to fall in with peasant speech and winking at me the while.

"We did that, father of mine, all through your gracious

142

favor. Signed the papers day before yesterday. The folks from Hlynov got uppity at first—they got uppity, my father, true enough. They made demands . . . they made demands . . . well, they made God knows what demands. But then they're just a pack of fools, father of mine—a stupid lot. But we, father of mine, through your gracious favor, showed our gratitude to Micholai Micholaich, the mediator, and made it up to him; we acted according to your orders throughout, father of mine; just as you deigned to order us, so did we act, and we acted throughout with the full knowledge of Egor Dmitrich."

"Egor reported the matter to me," Arcadii Pavlych commented with an important air.

"Of course Egor Dmitrich did, father of mine; of course he did."

"Well, in that case, are all of you satisfied now?"

This was all that Sophron had been waiting for. "Ah, there, our father, our gracious benefactor!" he struck up his chant again. "Yea, be gracious unto me! Yea, our father, we pray to the Lord God day and night for you. . . . Of course, there's little land, kind of—"

Penochkin cut him short: "There, it's all right, it's all right, Sophron; I know that you are my zealous servant. Well, now, what about the threshing?"

Sophron sighed. "Well, our father, the threshing come out none too good. But then, Arcadii Pavlych, father of mine, let me tell you what sort of a little matter has come up." At this point he drew nearer to Penochkin, Esq., with his arms outspread, bent over, and puckered up one eye. "A dead body turned up on our land."

"How so?"

"Can't figure it out myself, father of mine and our father—looks like the trick of some enemy. But, as good luck would have it, it turned up near the boundary of another field than ours; however, there's no use trying to cover up a bad thing: the body was on our land. So I ordered it to be dragged over to the other strip of land right off, whilst we had the chance, and put a guard over it, and gave strict orders to my people: 'Not a word of this!' I told them. As to the constable, I explained what was what to him, just in case: 'The things that go on!' I told him, and treated him to tea, and slipped him something to show my gratitude. Well, and what do you think, father of mine? Why, it was the

143

others that were stuck with it—and yet a dead body means a fine of two hundred rubles, sure as little apples."

Penochkin, Esq., laughed a great deal at his steward's dodge and told me repeatedly, nodding in the other's direction: *"Quel gaillard, ah*—what a clever fellow, eh!"

In the meanwhile it had grown altogether dark out of doors; Arcadii Pavlych ordered the table to be cleared and hay to be brought. A flunky spread the sheets for us and placed the pillows; we lay down. Sophron went off to his room after receiving his orders for the next day. Arcadii Pavlych, even as he was falling off to sleep, discoursed a little more about the sterling merits of the Russian peasant, and while he was at it remarked that since the beginning of Sophron's management the peasants in Shipilovka weren't in arrears by as much as a copper. . . . The night watchman took to pounding his board; a baby, which apparently hadn't yet managed to become imbued with a feeling of proper self-abnegation, started mewling somewhere in the hut. . . . We fell asleep.

Next morning we got up rather early. I was all set to drive to Ryabovo, but Arcadii Pavlych wished to show me over his property and persuaded me to remain. Besides, I myself did not mind actually ascertaining the points of excellence of that statesman Sophron.

The steward appeared. He had on a peasant overcoat of blue, girded with a broad red belt. He talked considerably less than yesterday, looked keenly and intently into the eyes of his master, answered fluently and in a businesslike way. We set out with him for the threshing barn. Sophron's son, the seven-foot headman, quite a foolish fellow to judge by all the signs, also came tagging along, and Thedoseich, the village constable, likewise attached himself to us: he was a quondam soldier with enormous mustachios and the oddest of expressions—just as if quite a long while ago he had been extraordinarily astonished by something and ever since then had not come to himself.

We inspected the threshing barn, the corn kiln, the silos, the sheds, the windmill, the cattle barn, the vegetable patches, the hemp fields; everything was, in fact, in excellent order: the despondent faces of the muzhiks alone gave me some pause for wonder. Outside of things utilitarian, Sophron also took thought of things which afford aesthetic pleasure: he had bordered all the ditches with base-trefoil; between the hayricks near the threshing barn he had laid out paths and strewn them with fine sand; atop the windmill he had contrived a weathervane in the shape of a bear with gaping maw and red tongue; onto the cattle barn, which was of brick, he had slapped something in the nature of a Greek pediment, and under this pediment he had inscribed, in white lead: KONSTRUCKTED IN THE SETLEMINT OF SHIPILOFKA IN THE YR OF EITEEN HUNDERD & FOURTY. THIS CATTEL BARN.

Arcadii Pavlych went all to pieces, he was that touched, and embarked on expounding to me, in French, all the benefits of the quitrent system, at the same time noting, nevertheless, that serf labor was better for landowners—but then, this world was full of all sorts of things!

He started in giving the steward bits of advice: on how to plant potatoes, on how to prepare feed for the cattle, and so on. Sophron would hear his master's speech out to the end with attention, now and then offering opinions of his own in reply, but he no longer glorified Arcadii Pavlych either as his father or his gracious benefactor, and constantly kept pressing the point that they hadn't any too much land, now; that it wouldn't hurt none to buy some additional acreage.

"Well, then, buy some," Arcadii Pavlych told him. "I wouldn't mind, if it's in my name."

To these words Sophron made no reply whatsoever, merely stroking his beard.

"However, it mightn't be amiss to take a ride into the forest," Penochkin, Esq., remarked.

Saddle horses were led up for us at once; we went off into the forest—or *zakaz*, as we say in our district. In this *zakaz* we came upon tanglewoods and stretches of frightful wilderness, something for which Arcadii Pavlych praised Sophron and gave him a pat on the shoulder. Penochkin, Esq., adhered, as far as forestry was concerned, to Russian concepts and, right then and there, told me a most amusing (to quote him) incident, of how a certain wag of a landowner had gotten some sense into his forester by yanking out about half of the other's beard, by way of proving that a forest won't grow any thicker if you fell its trees. . . . In other respects, however, both Sophron and Arcadii Pavlych did not shy away from innovations. On our return to the village the steward led us off for a look at a winnowing machine he had recently ordered by mail from Moscow. The winnowing machine actually worked well, but had Sophron known what an unpleasantness awaited both him and his master during this last excursion he would probably have stayed at home with us.

What happened was this. On coming out of the shed housing the winnowing machine we beheld the following sight: standing a few paces away from the door of the shed, close to a muddy puddle in which three ducks were plashing with never a care in the world, were two muzhiks: one an old man of sixty, the other a lad of twenty, both of them in patched shirts of homespun, both barefooted and with ropes by way of belts. Thedoseich, the village constable, was being zealously officious with them and probably would have managed to persuade them to make themselves scarce if we had tarried in the shed, but, on catching sight of us, he drew himself up as if on parade and froze in his tracks. Standing right here, too, was the headman, with his mouth hanging open and fists that were utterly at a loss. Arcadii Pavlych's brow became overcast; he bit his lips and approached the petitioners. Both, in silence, bowed down to his very feet.

"What do you want? What are you petitioning about?" he asked in a stern voice and somewhat through his nose. The muzhiks exchanged looks but did not utter as much as one word; they merely puckered up their eyes, as if against the sun, and their breath was coming faster now. "Well, what is it?" Arcadii Pavlych went on, and immediately turned to Sophron: "What family are they from?"

"The Toboliev family," the steward answered slowly.

"Well, what are you after?" Penochkin, Esq., began again. "Have you no tongues, or what? Speak up, you—what do you want?" he added, nodding to the old man. "There, don't be afraid, you fool."

The old man craned his dark-brown wrinkled neck, opened his twisted livid lips wide, and uttered "Protect us, our lord and master!" in a husky voice and knocked his forehead against the ground once more. The young muzhik kowtowed in his turn. Arcadii Pavlych eyed the napes of their necks with dignity, threw his head back, and shifted his legs a little wider apart. "What is it? Whom are you complaining against?"

"Have mercy upon us, our lord and master! Give us a chance to catch our breath. . . . We've been tortured to death entirely." The old man spoke with difficulty.

"Who tortured you to death?"

"Why, Sophron Yakovlevich, father of mine."

Arcadii Pavlych kept silent for a space.

"What's your name?"

"Antip, father of mine."

"And who might this be?"

"Why, my young son, father of mine."

Arcadii Pavlych kept silent for another space and his mustache twitched.

"Well, just how has Sophron Yakovlevich tortured you to death, now?" he began speaking again, regarding the old man through his mustache.

"He has ruined me altogether, father of mine. Two of my sons he has turned over as recruits, out of their turns, and now he's taking the third one away as well. Yesterday, father of mine, he led my last little cow out of my yard and beat up my good woman—there, that's his gracious self over there—" He indicated the headman.

"Hm!" hm'd Arcadii Pavlych.

"Don't let us be ruined altogether, our provider!"

Penochkin, Esq., frowned. "What's the meaning of this, though?" he asked the steward in an undertone and with a displeased air.

"A hard-drinking fellow, sir," answered the steward, using the formal address for the first time. "He won't work. Can't get out of his arrears for the fifth year by now, sir."

"Sophron Yakovlevich paid in the arrears for me, father of mine," the old man went on. "There, it's the fifth year he's paid them in, but once he paid them in he got me into bondage to him for sure, father of mine, and that's the way things stand now—"

"But how did you come to get into arrears?" Penochkin, Esq., asked awesomely. The old man let his head droop. "You like to get drunk, to go traipsing from pothouse to pothouse, likely enough?" The old man was just about to open his mouth. "I know your kind!" Arcadii Pavlych went on, flaring up. "All you know is to drink and loaf on the ledge atop the oven; but it's a good muzhik that has to be held responsible for the likes of you."

"And he's an impudent fellow besides," the steward added his bit to the master's diatribe.

"Well, naturally, that goes without saying. That's always the way. That's something I've already noticed, more than once. All year long he leads a loose life and carries on impudently, but now he's wallowing at my feet."

"Father of mine, Arcadii Pavlych," the old man spoke up in desperation, "be merciful, protect us—what sort of impudent fellow am I? Speaking as before the Lord God, I'm telling you things are getting past all bearing. He's taken a dislike to me, has Sophron Yakovlevich; as to why he has taken this dislike against me, let the Lord be his judge! He's ruining me altogether, father of mine. There, this is the last of my little sons—well, he's taking even him. . . ." A teardrop glistened in the old man's eyes with their crow's-feet. "Be merciful, our lord and master, protect us—"

"And we're not the only ones he's got it in for—" the young muzhik tried to speak.

Arcadii Pavlych suddenly flared up: "Why, who's asking you anything, eh? Nobody's asking you, so you keep quiet. What's all this? Quiet, I'm telling you! Quiet! Ah, my God! Why, this is nothing short of a riot! No, brother, I don't advise you to riot—I won't have it. I won't have it—" Arcadii Pavlych took a step forward, but probably recalled my presence, turned away, and put his hands in his pockets. *"Je vous demande bien pardon, mon cher*—I ask you to excuse me, my friend," said he with a constrained smile, lowering his voice significantly. *"C'est le mauvais côté de la médaille* —this is the reverse side of the medal. Oh, very well, very well," he went on, without looking at the muzhiks. "I'll issue orders. All right—be off with you." The muzhiks would not get up from the ground. "Why, I've told you—it's all right. Be off with you, then; I'll issue orders, I'm telling you."

Arcadii Pavlych turned his back on them. "These eternal unpleasantnesses," he got out through his teeth and started off for his quarters with great strides. Sophron set out after him. The village constable popped out his eyes, as though he were getting set to jump a very great distance in some direction or other. The headman shooed the ducks out of the puddle. The petitioners stood a while longer where they were, then looked at each other and, without as much as a backward glance, went their plodding way.

Two hours later I was already in Ryabovo and, together with Anpadist, a muzhik of my acquaintance, was getting ready to set out hunting. Penochkin had kept sulking at Sophron up to my very departure. I got into talk with Anpadist about the peasants at Shipilovka, about Penochkin, Esq., and asked him if he didn't happen to know his steward there.

"Sophron Yakovlevich, you mean? I should say so!"

"And what sort of man may he be?"

"He's a dog and not a man—you wouldn't find such another dog if you was to search as far as Kursk itself."

"How is that?"

"Why, that there Shipilovka belongs to this—what d'you-call-him?—this Penochkin. It belongs to him in name only; for it's not him that owns it: it's owned by Sophron."

"Is that really so?"

"He owns it like it was his own property. All the peasants there are up to their ears in debt to him; they work for him like they were his hired hands: he'll send this one off in charge of a wagon train, and another somewhere else; he's got them all run ragged."

"They haven't got much land there, I think?"

"Not much? Why, he's got two hundred sixteen acres on lease from the Hlynov folk alone, and three hundred twenty-four from us—and that's well over five hundred acres you've got right there. And it isn't land alone that he makes money on; he makes money on horses, and on cattle, and on birch tar, and oil, and hemp, and this and that. He's smart, powerful smart, and is he rich, the villain! But here's his worst trait—he fights. A wild beast and not a man; a dog, like I told you; a hound, that's what he is, a downright hound."

"But how is it they don't complain against him?"

"Come, now! What need has the master to concern himself? There are no arrears, so what difference does it make to him? Yes, you just go and try," he added after a short silence, "try to complain. Why, he'll take you and . . . you just go and try it. . . . No, he'll take you, like this, see—"

I recalled Antip and told Anpadist what I had seen.

"Well," he declared, "he'll eat him up alive now: he'll eat the man up alive, entirely. The headman will now be the death of him. What a poor hapless fellow it is, when you think of it! And what a thing he has to be suffering for! Had an argument with him at a meeting—with the steward, that is; things got so he couldn't hold out any more, I guess. A great matter! So he took to pecking away at him—at Antip, that is. Now he'll gobble him up for good and all. Why, he's such a hound, such a dog, the Lord forgive me my transgression in speaking thus; he knows whom he can bear down on. The old-timers, now, those who are better off, those whose families are larger, he won't touch, the bald-headed devil—but here, now, he's let himself all out! Why, he sent Antip's sons up as recruits, outside their turn, the unforgivable swindler, the hound, may the Lord forgive me my transgression!"

We set out hunting.

Salzbrünn, in Silesia,
July, 1847.

THE OFFICE

THIS HAPPENED during autumn. I had been roving the fields
with a gun for several hours already and, probably, would
have stayed away until evening from the inn on the main
Kursk highway where my troika was waiting for me, had it
not been for an exceedingly fine and chill drizzle which had
been nagging away at me since the very morning as indefati-
gably and relentlessly as any old wench and had at last compelled me to seek refuge, if only a temporary one, somewhere
nearby. While I was still considering what direction I ought
to take my eyes were unexpectedly confronted by a low
wickiup standing near a field sown to peas. I approached this
primitive shelter, peeped in under its straw thatch, and beheld an ancient so decrepit that I instantly bethought me of
that dying goat which Robinson Crusoe had come upon in
one of the caves on his island. The ancient was squatting on
his heels, puckering up his tiny dimmed eyes and hurriedly
and cautiously, as if he were a rabbit (the poor fellow
hadn't a tooth in his head), was chomping away at a hard and
dried pea, incessantly rolling it from one side of his mouth
to the other. He was so deeply engrossed in his occupation
that he had not noticed my arrival.

"Hi, Grandpa! Hi there, Grandpa!" said I.

He stopped chewing, raised his eyebrows high, and opened
his eyes with an effort.

"What is it?" he got out in a wheezing mumble.

"Any village close by?"

The ancient fell to chomping again. He had not heard me
clearly. I repeated my question more loudly than before.

151

"A village? Come, what is it you want?"

"Why, to get in out of the rain."

"What is it?"

"To get in out of the rain!"

"So!" he scratched the nape of his sunburned neck. "Well, now, you head that way," he suddenly began, waving his hands at random, "then . . . then, when you find yourself going past a patch of woods—well, when you'll be going that way, you'll hit on the road right there; well, you leave it behind you—the road, that is—and just keep bearing to the right all the time, now . . . to the right, to the right, to the right. . . . Well, then, that's just where you'll hit on Ananievo. And, like as not, you'll even get to Sitovka."

I found it difficult to understand the old man. His mustache interfered with his speech and his tongue, too, obeyed him but poorly.

"And where are you from?" I asked him.

"From Ananievo."

"What are you doing here, then?"

"What's that?"

"What are you doing here?"

"Why, I've been put here as a watchman."

"But what are you watching?"

"Why, the peas."

I could not help laughing. "Come, now—how old are you?"

"Why, God knows."

"I guess you don't see well."

"What's that?"

"You don't see well, I guess?"

"No, not well—there's times I don't hear a thing."

"Well, then, how can you be a watchman?"

"Why, them that's older than me knows best."

"Those older than he!" I reflected and, not without pity, took a good look at the old man. His hand groped over his breast and, pulling a hunk of stale bread out of the bosom of his shirt, he took to sucking at the crust like a child, drawing in his cheeks (sunken enough even as it was) with an effort.

I set out in the direction of the patch of woods, kept turning to the right all the time, as the old man had advised me to do, and at last made my way to a large settlement with a stone church in the new style—with a colonnade, that is—and a spacious manor house (likewise with a colonnade). Even from afar, through the fine lacery of the rain, I

had noticed a hut somewhat higher than the others, with a
roof of hewn timbers and two chimneys—in all probability
the dwelling of the headman—and I bent my steps in that direction in the hope of finding at his place a samovar, tea,
sugar, and not entirely curdled cream. Accompanied by my
thoroughly chilled dog I went up on the little porch, then
stepped into the entry and opened a door, but instead of
the usual furnishings of a hut I beheld several tables cluttered with papers; two red-painted closets; spattered inkwells;
sand sprinklers for drying ink, of pewter and looking as if
they weighed thirty pounds each; the longest of quills; and
so on. Perched on one of the tables was a lad of twenty, with
a puffy and sickly face, diminutive eyes, a greasy forehead,
and endless temples. He was, fittingly enough, dressed in a
gray nankeen caftan, glossy with grease at the collar and in
the region about the belly.

"What do you wish?" he asked me with an upward jerk of
his head, like that of a horse that had been unexpectedly
grabbed by its muzzle.

"Is this where the steward lives, or—"

"This is the owner's main office," he cut me short. "I'm on
duty now. Didn't you see the sign outside, by any chance?
That's what the sign was put up for."

"But where could I get dry? Is there anybody in the village
that has a samovar?"

"Why wouldn't there be samovars?" the lad in the gray
caftan retorted with dignity. "Go to Father Timothei, or to
the servants' quarters, or to Nazar Tarassych, or else to
Agraphena, who's in charge of the poultry."

"Whom are you talking to, you blockhead, you? You
won't let me sleep, you blockhead!" a voice came from an adjoining room.

"Why, some gentleman or other has dropped in, asking
where he may get dry."

"What sort of gentleman?"

"Why, I don't know. He's got a dog and a gun."

A bed creaked in the adjoining room. Its door opened and a
man of fifty entered, stout, short, with the neck of a bull, goggling eyes, unusually rounded cheeks, and the sheen of sweat
was all over his face. "What do you wish?" he asked me.

"To get dry."

"This is no place for that."

"I didn't know this was an office; however, I am prepared to pay—"

"Well, you can use this place, if you like," answered the stout man. "This way, now, if you'll be so kind." He led me to another room—not the one from which he had issued, however. "Will this be all right for you?"

"Right enough. But couldn't I get tea and cream?"

"At once, if you wish. In the meanwhile, if you wish, you can take your things off and rest up a bit; as to the tea, it'll be ready in just a minute."

"And whose estate may this be?"

"Madam Losnyakova's—Ellena Nicholaievna Losnyakova's."

He went out. I looked about me: along the partition dividing off my room from the office there stood an enormous leather divan; two chairs, likewise upholstered in leather, with the highest of backs, stiffly flanked the window which looked out on the street. On the walls, papered in green with pink arabesques, hung three enormous pictures done in oils. One depicted a setter in a blue dog collar inscribed with "This Is My Solace"; a river flowed at the dog's feet, while sitting on the opposite bank, under a pine, was a rabbit of inordinate size, with one ear cocked. The other picture showed two old men eating a watermelon; peeping out from behind the watermelon, in the distance, was a small Greek portico, inscribed "Temple of Requitement." The third picture represented a female seminude in a recumbent position *en raccourci*,[1] with raddled knees and exceedingly thick heels.

My dog, without wasting any time, crawled under the divan after preternatural exertions and, apparently, must have come upon a great deal of dust there, because she went off into a frightful spell of sneezing. I walked over to the window. Boards were laid out in an oblique direction from the manor house to the office: quite a useful precaution since, owing to our black loam soil and the prolonged rain, the mud all around was frightful. Near the manor house, which had its rear to the street, the activities which usually go on in the vicinity of manor houses were going right on: wenches in dresses of faded calico were darting to and fro; house serfs were meandering through the mud, pausing every now and then to scratch their backs reflectively; the village

[1] In foreshortened perspective.—*Trans.*

constable's hitched horse was lazily swishing its tail and, reaching high with its muzzle, was gnawing away at the fence; hens clucked; consumptive turkey hens were incessantly calling to one another. Upon the tiny porch of a time-darkened and rotted structure (probably the bathhouse) a husky lad with a guitar was sitting and, not without bravado, was singing in a low voice a well-known sentimental ballad, mangling the words:

> Me, to far deserts I'm a-going,
> For, mid the be-ay-utiful scenes all about me—

The stout man came into the room where I was.

"There, they're bringing you tea," he informed me with a pleasant smile.

The young fellow in the drab caftan who was on duty in the office disposed on a folding table the samovar, a teapot, a tumbler on a cracked saucer, a crock of cream, and a string of Bolhov cracknels which were as hard as flint. The fat man walked out.

"Who's he?" I asked the young man on duty. "A clerk?"

"By no means, sir. He was the head cashier, once, but now he has been made the head of this office—"

"Why, have you no clerks?"

"By no means, sir. We have a steward—Michaila Vikulov—but no clerk."

"Is there an estate manager, then?"

"Of course there is—Lindamanndohl, Karlo Karlych; the only thing is, he don't see to things."

"Who does, then?"

"The mistress herself."

"So that's it! Well, now, have you a great many people assigned to this office?"

The young fellow was in deep thought for a while.

"There's six men here."

"And just who may they be?"

"Why, here's who: first of all there's Vassilii Nicholaievich, the head cashier; then there's Peter, the bookkeeper; Peter's brother Ivan, a bookkeeper; another Ivan, also a bookkeeper; Koskenkin Narkizov, likewise a bookkeeper; then there's myself, now—why, you couldn't count them all."

"Your mistress has a lot of house serfs, I guess?"

"No, you couldn't say there's a lot of them, exactly—"

"Still, how many are there?"

"They would run to a hundred and fifty, like as not."

We both kept silent for a while.

"Well, now, are you a good penman?" I began again.

The young fellow's grin distended his whole mouth; he nodded, went into the office, and brought back a sheet of paper covered with writing.

"Here's something I've written," said he, still grinning.

I looked at it: on the quarto sheet of grayish paper, in a beautiful and bold hand, was written the following:

ORDER

From the Main Proprietorial Domestic Office at Ananievka, to Michailo Vikulov, Steward; No. 209:

You are ordered, immediately upon receipt of this, to investigate: who was the party that last night, whilst in a State of intoxication and singing indecent Songs, did pass through the Anglish garden, awakening and Disturbing Mme Engenie, the French governess? And why did the watchmen overlook this, and who was the watchman on Duty in the garden? And why did he permit Disorderly actions of such a Nature to take Place?

You are hereby ordered to investigate the entire Matter abovementioned in full detail, and to submit a Report thereon to this Office forthwith.

Signed:

NICHOLAI HVOSTOV, Chief Clerk.

Attached to the order was an enormous armorial seal bearing the inscription SEAL OF THE MAIN PROPRIETORIAL OFFICE AT ANANIEVKA, while toward the bottom there was a subscript: "To be carried out exactly. Ellena Losnyakova."

"Did your mistress add that herself—is that it?" I asked.

"Of course, sir; it were none other than she. Why, the order wouldn't be in force otherwise."

"Well, now, are you going to send this order to the steward?"

"No, sir. He'll come himself and read it. That is, it'll be read to him—for he's one of those amongst us who don't know their A B C's." The clerk on duty was silent for another spell. "Well, now," he added with a smirk, "it's written well, isn't it, sir?"

"It is."

"It weren't me that made it up, though, I confess. Kosken-kin is a master at that sort of thing."

"What—are your orders actually made up first?"

"Why, how else, sir? You can't write one out just so, without a preliminary draft."

"And what salary are you getting?" I asked.

"Thirty-five rubles a year, and five rubles allowance for boots."

"And you're satisfied?"

"I am, naturally. It isn't everybody amongst us that can get a place in the office. In my case, I confess, God Himself willed it: my uncle has the post of butler."

"And are you doing well?"

"Right well, sir. To tell you the truth," he went on, with a sigh, "our sort, now, is much better off amongst the merchants. Amongst merchants our sort is very well off. There, a merchant from Venevo came to us the other evening, so his hired man was telling me things. You're well off with merchants, there's no use talking—well off."

"Why, how is that? Are merchants offering bigger pay?"

"God forbid! Why, a merchant would throw you out neck and crop if you were to ask him for too much pay. No, if you're living at a merchant's you've got to trust and fear him. He gives you food, and drink, and clothing, and all found. If you please him, he'll give you still more. What does your salary mean—there's no need of it at all! And the merchant, now, he lives after a simple fashion, after the Russian fashion, after the fashion of our own kind—why, you go on the road with him, and he's drinking tea, well, you drink right with him; whatever he eats, you eat the same. A merchant does his best for you; a merchant don't act the way one of the gentry does. A merchant don't go in for whims—well, supposing he gets angry at you: he'll give you a drubbing and that's the end of the matter. He don't go in for whittling you down, a chip at a time; he don't go in for making small of you. But when you have to do with one of the gentry it's sheer misery! Nothing suits him at all: this thing isn't done right, and that thing don't please him. Bring him a glass of water or some food: 'Ah, the water stinks! Ah, the food stinks!' So you take it away and stand on the other side of the door a while and then bring it in again: 'There, now, that's good; there, now, that don't stink.' And I must tell you that when it comes to highborn

157

ladies—when it comes to highborn ladies, they're something! And then there's the highborn young ladies, too—"

"Fediushka!" the stout man's voice came from the office.

The man on duty left my room briskly. I finished my glass of tea, lay down on the divan, and fell asleep. I slept for a couple of hours.

On awaking I was about to get up, but laziness got the best of me; I shut my eyes—without, however, going back to sleep. A very quiet conversation was going on on the other side of the partition, in the office. I involuntarily took to listening.

"That's how it is, sir; that's how it is, Nicholai Eremeich," one of the voices was saying. "That's how it is, sir. You can't help taking that into consideration—you can't help it, to be sure. Hm—" here the speaker coughed.

"Do believe me, Gavrila Antonych," the stout man's voice retorted, "who if not I should know how things are done hereabouts? Judge for yourself."

"Yes, who else should know that, Nicholai Eremeich? You are, one may say, the foremost personage here, sir. Well, what's it to be, sir?" the voice, which was unfamiliar to me, went on. "What shall we decide on, Nicholai Eremeich—if I may be so curious?"

"Yes, what shall we decide on, Gavrila Antonych? It's you that the matter depends on, so to say—you're none too willing, it looks like."

"Mercy on us, Nicholai Eremeich—whatever are you saying, sir? Our business is trading, merchantly; it's our business to buy. That's what we depend on, Nicholai Eremeich, so to say."

"Eight rubles a hundredweight," the stout man uttered drawlingly.

I caught a sigh.

"That's a mighty high price you're pleased to ask, Nicholai Eremeich."

"Can't do otherwise, Gavrila Antonych; I'm saying this as if before the Lord God Himself—I can't."

A silence ensued. I raised myself, ever so quietly, and peeped through a crack in the partition. The stout man was sitting with his back to me. Sitting with his face to me was a merchant of forty, spare and with a face as pallid as if it had been smeared with sunflower-seed oil. He was incessant-

158

ly fiddling with his beard and was twitching his lips and blinking very rapidly.

"The standing crops are most amazing this year, sir, one may say," he spoke up again. "I was admiring them all the while I was driving here. They began to amaze one from Voronezh itself—first-rate crops, one may say."

"The standing crops aren't bad, true enough," answered the office manager. "But then as you know, Gavrila Antonych, fall disposes as spring proposes."

"That's truly so, Nicholai Eremeich; everything depends on God's will; it's downright truth you are pleased to utter. But perhaps your guest has awakened, sir."

The stout man turned around and cocked an ear.

"No, he's sleeping. However, one might as well make sure—" he came over to the door. "No, he's sleeping," he repeated and went back to his seat.

"Well, now, what's it going to be, Nicholai Eremeich?" the merchant resumed. "We've got to finish our little deal. So be it, then—so be it," he went on, blinking incessantly. "Two lovely gray notes and a lovely little white one to your gracious self, and as for them over there"—he nodded in the direction of the manor house—"they'll get six and a half rubles a hundredweight. Shall we strike the bargain?"

"Four grays and a whitey," countered the chief clerk.

"Make it three!"

"Four grays and forget the whitey."

"Three grays, Nicholai Eremeich!"

"Three grays and a half, and not a kopeck less."

"Three grays, Nicholai Eremeich."

"Don't even mention any such sum, Gavrila Antonych."

"What a hard man you are to talk over!" muttered the trader. "If that's the case I'd better close the deal with the proprietress myself."

"Just as you wish," responded the fat man. "You should have done that long ago. Really, now, why should you put yourself out? And it'll be far better, at that!"

"There, that'll do, that'll do, Nicholai Eremeich. There, the man had to go and get riled right off! Why, I said that there just so."

"No, why not, really—"

"That'll do, I say. As I say, I was just having a bit of fun. There, take your three grays and a half—what can a fellow do with you."

"It should have been four grays [2] but, like a fool, I was in too much of a hurry," grumbled the fat man.

"And so, over there—at the house, that is—the price will be six and a half: the grain will go for six and a half?"

"Six and a half—I've already told you that."

"Well, in that case let's strike the bargain, Nicholai Eremeich." The trader struck his outspread fingers on the chief clerk's palm. "And so, Nicholai Eremeich, father of mine, I'm going to the proprietress now, sir, and will order myself to be announced, and that's just what I'll tell her: 'Nicholai Eremeich, now, has settled, ma'am, on six and a half rubles a hundredweight, ma'am'."

"Say that very thing, Gavrila Antonych."

"And now, here's yours, if you'll be so kind."

The trader handed the chief clerk a small packet of papers, bowed, tossed his head, picked up his hat daintily with two fingertips, twitched his shoulders, and bestowing an undulant motion to his torso, went out, his half boots creaking decorously. Nicholai Eremeich drew close to a wall and, as far as I was able to make out, began to go through the papers the merchant had handed him. A red head with luxuriant side whiskers thrust itself in at the door.

"Well, now?" asked the head. "Everything in order?"

"Everything's in order."

"How much?"

The fat fellow gestured with his hand in vexation and pointed to my room.

"Ah, very well!" the head retorted and disappeared.

The fat man walked over to the table, sat down, opened a ledger, reached for an abacus, and fell to subtracting and adding the bone counters, using, instead of the index finger, the middle finger of his right hand, which is considered more seemly.

The man on duty entered.

"What do you want?"

"Sidor has come here from the Goloplek settlements."

---

[2] On a carefully considered assumption, the "little deal" involved *assignatsia's*, or government obligations. A note overprinted with *gray* had a face value of fifty rubles; *white* notes came in many denominations; in all human likelihood the white note here was for twenty-five rubles. But since this paper currency was worth only 1/3 of its face value, the fat influence peddler received, instead of the nominal 175 rubles, only the equivalent of about 58 rubles in silver (roughly, $29) for his betrayal of trust.—*Trans.*

"Ah! Well, call him in. Hold on, hold on—go first and see what the strange gentleman is doing: is he still sleeping or has he waked up?"

The man on duty cautiously entered the room I was in. I had put my head on the gamebag that served me as a pillow and shut my eyes. "He's sleeping," he whispered on his return to the office.

The fat fellow grumbled a while through clenched teeth. "Well, call in Sidor," said he at last.

I raised myself up anew. A muzhik of enormous stature entered—about thirty, husky, red-cheeked, with ruddy hair and a small curly beard. He prayed before a holy image, bowed to the chief clerk, clutched his hat in both hands, and straightened up.

"Greetings, Sidor," the fat man let drop, clicking away on his abacus.

"Greetings to you, Nicholai Eremeich."

"Well, now, how was the road?"

"Good, Nicholai Eremeich. A trifle on the muddy side." The muzhik spoke unhurriedly and not at all loudly.

"Your wife in good health?"

"What should she know of ill health!"

The muzhik sighed and put one foot forward. Nicholai Eremeich tucked his quill behind his ear and blew his nose.

"Well, now, what's your reason for coming here?" he went on questioning the other, pocketing his checked bandanna.

"Why, I've heard a call's gone out for the carpenters amongst us."

"Well, what of it—aren't there any among you, or what?"

"Why shouldn't there be, Nicholai Eremeich, when it's all wooded country—everybody knows that. Only it's a busy time now, Nicholai Eremeich."

"A busy time! That's just it: you're willing to work for others, but you don't like to work for your own mistress. It's still work, all the same!"

"The work, now, is work all the same—that's true enough, Nicholai Eremeich . . . but then—"

"Well?"

"The pay is mighty . . . poor . . . you know—"

"If it's not one thing it's another! See how spoiled they've become! Get along with you!"

"And it must also be said, Nicholai Eremeich, there'll be

work for only a week or so, yet they'll keep us here for a month. Either the material will run out, or else they'll just send us to sweep the paths in the garden."

"If it's not one thing, it's another! The mistress herself deigned to issue that order, so there's nothing here for you and me to discuss."

Sidor fell silent and took to shifting from foot to foot. Nicholai Eremeich, his neck slewed over to one side, started clicking the bone counters of his abacus assiduously.

"Our muzhiks, now, Nicholai Eremeich," Sidor spoke up at last, stumbling at each word, "have ordered me to . . . for your gracious self . . . you'll find something . . . here—" he shoved his ham of a hand into the bosom of his short sheepskin overcoat and started dragging out therefrom something bundled in a red-striped towel.

"What are you up to, you fool? What are you up to? Have you gone out of your mind, or what?" the fat man harshly cut him short. "Go on—go to my hut," he continued, almost hustling the bewildered muzhik out. "Ask my wife there— she'll give you tea. I'll come right away—go on! There, don't be afraid; go on, I'm telling you."

Sidor went out.

"What a . . . bear!" the chief clerk muttered after him, shook his head, and tackled his abacus anew.

Suddenly shouts of "Kuprya! Kuprya! You can't keep Kuprya down!" resounded out in the street and on the porch, and a little later a man of rather short stature entered the office; he had a consumptive look, his nose was unusually long, his eyes were big and unmoving, and his bearing was quite haughty. He was dressed in a quite old, tattered surtout of Adelaide (or, as we say in our region, "odelloid") hue, with a plush collar and tiny buttons. He was toting a bundle of firewood over his shoulder. Five house serfs were crowding around him and all five were shouting: "Kuprya! You can't keep Kuprya down! They've promoted him to furnace stoker, to furnace stoker!" But the man in the surtout with a plush collar paid not the least heed to the boisterousness of his comrades, and his face did not betray any change of expression. With measured steps he reached the stove at last, cast off his burden, straightened up, took a snuffbox out of a hip pocket, goggled his eyes, and began to stuff his nose with a bogus rappee of hart clover mixed with ashes.

At the entrance of the noisy band the fat man had at first

162

knit his eyebrows and gotten up from his place but, on seeing what was up, smiled and merely bade them not to shout: there was a hunter, now, sleeping in the next room.

"What sort of a hunter?" the voices asked in unison.

"A landowner."

"Ah!"

"Let them make noise," the man with the plush collar began, spreading his arms. "What's it to me! So long as they leave me be. I've been promoted to furnace stoker—"

"To furnace stoker! To furnace stoker!" the crowd joyfully caught up.

"It's the mistress' orders," he went on with a shrug. "As for all of you, you just bide a while—you'll be promoted to swineherds yet. But the fact that I am a tailor, and a good tailor at that, who learned his trade from the foremost masters in Moscow and who tailored for generals—that's something no one can take away from me. However, what are you putting on such brave airs about? What about? You're all a pack of freeloaders, of lazy good-for-nothings, no more. Set me free—I won't die from hunger, I won't perish; give me a passport, and I'll pay in a good quitrent and will satisfy the masters. But what about you? You'll perish, like so many flies, and that's all there is to it!"

"There, you've gone and told a lie," a pockmarked and exceedingly fair lad, in a red cravat and a coat out at the elbows, cut him short. "For you did go about with a passport, but the masters never saw a kopeck of quitrent from you, and you never earned a copper for yourself; it was all you could do to drag yourself back home, and ever since then you've been living in that miserable thing you've got on."

"Well, what's one to do, Constantin Narkizych!" Kuprian retorted. "A man falls in love—and that man is done for, and perishes. You first live what I have lived through, Constantin Narkizych, and only then go ahead and condemn me."

"And what he found to fall in love with! A downright freak!"

"No, don't you be saying that, Constantin Narkizych."

"Why, whom are you trying to convince? For I saw her—I saw her last year in Moscow, with my own eyes."

"Last year she did lose a little of her looks, actually," Kuprian remarked.

163

"No, gentlemen, I'll tell you what," a man of tall stature, gaunt, his face sprinkled with pimples, his hair becurled and slicked down with butter (a valet, in all probability), spoke up in a disdainful and flippant voice. "There, let Kuprian Athanassich sing his little song for us. Come now, begin, Kuprian Athanassich!"

"Yes, yes!" the others caught up. "Oh you Alexandra! You've tripped up Kuprya, it's no use talking. . . . Sing, Kuprya! Good for you, Alexandra!" (House serfs frequently, when speaking of a man, resort to feminine endings, to make the thing sound more affectionate.) "Sing!"

"This is no place to sing," Kuprian objected with firmness. "This is the mistress' office."

"Why, what's that to you? Guess you're aiming to become a clerk yourself!" Constantin answered with coarse laughter. "That must be it!"

"Everything depends on the mistress' will," the poor fellow remarked.

"See? See where he's aiming at—see what a fellow it is?" This was followed by ululations, and they all went off into peals of laughter; some started cavorting. The loudest peals of all came from a hobbledehoy of fifteen, probably the son of some aristocrat among the house help; he was wearing a cravat of lilac hue and a waistcoat with bronze buttons, and had already managed to cultivate something of a potbelly.

"Look here, though, Kuprya—own up," Nicholai Eremeich began smugly, visibly amused in the extreme and in ever so affectionate a mood, "it's tough to be a furnace stoker, now, isn't it? It's a trifling occupation altogether, I guess?"

"Well, if it comes to that, Nicholai Eremeich," Kuprian began in his turn, "why, you're now our chief clerk, to be sure; to be sure, there's no disputing it; and yet you, too, were out of grace once, and you, too, did your stretch of living in a muzhik hut."

"I say, you'd better watch out and don't forget yourself when you're talking to me," the fat man flared up and cut the other short. "People are having a little fun with you, you fool; you fool, you ought to appreciate that people are taking an interest in you and thank them for it, fool that you are."

"That was just by the bye, Nicholai Eremeich—excuse it."

"It had better be by the bye!"

The door opened, and a serving lad in a cossackeen ran in.

"Nicholai Eremeich, the mistress demands that you come to her."

"Who's with the mistress?" he asked the lad.

"Axinia Nikitishna and the trader from Vanevo."

"I'll be there in just a minute. As for you, brothers," he went on in a persuasive voice, "you'd better go on out of here with the newly appointed stoker, now; the German might drop in by ill luck, and he'll be sure to complain."

The fat man smoothed down his hair, coughed into his fist (which was almost hidden by his coat sleeve), buttoned up, and set off to see the proprietress, setting his feet wide apart as he walked. Shortly afterward the whole band, together with Kuprya, ambled out after him. My old acquaintance, the man on duty, was the only one to remain. He had at first busied himself with mending quills, but had fallen asleep as he sat there. Several flies immediately utilized the happy chance and clustered about his mouth. A mosquito perched on his forehead, disposed its slender legs in the correct stance, and slowly sank its whole sting into the victim's soft flesh. The side-whiskered red head I had seen before again showed itself from behind the door, took a look, then another, and came into the office together with its quite ungainly torso.

"Fediushka? Hey, Fediushka! You're forever sleeping!" the red head declared. Fediushka opened his eyes and got up from his chair. "Has Nicholai Eremeich gone to see the mistress?" continued the newcomer.

"He has, Vassilii Nicholaich."

"Oh, oh!" said I to myself. "There he is, the head cashier."

The head cashier took to pacing the room. However, he padded along stealthily rather than walked and, all in all, was not unlike a cat. An old black frock coat with very narrow tails hung loosely on his shoulders; one hand he kept on his chest, while with the other he was constantly taking hold of his high and narrow neckcloth of horsehair as, all on edge, he kept twisting his head this way and that. He was wearing morocco boots which did not creak, and his tread was ever so soft.

"The landowner from Yagushka was asking for you today," added the man on duty.

"Hm! He was? Just what did he have to say?"

"He said, now, that he was dropping in at Tuturev's this evening and would be expecting you. 'There's a certain matter I've got to talk over with Vassilii Nicholaich, now,' but what that matter was he didn't say. 'Vassilii Nicholaich is sure to know,' he said."

"Hm!" retorted the head cashier and walked over to the window.

"Is Nicholai Eremeich in the office?" a loud voice sounded in the entry, and a tall man, neatly dressed, obviously irate, with a face the features of which were irregular yet which was expressive and courageous, stepped over the threshold. "Isn't he here?" he asked after looking about him quickly.

"Nicholai Eremeich is at the mistress'," answered the cashier. "Tell me whatever you have to say, Pavel Andreich; you can tell me. What do you wish?"

"What do I wish? You want to know what I wish?" The cashier painfully nodded. "I want to teach him a good lesson, the worthless potbelly, the low-down instigator—I'll show him what it means to instigate!" The speaker dropped into a chair.

"Come, come, Pavel Andreich! Calm down. How is it you're not ashamed? Don't forget whom you're speaking of!" the cashier began to babble.

"Whom I am speaking of? Why, what's it to me that he's been appointed chief clerk? There, I must say, they've found someone to appoint! There, one may truly say, they've set a wolf to watch the sheep!"

"That'll do, that'll do, Pavel Andreich—that'll do! Drop it! What sort of nonsense is this!"

"There, Milady Vixen has started wagging her brush! I'll wait till he comes," Pavel let drop with hearty vexation and slapped the table with the flat of his hand. "Ah, here he is, condescending to pay us a visit," he added after a look through the small window. "Speak of the Devil. . . . You're right welcome!" He stood up.

Nicholai Eremeich came into the office. His face was aglow with gratification, but at the sight of Pavel he was somewhat taken aback.

"Greetings, Nicholai Eremeich," Pavel uttered meaningfully, advancing slowly toward him. "Greetings!"

The chief clerk made no reply. The merchant's face appeared in the doorway.

166

"How is it you don't deign to answer me?" Pavel went on. "But no—no," he added, "this is no way to go about it; one will gain nothing by shouting and abuse. No, you'd better tell me of your own goodness, Nicholai Eremeich: what's your reason for persecuting me? What's your reason for wanting to ruin me? There, now, speak up—speak up!"

"This is no place for an explanation with you," the chief clerk retorted, not without agitation, "and it's not the time for it, either. But, I confess, there is one thing I wonder at: what gives you the idea that I wish to ruin you, or that I'm persecuting you? And, finally, how could I be persecuting you? You're not attached to my office."

"Oh, sure! That would be the only thing lacking! But why do you pretend, Nicholai Eremeich? For you do understand me."

"No, I don't."

"No, you do."

"No, by God, I don't!"

"You're swearing by God, actually! Well, if it comes to that, tell me: come, now, is there no fear of God in you? Well now, why won't you let a poor wench live? What do you want of her?"

"Whom are you speaking of, Pavel Andreich?" the fat man asked with feigned astonishment.

"So that's it! The fellow doesn't know, I guess? It's Tatiana I'm speaking of. Put the fear of God in you—what are you so vengeful about? You ought to be ashamed—you, a married man, with children as big as myself by now; as for me, I have nothing else in mind except wanting to marry her. I'm acting honorably."

"Wherein am I to blame here, Pavel Andreich? The mistress won't allow you to marry—that's her will as the mistress. What do I count in this?"

"What do you count? Why, you aren't in cahoots with that old witch, the housekeeper, are you? You don't go in for whispering in the mistress' ear, do you? Tell me, aren't you bringing up all sorts of impossible lies against the defenseless wench? It wasn't through your good offices, was it, that she was demoted from laundress to scullery maid? And isn't it through your good offices that they're beating her and keeping her in calico rags? You ought to be ashamed of yourself—you ought to be ashamed, a man of your age!

167

Why, first thing you know you'll be having a paralytic stroke —you'll have to answer to God."

"Keep on cursing, Pavel Andreich—keep on cursing. Will you have a chance to keep cursing for long, though!"

"What! You've gotten the notion of threatening me?" the other flared up. "Do you think I'm afraid of you? No, brother, you haven't run up against one of that sort here! What have I to be afraid of? I'll manage to earn my bread anywhere. But you, now—that's something else again! The only thing for you is to live here, and instigate, and thieve—"

"See what high and mighty notions he's gotten in his head!" the chief clerk, who was also beginning to lose his temper, broke in on him. "A country doctor, just a country doctor, a no-account pill-roller, but you just listen to him— hoity-toity, what an important person!"

"Yes, a country doctor—yet if it hadn't been for that country doctor your gracious self would now lie rotting in the graveyard. The Foul One sure egged me on to cure him!" he added through clenched teeth.

"You cured me? No, you wanted to poison me; you doused me with aloes," the chief clerk caught him up.

"Well, what of it, when nothing but aloes would work on you."

"The use of extract of aloes is prohibited by the Medical Board," Nicholai went on. "I may yet lodge a complaint against you. You wanted to do away with me, that's what! But the Lord wouldn't let that happen."

"That will do you, gentlemen, that'll do—" the cashier made an attempt to speak.

"You leave me alone!" the chief clerk yelled at him. "He wanted to poison me! Do you understand that?"

"I sure had great need of that. Listen, Nicholai Eremeich," Pavel began in despair, "I'm asking you for the last time . . . you've forced me to do so—things are becoming unbearable for me. You leave us in peace, understand? Or else, by God, one of us is bound to come to a bad end—and the one I'm talking about is you."

The fat man let himself go altogether. "I'm not afraid of you!" he started shouting. "Do you hear me, you milksop? I managed to get the better of your father, too—I cropped his horns for him as well, and let that be an example to you; watch out!"

"Don't remind me of my father, Nicholai Eremeich—don't remind me!"

"Is that so? Who are you to be telling me what to do?"

"I'm telling you—don't remind me!"

"And I'm telling you, don't forget your place. No matter how necessary you may be to the mistress in your way, still, if she should have to choose between the two of us, you won't stay put, dear man! Nobody's allowed to riot—watch yourself!" Pavel was trembling with rage. "As for that wench Tatiana, why, she's getting what's coming to her; bide a while—it's nothing to what's going to happen to her."

Pavel lunged forward with his hands raised and the chief clerk slid heavily to the floor.

"Put him in leg irons—in leg irons, now—" Nicholai Eremeich got out in a moan.

I do not undertake to describe the end of this scene; I am afraid I may have offended the reader's sensibilities as it is.

I got back home that same day. A week later I learned that Mme. Losnyakova had retained both Pavel and Nicholai in her service, but that she had exiled the wench Tatiana to another village: evidently she was expendable.

LONE WOLF

I WAS ALONE, returning at evening in a racing droshky after a hunt. I was about five miles from home; my mare, good-natured and a good trotter, was running briskly over the dusty road, breathing hard from time to time and twitching her ears; my tired dog did not lag a step behind the back wheels, just as though it were hitched to them. A thunderstorm was advancing upon us. Ahead of us an enormous lilac cloud was slowly rising from beyond the forest; long gray clouds were racing over me and toward me; the willow shrubs were stirring uneasily and murmuring. The stifling sultriness had been unexpectedly replaced by a humid chill; the shadows were rapidly intensifying. I struck the horse with one of the reins, descended into a ravine, made my way across the bed of a dried stream, now all grown over with low osiers, went uphill, and drove into a forest.

The road wound before me between hazel bushes, by now flooded with murk; I was moving ahead with difficulty. The droshky jounced over the tough roots of centenarian oaks and lindens incessantly cropping up across deep, elongated ruts—the tracks of cartwheels; my horse had taken to stumbling. A strong wind suddenly began to hum on high, the trees tossed tempestuously, big raindrops came pattering down sharply, slapping the leaves; there was a flash of lightning and the storm broke. The rain started falling in torrents. I slowed down to a walk, and shortly was forced to stop: my horse was getting mired; I couldn't see a speck. I sheltered myself as best I could near a spreading bush. Hunched up and with my face muffled I patiently awaited the end of the inclement spell, when suddenly, by the light of a lightning flash, I thought I saw a tall figure. I fixed my eyes in that direction—the same figure seemed to spring up out of the ground close to my droshky.

"Who's there?" asked a ringing voice.

"And who are you yourself?"

"I'm the forester here."

I gave him my name.

"Ah, I know! You're on your way home?"

"I am. But you see what a storm this is."

"Yes, it's a storm, sure enough," the voice answered.

A white lightning flash lit up the forester from head to foot; a short, crackling peal of thunder came on the heels of the lightning. The dear rain lashed down with redoubled force.

"It won't be over so soon," the forester resumed.

"What can one do!"

"I'll lead you to my hut, if you like," he said abruptly.

"You'd oblige me."

"Please get in."

He walked up to the horse's head, took the bit, and yanked it until the animal budged. We started off. I was holding onto the cushions of the droshky, the droshky itself rocked like "a bark upon the sea," and I kept calling the dog. My poor mare's hoofs sloshed heavily through the mud, she slipped, she stumbled; the forester swayed before the shafts now to the right, now to the left, just like an apparition. We went on for quite a long while; finally my guide stopped.

"There, we're home, master," he announced in a calm voice.

A wicket creaked; several puppies began barking in unison. I raised my head and, by the light of a lightning flash, saw a small hut in the middle of a roomy yard surrounded by a wattle fence. A light showed dully through a small window. The forester led my horse up to the entrance and fell to knocking on the door.

"Right away, right away!" came the highest of trebles; one could catch the patter of bare feet, the bolt creaked, and

171

a girl of twelve, in a tiny shift belted with a bit of tape, appeared on the threshold with a lantern in her hand.

"Light the way for the master," he told her. "I'm going to put your droshky under the overhang."

The girl glanced at me and went into the hut. I followed her in.

The forester's hut consisted of but one room, sooty, low-ceiled and bare, without any sleeping ledges or partitions. A torn sheepskin hung on one of the walls. A single-barreled gun was lying on a bench, a tumbled heap of rags filled one of the corners, two big pots stood by the oven. A rush light burned on the table, flaring up and dimming in mournful fits. A cradle, fastened to the end of a long pole, hung in the very middle of the hut.

The girl put out the lantern, sat down on a diminutive bench, and took to rocking the cradle with her right hand and trimming the rush light with her left. I looked about me: my heart ached naggingly—it isn't a cheery thing to enter a muzhik's hut at night. The baby in the cradle was breathing heavily and rapidly.

"Why, are you all alone here?" I asked the girl.

"I am that," said she; one could hardly make her out.

"Are you the forester's little girl?"

"I am that," she answered in a whisper.

The door creaked and, ducking his head, the forester stepped over the threshold. He picked up the lantern from the floor, walked up to the table, and lit a candlewick.

"Guess you aren't used to a rush light, are you?" he let drop and tossed his curly hair.

I looked at him. Rarely have I had occasion to see such a well-made fellow. He was tall, broad-shouldered, of a glorious build. The mighty sinews stood out in bold relief from under his wet shirt of homespun linen. A black curly beard half covered his austere and manly face; from under the broad eyebrows, which had grown into a single line, his small hazel-hued eyes gazed boldly. He lightly placed his arms akimbo and halted before me.

I thanked him and asked his name.

"They call me Thoma—and, by way of a nickname, Biriuk." [1]

[1] The name *Biriuk* is, in the Orlov province, bestowed on a lonely and morose man.—*Author.*
The term has also the specific meaning of "lone wolf."—*Trans.*

"Ah, so you're Biriuk himself?"

I looked at him with redoubled interest. From my Ermolai and others I had often heard stories of Biriuk the forester, whom all the muzhiks thereabouts dreaded worse than fire. To hear them tell it, the world had never yet seen such a master of his calling: "He won't let you get away with even a bundle of faggots; no matter what time it may be, even at very midnight, he'll come down on your head like a snowfall, and don't you even think of putting up a fight—he's as strong, now, and as nimble, as a fiend. And there's no way of getting around him—neither with drink nor money: he won't fall for any bait. It's more than once by now that good folks have gotten all set to rid the world of him, but no, he won't let them."

That's how the muzhiks of that neighborhood spoke of Biriuk.

"So you're Biriuk," I repeated. "I've heard about you, brother. They say you won't let anybody get away with anything."

"I do my job," he answered morosely. "So happens, I'm not eating my master's bread for nothing."

He took a hatchet out of his belt, squatted on the floor, and began splintering a rush light off a billet.

"You have no woman to see to things, have you?"

"No," he answered and swung his hatchet hard.

"She died—is that it?"

"No . . . yes . . . she died," he added and turned his head away.

I fell silent; he lifted up his eyes and looked at me.

"She ran off with a city fellow that was passing through," he got out with a harsh smile. The little girl cast down her eyes; the baby woke up and started crying; the girl walked up to the cradle.

"Here, give him this," said Biriuk, thrusting a soiled baby bottle into her hand. "There, she abandoned even him," he went on in a low voice, indicating the baby. He walked over to the door, paused, and turned around: "I guess, master," he spoke again, "you won't feel like eating our bread—and yet, outside of bread, I haven't a thing."

"I'm not hungry."

"Well, just as you know best. I'd put up a samovar for you, only I haven't any tea. . . . I'm going out to see how your horse is doing."

He walked out and slammed the door. I inspected my surroundings once more. The hut struck me as more dismal than ever. The acrid odor of stale smoke interfered unpleasantly with my breathing. The girl did not stir from her place; now and then she gave the cradle a push, or timidly put her shift back as it slid off her shoulder; her bare little legs hung down motionlessly.

"What's your name?" I asked.

"Ulita," she managed to say, dropping her small sad face still lower.

The forester came in and seated himself on a bench.

"The storm is passing," he remarked after a short silence. "If you want me to, I'll guide you out of the forest."

I got up. Biriuk picked up his gun and examined the priming pan.

"What's that for?" I asked.

"Why, there's mischief going on in the forest. They're chopping down a tree in Mare's Hollow," he added in answer to my questioning look.

"And it really can be heard all the way here?"

"You can hear it out in the yard."

We went out together. In the distance the ponderous cloud masses were still huddling together; long lightning flashes flared up at rare intervals, but over our heads we could already glimpse here and there the dark-blue sky; the tiny stars were glimmering through the tenuous, rapidly flying clouds. The outlines of the trees were beginning to stand out of the gloom. We listened closely. The forester took off his cap and stared at the ground.

"There . . . there, now," said he abruptly and stretched out his arm. "Just see what a night the man has picked out."

I could hear nothing save the noise of the leaves. Biriuk led out the horse from under the overhang.

"At this rate," he added audibly, "I may let him slip through my fingers, like as not."

"I'll go along with you. Do you want me to?"

"Very well," he answered and backed up the horse. "We'll catch him in a jiffy, and after that I'll guide you. Let's go."

We started walking, with Biriuk in the lead. God knows how he could tell the way, but he paused only rarely, and then only to hearken to the ax strokes.

"There," he kept muttering through clenched teeth, "you hear that? You hear that?"

"Why, where is it?"

Biriuk merely kept shrugging. We descended into a ravine; the wind quieted down for an instant: the measured strokes now reached my ears clearly. Biriuk glanced at me and shook his head. We went on over the wet lady ferns and nettles. There came a dull and prolonged crash.

"He felled it," Biriuk muttered.

Meanwhile the sky kept clearing; there was the least glimmering of light in the forest. We clambered out of the ravine at last.

"Wait here," the forester whispered to me, stooped over, and tipping up his gun, vanished among the bushes.

I began straining my ears. Through the incessant noise of the wind I imagined I caught faint sounds not far off: an ax hacking cautiously at branches, the creaking of wheels, the snorting of a horse.

"Where are you going? Hold on!" Biriuk's voice rang out suddenly, clangorous as iron. Another voice sent up a scream —piteously, like a snared rabbit. A struggle ensued.

"No, you don't. No, you don't," the gasping Biriuk kept saying. "You won't get away from me—"

I dashed off in the direction of the noise and, stumbling at every step, came at a run on the scene of the battle. The forester was fussing on the ground near the felled tree; he had the thief under him and was twisting the latter's arms behind his back, to tie them with a belt.

I approached. Biriuk raised the other to his feet. I saw a muzhik, sopping wet, in tatters, with a long disheveled beard. His wretched little nag, half covered with stiff matting, was standing right there, together with a cart the sides of which had been removed. The forester wasn't saying a word; the muzhik was also silent and merely kept tossing his head every now and then.

"Let him go," I whispered in Biriuk's ear. "I'll pay for the tree."

Biriuk silently took the horse by its forelock with his left hand; with his right he held the thief by the belt.

"There, get a move on, you crow," he let drop sternly.

"Take the ax along," muttered the muzhik.

"No use its getting lost!" said the forester and picked up the ax.

We set off. I brought up the rear. The rain had begun drizzling again, and then came down in torrents. We managed to reach the hut with difficulty. Biriuk left the captured nag in the middle of the yard, led the muzhik into the hut, eased up the knot of the belt that bound him, and made him sit in a corner. The little girl, who had fallen asleep near the oven, bounded up and with silent fright began eyeing us. I seated myself on a bench.

"Eh, damn it—how it's started pouring," remarked the forester. "Guess you'll have to wait till it's over. Wouldn't you like to lie down?"

"Thanks."

"I'd lock him up in that cubbyhole, for your honor's sake," he went on, indicating the muzhik, "but, you see, the bolt's out of order—"

"Leave him here. Don't touch him," I interrupted Biriuk. The muzhik glanced at me from under his brows. I inwardly vowed to set the poor fellow free, at any cost. He was sitting motionlessly on the bench. By the light of the lantern I could make out his drink-ravaged, wrinkled face, beetling yellow eyebrows, restless eyes, gaunt limbs. The little girl had lain down on the floor, near his very feet, and fallen asleep again. Biriuk was sitting at the table, his hands propping up his head. A cricket was chirping in a corner . . . the rain pattered on the roof and glided down the windowpanes; we were all silent.

"Thoma Kuzmich," the muzhik suddenly began in a stifled and broken voice. "Oh, Thoma Kuzmich!"

"What do you want?"

"Let me go."

Biriuk made no answer.

"Let me go . . . I done it out of hunger. Let me go!"

"I know your kind," the forester retorted glumly. "Your whole borough is like that, thief upon thief."

"Let me go," the muzhik kept on. "We've got a manager, now . . . he's ruined all of us, that's what. Let me go!"

"Ruined, are you! Nobody's got any call to steal."

"Let me go, Thoma Kuzmich—don't be the death of me. Your master, now, you know yourself, will eat me up alive, that's what."

Biriuk turned away. The muzhik kept shuddering, as if he were shaken by ague. He kept tossing his head and was breathing unevenly.

"Let me go," he repeated with the despondence of despair. "Let me go, by God—let me go! I'll pay, that's what—by

176

God, I will! By God, I done it out of hunger . . . the little ones squalling—you know how it is yourself. It's hard going, that's what."

"But, just the same, don't you be going out to steal."

"There's the little nag," the muzhik went on. "That little nag, now—you might spare it, at least . . . that's all the livestock I got. Let me go!"

"Can't be done, I'll telling you. I'm not a free man either; I'll be called to account. And besides, there's no need of pampering your kind."

"Let me go! It's my need drove me to it, Thoma Kuzmich —need, that's what it was . . . let me go!"

"I know your kind!"

"Come, let me go!"

"Eh, what's the use of arguing with you; sit there quietly, or else you know what you'll get from me, don't you? Can't you see there's a gentleman here, now?"

The poor fellow cast his eyes down. Biriuk yawned and put his head on the table. The rain still persisted. I waited to see what would happen.

The muzhik suddenly straightened up. His eyes caught fire, and color came to his face:

"Well, then, go ahead and eat me up alive—here, may you choke! Here!" he began, narrowing his eyes and letting the corners of his mouth drop. "Here, you accursed destroyer of souls—drink Christian blood; go ahead, drink it!"

The forester turned around.

"It's you I'm talking to, you—you heathen, you bloodsucker! You and none other!"

"Are you drunk, or what, that you've gotten a notion of cursing?" the forester began in amazement. "Have you gone out of your mind, or what?"

"I am drunk! But it's not on your money, you accursed destroyer of souls—you wild beast! Beast, beast!"

"Ah, you . . . why, I'll take you and—"

"Well, what does it matter to me? It's all one—I've got to perish anyway: where would I go without a horse? Go on and finish me off—it's all the same in the end whether it's from hunger or this way: it's all one. Let everything perish: wife, children—let them all peg out. . . . But as for you, you just wait—we'll get at you in good time!"

Biriuk stood up.

"Go on, beat me, beat me!" the muzhik put in in a ferocious voice. "Beat me, there, beat me!" The little girl hastily bounded up from the floor and stared at him. "Beat me—beat me!"

"Keep still!" thundered the forester and took a couple of steps forward.

"That'll do, that'll do, Thoma!" I cried out. "Leave him alone. God be with him!"

"I'm not going to keep still," the poor wretch went on. "This means pegging out, anyway. You're a destroyer of souls, and a wild beast; there's no sending you to hell. But you just bide a while; you won't be strutting around for long! You'll get a tight fit around your windpipe yet—just bide a while!"

Biriuk seized him by the shoulder. I rushed to the muzhik's aid.

"Keep your hands off, master!" the forester shouted at me.

His threat would not have deterred me, and I had already put out my arm but, to my extreme amazement, at a single sweep he snatched the belt off the muzhik's elbows, seized him by the scruff of his neck, shoved his cap down over his eyes, and thrust him outside.

"Take yourself to the Devil together with your horse!" he shouted after him. "And watch out—another time you won't fare so well at my hands—"

He came back into the hut and busied himself in a corner.

"Well, Biriuk," I said at last, "you're a splendid fellow, I can see that."

"Eh, that'll do, master," he cut me short in vexation. "Only thing is, please don't say anything about this. There, I'd better guide you," he added. "Guess you're not likely to outwait the rain."

The wheels of a peasant cart rattled out in the yard.

"Listen to him plodding off!" Biriuk muttered. "Why, I'll take him and—"

Half an hour later he told me goodbye at the edge of the forest.

TWO LANDOWNERS

I HAVE ALREADY had the honor, my indulgent readers, of presenting to you certain of my neighbors among the gentry; permit me now, while the opportunity offers itself (for us of the writing fraternity everything offers an opportunity), to acquaint you now with two more landowners, on whose estates I have often hunted, men who are quite estimable, well intentioned, and who enjoy the general respect of several districts.

First of all I shall describe for you Major General Vyacheslav Ilarionovich Hvalynsky (Retired). Picture to yourselves a man who is tall and who once had been graceful but is now somewhat flabby, yet not at all decrepit, not even elderly—just a mature man in, as they say, his very prime. True, the features of his face, features which were once regular and which are even now pleasing, have changed a trifle: the cheeks have sagged; crow's-feet, close together, have disposed themselves in rays about his eyes; certain teeth no longer are as Saadi (so Pushkin assures us), has put it; his ruddy hair (at least what is left of it) has turned to lilac, thanks to a preparation he had bought at the Romen horse fair from a Jew who posed as an Armenian. But Vyacheslav Ilarionovich steps out spryly, laughs ringingly, jingles his spurs, twirls his mustache, and to wrap the thing up, styles himself an old cavalryman—and yet, as everybody

179

knows, men who are really old never style themselves old men.

He usually wears a surtout buttoned right up to the neck, a high cravat with a starched collar, and trousers of a military cut, gray, with tiny red dots; as for his hat, he wears it right over his forehead, leaving the nape of his neck entirely exposed. He is a very kindly man but with notions and habits that are quite odd. For instance: he simply cannot treat those of the gentry who are not rich or have no rank as his equals. When he converses with such he usually gives them the sidelong look, his cheek pressing against his stiff and white collar, or he will suddenly up and let the light of his clear and stony stare beat full upon them, fall silent for a spell, and then wriggle his whole scalp; he even pronounces his words in a different manner on such occasions and will not say, for example: "Thank you, Pavel Vassilich" or "Please come here, Michailo Ivanych," but rather: "Thank yo', Pa'el 'Assilich" or "Pul-lease c'm' here, Michal' 'Vanych." As to people situated on the bottom-most rungs of society, his behavior toward them is still odder: he doesn't look at them at all and, before explaining to them what his wish is, or giving them an order, he will repeat, several times in succession, and with a preoccupied and meditative air: "What do they call you? What do they call you?"—stressing the "what" with exceptional abruptness but pronouncing the other words very rapidly, which gives his whole delivery a quite close resemblance to the call of a cock quail.

He is a dreadful fussbudget and skinflint yet a poor manager: he has taken on as his superintendent a retired quartermaster, a Little Russian who is extraordinarily stupid. However, in this business of fussing with an estate none in our region has yet topped a certain important official in St. Petersburg who, perceiving from the reports of his manager that the corn kilns on his estate were prone to frequent fires, which occasioned the loss of much grain, issued a most strict order: in the future to put no sheaves in any kiln until the fire in it was all out. That same grandee also got the notion of sowing all his fields with poppies—in consequence of an apparently quite common-sense reckoning: poppyseed, you see, fetched more than rye; ergo, it was more profitable to sow poppies. It was he, too, who ordered his female serfs to wear the ancient high-fronted and ornate headdress, fashioned after a sample which he sent from St. Petersburg, and, actually, the country wives on his estate are wearing these headdresses to this day—only they are wearing them atop their headkerchiefs, which are folded diagonally.

However, let us get back to Vyacheslav Ilarionovich. Vyacheslav Ilarionovich is a terrific admirer of the fair sex and, no sooner does he espy some pretty little thing on the boulevard in his district capital than he immediately sets off after her, but goes lame right then and there—and what a remarkable circumstance that is! Play at cards is something he is fond of, but only with persons of a lower station; they, now, keep "Your Excellency"-ing him, but he goes on trimming and berating them to his heart's content. Whenever he happens to be playing with a governor general, however, or with some person of official standing, he undergoes an amazing change, keeps smiling, now, and nodding, too, and peering into the eyes of the others—the man simply reeks of honey. He even loses—and never complains.

It is but little reading Vyacheslav Ilarionovich does: when he does read he keeps ceaselessly working his mustache and eyebrows, as though he were sending a wave up his face. Especially noticeable is this undulant motion on the face of Vyacheslav Ilarionovich whenever he happens (in the presence of guests, of course) to be running through the columns of the *Journal des Débats*. At the elections held by the gentry he plays quite a significant role but, out of stinginess, declines the honorable post of marshal of the nobility. "Gentlemen," he tells the gentry who are usually pressing him to accept the office, and tells them in a voice filled with condescension and independence, "I am very grateful for the honor, but I have decided to consecrate my leisure to solitude." And, having uttered these words, he will work his head right and left several times and then, in a dignified sort of a way, let his chin and jowls lap over his cravat.

In the years of his youth he had served as an adjutant for some important person or other, whom he never failed to call otherwise than by his first name and patronymic; it would seem, the way they tell it, that it wasn't only an adjutant's duties which he took upon himself; it would seem (to give an example) that, having clothed himself in full uniform as if for a parade, even to the extent of fastening every hook and eye, he used to assist his superior in the steam room of the baths—but then you can't believe every story you hear. However, even General Hvalynsky himself doesn't like to talk of his career in the service, which, on the whole, is quite strange; he has never been in any war, either, it would seem.

General Hvalynsky lives all by himself in a small house; he has never had a taste of connubial bliss in his life, and for that reason he is to this day considered an eligible candidate for marriage—and an advantageous candidate, at that. But then, he has a housekeeper, a woman of thirty-five, dark-eyed, dark-browed, full-fleshed, fresh-looking, and with a mustache; of weekdays she goes about in starched dresses, while on Sundays she puts on one that has muslin sleeves as well.

Vyacheslav Ilarionovich cuts a fine figure at the great banquets given by the landowners for governors general and others in authority; here, one may say, he is right in his element. On such occasions he usually sits, if not on the governor's right hand, then at least at no great distance from him; at the beginning of the dinner he is usually taken up with maintaining a sense of his personal dignity and, leaning far back, but without turning his head, lets a sidelong glance wander downward over the bulging scruffs and the stiff high collars of the guests; but then, as the feast nears its end, he grows merry, takes to smiling right and left (he had been smiling in the direction of the governor general even from the very start of the banquet), while at times he actually proposes a toast in honor of the fair sex—the adornment, as he puts it, of our planet. Nor is General Hvalynsky at all bad when it comes to all solemn and public functions, examinations, assemblies, and exhibitions; when he approaches to receive a priest's blessing he does that, too, in a masterly sort of way.

Vyacheslav Ilarionovich's servants do not raise a fuss and do not shout whenever gatherings are breaking up, or at ferry crossings and the like; on the contrary, as they clear a path through the crowd or call out for his carriage they say: "If you please, if you please—allow General Hvalynsky to pass" or "General Hvalynsky's carriage!" And they say this in an agreeable, throaty tenor. General Hvalynsky's carriage is, true enough, a rather antique model, the liveries of his flunkies are rather threadbare (that they are gray and with red facings it would seem hardly necessary to mention), and the horses, too, have lived and served rather long in their time; but then Vyacheslav Ilarionovich lays no claims to elegance and even does not consider it seemly for one in his station to be throwing dust in people's eyes. Hvalynsky has no particular mastery of the gift of speech or, perhaps, has no occasion to evince his eloquence, because he will not stand for the least contradiction, let alone any actual discussion, and takes pains to avoid any protracted conversations, especially with young people. This is, actually, the safest course of all, for otherwise one is bound to run into trouble with the kind of folk one meets nowadays: first thing you know they'll drop all deference and lose respect for you. Before persons of a higher station Hvalynsky for the most part keeps mum, but as for persons on a lower level, whom he evidently despises, yet who are the only ones he mingles with, he keeps to abrupt and brusque speech, incessantly using such expressions as: "However, the things you're saying are ut-ter non-sense" or "After all, I find it necess'ry to point it out to you, m'dear sir" or "After all, you really ought to be aware whom you're dealing with," and so on.

It is the postmasters, permanent chairmen of sundry committees, and posting-station supervisors who dread him most of all. At home he does not receive anybody and, one hears, lives like a kopeck-pincher. For all that, he is a fine landowner. "An old hand who has served well, a disinterested man, with principles, *vieux grognard*—an old grumbler," his neighbors say of him. The public prosecutor of the province alone permits himself a smile whenever General Hvalynsky's outstanding and substantial merits are mentioned in his presence—but then, what lengths won't envy go to!

However, let us now pass on to the other landowner.

Mardarii Apollonych Stegunov did not resemble Hvalynsky in any respect; it was hardly likely that he had served anywhere and he had never been considered an Adonis. Mardarii Apollonych is a very short, very plump little ancient, bald, with a double chin, soft little hands, and quite something of a little potbelly. He is a great one for hospitality and a merry fellow; he lives, as they say, to pleasure himself; winter and summer he goes about in a striped, cotton-quilted dressing gown. In one respect only has he anything in common with General Hvalynsky: he, too, is a bachelor. He owns five hundred souls. The interest Mardarii Apollonych takes in his estate is quite superficial; ten years ago, so as not to be behind the times, he did buy a threshing machine from the Butteknopf firm in Moscow, then locked it up in a barn and thus set his mind at rest. He may, of course, if it's a fine summer day, order a racing droshky to be harnessed and take a ride out into the fields for a look at the grain crops and to pick a posy of cornflowers.

Mardarii Apollonych lives in perfect keeping with the old ways. His house, too, is along the old lines: the entry has the proper smells of bread-cider, tallow candles, and leather; here, too, on your right, is a sideboard with pipes and ornamental towels; in the dining room you will find portraits, flies, a big pot of geraniums, and a grand piano with not a note in it that isn't sour; in the parlor, three divans, three tables, two mirrors, and a wheezy clock with blackened enamel and hands of fretted bronze; in the study, a writing table cluttered with papers, a screen of a bluish color with illustrations cut out from various works of the last century pasted upon it, closets with fusty books, spiders, and black dust, an overstuffed armchair, an Italian window, and a door into the garden, all nailed up. In a word, everything is just as it should be.

Of domestics Mardarii Apollonych has a multitude, and all of them garbed after the old fashion: in long blue caftans with high collars, trousers of an indefinite muddy hue and rather short, rather yellowish waistcoats. They address a guest as "father of mine." His estate is run by a steward of muzhik origin, with a beard that spills down the entire front of his sheepskin jacket; his house, by a crone in a brown headkerchief, who is all wrinkles and miserliness. Thirty horses of all sorts and sizes stand in Mardarii Apollonych's stables; he rides out in a home-built carriage weighing well over two tons and a half. He receives his guests most cordially and regales them gloriously—that is, thanks to the stupefying nature of Russian cooking, he deprives them up to the very evening of any possibility of occupying themselves with any activity more strenuous than playing preference. As for himself, he is never occupied with anything, and has given up reading as much as a dream book.

However, of such landowners there is still quite a plenty among us in Russia; apropos of what, then (it may be asked), had I begun to speak of him, and whatever for? Well, now, instead of answering that, permit me to tell you about one of my visits at Mardarii Apollonych's.

It was about seven of a summer evening when I arrived at his place. He had just gotten through with vespers and the priest, a young man, evidently quite timid and not long out of the seminary, was sitting in the parlor, near the door, perched on the very edge of his chair. Mardarii Apollonych received me, after his wont, with exceeding kindness; he was unfeignedly glad to see every guest, and besides that he was, in general, the kindliest of men. The priest rose and picked up his hat.

"Bide a while, bide a while, Father." Mardarii Apollonych spoke up without letting go of my hand. "Don't go away. I've ordered them to bring you some vodka."

"I don't drink, sir," the priest mumbled in confusion and turned red to his very ears.

"What nonsense!" Mardarii Apollonych retorted. "Mishka! Iushka! Some vodka for the Father!" Iushka, a tall and gaunt ancient of eighty, entered with a tumbler of vodka on a wooden tray painted a dark color and mottled with flesh-colored blotches. The priest declined at first. "Drink it, Father; stop putting on airs—it's not right," the landowner commented reproachfully. The poor young man submitted. "Well, now you can go, Father." The priest began bowing and scraping. "There, that'll do, that'll do; you can go. . . . A fine fellow," Mardarii Apollonych went on, following him with his eyes. "I'm very much satisfied with him; the only thing is, he's still young. Well, now, and how about you, father of mine? How are you, what are you doing? Let's go out on the balcony—there, see what a glorious evening it is."

We went out on the balcony, sat down, and got into talk. Mardarii Apollonych glanced down and suddenly became dreadfully agitated.

"Whose hens are those? Whose hens are those?" he began shouting. "Whose hens are those strutting about in the garden? Iushka! Iushka! Go and find out whose hens those are, strutting about in the garden! Whose hens are those? How many times have I forbidden it—how many times have I said—"

Iushka went off at a run.

"What disgraceful goings on!" Mardarii Apollonych kept repeating. "This is dreadful!"

The wretched hens—two white-spotted guinea fowl and one white, with a tuft (I remember the thing as if it were now)—kept strutting about under the apple trees, as unruffled as you please, expressing their feelings every now and then by prolonged clucking, when suddenly Iushka, bareheaded, stick in hand, and two other mature house serfs all pounced on them as one. Then the fun began. The hens squawked, flapped their wings, leaped about, clucking deafeningly; the house serfs ran hither and yon, stumbled, fell; their master, as if in a frenzy, kept shouting from the balcony: "Catch them, catch them! Catch them, catch them, catch them, catch them, catch them! Whose hens are they? Whose hens are they?"

Finally one of the house serfs succeeded in catching the tufted hen by crushing her to the ground with his chest, and at that very point a girl of eleven, all tousled and with a dead twig in her hand, appeared in the lane and jumped over the wattled garden fence.

"Ah, so that's whose hens they are!" the landowner exclaimed in triumph. "They're Ermilla the coachman's hens. There, he sent out his Natalka to chase them home. Didn't send out Parasha, never fear," the landowner added in a low voice and smirked significantly. "Hey, Iushka! Leave the hens be, now—you just catch Natalka for me."

But before Iushka, all out of breath, had a chance to run up to the thoroughly frightened little wench, the housekeeper bobbed up from none knows where, seized her by the arm, and slapped her back several times.

" 'At's it, 'at's it, now!" the landowner added his bit. "My, my, my! My, my, my! As for the hens, you take them from her, Avdotia," he added in a loud voice and, with a radiant face, turned to me: "What think you of that for a hunt, father of mine—eh? Just see, I've actually worked up a sweat." And Mardarii Apollonych broke into peals of laughter.

We remained on the balcony. The evening really was unusually fine. Tea was brought out for us.

"Do tell me, Mardarii Apollonych," I began, "was it your people who resettled those farms—the ones along the road, beyond the ravine?"

"They're mine—but why do you ask?"

"Come, how could you do it, Mardarii Apollonych? Why, it's a sin. The little huts you have assigned to the muzhiks are wretched, cramped; there's not the smallest tree to be seen around there; there isn't as much as a pond, not even a small one; there's only one well, and that one no good. Couldn't you possibly have found another spot? And—so they say—you've taken away even their old hemp fields."

"But what is one to do when it comes to reallotting the land?" Mardarii Apollonych said by way of answer. "That reallotment is a pain to me right here." He indicated the nape of his neck. "And I foresee no good whatsoever from this reallotment. And as for my having taken away their hemp fields, and not having dug any ponds, or whatever— that, father of mine, is something I really don't know anything about. I'm a simple man—I act in accordance with the old ways. To my way of thinking, if you're a master, then be a master; if you're a muzhik, then be a muzhik. That's what!"

To so clear and convincing an argument there was, naturally, no answer.

"And besides that," he continued, "those muzhiks are a bad lot—in disgrace, all of them. Particularly two families there; even my late father, may God grant him the Kingdom of Heaven, wasn't favorably inclined toward them—very far from favorably inclined. And as for me, I must tell you there's one observation I go by: if the father is a thief, then the son is a thief likewise, no matter what you may think. Oh, family blood, family blood—it's a great thing! I, I must confess to you frankly, have sent up men from one of those families for recruits out of their turn, and have shoved them in this place and that, wherever I could; but what can one do—there's no end to them! They're prolific, damn them!"

In the meanwhile the air had become utterly calm. Only at rare intervals would the wind rise in currents, and as it finally died away close to the house, it brought to our ears the sound of measured and frequent strokes, coming from the direction of one of the stables. Mardarii Apollonych had just brought up to his lips a saucerful of tea and had already distended his nostrils (something without which, as everybody knows, not a single trueborn Russ will inhale his tea), but he stopped, hearkened, nodded, took a sip, and placing the saucer on the table, uttered with the kindliest of smiles and as if involuntarily echoing the strokes: *"Chiukki-chiukki-chiuk! Chiukki-chiuk! Chiukki-chik!"*

"Just what is that?" I asked in astonishment.

"Why, they're punishing a little mischief-maker there, at my orders. Do you happen to know Vassya the butler?"

"What Vassya?"

"Why, the fellow that waited on us at dinner a little while back. He's got such great side whiskers, too—"

The most ferocious indignation would not have been able to withstand Mardarii Apollonych's radiant and mild gaze.

"What do you mean, young man, what do you mean?" he began, shaking his head. "What am I, an evildoer or something, that you stare at me so? Love yet chastise—you know that saying yourself."

A quarter of an hour later I said goodbye to Mardarii Apollonych. As I was riding through the village I caught sight of Vassya the butler. He was walking along the street and crunching nuts. I ordered the coachman to stop the horses and called the butler over.

"Well, now, brother, did they punish you today?" I asked him.

"But how come you to know it?" Vassya parried.

"Your master happened to tell me."

"The master himself did?"

"What did he order you to be punished for, now?"

"Why, I had it coming to me, father of mine; I had it coming to me. They don't punish you for trifles here; that's not the way things are done here, no siree! Our master is not that sort; our master—why, you couldn't find such another master in all the province."

"Drive on!" I told the coachman. "There it is, Old Russia itself!" I reflected on my way back home.

LEBEDYAN

ONE OF THE main advantages of hunting, my amiable readers, consists of its compelling you to be incessantly on
the move from place to place, which is quite a pleasant thing
for a man with nothing in particular to do. True, at times (especially during a rainy spell) it is none too gay to be riding
at random over byroads, "going it blind," stopping every muzhik with the question: "Hey there, dear man, how could we
get to Mordovka?"—and, in Mordovka, trying to draw out of
some dull-witted country wife (all the workers, now, are out
in the fields) as to whether it's far to any small inns along the
high road, and how would a body get to them—and, after
driving for seven miles, instead of coming upon any wayside inns finding oneself in the proprietorial hamlet, gone all
to rack and ruin, of Churchmouseville, to the extreme
amazement of a whole herd of swine, plunged up to their
ears in dark-brown mud in the very middle of the main street
and who had not at all been expecting to be disturbed.
    There is also nothing gay about making one's way over
tiny bridges that quiver as if they were living flesh and
blood, or descending into ravines, or fording quaggy
streams; there's nothing gay about driving, driving the clock
around, over the greenish sea of highways or (God save you
from this!) getting bogged down for several hours before
a striped milepost with the figures 22 on one side and 23 on
the other; there's nothing gay about subsisting, for weeks at a

189

stretch, on eggs, milk, and the bepraised rye bread. All these inconveniences and mishaps are, nevertheless, redeemed by advantages and pleasures of another sort. However, let's get down to the story itself.

In view of all that has been said above it would be pointless for me to explain to the reader just how I came to be in Lebedyan five years ago, at the very height of its fair. Anyone of our hunting brotherhood is apt to ride out of his more or less hereditary estate one fine morning with the intention of returning on the evening of the next day and, little by little, little by little, without ceasing to shoot snipe, will at last reach the blessed banks of the Pechora; besides that, every devotee of the gun and the dog is also a passionate votary of the noblest animal in the world—the horse. And so I arrived at Lebedyan, put up at a hotel, changed my clothes, and set out for the fair. (The waiter *cum* bellboy, a lanky and spare fellow of twenty, with a sweet, nasal tenor, had already managed to inform me that His Illustrious Highness, Grand Duke N., in charge of remounts for the —— Regiment, had put up at their place; that there had been an influx of many other guests, that of evenings there were singing Gypsies and *Pan Tvardovski* was put on at the theater; that hosses, now, were fetching high prices—on the whole, though, the hosses brought to the fair were good ones.)

Endless rows of carts stretched away into the distance on the fair site, while behind the carts were horses of all possible breeds: racers, studs, Percherons, draft-, stagecoach-, and ordinary plow-horses. Some, well fed and sleek of hide, matched according to colors, covered with varicolored cloths, and hitched closely to tall posts, were eyeing askance the too-familiar whips of their masters, the dealers; the steeds of the landowners, sent by steppe squires for a hundred or even two hundred versts around, under the supervision of some decrepit coachman and two or three hardheaded ostlers, were tossing their long necks, stamping their hoofs, gnawing their breast-high bars out of sheer boredom; roans of the Viatka breed snuggled right up against one another; in a majestic immobility, lionlike, stood the broad-beamed racers with wavy tails and shaggy fetlocks—dappled gray, raven-black, sorrel. Good judges of horseflesh halted before them in respect. In the lanes formed by the carts people of every calling, age, and appearance were swarming: horse dealers in long blue caftans and tall caps were slyly on the watch and wait for buyers; popeyed, curly-headed Gypsies darted to and fro as if they had inhaled charcoal fumes, examining the horses' teeth, lifting up their legs and tails, shouting, squabbling, serving as intermediaries, drawing lots, or wriggling about some officer in charge of remounts in cap and military overcoat trimmed with beaver. A stalwart Cossack towered on a gaunt gelding with the neck of a stag and was selling him "as found"—i.e., with saddle and bridle.

Muzhiks, their sheepskin jackets torn under the armpits, were desperately barging through the crowd, piling up by the score into a cart harnessed to a horse that had to be "tried out" or, somewhere off to one side, with the help of an eel-like Gypsy, were dickering to exhaustion, striking hands a hundred times in a row, each one insisting on his own price, while the object of their contention, some wretched little nag covered over with warped matting, merely kept on batting her eyes as though the matter did not concern her at all. And really, wasn't it all one to her who would be beating her! Wide-browed landlords with dyed mustachios and an expression of dignity on their faces, in jackets of a military cut and overcoats of camlet, one arm in its sleeve, the other free, condescendingly entered into conversation with paunchy merchants in downy hats and green gloves. Officers from different regiments were also milling about here; an unusually lanky cuirassier, of German origin, was coolly asking a lame dealer: How much did he desire to receive for this red horse? A flaxen-haired little hussar of nineteen was trying to match an off horse for his lean, thorough-paced pad-nag; a stagecoach driver, in a low hat wound around with a peacock feather, a fawn-colored overcoat, and with leather gauntlets thrust into his narrow, greenish belt, was looking for a shaft horse. Coachmen were plaiting the tails of their horses, moistening their manes, and offering deferent advice to their masters. Those who had consummated deals were hastening to inn or pothouse, depending on their means. . . . And all this was bustling, shouting, fossicking, squabbling and making up, bandying curses and laughing, in mud up to its knees.

I wanted to buy a team of three tolerable horses for my surrey; the horses I had were beginning to go back on me. I found two, but hadn't time enough to match the third. After a dinner which I do not undertake to describe (even Aeneas, in his day, knew how disagreeable it is to recall past grief), I set out for a coffeehouse, so called, where remount officers, owners of stud farms, and other arrivals used to congregate every evening. There were some twenty people in the billiard room, flooded with leaden-hued billows of tobacco smoke. Here were free-and-easy young landowners in Hungarian jackets and gray pantaloons, with long locks at the temples and minuscular waxed mustaches, looking about them in a noble and bold sort of a way; other squires in cossackeens, with extraordinarily short necks and little eyes sunk in fat, were right there, agonizingly wheezing; certain smart-looking merchants were sitting off to one side—all by their lonesome, as the phrase goes; the army officers were talking unconstrainedly with one another.

Young Grand Duke N. was playing billiards—a young man of two and twenty with a gay and somewhat disdainful face, in a jacket all unbuttoned, a blouse of red silk, and velvet trousers so wide that they ballooned over the tops of his boots; he was playing with Victor Hlopakov, an ex-lieutenant.

Ex-lieutenant Victor Hlopakov, a swarthy little, thin little man of thirty, with short black hair, brown eyes, and a blunt, upturned nose, was an assiduous attendant at all the county elections of the gentry and all the fairs. He hopped a little as he walked, gesticulated devilishly with his rounded arms, wore his cap tilted to one side, and turned back the sleeves of his military coat, which was lined with dove-gray calico. Monsieur Hlopakov possessed the ability of making up to rich gay blades from Petersburg; he smoked, drank, and played cards with them; he addressed them with the utmost familiarity. Why they favored him was rather difficult to fathom. He wasn't clever, he wasn't even funny; as a jester, too, he was hardly the thing. True enough, they treated him with a friendly disregard, like a good but shallow fellow; they'd be bosom pals with him for a fortnight or so, and then suddenly wouldn't as much as bow to him, and by that time he himself wasn't bowing to them, either. Lieutenant Hlopakov's speciality consisted of his constantly repeating for the duration of a year, or even two years, the one and the same expression, in season and out—an expression not in the least amusing but which, God knows why, moved everybody to mirth. Eight years ago he used to say, at every step: "My compliments to you; I am ever so humbly grateful," and his then patrons would simply die laughing every time and compel him to repeat this "My compliments" bit; then

he took to using a rather complicated expression: "No, you're just *qu'est-ce que ça*-ing, now—that's how it's turned out it turns out," and this met with the same brilliant success; two years ago, or thereabouts, he thought up a new sally: *"N'est vous* so hot *pas,* O man of God, in a ram's hide shod," and so on. Well, what do you think? These little *mots,* not at all ingenious as you can see, provided him with food, drink, and raiment. (His estate he had long since sent down the drain, and he now lived solely at the expense of his friends.)

Mark you this: there were absolutely no other amiable points about him; true enough, he would smoke a hundred pipefuls a day of the good Zhukov tobacco, while at billiards he had a way of heaving his right leg higher than his head and, as he frenziedly took aim, kept jiggling the cue in his hand—but then, it wasn't every man who had a relish for such fine points. He was also a good man with a bottle—however, in our Russia it's rather difficult to gain distinction thereby. In a word, his success was an utter puzzle to me. Unless it was explained by one thing: he was discreet; he wouldn't wash anybody's linen in public, wouldn't breathe even one bad word against anybody.

"Well," I mused on catching sight of Hlopakov, "what's his favorite bit of patter now?"

The Grand Duke played the cue ball.

"Thirty—and nobody's," vociferated the consumptive marker, dark of face and with leaden pouches under his eyes.

The Grand Duke sent the yellow ball crashing into the corner pocket.

"Uh!" A rather plump merchant, sitting in a corner at a rickety one-legged table, emitted an approving and full-bodied grunt—he emitted the grunt and became abashed. Fortunately, however, no one noticed him. He sighed in relief and ran his hand over his beard.

"Thirty-six—and mighty little!" the marker shouted nasally.

"Well, how does it strike you, brother?" the Grand Duke asked Hlopakov.

"Well, naturally, it's a rrrrapscallio-o-on—a rrrrapscallio-o-on, for a fact!"

The Grand Duke snorted with laughter. "How, how? Say that again!"

"A rrrrapscallio-o-on!" the ex-lieutenant said it again smugly.

"There, that's it—that's the *mot,* now!" I reflected.

The Grand Duke shot the red ball in a pocket.

"Eh! That's no way, Duke—that's no way," a flaxen-haired little officer with reddened eyes, a tiny button of a nose, and a babyishly sleepy face suddenly began to babble. "You're not playing it right—you should've . . . that's no way!"

"How then?" the Grand Duke asked him over his shoulder.

"You should have . . . now . . . made it a triple combination."

"Really?" the Grand Duke muttered through his teeth.

"I say, Duke, are you going to the Gypsies tonight?" the confused young man hurriedly went on. "Steshka is going to sing . . . and Iliushka—"

The Grand Duke did not bother to answer him.

"Rrrrapscallio-o-on, little brother," Hlopakov let drop, slyly puckering his left eye.

And the Grand Duke went off into peals of laughter.

"Thirty-nine—and nobody's," proclaimed the marker.

"Nobody's . . . just watch me get that yellow ball, now—" Hlopakov jiggled the cue in his hand, took aim—and muffed the shot. "Eh, rrrapscallio-on!" he shouted in vexation.

The Grand Duke broke into laughter again.

"How? How? How?"

But Hlopakov did not feel like peddling his cabbages twice: after all, there is such a thing as being coaxed.

"You scratched that time," the marker put in. "Let me chalk your cue. . . . Forty—and mighty little!"

"Yes, gentlemen," the Grand Duke spoke up, turning to all those present—without looking at anybody in particular, however. "Verzhembitskaya ought to get a lot of curtain calls from you at the theater tonight, you know."

"Of course, of course—without fail," several gentlemen responded loudly, vying with one another, amazingly flattered at the chance of responding to the speech of a Grand Duke. "Verzhembitskaya."

"Verzhembitskaya is an excellent actress, far better than Sopniakova," a miserable little specimen with a tiny mustache and in spectacles squeaked out from his corner. The unfortunate! In secret he was sighing like a furnace after Sopniakova—yet the Grand Duke had not deemed him worthy of even a glance.

"Eh, waitah . . . bring me a pipe," some tall gentleman with a chiseled face and the noblest of bearings—a cardsharp, by all the signs—spoke into his cravat.

The waiter darted off after a pipe and, on his return, informed His Excellency that, now, Baklaga, the driver, was askin' for him.

"Ah! Very well; tell him to wait—and bring him some vodka."

"Right, sir!"

Baklaga, as I was told afterward, was the name of a young, handsome, and exceedingly spoiled driver; the Grand Duke loved him very much, presented him with horses, raced against him, spent whole nights in his company. . . . Nowadays you'd never recognize this same Grand Duke, the one-time gay blade and profligate. How perfumed he is, how laced in (and strait-laced), how proud! How taken up he is with his government duties! And, above all, how circumspect!

However, the tobacco smoke was beginning to corrode my eyes. Having listened attentively for the final time to Hlopakov's interjection and the Grand Duke's loud laughter I went to my room, where my man had already made my bed on the narrow and broken-springed horsehair divan with its high curved back.

The next day I set out to look over the horses the copers had to offer, beginning with the well-known horse dealer Sitnikov. I entered through a wicket into a sand-strewn yard. Standing before the wide-open door of the stable was the owner himself, a man no longer young; tall and stout, he wore a short jacket lined with rabbit fur, the collar raised and tucked in. On seeing me he slowly came forward, held his hat up over his head with both hands for a while, and uttered in singsong:

"Ah, our compliments to you! You're wanting to look some little hosses over, I take it?"

"Yes, I've come to look over some little horses."

"And just what kind, if I may ask?"

"Let's see what you have."

"That'll be a pleasure for us."

We went into the stable. Several white, distinctly unpedigreed sheep dogs got up from the hay and ran up to us, wagging their tails; an old, long-bearded billy goat withdrew to one side in displeasure; three ostlers in stout but greasy sheepskin jackets bowed before us without speaking. To the right and left, in artfully raised stalls, stood some thirty horses, gloriously groomed and currycombed. Pigeons were fluttering from crossbeam to crossbeam and cooing.

"What purpose would you be wantin' a little hoss for, now—for ridin' or for stud?" Sitnikov asked me.

"Both for riding and for stud."

"We understand, we understand, we understand," the dealer got out, pausing at every word and adding "sir" after each phrase. "Petie, show the gentleman Ermine."

We went out into the yard.

"Would you care for a bench to be brought out of the house? You don't need it? Just as you wish."

Hoofs thundered over planks, a whip snapped, and Petie, a fellow of forty, pockmarked and swarthy, leaped out of the stable together with a gray, rather stately stallion, let him rear up on his hind legs, ran him around the yard a couple of times, and deftly brought him up short at an indicated spot. Ermine drew himself up, snorted whistlingly, threw up his tail, wrinkled his nose and lips, and looked at us out of the corner of his eye.

"A well-trained article!" I reflected.

"Give him a free rein, give him a free rein," said Sitnikov to Petie and fixed me with his eyes. "Well, sir, how does he strike you?" he asked at last.

"Not a bad horse—forelegs not altogether reliable."

"He's got excellent legs!" Sitnikov retorted with conviction. "And the beam on him—just look at it, if you please—broad as a ledge atop an oven, for sure—you could sleep all night on it!"

"His pasterns are too long."

"Long, you say? Have a heart! Run with him, Petie, now—run with him, but at a trot, at a trot, at a trot—don't let him gallop."

Petie again ran through the yard with Ermine. We all kept silent for a while.

"Well, put him back in his stall," said Sitnikov, "and let's have Falcon."

Falcon, black as a beetle, a stallion of the Dutch breed, gaunt and with a low-slung croup, turned out to be a trifle better than Ermine. He belonged to that category of horses

concerning whom judges of horseflesh say that they chop and
they lop and take prisoners of war—that is, they twist and
throw out their forelegs right and left on the run, yet make
but little headway. Middle-aged merchants are rather fond
of horses like that; their gait recalls the dashing stride of a
sprightly waiter; they're good horses harnessed all by themselves for a pleasure ride after dinner; stepping out like a
dandy and arching its neck, a horse like that will zealously
draw along a cumbersome droshky, freighted with a coachman who has eaten himself groggy, a depressed merchant suffering from heartburn, and his spongy lady in a mantle of
blue silk and with a small lilac kerchief on her head. I
turned down Falcon as well. Sitnikov showed me a few
more horses. At last one, a dappled gray stallion of the fa-
mous Voiekovsky breed, proved to my liking. I could not
restrain myself, and it was a pleasure to pat his withers. Sitnikov immediately assumed an air of indifference.

"Well, now, does he ride well?" I asked. (You don't say
"run" when referring to a trotter.)

"That he does," the dealer answered calmly.

"Couldn't I see him at it?"

"Of course; why not, sir. Hey there, Kuzya, harness Over-
take to a droshky!"

Kuzya, a horseman who was a master of his craft, drove
past us in the street three times. The horse did well, didn't
start off with the wrong foot, didn't toss up his croup,
brought each leg up freely, held his tail right, and kept his
gait—a rare trotter.

"And what are you asking for him?"

Sitnikov came out with an unheard-of price. We fell to
dickering on the spot, out on the street, when suddenly, from
around a corner, a masterfully matched troika came flying
and stopped with a flair, before the gates of Sitnikov's house.
Sitting in a dandified hunter's cart was Grand Duke N.;
sticking close to him was Hlopakov. Baklaga was driving the
horses, and how he was driving them! He could have driven
them through an earring, the brigand! The off horses, small,
lively, dark-eyed bays, were simply afire, simply like coiled
springs: just whistle, and they would vanish! The shaft horse,
a dark bay, stood minding his own business, his neck thrown
back, like a swan's, chest out, legs like arrows, tossing his
head every little while, narrowing his eyes proudly. . . . A
fine sight! Fit for any man to go dashing with at Eastertide!

"Your Excellency! You're right welcome!" Sitnikov called out.

The Grand Duke leaped down from the cart. Hlopakov slowly climbed down on the other side.

"Greetings, brother. Got any horses?"

"For Your Excellency? How else! Step in, please. Petie, bring out Peacock. And tell them to get Praiseworthy ready. As for you, my father," he went on, turning to me, "we'll finish the deal some other time. A bench for His Excellency, Thomka!"

Out of a special stable, which I had not noticed at first, they led out Peacock. The mighty, dark-sorrel steed simply spiraled with all four legs into the air. Sitnikov actually turned his head away and puckered his eyes.

"Oo, rrapscallion!" Hlopakov proclaimed. *"La gemme, ça."*

The Grand Duke broke into laughter.

It was not without difficulty that they brought Peacock to a halt. He contrived, in spite of everything, to drag the hostler through the yard; finally they backed him up against a wall. He was breathing hoarsely, trembling, and coiling to buck, yet, on top of that, Sitnikov was egging him on, brandishing his whip at the animal:

"Where's your eyes? There, I'll fix you! Oo!" the dealer was saying, caressingly threatening, himself involuntarily admiring his steed.

"How much?" asked the Grand Duke.

"Seeing it's for Your Excellency, five thousand."

"Three!"

"Can't be done, sir, Your Excellency. Have a heart—"

"Three, you're told, rrapscallion," Hlopakov chimed in.

I didn't wait for the end of the deal and left. On a corner, at the very end of the street, I had noticed a large sheet of paper glued upon the gates of a small, grayish house. Drawn with a quill at the top of the sheet was a steed with a tail like a trumpet and an endless neck, while underneath the hoofs of the steed were the following words, written in an old-fashioned hand:

FOR SALE HERE

Horses of Various Colors, brought to the Lebedyan Fair from the Well-Known Steppe Stud Farm of Anastassey Ivanych Chernobai, a Squire of Tambov. These

Horses are of Excellent Qualities; Train'd to Perfection, and most Gentle in Temper. Gentlemen Wishful to Purchase the Same, Will Please be Kind Enough to Ask for Anastassey Ivanych Himself; but, should He be Away, Please to ask for Nazar Kubyshkin, the Hostler. Gentlemen and Purchasers, We Ask You to Honor an Old Gentleman!

I stopped. "Let's have a look," I reflected, "at the horses of Squire Chernobai, the well-known horse breeder of the steppes."

I was about to enter through a side gate but, contrary to usage, found it shut tight. I knocked.

"Who's there? A buyer?" a woman's voice squeaked out.

"I am."

"Right away, father of mine, right away!"

The side gate opened. I saw a country wife of fifty, bareheaded, in boots and an unbuttoned sheepskin jacket.

"Please to enter, our provider, and I'll go and tell Anastassey Ivanych right away. Nazar—oh, Nazar!"

"What is it?" the voice of a toothless septuagenarian came from the stable.

"Get the hosses ready; there's a buyer come."

The crone ran off into the house.

"A buyer, a buyer," Nazar growled back at her. "I ain't washed all their tails yet."

" 'Oh, Arcadia!' " I mused.

"Greetings, father of mine—you're right welcome," a slow, succulent, and pleasing voice came from behind me. I turned around: standing before me in a blue, long-skirted overcoat was an old man of medium height, with white hair, an amiable smile, and splendid light-blue eyes.

"Is it hosses you're after? By all means, father of mine, by all means. But wouldn't you like to drop in on me and have a dish of tea first?"

I declined, with thanks.

"Well, just as you wish. You excuse me, father of mine —for I do things in the old way." Squire Chernobai spoke leisurely, and stressed his *o*'s. "I hold to simplicity in all things, you know. Nazar—hey, Nazar," he added drawlingly and without raising his voice.

Nazar, a wrinkled mite of a gaffer with a tiny nose like

a falcon's beak and a small goatee, appeared at the threshold of the stable.

"What sort of hosses are you needing, father of mine?" Squire Chernobai went on.

"Not too dear, broken to harness, for a tilt-cart."

"By all means; I've got that sort, too—by all means. Nazar, Nazar, show the master that little gray gelding; you know, the one in the end stall; and the bay mare with the bald patch; or no, make it the other bay mare, the one out of Little Beauty—you know which?"

Nazar went back into the stable.

"Yes, and bring them out without halters, just as they are," Squire Chernobai called after him. "I don't do things, father of mine," he went on, looking me in the face serenely and meekly, "the way the dealers do—bad cess to them! They go in for ginger and all that stuff, and salt, and malt grains [1]—God be with them altogether! But with me, as you'll see for yourself, everything is out in the open, as if it were on the palm of your hand, without any dodges."

Some horses were led out. They didn't prove to my liking.

"Well, put them back in their stalls—God be with them," Anastassey Ivanych let drop. "Show us some others."

They showed us others. I finally chose one, of the cheaper sort. We fell to dickering. Squire Chernobai did not grow heated; he spoke so reasonably, with such gravity, that I couldn't but "honor the old gentleman"—I gave him a deposit.

"And now," uttered Anastassey Ivanych, "allow me, according to the old custom, to hand the hoss over to you, from coat skirt to coat skirt. . . . You'll be thanking me for it—for it's such a fresh hoss! Sound as a nut, untouched, born and bred out on the steppes! It'll go in any sort of harness."

He crossed himself, placed a skirt of his overcoat over his arm, took the halter, and handed the horse over to me.

"Own it with God's blessing, now. But you still don't care for a dish of tea?"

"No, thanks ever so much. It's time I was getting home."

"Just as you wish. And is my stableboy to lead the hoss after you now?"

[1] A horse will put on weight in a short time from malt grains and salt.—*Author*.

"Yes, now, if you will permit it."

"By all means, dear man, by all means. Vassilii—oh, Vassilii—you'll go with this gentleman; bring the hoss there and get the money. Well, goodbye, father of mine, and God go with you."

"Goodbye, Anastassey Ivanych."

The horse was brought to my place. The very next day it turned out to be broken-winded and lame. I got the notion of harnessing it to a carriage: my horse kept backing away, but when the whip was put to it, it turned mulish, kicked, and then lay down. I set out for Squire Chernobai's at once.

"Is he home?" I asked.

"He is."

"Well, now," I began, "it turns out you sold me a broken-winded horse."

"Broken-winded? God forbid!"

"And it's lame besides—and has a mean temper, to top it all off."

"Lame? I wouldn't know. Looks like your stableboy injured it somehow. As for me, I swear to you as before the face of God—"

"You really ought to take it back, Anastassey Ivanych."

"No, father of mine, don't be wroth with me—once it's out of my place the deal is closed. You should have looked it over beforehand."

I understood the whole thing, submitted to my lot, had a good laugh, and went away. Fortunately, I hadn't paid too much for my lesson.

Two days later I left, and a week afterward turned in at Lebedyan again, on my way back. In the coffeehouse I found almost the same faces, and again found Grand Duke N. at billiards. But the usual change in the fortunes of Lieutenant Hlopakov had already taken place. The flaxen-haired little officer had replaced him in the good graces of the Grand Duke. The poor ex-lieutenant made one more attempt while I was there to give currency to his little *mot*—perhaps, even now, it might find the same favor as before—but the Grand Duke not only didn't smile, he actually knit his brows and shrugged a shoulder. Monsieur Hlopakov became downcast, shrank into himself, made his way into a corner nook, and there fell to stuffing his little pipe, ever so quietly. . . .

201

TATIANA BORISOVNA
AND HER NEPHEW

LET ME HAVE your hand, amiable reader, and let's ride off together. The weather is splendid; the May sky is mildly blue; the smooth young leaves of the willows glisten, just as if they had been laved; the broad level road is grown over with that short, reddish-stemmed grass which the sheep nibble so eagerly; to right and left, along the low slopes of gently rising knolls, the green rye ripples in wavelets; the shadows of small clouds glide over it in tenuous splotches. In the distance woods show darkly, ponds sparkle, villages gleam yellowly; skylarks rise in their hundreds, sing, plummet headlong, cling to small clods with their little necks craned; the rooks on the road pause, stare at you, flatten themselves against the ground—then, having allowed you to ride by, give a couple of hops and fly off heavily to one side; up on a hill, beyond a gully, a muzhik is plowing; a dappled colt, with a stump of a tail and his little mane all rumpled, is running on uncertain legs after his dam—you can hear her high-pitched whinny.

We roll into a grove of birches: the pungent fresh odor pleasantly constricts our breath. Here is enclosed pasture-land. The driver gets down; the horses snort—the off horses turn to look back, the shaft horse switches its tail casually and leans its head against the shaft bow. The huge gate creaks open. The driver resumes his seat. Get going!

There's a small village ahead of us. After passing five homesteads we come down into a small hollow and drive up on a dam. Beyond a small pond and peeping over the rounded tops of apple trees and lilac bushes is a planked roof—it had been red on a time and has two chimneypots; the driver keeps close to a fence on the left and, amid the shrill and wheezy barking of three most ancient sheep dogs, drives in at the wide-open gates, makes a dashing circuit of the spacious yard, past a stable and a shed, bows gallantly to the old housekeeper who has sidled over the high threshold into the doorway of a storehouse, and halts at last before the small porch of the dark little house with its bright windows. We are at Tatiana Borisovna's. Why, there she is herself, opening one of the small hinged windowpanes and nodding to us. Greetings, mother!

Tatiana Borisovna is a woman of fifty, with big, gray bulging eyes, a somewhat blunted nose, rosy cheeks, and a double chin. Her face emanates welcome and kindliness. She had been married once upon a time but had shortly become a widow. Tatiana Borisovna is quite a remarkable woman. She lives on her small estate without ever leaving it, has little to do with her neighbors, and receives and likes young people only. By birth she belonged to a quite poor family of landowners and had received no education whatsoever—that is, she doesn't talk French; she has never been to Moscow, even. Yet, despite all these shortcomings, she conducts herself so simply and well, her feelings and opinions are so free, she's so little infected with the usual ailments of the mistress of a small estate that, truly, one cannot help but wonder at her. And, really: here is a woman who lives the year round in a village, out in the sticks—and she neither gossips, nor speaks in a squeak, nor curtsies, nor gets excited, nor chokes at table, nor quivers from curiosity. Miracle upon miracle!

She usually goes about in a gray taffeta dress and a white cap with dangling lilac ribbons; she likes to eat well but not to excess; the cooking of jams, the drying of fruits, and pickling she relegates to the housekeeper. What, then, does she busy herself with all day long? you will ask. Does she read? No, that she doesn't—and, truth to tell, it isn't for the likes of her that books are printed. If she isn't receiving

203

a caller, my Tatiana Borisovna sits by the window and knits away at a stocking—if it's wintertime, that is; in the summer she goes into the garden, plants and waters flowers, plays with kittens for hours on end, feeds the pigeons. . . . She occupies herself but little with running the house. But should a guest drop in, some young neighbor or other whom she favors, Tatiana Borisovna becomes all animated: she will seat him comfortably, drench him with tea, listen to his stories, laugh, pat his cheek now and then, but will have little to say herself: if there's any trouble, any woe, she'll console him, offer good counsel.

How many folks have confided their soulmost family secrets to her, have shed their tears upon her hands! Times were, she'd take a seat facing her guest, lean ever so gently on her elbow, and look into his eyes with such sympathy, with so friendly a smile, that he could not help but think: "Really, what a fine woman you are, Tatiana Borisovna! Come, I'll tell you what weighs on my heart!"

A man feels fine and warmed in her small cozy rooms; it's always fine weather in her house, if one may use such an expression. An amazing woman is Tatiana Borisovna— and yet no one is amazed at her: her common sense, firmness, and freedom, her fervent sympathy when it comes to the troubles and joys of others—all her good qualities, in short—seem to have been born at the same time she was: they had cost her no exertions and pains. It is actually impossible to imagine her as being any different; consequently, there is actually nothing to thank her for.

She is particularly fond of looking on at the games and capers of young people; she'll fold her hands on her heart, throw her head back, pucker up her eyes and sit there, smiling—then suddenly sigh and say: "Ah, you little ones —my little ones!" There were times when one could not but feel like walking up to her, taking her hand, and saying: "Look here, Tatiana Borisovna—you don't know your own worth; why, for all your simplicity and lack of schooling, you are an extraordinary being!"

Her very name has a certain familiar ring about it, a ring of welcome; one utters it eagerly, it brings forth an amiable smile. How many times, for instance, have I had occasion to ask some chance-met muzhik: "How does one get to Grachevka, now, brother?" — "Why, father of mine, you head for Viazovoye first, and from there to Tatiana

Borisovna's—and from Tatiana Borisovna's anybody will show you the way." And, as he utters her name, the muzhik will give a special sort of toss to his head.

The staff of servants she maintains isn't large, in keeping with her means. Her house, laundry, storeroom, and kitchen are presided over by Agatha, the housekeeper, who had been her nurse—the kindest of rheumy-eyed, toothless creatures; two stalwart wenches with cheeks firm and ruddy as winesaps are under her command. The posts of valet, majordomo, and butler are filled by the septuagenary servant Polycarp, an extreme eccentric, a man of wide reading, an ex-soldier, a worshiper of the violinist and composer Viotti and a fiddler himself, a personal foe of Bonaparte (or, as he puts it, that "miserable little scalawag Boney)", and a passionate lover of nightingales. He always keeps five or six of them in his room; in early spring he sits for days on end by their cages biding their first "chopping" and, his wait rewarded at last, covers his face with his hands and moans: "Oh, 'tis pitiful, pitiful!"—and bursts into torrential tears.

It is none other than Vassya, his own grandson, who has been assigned to assist Polycarp—a boy of twelve, curly-headed and with quick-darting eyes; Polycarp loves him beyond all reason and grumbles at him from morning till night. It is he, too, who has taken the boy's education upon himself.

"Vassya," he'll begin, "say: 'That miserable little scalawag Boney is a highwayman.' " — "But what will you give me, Grandpa?" — "What'll I give you? I won't give you a thing. Come, what are you? Are you a Russian?" — "I'm an Amchanin, Grandpa—I was born in Amchensk." [1] — "Oh, you dunderhead! But where is this Amchensk, now?" — "Why, how should I know?" — "Amchensk is in Russia, stupid!" — "Why, how should I know?" — "Amchensk is in Russia, stupid!" — "Well, suppose it is in Russia— what of it?" — "What do you mean, what of it? It was His Most Illustrious Excellency, the late Prince Michailo Ilarionovich Golenishchev-Kutuzov, who, with God's help,

---

[1] Among the common folk the city of Mtsensk is called Amchensk, and its inhabitants are called Amchanins. The Amchanins are lively lads: it is not for nothing that, among us, one wishes to somebody who is no friend: "May you get an Amchanin into your household!" —*Author.*

was pleased to drive that miserable little scalawag Boney out of the confines of Russia. There was even a song made up to mark that occasion: 'Bonaparte don't want to dance, 'cause he's gone and tore his pants.' Do you understand, the Prince liberated your fatherland." — "But what's that got to do with me?" — "Ah, you stupid boy! You stupid! Why, if the Most Illustrious Prince Michailo Ilarionovich hadn't driven out that miserable little scalawag Boney, some M'sieu' or other would be pounding your noggin with a stick right now, for sure. He'd walk up to you, like this, say: *'Comment vous portez vous?'*—meaning 'How do you do'—and then go *tap, tap!"* — "Well, I would sink my fist in his belly." — "But then he'd say to you: *'Bon jour, bon jour, venez ici!—*good day, good day, come here!'—and grab you by the topknot—by the topknot, now!" — "Well, I'd go after his feet, his buniony feet." — "That's true enough; they do have buniony feet. But then, suppose he were to tie your hands?" — "Well, I wouldn't give in. I'd yell for Mihei our coachman to help me." — "Come to think of it, Vassya, there's no Frenchman could stand up to Mihei, is there?" — "How could he? Mihei is *that* strong, now!" — "Well, and just what would the two of you do to him?" — "We would start working on his back—on his back all the time, that's what!" — "But he'd begin screaming for pardon—*'Pardon, pardon, s'il vous plâit!'* " — "Then we'd tell him: 'There's no *sivooplay* for you, Frenchy that you are!' " — "Good boy, Vassya! Well, then, let's hear you shout: 'That miserable little scalawag Boney is a high-wayman!' " — "You just give me some sugar, then." — "What a fellow that is!"

With the lady landowners Tatiana Borisovna has little to do: they are none too eager to call on her, and she doesn't know how to entertain them; she dozes off to the murmur of their conversation, awakes with a start, tries her hardest to open her eyes, and dozes off anew. Tatiana Borisovna has, as a general thing, no liking for women. One of her good friends, a fine and quiet young man, had a sister, an elderly maiden of thirty-eight and a half, the kindest of beings yet warped, constrained, and given to exalted moods. Her brother had often spoken to her about his neighbor. One fine morning my elderly maiden (meaning no evil by the phrase) ordered a horse saddled and set out for Tatiana Borisovna's. In her long habit, with a green veil on her riding hat and her curls loose, she stepped into the entry and, bypassing the bewildered Vassya, who had taken her for a water-nixie, dashed into the reception room. Tatiana Borisovna became frightened; she was about to stand up but her knees buckled.

"Tatiana Borisovna," her caller began in an imploring voice, "pardon my presumption; I am the sister of your good friend Alexis Nicholaievich, and I have heard so much from him about you that I've decided to make your acquaintance."

"I am greatly honored," murmured the astonished hostess.

The caller threw off her hat, gave a toss to her curls, settled herself next to Tatiana Borisovna, and took her hand.

"And so, here she is," she began in a pensive and touched voice. "Here is that kind, radiant, noble, saintly being! Here she is! That simple and, at the same time, profound woman! How glad I am—how glad I am! How we will love each other! I am going to find repose at last! It is precisely thus that I imagined her to myself," she added in a whisper, fixing Tatiana Borisovna's eyes with her own. "You aren't angry at me. Isn't that so, my kind, my splendid one?"

"Goodness, I'm very glad. . . . Wouldn't you like some tea?"

The caller smiled condescendingly.

"*Wie wahr, wie unreflectirt*—how real, how unaffected!" she got out in a whisper, as though to herself. "Allow me to embrace you, my darling!"

The elderly maiden sat through three hours at Tatiana Borisovna's, without falling silent for even an instant. She was trying to make clear to her new acquaintance the latter's own worth. Immediately after the departure of the unexpected visitor the poor landed proprietress headed for the bathhouse, drank copiously of linden-leaf tea, and took to her bed. But the very next day the elderly maiden was back, sat for four solid hours, and as she left promised to visit Tatiana Borisovna every day. She'd gotten the notion, if you please, of thoroughly developing such a rich nature, as she put it, and rounding out her education and, in all probability, would have proved the end of her altogether, had it not been for her having become, first of all, "fully" disenchanted about her brother's friend after a fortnight or so and, secondly, falling in love with a transient young student with whom she had immediately entered into

207

active and ardent correspondence: in her missives she, as is usual, gave him her blessing to lead a holy and splendidly beautiful life, offered up "all of herself" as a sacrifice, demanded only the status of a sister, went in for descriptions of nature, referred to Goethe, Schiller, Bettina von Arnim, and German philosophy—and, in the end, brought the poor youth to dark despair. But youth had its way: one fine morning he awoke with such furious hatred for his "sister and best friend" that, in the first heat of his temper, he almost beat his valet and, for a long spell afterward, all but snapped at people whenever there was the least hint at exalted and disinterested love. . . . And it was from then on that Tatiana Borisovna took to shunning still more any rapprochement with her fair neighbors.

Alas! Nothing is permanent on earth. All I have told you about the days and ways of my good landed proprietress is a thing of the past. The tranquillity that reigned in her house has been disrupted for all time. For more than a year now her nephew, an artist from St. Petersburg, has been staying at her place. Here is how it all came about.

Eight years ago Tatiana Borisovna had a boy of twelve living with her—Andriusha, a total orphan, the son of her late brother. Andriusha had great, radiant, humid eyes, a tiny mouth, a chiseled nose, and a splendid towering forehead. He spoke in a quiet and sweet voice, kept himself neat and behaved decorously, sought the caresses of visitors and made himself useful to them, and, whenever he kissed his aunt's hand, did so with the sensitiveness of an orphan. You would hardly appear on the scene when you saw him already bringing up an armchair for you. He didn't go in for mischief of any kind; he wouldn't make the least noise but just sat there minding his business in his nook over his little book, and that ever so well behaved and meek—not leaning against the back of his chair, even. If a guest entered, my Andriusha would stand up, smile politely, and blush; as soon as the guest left the boy would sit down again and, getting a tiny mirror and a small brush out of his little pocket, would slick down his hair.

He had felt an attraction for drawing from his earliest years. If a scrap of paper happened to come his way he lost no time in wheedling a pair of scissors from Agatha, the housekeeper; and, painstakingly cutting a regular quadrangle out of the scrap, he would rule a neat border all around

208

it and set to work: he'd draw an eye with an enormous pupil, or a Grecian nose, or a house with a chimney belching smoke in a screw-shaped swirl; or it might be a dog *en face* yet looking like the side view of a bench, or a sapling with a pair of doves. He would make the drawing and then sign it: "Drawn by Andrew Belovzorov, on such and such a date, in such and such a year, in the village of Little-Kicks."

With particular assiduity did he toil for the fortnight or thereabouts preceding Tatiana Borisovna's birthday; he would be the first to come to felicitate her and would offer her a scroll tied with a bit of pink ribbon. Tatiana Borisovna would kiss her nephew on the forehead and untie the bow: the scroll, opening, revealed to the curious gaze of the beholder a spirited wash drawing of a circular temple with columns and, in its center, an altar; flaming on the altar lay a heart and, on top of the heart, a wreath, the whole affair surmounted by a streaming banderole neatly lettered with: "To My Aunt and Benefactress, Tatiana Borisovna Bogdanova, from Her Respectful and Affectionate Nephew, as a Mark of the Profoundest Attachment." Tatiana Borisovna would give him another kiss and present him with a silver ruble. She did not, however, feel any great attachment for him: Andriusha's servility was not at all to her liking.

In the meanwhile Andriusha was growing up; Tatiana Borisovna was beginning to feel concerned about his future. An unexpected incident led her out of the difficult situation.

To be precise: one day, eight years ago, a certain gentleman by the name of Peter Michailovich Benevolenski, a collegiate councilor and a gallant gentleman, happened to pay her a visit. He had at one time served in the nearest county town and had assiduously cultivated Tatiana Borisovna; then he had gone to St. Petersburg, entered a ministry, attained quite an important post, and during one of his frequent trips on official business had recalled his acquaintance of old and made a side excursion to her place with the intention of resting up from his official worries for a day or two "in the bosom of rustic quiet." Tatiana Borisovna had received him with her usual cordiality, and Benevolenski himself . . . however, before we go on with the story proper, permit me, amiable reader, to acquaint you with this new personage.

M. Benevolenski was a stoutish man, of medium height,

apparently soft, with stubby little legs and chubby little hands; he wore a roomy and exceedingly neat frock coat, a high and wide cravat, linen as white as snow, a dainty gold chain across his silk waistcoat, a ring with a precious stone on his right index finger, and a flaxen toupee; he spoke convincingly and mildly, had a noiseless walk, smiled pleasantly, rolled his eyes pleasantly, and let his chin sink into his cravat in a pleasant sort of way: he was, in general, a pleasant fellow. The heart the Lord had endowed him with was of the kindliest also: he was easily moved to tears and rapture; on top of that, he was consumed by a disinterested passion for art, and disinterested it surely was since, if the truth were to be told, when it came right down to it M. Benevolenski knew absolutely nothing about art. The thing was actually astonishing: whence, through the operation of what incomprehensible laws had this passion sprung up in him? He was of the reliable sort, even rather ordinary . . . however, there are quite many such people in our Russia.

The love such persons bear for art and artists lends an inexplicable mawkishness to them: to have anything to do with them, to talk with them, is excruciating: they are downright dummies of wood, daubed all over with honey. They will never, for instance, call Correggio Correggio, or Raphael Raphael: "Inimitable de Allegris, divine Sanzio," say they—and say it, without fail, with a stress on the *o*. Every home-grown, self-centered, hoodwinked, and mediocre talent they will dignify as a genius—or, to convey it more closely, a "genious"—*the blue skies of Italy, the citron of the South, the fragrant vapors of the banks of the Brenta* are never off their lips. "Eh, Vanya, Vanya," or "Eh, Sasha, Sasha," they say to each other, "we ought to head South, you and I . . . for you and I are Greeks at soul, ancient Greeks!"

You can observe them at exhibitions, before certain works of certain Russian painters (it must be remarked that these gentry are, for the most part, frightful patriots). Now they will fall back a pace or two and throw their heads back, then move closer to the picture again; their dear little eyes become glazed over with an oleaginous moisture. . . .

"Really now . . . my God!" they will say at last in a voice breaking with emotion. "How much soul there is in that—how much soul! See how much there is of the heart

—the heart, now! See how much soul he's put into it, now!
The soul, there's no end to it! And the conception of it,
now! Masterly conception!"

And what pictures they have hanging in their own drawing rooms! What artists they have coming to their houses
of evenings, drinking tea with them, listening to their *con-
versazione*! What perspective views of their rooms the artists offer up to them, with a floor brush in the right fore-
ground, a small mound of rubbish on the waxed floor, a
lurid samovar on a table by the window, and the master
himself, in dressing gown and skullcap, with a bright blotch
of light on his cheek! What long-haired fledglings of the
muses come calling on them, smiling their feverishly con-
temptuous smile! What pale-green damsels caterwaul at their
grand pianos! For that's the way of things in our Russia: a
man can't devote himself to just one of the arts: you've got
to dish up all of them for him. And therefore it is not at
all to be wondered at that these amateur gentry extend a
powerful patronage to Russian literature, especially the dra-
matic. It is for them that the *Jacob Sanpazars* are written:
the struggle, depicted a thousand times, of unrecognized talent against men, against all the world, stirs their souls to
their very depths. . . .

On the very next day following the arrival of M. Benevolenski, Tatiana Borisovna bade her nephew, during tea, to
show his works to the guest.

"Why, does this boy of yours draw?" Benevolenski asked,
not without surprise, and turned with interest to little Andrei.

"Of course he draws," said Tatiana Borisovna. "He's a
great hand at it! And mind you, he's doing it all by himself, without anyone to instruct him."

"Ah, show me your drawings, show them to me," Benevolenski reacted quickly. The boy, blushing and smiling, offered his sketchbook to the guest, who took to turning its
leaves with the air of a connoisseur. "Well done, young
man," he declared at last. "Well done, very well done," and
he patted Andrei's neat little head. The latter caught the
guest's hand in midair and kissed it.

"What talent, one must say! I congratulate you, Tatiana
Borisovna, I congratulate you!"

"But what's the use, Peter Michailych—I can't unearth
an instructor for him here. To get one from town will come

211

too high; our neighbors, the Artamonovs, have a painter on their place, and an excellent one, they say, but the lady of the house forbids him to give lessons to outsiders. It'll spoil his taste, she says."

"Hm," Benevolenski let drop, then sank into thought and regarded little Andrei from under his brows. "Well, we'll discuss this matter further," he suddenly added and rubbed his hands.

That same day he asked his hostess for a private interview. They closeted themselves. Half an hour later they summoned Andrei. He came into the room. M. Benevolenski was standing by a window; his face was slightly flushed, and his eyes were glowing. The aunt was sitting in a corner and dabbing away at her tears.

"Well, Andriusha," she spoke at last, "thank Peter Michailych; he's taking you under his guardianship, carrying you off to St. Petersburg."

Andriusha was simply petrified.

"Tell me frankly," Benevolenski began in a voice overflowing with dignity and condescension, "do you desire to be an artist? Do you feel a sacred call to follow art?"

"I do desire to be an artist, Peter Michailych," Andrei confirmed, all aquiver.

"I'm very glad that is the case. Of course," Benevolenski went on, "it will be hard for you to part with your esteemed aunt; you are bound to feel the liveliest gratitude toward her."

"I adore my dear aunt," Andriusha broke in on him and took to blinking his eyes.

"Of course, of course; that's quite understandable and does you a great deal of credit; but then, imagine what joy time will bring . . . your successes. . . ."

"Take me around, Andriusha," murmured the kindly landed proprietress. Andrew threw himself on her neck. "Well, and now thank your benefactor—"

Little Andrei put his arms around Benevolenski's belly, stood up on tiptoes, and in the end managed to get at his hand, which the benefactor was, true enough, trying to extricate yet was in none too great a hurry to do so. After all, one must humor, one must gratify a child—and one may indulge oneself a little as well.

Two days later Benevolenski took his departure and bore off his new protégé.

During the course of the first three years he was away from his aunt Andrei wrote her quite frequently, at times enclosing drawings with his letters. On rare occasions Benevolenski also added a few words of his own—for the most part words of approval. Then the letters became rarer and rarer; finally they ceased altogether. For all of a year did the nephew keep silent; Tatiana Borisovna was actually beginning to worry, when she suddenly received a brief note, the contents of which were as follows:

> Dear Aunt:
> Four days ago my benefactor, Peter Michailych, passed away. The cruel stroke of paralysis deprived me of this last support. Of course, I am now going on twenty; in the course of seven years my accomplishments have been significant; I rely greatly on my talent and can live thereby; I do not despond—but still, if you can, send me 250 rubles in government notes for the time being.
> I kiss your hands, and remain, and so on.

Tatiana Borisovna sent the sum to her nephew. Two months later he demanded more; she scraped together her last money and sent him more. Hardly six weeks passed after the second remittance when he made a third request: he had, it would seem, to buy colors for a portrait that Princess Terteresheneva had commissioned him to do. Tatiana Borisovna turned him down. "In that case," he wrote her, "I intend to come to you, to mend my health in the country." And, sure enough, in May of that same year, Andriusha came back to Little Kicks.

Tatiana Borisovna failed to recognize him at first. Judging from his letter she had expected somebody sickly and gaunt, but what she saw was a stout fellow, wide in the shoulders, with a broad and red face, his hair curly and greasy. The ever so slender and pale Andriusha had turned into a husky Andrew Ivanov Belovzorov. Nor was it his appearance alone that had changed. The sensitive shyness, the circumspectness and neatness of his former years had been supplanted by negligent derring-do, by unendurable slovenliness; as he walked he rocked to right and left; he threw himself into his chair and put all his weight on a table; he lounged, yawned as loudly and gapingly as he could, and treated both his aunt and the servants with impudence, as much as to say "I'm an artist, a free Cossack! You might as well know what sort of folks us artists are!"

There were days when he would not touch a brush; if inspiration (so-called) would come upon him he would posture heavy-handedly, clumsily, noisily, as though he were getting over a spree; his cheeks would blaze up into a ruddy hue, his eyes become glazed; he would launch into disquisitions on his talent, on his successes, on how he was developing, forging ahead. In reality, however, it turned out that his abilities barely, barely sufficed for daubs that could pass as portraits.

He was an all-around ignoramus who did no reading whatsoever—and besides, why should an artist read? Nature, freedom, poesy, *these* are an artist's elements. All he has to know is how to toss his curls, and trill like a nightingale, and inhale Zhukov's fine latakia till the pipe gurgles! A fine thing is Russian bravado, but then there aren't many to whom it's becoming, whereas untalented, secondhand Polezhaevs are unbearable. Our Andrei Ivanych had found a snug berth at his aunt's: free board, it seemed, suited him right down to the ground. He induced a deathly boredom in all who came to the house. He used to sit him down at the piano (Tatiana Borisovna had even a grand piano around her place) and start picking out "The Dandy Troika" with one finger; he'd tackle chords, tap away at the keys, and for hours on end howl excruciatingly through the romantic ballads of Varlamov: "The Lonely Pine" or "No, Doctor, No— You Need Not Come," yet the eyes on him were sunk in blubber, and his cheeks were as glossy and taut as a drumhead. . . . Or else he would suddenly and thunderously break into "Subside, ye Passion's Agitations. . . ." All Tatiana Borisovna could do was shudder.

"It's an amazing thing," she remarked to me once, "what all the songs they make up nowadays are like—despairing songs, somehow. In my time they made up different songs; there were sad songs, too, but just the same it was a pleasure to listen to them. For instance:

> Come to the meadow, come where I wait—
> Where I wait for thee in vain;
> Come to the meadow, come where I wait,
> Where I shed my tears like rain. . . .

214

But when you come where I await
Alas, dear friend, 'twill be too late!"

Tatiana Borisovna smiled slyly.

" 'I su-uffer, I su-uffer!' " her nephew set up a howl in an adjoining room.

"That'll do you, Andriusha!"

" 'My soul pines away while we are parted!' " the irrepressible singer went right on.

"Oh, what these artists do to me!"

A year has passed since then. Belovzorov is living at his aunt's to this very day and is forever getting ready to go to St. Petersburg. In the country his breadth has come to exceed his height. His aunt—who would have thought it?—loves him more than her own soul, while all the young ladies thereabouts are falling in love with him. . . .

Many of her former acquaintances have stopped calling on Tatiana Borisovna.

DEATH

I HAVE A neighbor, young as a gentleman farmer and young as a Nimrod. One fine July morning I went over to his place on horseback, proposing that the two of us set out after grouse. He agreed.

"However," he told me, "let's ride through my small holdings, toward Zusha; while I'm at it I'll take a look at Chaplyghino. My oak forest, you know. I'm having some timber felled there."

"Let's."

He ordered a horse to be saddled, put on a bit of a green jacket with bronze buttons, each one a representation of a boar's head, slung a gamebag (embroidered in worsted) and a silver flask over one shoulder and a brand-new gun of a French make over the other, turned this way and that before a mirror for a while, not without satisfaction, and called to his dog Esperance, which had been presented to him by a cousin of his, an elderly maiden with a heart of gold but without any hair.

We set out. My neighbor took along Arhip, the village constable, a stout and squat muzhik with a quadrangular face and cheekbones the development of which was like that of an antediluvian troglodyte, and also Herr Gottlieb von der Kock, his recently hired manager, who hailed from the Baltic Provinces, a youth of nineteen, thin, fair-haired, purblind, with drooping shoulders and a long neck. My neighbor himself had only recently entered upon the possession

of his estate. It had come to him by inheritance from Kar-
don-Kataeva, an aunt of his, the widow of a state councilor,
an inordinately corpulent woman who used to grunt long
and plaintively even when lying in bed.

We rode into the "small holdings."

"You can wait a while for me, here on the meadow," said
Ardallion Michailych (such was my neighbor's name), addressing his retinue. The German bowed, got down off his
horse, drew a book out of his pocket (a novel of Johanna
Schopenhauer's, I believe it was), and sat him down under a
small bush; Arhip stayed out in the sun and, for all of an
hour, did not as much as stir.

My neighbor and I beat about the bushes and did not
flush even one covey. Ardallion Michailych announced that
he intended to set out for the forest. Somehow I myself did
not believe there would be good hunting that day; I ambled
off after him. We came back to the meadow. The German
marked his page, stood up, replaced the book in his pocket
and, not without difficulty, got up on his dock-tailed, con-
demned mare, which whinnied and bucked at the least
touch; Arhip perked up, started tugging at both reins and
pumping with his legs, and at last budged his stunned and
depressed little nag from her place. We were off.

Ardallion Michailych's forest had been familiar to me
since childhood. Together with my French tutor, Monsieur
Désiré Fleury, the kindest of men (who, nevertheless, all
but wrecked my health forever by compelling me to drink
Lerois' medicine nightly), I used to walk to Chaplyghino frequently. This whole forest consisted of some two or three
hundred enormous oaks and ash trees. Their graceful,
mighty trunks showed magnificently dark against the aureately translucent greenery of hazel bushes and rowans; and,
rising higher, they stood out in graceful design against the
clear azure, and only there did they spread their wide, angular boughs in a canopy. Hawks, merlins, kestrels darted,
whistling, beneath the motionless treetops; brightly plum-
aged woodpeckers tapped hard at their thick bark; the sonorous song of the blackbird would unexpectedly resound in
the thick leafage, right after the trilling call of the yellow
thrush; below, in the bushes, the hedge sparrows, siskins,
and pewits chirped and sang; the white hare stole along the
edge of the forest, cautiously, as if on crutches; a reddish-
brown squirrel would leap sprightly from tree to tree and

then suddenly sit up, its tail raised above its head. In the grass, near the tall anthills, under the light shade of the beautiful chiseled fronds of the lady fern, violets and lilies of the valley blossomed; agarics, yellowish mushrooms, pepper mushrooms, oak truffles, crimson toadstools—all grew there; in the dales, between the spreading bushes, strawberries glowed red. . . .

And what shade there was in that forest! At the sultriest, at noonday, it was like real night; stillness, fragrance, freshness. . . . Blithely did I pass my time in Chaplyghino and therefore, I confess, it was not without a feeling of sadness that I now rode into this forest, all too familiar to me. The murderous, snowless winter of 1840 had not spared my old friends, the oaks and the ash trees; withered, stripped, covered here and there with consumptive greenery, sadly did they rear over the young grove which "had taken their place without replacing them." [1] Some, their lower trunks still covered with leaves, were, as if in reproach and despair, raising aloft their lifeless and broken limbs; others had thick, dry, dead branches sticking out of their leafage, which was still rather dense, even though not as abundant, not as luxuriant as of yore; from some the bark had already fallen off; some, finally, had fallen altogether and were rotting upon the ground like corpses. Who could have foreseen it: of shade—this in Chaplyghino!—of shade one could find none! "Well, now," I mused, gazing at the dying trees, "you must feel shame and bitterness, I guess?" I recalled Koltzov:

> Whither have ye gone,
> Lofty-flowing speech,
> Strength in all its pride,
> Prowess meet for kings?
> Where is now all thy
> Greenwood sovereign might?

"But how did all this come about, Ardallion Michailych?" I began. "Why weren't these trees cut down the very next

---

[1] In 1840, during the cruelest frosts, no snow fell until the end of December; all the leafage was killed by frost, and many splendid oak forests did this pitiless winter destroy. To replace them is hard: the productive power of the earth is evidently growing poorer; upon the "bespoken" waste tracts (those which have been walked around with holy images) birches and aspens grow up of themselves—and as for cultivating groves in any other way, that is something we don't know how to do as yet.—*Author.*

year? For nobody will now give you one-tenth of what they would have fetched before."

He merely shrugged. "Ask my aunt that—and yet the dealers came to her, cash in hand, importuning her."

"*Mein Gott! Mein Gott!*" von der Kock kept exclaiming at every step. "What a pity, what a pity!"—and his mispronunciation of *zhalost* [pity] made it sound like *shalost* [mischief].

"What mischief do you mean?" my neighbor asked with a smile.

"That is, I meant to say how pitifulll it was." (It's well known that Germans, when they do at last get the upper hand of our letter *l*, will attack it amazingly hard.)

His regrets were particularly aroused by the oaks lying on the ground—and, truly, many a miller would have paid plenty for them. Arhip the constable, on the other hand, preserved an imperturbable calm and did not grieve in the least; on the contrary, it was not without actual pleasure that he jumped over them and flicked at them with his small whip.

We were making our way to the place where the felling was going on when, close upon the noise made by a tree in its fall, sudden shouting and loud talk broke out, and a few moments later a young muzhik, pale and disheveled, popped out of a thicket, heading toward us.

"What is it? Where are you running?" Ardallion Michailych asked him.

He immediately stopped. "Ah, Ardallion Michailych, father of mine, there's trouble!"

"What is it?"

"Maxim was crushed by a tree, father of mine."

"Just how did it happen? Was it Maxim the contractor?"

"The contractor it is, father of mine. We started chopping down an ash tree, and he stood there, watching. He stood and stood there, and then went off to the well for water—guess he wanted to drink—when all of a sudden the ash tree started cracking, falling right toward him. We shouted to him 'Run, run, run!' He should have dashed to one side, but he ups and starts running straight ahead—must have gotten scared, I guess. And that ash tree, now, it fell on top of him with its upper branches. And why it ever fell so quickly, the Lord alone knows. Unless the heartwood was rotted—"

"Well, and did it kill Maxim?"

"It did that, father of mine."

"Outright?"

"No, father of mine—he's still alive. But what's the use— his arms and legs are broken. I was running to get Seliver- stych, the doctor, now."

Ardallion Michailych ordered the constable to gallop to the village after Seliverstych, while he himself went at a full trot to where the felling was going on. I followed him.

We found poor Maxim on the ground, with half a score muzhiks standing around him. We got down from our horses. There was hardly a moan out of him; now and then he would open his eyes, and they widened, as though he were looking about him in wonder, and he bit his lips, which had turned blue. His chin was trembling; his hair stuck to his forehead, his breast heaved irregularly: he was dying. The light shadow of a young linden glided softly over his face.

We bent over him. He recognized Ardallion Michailych.

"Father of mine," he began speaking, "tell them . . . to send . . . for the priest. The Lord has punished me . . . my hands, my feet—the whole body is smashed up. Today is Sunday . . . but I . . . but I, now, wouldn't let the lads off—"

He fell silent. It was hard for him to breathe.

"As to my money, now . . . give it to my wife . . . to my wife, now . . . whatever's coming to me. There, Onissim knows . . . what I owe, and to whom—"

"We've sent for the doctor, Maxim," my neighbor began. "There's a chance you may not die, after all."

He opened his eyes and, with an effort, raised his eye- brows and lids.

"No, I'm going to die. There . . . there, it's drawing near— there it is, now. . . . Forgive me, lads, if I've been at fault in any way—"

"God will forgive you, Maxim Andreich," the muzhiks spoke up dully, as if with one voice, and took off their caps. "You must forgive us."

He suddenly shook his head in despair, thrust his chest out pathetically, and again sank back.

"However, we simply can't let him die there," Ardallion Michailych called out. "Let's take the matting off that cart, lads; we'll bring him over to the hospital."

A couple of men dashed over to the cart.

"I bought a horse yesterday . . . from Ephim . . . Sychovsky," the dying man began to babble. "Gave him a deposit . . . so the horse is mine . . . it goes to my wife, too—"

They started putting him on the matting. He quivered all over, like a shot bird, and straightened out. . . .

"He's dead," the muzhiks muttered.

We mounted in silence and rode away.

Poor Maxim's death made me somewhat thoughtful. It is amazing, the way the Russian peasant dies! His state before his end can be called neither apathy nor stolidity: he dies as if he were performing a rite: coolly and simply.

Several years ago, in a village belonging to another neighbor of mine, a muzhik was burned to death in a corn kiln. (He would have remained in the corn kiln to the end, had it not been for a burgher staying in the village, who dragged him out of there half alive: this neighbor soused himself in a tub of water and then, running full tilt, broke the door under its flaming overhang.) I dropped in at this muzhik's hut. It was dark in that hut, stuffy, smoky. I asked where the sick man was.

"Why, over there, father of mine, atop that ledge," a downcast peasant woman answered me in a singsong voice.

I approached; the muzhik was lying there, covered over with a sheepskin coat, breathing with difficulty.

"Well, how do you feel?"

The sick man started fussing on his sleeping ledge atop the oven, wanting to raise himself up, yet he was all wounds, at death's very door.

"Don't move, don't move, don't move. . . . Well, now. How are things?"

"In a bad way, it looks like," said he.

"Feel any pain?" He kept silent. "Do you need anything, perhaps?" He still kept silent. "Should I send you some tea, maybe?"

"No need of that."

I walked away from him and sat down on a bench. I sat there for a quarter of an hour, a half hour—there was a silence as of the grave in the hut. In a corner, at a table under the holy images, a girl of five was sitting unobtrusively, eating bread. The mother shook a warning finger at her every now and then. Out in the entry people were walking about, stomping, talking; a sister-in-law was chopping cabbage.

"Hey there, Axinia!" the sick man spoke up at last.

"What is it?"

"Let me have some bread-cider."

Axinia brought him some. Silence again. I asked, in a whisper, if the last rites had been administered to him.

"They were."

Well, in that case, everything was surely in order: he was biding for death, and that was that. I could not take it any more and went out.

Or else, I remember, I once happened to turn in on my way at an infirmary in the settlement of Krasnogorie, to see Kapiton, a country doctor of the secondary grade, who was a passionate hunter.

This hospital consisted of what had been a wing of the manor house; the place had been arranged by the landed proprietress herself—that is, she had ordered to be nailed up over the door a board lettered "Krasnogorie Hospital" in white against pale blue, and had herself put into the hands of Kapiton a handsome album wherein the names of the patients were to be registered. On the first sheet of this album one of the Lady Bountiful's lickspittles and toadies, ever-ready for any service, had indited the following versicles:

> Dans ces beaux lieux, où règne l'allégresse
> Ce temple fut ouvert par la Beauté;
> De vos seigneurs admirez la tendresse,
> Bons habitants de Krasnogorié! [2]

—while another gentleman had added underneath:

> Et moi aussi j'aime la nature!
> JEAN KOBYLIATNIKOV [3]

The secondary-grade medico had bought six beds at his own expense and, after blessing himself, started out to heal God's folk. The hospital had a staff of two besides himself: Paul, a woodcarver, who was subject to fits of madness, and Melectrissa, who filled the post of cook. Both of them prepared the medicines; they dried herbs and made infusions of them; it was they, likewise, who subdued delirious pa-

---

[2] Mid these fair scenes, where reigneth gaiety,
Beauty doth ope this temple to cure ills;
All your seigneurs admire the charity
Of the good folks now dwelling in Red Hills!

[3] And I, too, love Nature! Ivan Kobyliatnikov.

tients. The mad woodcarver was of morose appearance and niggardly of speech; of nights he sang a song about "beauteous Venus," and whenever there was a visitor he would approach him with an appeal for permission to marry Malania, some wench or other who had died long since. The peasant cook, one of whose arms was withered, used to beat him and made him take care of the turkeys.

Well, there I was one day, sitting at Kapiton's, the secondary-grade medico's. We had just begun talking over our last hunting trip when suddenly a cart drove into the yard; the cart was drawn by an extraordinarily fat horse, a gray, such as only millers go for. A corpulent muzhik, in a new overcoat and with a grizzled beard, was sitting in the cart.

"Ah, Vassilii Dmitrich," Kapiton shouted to him through the window, "you're right welcome! . . . The miller from Liubovshino," he whispered to me.

The muzhik, grunting, clambered down from the cart, entered the doctor's room, searched for the holy images with his eyes, and made the sign of the cross over himself.

"Well, Vassilii Dmitrich, what's new? Why, you must be ailing; your face doesn't look at all well."

"Yes, Kapiton Timotheich, something's gone wrong. I bought millstones in town not so long ago; well, I carted them home, but when I started getting them out of the cart, now, I must have strained myself, I guess; something plopped, sort of hard, in my belly, now, as if it had torn loose. Well, now, ever since then I've been ailing all the while. Today things are in a bad way—very much so, for a fact."

"Hm," Kapiton let drop and took a pinch of snuff. "That means rupture. And was it a long while ago this happened to you?"

"Why, it's going on the tenth day now."

"The tenth?" The doctor drew in the air through his teeth and shook his head. "There, let me feel you. . . . Well, Vassilii Dmitrich," he uttered at last, "I feel sorry for you, you're a man after my own heart, yet that business of yours is in a bad way; your illness is no trifle—stay on here at my place. For my part, I'll exert every effort, but at the same time I don't guarantee anything."

"Can it be as bad as all that?" muttered the astonished miller.

"Yes, Vassilii Dmitrich, it's bad; had you come to me a

223

couple of days sooner, why, it wouldn't have been anything; I'd have rid you of it at a snap, but now you have inflammation, that's what; first thing you know it'll turn into Saint Anthony's fire." Kapiton was using the folk name for erysipelas.

"Why, it just can't be, Kapiton Timotheich!"

"Well, I'm telling you it's so."

"But how can this be?" The doctor shrugged. "And am I to die because of this rubbish?"

"I'm not saying that—but you stay on here, just the same."

The muzhik thought and thought a while, looked at the floor, then at us, scratched the back of his neck—and picked up his cap.

"But where are you going, Vassilii Dmitrich?"

"Where? Anybody knows where—home, if things are as bad as all that. Ought to see to things, if that's the case."

"Why, good heavens, you'll do yourself harm, Vassilii Dmitrich—I wonder as it is how you ever managed to get here. Do stay on!"

"No, brother Kapiton Timotheich, if I'm going to die then let me die at home; for what's the sense of dying here? The Lord alone knows what will go on at home."

"It's still uncertain, Vassilii Dmitrich, how this case will go. . . . Of course it's dangerous, very dangerous, there's no disputing that. But for that very reason you ought to stay on here."

The muzhik shook his head:

"No, Kapiton Timotheich, I won't stay on . . . but if you should care to prescribe a bit of medicine—"

"Medicine by itself won't help."

"I'm not going to stay here, I'm telling you."

"Well, do as you wish. Mind you, don't blame me later!"

The doctor tore one of the small pages out of the album and, having written out a prescription, advised the patient as to what else he was to do. The muzhik took the scrap of paper, gave Kapiton a half-ruble coin, walked out of the room, and took his seat in the cart.

"Well, goodbye, Kapiton Timotheich; don't remember any ill of me, and don't forget the little orphans, should anything befall—"

"Eh, stay on here, Vassilii!"

The muzhik merely tossed his head, slapped his horse with a rein, and drove out of the yard. I came out into the street and followed him with my eyes. The road was muddy and full of ruts; the miller was driving carefully, in no hurry, deftly guiding the horse and bowing to those he met. . . . On the fourth day after that he died.

As a general thing, Russian folk have an amazing way about them when it comes to dying. Many who have died come to my memory now. I recall you, my friend of old, Avenir Sorokoumov—a student who had never finished his studies, the most splendid, the noblest of men! I see anew your consumptive, greenish face, your scant, ruddy hair, your meek smile, your enraptured gaze, your lanky limbs; I hear your weak, kindly voice. You lived at the house of Gur Krupyanikov, a landowner of Great Russia, teaching his children Fofa and Zezya their Russian letters and geography and history, patiently bearing up under the heavy-handed jests of Gur himself, the coarse amenities of his major-domo, the vulgar pranks of his malicious little boys; not without a bitter smile, yet at the same time without murmuring, did you carry out the capricious demands of the bored mistress. But then, how you used to rest, how beautified were your evenings when, after supper, having at last done with all duties and lessons, you would sit down before a window, light your pipe thoughtfully, or turn with avidity the pages of a mutilated and soiled issue of some thick periodical which had drifted to you from town together with some surveyor, the same sort of homeless, hapless fellow as yourself! How you relished at such times all kinds of poems, all kinds of novels, how easily the tears came to your eyes, with what delight you laughed, with what sincere love for people, with what noble sympathy toward all things that were kindly and splendidly beautiful was your soul permeated then—a soul as pure as that of an infant!

One is bound to tell the truth: you weren't distinguished for any excessive wit; nature hadn't bestowed upon you the gift of memory or application; at the university you were one of the worst students; during the lectures you dozed, during oral examinations you maintained a solemn silence —yet whose eyes shone with joy, whose breath came in gasps, at the triumph, at the success of a comrade? Avenir's! Who had blind faith in the high calling of his friends, who sang their praises, who raged in their defense? Who knew no envy or ambition; who was it that submitted willingly to people who weren't worthy of tying his shoe-laces? You, always—always you, our kindhearted Avenir!

I remember: with a stricken heart did you say farewell to your friends as you were going off "to tutor"; you were tormented by evil premonitions. . . . And sure enough: things turned out to be bad for you in the country; in the country there was no one to whom you might listen reverently, no one to wonder at, no one to love. Both the steppe squires and the cultured landowners treated you as a schoolmaster: the first sort rudely, the second negligently. Besides that, your figure wasn't prepossessing, either; you had a way of growing timid, of turning red, of breaking into a sweat, of stammering. Nor did the country air improve your health: you wasted away like a candle, poor fellow! True: your tiny room did look out on a garden; the wild cherry trees, the apple trees, the lindens scattered their light petals upon your desk, upon your inkwell, upon your books; hanging on one of your walls was a little cushioned watch-holder of pale-blue silk, presented to you at the hour of farewell by a little kindhearted, sentimental German lady, a governess with flaxen curls and small blue eyes; now and then some old friend from Moscow would look you up and cause you ecstasy by reading verse to you—that of others, or even his own. But what of solitude, what of the unbearable slavery of the schoolmaster's calling, what of the impossibility of freeing oneself, what of the never-ending autumns and winters, what of your illness, which never let up. . . . Poor, poor Avenir!

I paid Sorokoumov a visit not long before his death. By then he was almost unable to walk. Gur Krupyanikov, the landowner, did not drive him out of the house, but he had ceased paying him any salary and had hired another teacher for Zezya—Fofa was placed in a cadet corps. Avenir was sitting by a window, in an ancient easy chair. The weather was splendid. The radiant sky of autumn was a blithe pale blue over the ranged dark-brown, denuded lindens; here and there the last, vividly golden leaves upon them stirred and babbled. The earth, which had been gripped by frost, was sweating and thawing out in the sun, whose rosy oblique rays beat upon and glided over the wan grass; one imagined a slight crackling in the air; the voices of the men at work in the garden sounded clearly and distinctly.

Avenir had on a Bukhara dressing gown; a green necker-

chief cast a tinge as of death upon his face, which had
become frightfully emaciated. He was quite overjoyed at
my coming, held out his hand to me, started to speak, and
went off into a fit of coughing. I let him calm down and
took a seat near him. A notebook in which the poems of
Koltzov had been painstakingly transcribed was lying on
his knees; he tapped it with his hand, smiling.

"There's a poet for you," he managed to murmur, and
at once launched into declaiming, in a barely audible voice:

> "Are a falcon's wings
> Closely bound and tied?
> Are the air's free ways
> All to him denied?"

I stopped him: the physician had forbidden him to talk.
I knew how to please him. Sorokoumov had never "followed" science (as they put it), but he was curious to
know: How far had the great minds gone, now? There were
times when he would corner some comrade and fall to
questioning him; he would listen, be amazed, take the other
at his word, and ever afterward simply go on repeating
what the other had said. It was German philosophy that
interested him in particular. I began expounding Hegel to
him (matters of auld lang syne, as you see). Avenir kept
nodding his head in affirmation, raising his eyebrows, smiling, whispering "I understand, I understand! Ah, that's fine,
that's fine!" The childlike love of knowledge in the poor,
dying, shelterless, and neglected fellow moved me, I confess,
to tears. I must remark that Avenir, unlike all consumptives,
did not deceive himself in the least as to his sickness.
And, would you believe it?—he did not sigh, did not grieve,
and did not hint even once at his condition.

Having gathered strength, he began speaking of Moscow,
of his friends, of Pushkin, of the theater, of Russian literature; he recalled our little feasts, the ardent debates of our
small circle, mentioned, with regret, the names of two or
three friends who had died. . . .

"Do you remember Dasha?" he added finally. "There was
a soul of gold! There was a heart! And how she loved
me. . . . What has become of her now? Guess she's all
dried up, all wasted away, the poor little thing?"

I hadn't the heart to disillusion the sick man—and, really,
why should he know that Dasha was now greater in girth

than in height, that she was now running around with the merchantly brothers Kondachkov, using whitening and rouge, that she spoke in a squeak and was quarrelsome?

However (it occurred to me as I contemplated his exhausted face), wasn't there a chance of dragging him out of here? Perhaps there was still a possibility of curing him. But Avenir wouldn't let me finish my proposition.

"No, brother, thanks," said he. "It doesn't matter where one dies. For I won't live until winter. Why put people to trouble all for nothing? I've gotten used to this house. True, the masters here—"

"Are they ill tempered or what?" I caught him up.

"No, it's not that! They're just so many wooden sticks, sort of. But on the whole I can't complain about them. There are neighbors: Kassatkin, a landowner, has a daughter—educated, amiable, the kindest-hearted girl . . . not at all proud—"

Sorokoumov went off into another severe coughing spell.

"Still, things wouldn't be so bad," he went on after resting a little, "if only they'd let me me smoke just a pipeful. . . . But there, I'm not going to die just like that—I will smoke a pipeful to the end!" he added with a sly wink. "Thank God, I've lived long enough, have been among good people—"

I interrupted him. "Well, you might at least write to your relatives."

"What's the use in writing to relatives? If it's for help, help me they can't; if I die, they'll learn about it anyway. But what's the use of talking about that? Better tell me what you saw abroad—"

I began telling him. His eyes simply plunged into me. Toward evening I went away, and ten days or so later I received the following letter from Krupyanikov:

I have the honor of informing you hereby, my Dear Sir, that your friend, Avenir Sorokoumov, the student residing in my house, has died on the fourth inst., at two in the afternoon, and that he was buried this day, at my expense, at the parish church. He requested me to send on to you the books and notebooks transmitted herewith. The money he left amounted to 22 rubles and a half, which, together with his other belongings, will be duly delivered to his relatives. Your friend was fully in his senses when his end came and, one may say, was as fully insensitive, expressing no signs of regret whatsoever, even when I and my whole family were bidding him farewell. Cleopatra Alexandrovna, my spouse, sends you her regards. The death of your friend could not but have an effect upon her nerves; as for me, I am, thank God, in good health, and have the honor to remain,

Your most obedient Servant,

G. KRUPYANIKOV

Many other instances come to mind, but there's no telling them all.

A landed proprietress, a little crone, lay dying in my presence. The priest began saying the prayer for the departing over her, but he suddenly noticed that the sick woman actually was departing and handed her the cross as quickly as he could. The landed proprietress drew back with displeasure.

"What's your hurry, Father?" she got out with a tongue that was growing numb. "You've got plenty of time."

She put her lips to the cross, was about to thrust her hand under her pillow—and breathed her last. There was a silver ruble lying under her pillow: she had wanted to pay the priest herself for saying the prayer for her own departure.

Yes, Russian folk have an amazing way about them when it comes to dying!

THE SINGERS

THE TINY HAMLET of Kolotovka, which once had belonged to a landed proprietress who had been nicknamed throughout the district as the Dockmaned Filly because of her dashing and spirited nature (her real name remains unknown), but which now belongs to a German from St. Petersburg, lies on the slope of a bare knoll, cleft from top to foot by a frightful ravine which, yawning like an abyss, winds along with its pits and washouts down the very middle of the village street and bisects the miserable little hamlet more disastrously than any river would—for, in the case of a river, you can at least throw a bridge across. A few scrawny willows crawl timorously down the sandy sides of this ravine; at its very bottom, which is dry and as yellow as brass, lie enormous slabs of clayey stone. A far from cheerful view, one is bound to admit, and yet the way to Kolotovka is well known to all the denizens of that region; they make trips to this hamlet willingly and often enough.

At the very head of this ravine, a few paces from that point where it begins as a narrow crevice, stands a small foursquare hut; it stands all by its lonesome, remote from all the others. It is thatched with straw and has a chimney; one window is turned, just like a vigilant eye, upon the ravine, and of winter evenings, when it shows the light within, it can be seen a long way off through the dull haze of the frost and glimmers like a guiding light for many a lowly muzhik driving by. A small board, painted blue, is nailed up over the doorway of this little hut: it's a pot-house, is this little house, named the Hunter's Rest. It isn't at all likely that the liquor in this pothouse is sold below the prevailing price, yet the place is frequented far more assiduously than all the establishments of this sort there-abouts. The reason for this is to be found in its host and tapster, Nicholai Ivanych.

Nicholai Ivanych—once a well-built, curly-headed, and rosy-cheeked lad, but now an inordinately stout man, al-ready gray, with bloated face, slyly amiable eyes, and a greasy forehead tautened with wrinkles that look like stitches —has been living in Kolotovka for more than twenty years. He is an up-and-doing shrewd fellow—as tapsters are, for the most part. Without being notable for any particular ami-ability or chattiness he nevertheless has the gift of attract-ing and keeping his patrons, who find it cheery, somehow, to sit before his bar under the calm and genial gaze of their phlegmatic host. He has a great fund of common sense; familiar to him is the landowners' way of life, and that of the peasants, and of the burghers as well; when difficult situations arise he could give you counsel . that would be not at all stupid; however, as a man of caution and an egoist, he prefers the role of a bystander, and only through roundabout hints, perhaps, uttered apparently with-out any intent, does he steer his habitués—and only his favorite habitués, at that—onto the right path.

He knows what's what in everything that is of import or of engrossing interest to the Russian: in horses and live-stock, in timber, in brick, in crockery, in dry goods and leather articles, in songs and dances. When there is no trade he usually sits on the ground before the door of his hut, as passive as a stacked sack of grain, with his spindly legs tucked in under him, and exchanges an amiable word or two with all the passersby. A great deal has he seen in his life; he has outlived more than one score of the squireens who were in the habit of dropping in at his place for a tot of "rectified" stuff; he knows everything that is going on for six and sixty miles around and will never blab any-thing, won't as much as let on that he knows even that which the most perspicacious district police officer hasn't as much as an inkling of. He just goes on keeping his

231

lips buttoned, and minding his own business, and chuckling a mite, and shifting his shot glasses about. He is held in respect by his neighbors: General Shcherspetenko, now retired, the highest ranking of all the landowners in the district, bows to him condescendingly whenever he rides by his small hut.

Nicholai Ivanych is a man of influence: he made a notorious horse thief bring back a horse that had been spirited away from the barnyard of a man whom the tavern keeper knew; he brought to their senses the muzhiks of a village nearby who had turned mulish about accepting a new estate manager, and so on. However, it must not be thought that he does all these things out of love for justice, out of zeal for his fellow men—not at all! He simply tries to forestall everything that might in any way upset his tranquillity.

Nicholai Ivanych is married and has children. His wife —spry, sharp-nosed, with quick-darting eyes, and from a family of burghers—has also put on some weight lately, just like her husband. He relies upon her in all things, and it is she who keeps the key to their cashbox. Those who are noisy in their cups go in fear of her—she has no great liking for them: there's much cry but little wool from them; it is the taciturn, glum drinkers who are more after her heart. Nicholai Ivanych's children are still small: those who came first have all died off, but those who are left have taken after their parents: it does one's heart good to look upon the clever little faces of those sturdy urchins.

It was an unbearably hot July day when I, barely able to drag my feet, was slowly going uphill together with my dog along the Kolotovka ravine, heading for the little pothouse of the Hunter's Rest. The sun was blazing up more and more in the sky, as if it were working itself into a rage; the humidity and the sunbake would not let up; the air was shot through and through with stifling dust. The rooks and crows, their feathers all glazed, their beaks gaping, eyed the passersby piteously, as though imploring their compassion; the sparrows alone were not down at the mouth and, ruffling their tiny feathers, were chirking and fighting along the fences more frenziedly than ever, swirling up from the dusty road all at the same time, darting in gray clouds over the green fields of hemp. I was tortured by thirst. There was no water close by: the muzhiks of Kolotovka, having no springs or wells (as is the case in so many other steppe villages), drank some sort of liquefied mud out of a pond. Well, who would ever dignify such revolting swill by the name of water? What I wanted was to order a glass of beer or bread-cider from Nicholai Ivanych.

Kolotovka does not, truth to tell, present a heart-gladdening sight at any time of the year, but it evokes an especially depressing feeling when the dazzling July sun floods with its implacable rays not only the tawny roofs of half-scattered thatching, but even this deep ravine, and the sun-baked, dust-covered common over which scrawny long-legged hens are wandering forlornly, and the framework of a house (its aspenwood weathered to gray, with holes where the windows should have been—all that is left of a manorial dwelling, surrounded and grown over with nettles, bushy weeds, and wormwood), and the black pond, which seems to be glowing at red heat (with an edging of half-dried mud and with goose down covering its surface), with a dam knocked all askew, near which, upon earth that has been so trodden down that it is now like fine ashes, some sheep, barely able to breathe and sneezing because of the heat, are dismally huddling to one another and in despondent patience let their heads droop as low as possible, as though biding the time when this unbearable sultriness will be over at last—and when would that be?

With wearied steps I was approaching Nicholai Ivanych's dwelling, arousing, in the usual way of things, a wonder that attained to a tensed, vacant contemplation on the part of the small fry and, on the part of the dogs, an indignation which they expressed by barking, so very hoarsely and malevolently that it sounded as if all their inwards were tearing loose, for they themselves had to gasp and choke for breath afterward—I was approaching Nicholai Ivanych's little pothouse when there suddenly appeared on its threshold a man of tall stature, bareheaded, in a frieze overcoat girded low with a narrow belt of light blue. He looked, at first glance, like a house serf; his thick gray hair rose in a scarecrow shock over a gaunt and wrinkled face. He was calling somebody, hurriedly flailing his arms, which evidently were swinging far more widely than he himself wished them to. One could perceive that he had already found time for a drop or two.

"Come on—come on, now!" he began to babble, raising

his shaggy eyebrows with an effort. "Come on, Blinky, come on! What a man you are, brother; just creeping along, I must say. That's not right, brother. You're being waited for inside, but here you are, just creeping along. Come on!"

"There, I'm coming, I'm coming!" a jarring voice burst forth and a squat little man, stout and gimp-legged, appeared from around the corner of a hut to the right. He was wearing a quite neat short overcoat of broadcloth, with one arm through a sleeve and the other free; a tall conical cap, pulled down right over his eyebrows, added a sly and mocking expression to his round, plump face. His small yellow eyes were simply darting about; a restrained, forced smile never left his thin lips, while his nose, pointed and long, jutted out brazenly, like a rudder. "I'm coming, dear man," he spoke again, hobbling in the direction of the drinking establishment. "Why are you calling me? Who can be waiting for me?"

"Why am I calling you?" the man in the frieze overcoat echoed him reproachfully. "What a queer stick you are, brother Blinky; you're called for at the pothouse—but no, you've got to be asking why! Well, the folks waiting for you are all a good sort: Yashka the Turk, and the Wild Squire, and the Shopman from Zhizdra. Yashka, now, has made a bet with the Shopman—the stake is a pot of beer for whoever wins; whoever will sing better, that is. Understand?"

"Yashka is going to sing?" the man nicknamed Blinky asked with lively interest. "And you're not lying, Featherbrain?"

"I am not," Featherbrain replied with dignity, "but it's yourself that's shooting off your mouth, now. Sure he's going to sing, seeing as how he's laying a bet on it, you ladybug, Blinky, you scalawag, you!"

"Well, let's go, Simple-minded," Blinky countered.

"Why, give us a kiss at least, my soul," Featherbrain fell to babbling, flinging his arms wide.

"My, what a softhearted scarecrow!" Blinky retorted contemptuously, elbowing the other aside, and both, stooping a little, stepped through the rather low doorway.

The conversation I had overheard had greatly whetted my curiosity. Rumors that this Yashka the Turk was the best singer in the region had reached me before, more than once, and now an opportunity had suddenly presented itself of my hearing him in competition with another master-singer. I redoubled my pace and entered the drinking establishment.

Probably few of my readers have had occasion to drop in at village taverns—but as to us hunters, where won't we go! The layout of such places is exceedingly simple. It usually consists of a dark entry and a main room, divided in two by a partition, behind which none of the frequenters has any right to enter. This partition has a big wide opening, cut out above a broad oaken table. It is over this table, or bar, that the drinks are sold. Bottles of different sizes and bearing seals are ranged on shelves flanking the opening. In the fore part of the hut, given over to the frequenters, one can find benches, two or three empty kegs, a table in a corner. Village pothouses are, for the most part, quite dark, and hardly ever will you see upon their log walls any of those brightly colored chromos which very few huts can do without.

When I entered the Hunter's Rest a quite numerous company was already gathered there.

Behind the bar (which, as is usually the case, extended along the entire width of the opening) Nicholai Ivanych, in a calico shirt of many colors, was standing with a slight lazy smile crinkling his plump cheeks as he poured out with a chubby white hand two glasses of spirits for Blinky and Featherbrain, the two cronies who had just come in, while behind him, in a corner near a window, one could catch a glimpse of his sharp-eyed wife. Standing in the middle of the room was Yashka [Jake] the Turk, a thin and well-made fellow of twenty-three, dressed in a long-skirted caftan of blue nankeen. He looked like a dashing lad, a factory hand, and judging by his appearance, could hardly boast of being in excellent health. The sunken cheeks, the big, restless gray eyes, the straight nose with fine mobile nostrils, the white sloping brow revealed by the tossed-back light-ruddy locks, the lips, large yet handsome and expressive—his whole face indicated an impressionable and passionate nature. He was in a state of great excitement: he kept blinking, his breathing was uneven, his hands were shaking as in a fever. And, true enough, he was in a fever, that sudden fever of nervousness which is so familiar to all those who speak or sing before an audience.

235

Standing near him was a man of forty, broad of shoulder, broad of cheekbone, with a low brow, narrow Tatar eyes, a nose short and flat, a square chin, and black glossy hair as coarse as bristles. The expression of his face, a face swarthy, with a leaden tinge—especially the expression on his pallid lips—might have been called well-nigh ferocious, had that face not been so calmly pensive. He hardly stirred and merely looked about him slowly from time to time, like an ox from under a yoke. He was clad in some sort of much-worn surtout with smooth brass buttons; an old kerchief of black silk muffled his enormous neck. He was the one they called the Wild Squire.

Directly opposite him, on a bench under the holy images, sat Yashka's rival, the Shopman from Zhizdra: a robust man of thirty, not so very tall, pockmarked and curly-headed, with a nose both blunt and snub, animated eyes of a hazel hue, and a short scanty beard. He was looking about him briskly with his hands tucked in under him, chatting with never a care in the world and now and then tapping his feet, which were shod in dandified boots with fancy tops. He had on a new peasant overcoat, short, plush-collared, of fine gray broadcloth, from under which the tails of his scarlet shirt, tightly buttoned around the throat, stood out in sharp relief.

In the opposite corner, to the right of the door, sitting at a table, was some little muzhik or other in a tight threadbare Ukrainian overcoat with an enormous rent on one of the shoulders. The sunlight was streaming in in a tenuous yellow torrent through the dust-covered panes of the two small windows and, apparently, could not overcome the customary murkiness of the room: all the objects in it were lit niggardly, as if in blotches. But then it was almost cool in here, and the feeling of suffocation and sultriness fell off my shoulders just like an oppressive burden as soon as I crossed the threshold.

My arrival (I could notice this) at first embarrassed Nicholai Ivanych's guests to some extent but, on seeing him bow to me as to someone he knew, they were reassured and paid no further heed to me. I asked for beer and took my seat in a nook, next to the muzhik in the tattered overcoat.

"Well, what about it!" Featherbrain suddenly screeched, having tossed off his glass of spirits at one breath, and accompanied his outburst with those odd flailing gestures, something without which he evidently could not utter a single word. "What else are we going to wait for? If you're going to begin, then go ahead and begin. Eh, Yasha?"

"Begin, begin," Nicholai Ivanych chimed in approvingly.

"We can begin, if you like," the Shopman let drop with *sang-froid* and a self-assured smile. "I'm all set."

"And so am I," Yakov got out in agitation.

"Well, begin, lads—begin," Blinky urged in his squeaky voice.

Yet, despite this unanimously expressed wish, neither contestant would begin; the Shopman didn't even get up; all those present seemed to be waiting for something.

"Begin!" the Wild Squire let drop morosely and sharply.

Yakov was startled. The Shopman stood up, adjusted his belt, and cleared his throat.

"But who's to begin?" he asked in a slightly changed voice, addressing the Wild Squire who was standing motionlessly in the middle of the room, his thick legs wide apart and with his mighty hands thrust almost up to the elbows in the pockets of his extremely wide trousers, ballooning over the tops of his boots.

"You, Shopman—you!" Featherbrain began to babble. "You, brother!"

The Wild Squire gave him a look from under his brows. Featherbrain emitted a faint squeak, became flustered, looked at some indefinite spot on the ceiling, shrugged, and did not utter another word.

"Draw lots," the Wild Squire said with deliberation. "And put the pot of beer on the counter." Nicholai Ivanych bent down and, with a grunt, lifted a pot of beer up from the floor and placed it on the long table. "Well?" the Wild Squire let drop after giving Yakov a look.

Yakov started rummaging in his pockets, came up with a two-kopeck copper, and marked it with his teeth. The Shopman pulled a brand-new leather purse out from under the skirts of his caftan, untied the strings, taking his time about it, and, having poured out a lot of small change on his palm, picked out a copper, likewise a two-kopeck coin but one fresh from the mint. Featherbrain put down his greasy cap, its peak broken and dangling; Yakov tossed his coin in; the Shopman tossed in his.

"You'll pick out the coin," announced the Wild Squire, turning to Blinky.

Blinky gave a self-satisfied smirk, picked up the cap with both hands, and began shaking it. On the instant a profound silence fell: the coins clinked faintly. I looked about me attentively: all the faces expressed a strained expectancy; even the Wild Squire narrowed his eyes; my neighbor, the little muzhik in the torn coat—well, even he was craning his neck in curiosity. Blinky shoved his hand into the cap and took out the Shopman's coin: they all sighed in relief. Yakov turned red; the Shopman ran his hand over his hair.

"See, I told you so!" Featherbrain called out. "I sure told you so!"

"There, there, stop making a noise like a frightened hawk!" the Wild Squire remarked contemptuously. "Begin," he went on, nodding to the Shopman.

"But what song am I to sing?" asked the latter, becoming flustered.

"Whichever one you wish," answered Blinky. "Whichever one pops into your head, why, you just go ahead and sing it."

"Of course, let it be whichever song you wish," added Nicholai Ivanych, slowly crossing his arms on his chest. "Nobody's giving you orders about that. Sing whichever song you wish; the only thing is, sing it well; and as for us, we'll decide all fair and square."

"All fair and square, of course," chimed in Featherbrain and gave the rim of his empty glass a lick.

"Let me clear my throat a little, fellows," the Shopman spoke up, his fingers fiddling with the collar of his caftan.

"There, there, quit stalling! Begin!" the Wild Squire spoke with decision and fixed his eyes on the floor.

The Shopman pondered a little, gave his head a toss, and stepped forward. Yakov riveted his eyes upon him. . . .

However, before getting down to a description of the contest itself, I deem it not superfluous to say a few words about each of the *dramatis personae* in my story. The lives of some of them were already known to me at the time I met them at the Hunter's Rest; the data concerning the others I gathered later on.

Let us begin with Featherbrain. The man's real name was Eugraph Ivanov, but nobody anywhere in that locality ever called him anything but "Featherbrain," and he himself used that same nickname as if it were an honor, so closely had it come to cling to him. And, actually, nothing could have been more appropriate to his insignificant, perpetually agitated features. He was an unmarried house serf who had gotten entirely out of hand, whom his rightful owners had long since given up, and who, having no employment of any sort, receiving not a copper of wages, nonetheless found ways and means each day of enjoying a fling at somebody else's expense. He had a multitude of acquaintances who treated him to hard drink and tea without themselves knowing why they did so, inasmuch as he was not merely socially unamusing but, on the contrary, actually annoyed everybody with his senseless chatter, his unbearable importuning, feverish bodily movements, and incessant, unnatural laughter. He could neither sing nor dance; he hadn't, in all his born days, uttered one sensible word, let alone a witty one: he just kept on yammering away and telling whatever lies popped into his head—an out-and-out Featherbrain! And yet there wasn't a single drinking bout for twenty-five miles around which could possibly come off without his gangling figure's bobbing and weaving in and out among the guests— that's how accustomed all had become to him, enduring his presence as an ineluctable evil. True enough, they treated him with contempt; it was only the Wild Squire, however, who could subdue his ridiculous impulses.

Blinky did not resemble Featherbrain in the least. His sobriquet of "Blinky" was also suitable enough, even though he did not blink any more than others; but then, it is well known that the Russian folk are masters at dealing out nicknames. Despite my endeavors to find out the past of this man in greater detail, for me (and, probably, for others) his life has remained not without a number of dark spots, of passages shrouded (as bookmen put it) in the profound murk of the unknown. All I found out about him was that at one time he had been a coachman for a childless old grande dame, that he had run off with a team of three horses entrusted to him, had been lost sight of for all of a year, and, probably having become convinced by reality of the disadvantages of a vagabond's life, had come back of his own will, but lamed by now, had cast himself at the feet of his owner and, in the course of several years, having smoothed over his transgressions by his exemplary conduct, had little by little gotten into her good graces, had finally earned her complete confidence, becoming one of her clerks, and, upon the grande dame's death, it turned out (nobody knows in just what way) that he had been given his freedom; he enrolled himself among the burghers, took to leasing melon patches from his neighbors, grew rich, and was now living on the fat of the land. He was a man of experience who always kept Number One in mind, and was neither malicious nor kind but rather a shrewd article; a fellow who had been through the mill, this, who knew people and could use them to his advantage. He was as wary and, at the same time, as resourceful as a fox; he was as gabby as an old woman yet never let his tongue slip—but was far more likely and able to make everybody else spill everything to him. He didn't, however, play the little simpleton, as some other crafty fellows of his sort do—besides, it would have been actually hard for him to pretend: never had I seen more penetrating and intelligent eyes than his diminutive, cunning "peepers" (as the Orel folk call eyes, just as they call the mouth the "guzzler"). Those eyes never looked at you just so—they were always looking around and about, always spying things out.

At times Blinky would spend weeks on end thinking over some apparently simple undertaking; on the other hand, he would come to a sudden decision on some desperately bold scheme: there, you might think, that's where he's bound to come a cropper. But lo and behold!—everything went off well, slick as slick. He was lucky, and he believed in his luck, believed in omens. He was, as a general thing, exceedingly superstitious. He wasn't liked, because he himself wasn't concerned about anybody, but he was respected. His whole family consisted of but one little son whom he loved more than his soul and who, brought up by such a father, would probably go far. "Why, little Blinky sure takes after his father," the codgers were saying about him even now in low voices as they sat on the ledges in front of their huts of summer evenings and discussed things amongst themselves, and everybody understood what was meant by this and nobody needed to add another word.

When it comes to Yakov the Turk and the Shopman, there is no great need of describing them at any great length. Yakov, nicknamed the Turk because he actually was the offspring of a captured Turkish woman, was, at soul, an artist in every sense of the word, while by calling he was a dipper in a certain merchant's paper factory. As to the Shopman, whose further fate, I confess, has remained unknown to me, he struck me as a city slicker, spry and full of dodges.

But as to the Wild Squire, he deserves being discussed in somewhat greater detail. The first impression which the appearance of this man aroused in one was a sense of some coarse, oppressive yet irresistible power. He was clumsily built—"slapped together," as they say among us—but he simply exuded insuperable health and (a strange thing!) his rather bearlike figure was not devoid of a certain grace all its own, springing, it may be, from an utterly placid confidence in his own might. It was hard to decide at first to what class this Hercules belonged; he did not look like a house serf, nor a burgher, nor an impoverished clerk in retirement, nor a small-propertied, ruined nobleman—a dog lover and a brawler: he was, verily, *sui generis*. Nobody knew whence he had tumbled into our district; it was said that by origin he was a freeholder, or petty squire, and that, apparently, he had formerly been in the civil service somewhere; however, nothing positive was known about that —and besides, whom could you learn all that from? Not from himself, surely: there never was a body more taciturn and morose. In the same way, nobody could have said positively what he lived on; he followed no trade, never called on anybody, had almost no associates, yet he did have money—not a great deal, it's true, but still he did have some.

His conduct wasn't what one might call modest—there was, in general, nothing of the modest about him—but calm, rather; he lived as though he did not notice anyone about him and had absolutely no need of anyone. The Wild Squire (thus had they nicknamed him; his real name, however, was Perevlessov) exerted an enormous influence throughout the region; he was obeyed at once and willingly, even though he not only had no right whatsoever to give any orders to anybody at all, but even himself did not evince the least claim to the obedience of the people he chanced to come in contact with. He spoke—they submitted to him: strength will always have its way. He drank hardly any spirits, kept away from women, and had a passionate love of singing. There was much that was enigmatic about this man; certain tremendous forces were, it seemed, in somber repose within him, as though aware that once they had become aroused, once they had broken free, they would be bound to destroy both themselves and everything they touched—and I am grievously mistaken if some such eruption had not already taken place in this man's life—if, having learned a lesson from experience and having barely saved himself from perdition, he was not now inexorably keeping an iron grip on himself. I was especially struck by the mixture in him of some innate, natural ferocity and a nobility likewise innate: a mixture which I had never come across in anyone else.

And so, the Shopman stepped forward, half-closed his eyes, and began singing in the highest of falsettos. His voice was quite pleasant and sweet, even though somewhat husky; he toyed with this voice and made it waver like a humming top, continually going off into trills and descending runs, but continually reverting to the higher notes, which he took particular pains to sustain and prolong; he would fall silent and then suddenly pick up the preceding tune with some sort of devil-may-care, chip-on-the-shoulder bravado. His transitions were at times quite daring, at others quite amusing: to a connoisseur they would have given great pleasure, while a German would have been moved to indignation by them. Here was a Russian *tenore di grazia*, a *ténor léger*. The song he was singing was a lilting one, its air meant to be danced to; its words, as far as I could catch them through the endless grace notes and added consonants and interjections, were:

> For thee, fair young maid,
> A small patch I'll plow;
> For thee, fair young maid,
> Poppies red I'll sow. . . .

He sang; they were all listening to him with great attentiveness. He evidently sensed that he had to do with folks who knew what good singing was, and for that reason he was, as they say, doing his darnedest. And truly, the folks in our parts do know what's what when it comes to singing, and it's not in vain that the settlement of Serghievskoe, which lies close to the Orel highroad, is celebrated all over Russia for its particularly delightful and harmonious melody making.

For long did the Shopman sing without arousing too great a response from his auditors; he lacked the support of a chorus. At last, during one especially successful transitional

242

passage, which compelled even the Wild Squire himself to smile a little, Featherbrain couldn't keep himself back any longer and let out a cry of pleasure. Everybody perked up. Featherbrain and Blinky began to chime in, *sotto voce,* helping the singer along, giving occasional shouts of encouragement: "Great! Hit that note, you hoss thief! Hit that note, draw it out, you varmint! Draw it out some more! Keep it up—more, more, you dog you, you hound! Damn your body and soul!" And more in the same vein.

Nicholai Ivanych, behind the bar, took to swaying his head right and left in approval. Featherbrain, at last, started in stamping and mincing, with one shoulder twitching; as to Yakov, his eyes burst into a glow, for all the world like live embers; he trembled all over, like a leaf; and his smile was distraught. The Wild Squire alone had not changed countenance and, as before, did not stir from one spot, but his gaze, fixed upon the Shopman, had softened somewhat, although the expression on his face was still disdainful.

Encouraged by these marks of general gratification the Shopman let himself out to the full in a very whirlwind of sounds, and by now had launched into such well-turned flourishes, such chopping and drumming effects produced by the tongue, putting his throat into such frenzied play, that when at last, worn out, pale, and bathed in hot perspiration, throwing his whole body back, he released his final, swooning note, they all responded to him in a frenzied outburst, their shouts blending into one. Featherbrain threw himself upon the Shopman's neck and fell to crushing him with his long bony arms; color appeared on the fleshy face of Nicholai Ivanych, and he seemed to have become rejuvenated. "Good lad, good lad!" Yakov was shouting as if he had gone mad; even my neighbor, the muzhik in the tattered overcoat, could not hold out and, thumping his fist on the table, cried out: "A-ha! That was great, Devil take it—that was great!" and spat aside to clinch the declaration.

"Well, brother, you sure have pleasured us!" Featherbrain kept shouting without letting the exhausted Shopman out of his clutches. "You've pleasured us, I must say! You've won, brother, you've won! I congratulate you, the pot of beer is yours. Yashka will have to go some to catch up with you. He'll have to go some, I'm telling you—you just take my word for it!" And he again hugged the Shopman to his breast.

"There, let go of him, let go, you she-gadfly," Blinky put in with vexation. "Give him a chance to sit down on the bench; you can see he's all in! What a horse's tail you are, brother—a horse's tail for sure! What are you sticking so close to him for, like a birch leaf off a steambath besom?"

"Oh, well, let him sit down; me, I'll drink to his health," said Featherbrain, and he walked up to the bar. "At your expense, brother," he added, turning to the Shopman.

The other nodded, sat down on the bench, got a cloth out of his cap, and fell to toweling his face, while Featherbrain with hasty avidity drained his glass and, after the manner of all hopeless topers, assumed, as he gave a grunt, an expression of carking care.

"You sing well, brother, you sing well," Nicholai Ivanych commented in a kindly tone. "And now it's your turn, Yasha; watch out—don't lose heart. We'll see who will beat whom; we'll see. But the Shopman does sing well—he sings well, by God."

"Ve-ery well," remarked Nicholai Ivanych's wife, and she gave Yakov a smiling look.

"He sings well, ha!" my neighbor repeated in an undertone.

"Ah, a turn-aside Poleha!"[1] Featherbrain suddenly screamed and, walking up to the little muzhik with the tear on his shoulder, stuck out his finger at him, started hopping about, and went off into peals of cracked laughter. "Poleha! Poleha! Ha, be ye driving on, Turn-aside? What have you come here for, Turn-aside?" he kept shouting through his laughter. The poor muzhik was all rattled and was just about to get up when suddenly the voice of the Wild Squire rang out, as clangorous as copper:

"Why, what sort of an unbearable animal is this?" he uttered, gnashing his teeth.

"I don't mean any harm," Featherbrain started mumbling. "I don't mean any harm; I was just—"

"Well, all right—keep still, then!" the Wild Squire retorted. "Begin, Yakov!"

---

[1] A name bestowed upon the inhabitants of southern Polessie, a long belt of forests which begins on the boundary of the Bolhov and Zhizdra districts. These peasants are distinguished by many peculiarities in their way of life, their manners and speech. They are called "turn-asides" because of their suspicious and harsh nature. Polehas add the exclamations of "Ha!" and "Be ye!" to almost every word.—*Author.*

Yakov put his hand to his throat: "Don't feel right, some-how, brother . . . hm! I don't know, really, something's not quite right, now—"

"There, that'll do. Don't lose heart. You ought to be ashamed of yourself! What are you backing water for? Sing as God wills you to sing." And the Wild Squire cast down his eyes, waiting.

Yakov kept silent a while, looked about him, and put his hand over his face. They all seemed to rivet their eyes upon him, particularly the Shopman, on whose face, through his habitual self-assurance and the triumph of his success, there emerged an involuntary, faint uneasiness. He snuggled back against the wall and again tucked his hands in under him, but he was no longer dangling his legs. And when Yakov uncovered his face at last it was as pale as that of a dead man; his eyes were barely gleaming through their lowered lashes. He sighed deeply and launched into song. . . . The first sound of his voice was faint and uneven and, it seemed, was issuing not out of his breast but had come wafting from afar, as though it had fluttered into the room by chance. A strange effect did this quavering, ringing sound have upon all of us; we looked at one another, while Nicholai Ivanych's wife actually drew herself up.

This first sound was followed by another, firmer and more prolonged, but still obviously as vibrant as a string when, after suddenly sounding at the plucking of a strong finger, it throbs in a final, rapidly expiring throb; the third sound followed and, gaining fire and expanding little by little, there poured forth a despondent song. " 'There was more than one little path leading through the field,' " he sang, and all of us felt ourselves being overcome by a delectable and un-canny feeling. Rarely, I confess, have I chanced to hear such a voice; it was a little overworked, and it rang as if it were slightly cracked; at first it even had a hint of something painful about it, yet there were in it, as well, an uncounter-feited, profound passion, and youth, and strength, and sweet-ness, and some sort of enticingly heedless sorrowing. A Rus-sian soul, true and ardent, sounded and breathed in it, and simply plucked at your heart, plucked right at its Russian chords. The song grew, spread like a flood of waters. Yakov was falling into a transport before our eyes; he no longer felt timid, he was giving himself up wholly to his happiness; his voice was no longer quavering—it was tremulous, but

245

only with that barely perceptible inner tremor of passion which plunges like an arrow into the soul of him who hears it, and was growing ever stronger, firmer, and expanding more and more. I remember once seeing, at evening, as the tide was ebbing on the flat sandy shore of a sea that was awesomely and deeply surging in the distance, a great white gull; it sat without stirring, offering its silky breast to the crimson of the evening glow, and only at infrequent intervals would it spread out its long wings in greeting to the sea it knew so well, to the low, deep-red sun: I recalled this as I listened to Yakov.

He sang, having utterly forgotten not only his rival but all of us, yet evidently buoyed up, like a vigorous swimmer by the waves, by our silent, passionate sympathy. He sang, and from every sound of his voice there was wafted something near and dear and unencompassably vast, as though the familiar steppe were unrolling before us, receding into the infinite distance. Tears, I felt, were seething in my heart and welling up in my eyes. I was suddenly struck by the sound of deep, restrained sobs and looked over my shoulder: the tavern keeper's wife was weeping, her bosom pressed against the window. Yakov threw a quick look at her and went off into trills still more ringing, still more delectable. Nicholai Ivanych cast down his eyes; Blinky had turned his face away; Featherbrain, all unnerved, stood with his mouth gaping; the drab little muzhik was softly sniveling in his corner, swaying his head as he grieved in a whisper, and down the iron face of the Wild Squire, from under brows that were now absolutely beetling, a heavy teardrop coursed slowly; the Shopman had brought a hard-clenched fist up to his brow and sat without stirring. . . .

I have no idea just how the general tension would have been broken if Yakov had not ended abruptly on a high, extraordinarily shrill sound—as though his voice had snapped. No one cried out nor as much as stirred; it was as though all were awaiting whether he would go on singing; but he opened his eyes, as though struck by our silence, ran them with a questioning look over all those there, and saw that the victory was his.

"Yasha," uttered the Wild Squire, placed his hand on the singer's shoulder—and fell silent.

We were all standing as if transfixed. The Shopman quietly got up and walked over to Yakov: "You . . . you've won.

The victory is yours," he at last managed to say, not without difficulty, and dashed out of the room.

His rapid, decisive move seemed to disrupt the spell; everybody quickly broke into noisy, joyous talk. Feather-brain bounded up, started babbling, brandishing his arms like the wings of a mill; Blinky hobbled up to Yakov and fell to kissing him; Nicholai Ivanych raised himself a little from his seat and solemnly announced that there would be another pot of beer, on the house; the Wild Squire laughed now and then, and his laughter was somehow good-natured, something which I had not at all expected to see on his face; the drab little muzhik in his corner kept reiterating, every so often, mopping his eyes, cheeks, nose, and beard with both his sleeves: "My, but that was fine; it was fine, by God; there, I'll be a son of a dog, but it was fine!"— while Nicholai Ivanych's wife, all flushed by now, got up and quickly withdrew. Yakov was as delighted as a child with his triumph; his whole face had become transfigured: his eyes especially—they had burst into a downright glow from happiness.

They dragged him toward the bar; he called the drab little muzhik to come over, too, and sent a little son of the tavern keeper's to fetch the Shopman (the little boy failed to find him, however), and the revel began.

"You'll sing for us again—you'll sing for us until evening," Featherbrain kept on saying, raising his hands high.

I took one more look at Yakov and went out. I did not want to remain. I was afraid of spoiling my impression. But the sultriness was as unbearable as ever. It seemed to be hanging right over the ground in a dense, heavy layer; against the deep-blue sky certain radiant small flames were apparently swirling through the exceedingly fine dust, which was almost black. Silence brooded over all things; there was something hopeless, crushed, in this profound silence of ex-hausted nature. I managed to make my way to a hayloft and lay down on the new-mown yet already dried grass. For a long while I could not doze off; for a long while did the irresistible voice of Yakov keep sounding in my ears. At last, however, heat and fatigue had their way and I fell dead asleep.

When I awoke everything had already grown dark; the cut grass tedded all around gave off a strong scent and had become just a trifle damp; through the thin rafters of the half-open roof small wan stars were faintly twinkling. I went out. The evening glow had long since died out, and the last trace of it showed only as a barely discernible whitishness on the horizon, but in the air, so recently incandescent, one could still feel warmth through the night freshness, and one's breast still yearned after a breath of coolness. There was no wind, nor were there any clouds; the sky all around remained absolutely clear and transparently dark, softly aglimmer with countless yet barely perceptible stars. The village was dotted with little flickering dots; from the pothouse, not far off and brightly lit, there was borne a discordant, indistinct din, amid which (so I thought) I could recognize Yakov's voice. Now and then furious laughter sprang up there, in gusts.

I walked up to one of the small windows and put my face against a pane. The tableau I saw was not at all gay, even though it was motley and animated enough. All those within were drunk—all of them, beginning with Yakov. He was seated on a bench with his breast bared and, as he softly sang in a husky voice some street catch with a lilting air, was listlessly fingering and plucking the strings of a guitar. His damp hair came down in tufts over his face, which had turned frightfully pale by now. Featherbrain, "higher than a kite" and without his caftan, was dancing in the middle of the pothouse, trying to outleap the muzhik in the drab overcoat, while the muzhik in his turn was having a hard time just stomping and scraping his logy feet, and, as he smiled senselessly through his rumpled beard, would wave his hand every now and then, as if to say: "Eh, come what may!" Nothing could have been more mirth-provoking than his face: no matter how he strove to twitch his brows upward, the lids, grown heavy, would not go up but just drooped over the small eyes, barely visible, drink-sodden yet cloyingly sweet. He was in that appealing state when a man is three sheets in the wind and every passerby, after a glance at his face, is bound to say: "You're all right, brother, you're all right!" Blinky, all as red as a lobster and with his nostrils distended, was caustically grinning from time to time in his corner; Nicholai Ivanych alone, even as befits a true tapster, preserved his never-changing *sang-froid*. Many new faces had gathered in the room, but I did not see the Wild Squire there.

I turned away and with rapid steps began going down the knoll upon which Kolotovka lies. A broad plain spreads at the foot of this knoll; flooded with the murky billows of the evening mist it seemed still more unencompassable and blended, as it were, with the darkened sky. I was descending with great strides over the road along the ravine, when suddenly, from somewhere far off on the plain, a boy's voice rang out:

"Antropka! Antropka!" he kept shouting in stubborn and weepy desperation, drawing the last syllable out for ever so long.

He would fall silent for a few moments and then start shouting anew. His voice rang and spread through the still, lightly slumbering air. Thirty times at least had he shouted Antropka's name when unexpectedly, from the opposite end of the meadow, as though from the other world, there came floating a barely audible response:

"Wha-a-at is it?"

The boy's voice was immediately raised in gleeful malice:

"Come here, you devil—you crazy loo-oo-oo-oon!"

"Wha-a-at for?" the other shouted back after a long interval.

" 'Cause daddy wants to beat the daylights out of you!" the first voice shouted hastily, drawing out the last word inordinately.

The second voice made no further response, and the boy again took to calling this Antropka. His outcries, becoming ever less frequent and sounding fainter and fainter, still came floating to my ears when it had grown altogether dark and I was turning the edge of the forest which surrounded my little village and which was situated at a distance of three miles or so from Kolotovka.

"Antropka-a-a!" I thought I could still hear floating in the air, now thronged with the shadows of night.

PETER PETROVICH KARATAEV

FIVE YEARS AGO or thereabouts, in the autumn, on the way from Moscow to Tula, I happened to get stuck for almost all of a day at a posting station, owing to a shortage of horses. I was returning from a hunting trip, and had been careless enough to send my team of three horses ahead. The stationmaster, a man of advanced years, morose, with hair hanging down over his very nose, his small eyes sleepy, replied to all my complaints and requests by abrupt grumbling, slammed the door in hearty vexation, as though he himself were cursing his job, and, stepping out on the front porch, upbraided the drivers who were plodding through the mud with thirty-pound horse collars in their arms, or lolling on benches, intermittently yawning and scratching themselves and not paying any particular heed to the wrathful outbursts of their superior. I had already sat down to tea three times; several times I had made vain attempts to doze off; I had read all the graffiti on the windows and walls; I was languishing under frightful boredom. I was regarding the uplifted shafts of my tarantass with a cold and hopeless despair when suddenly there came the tinkle of a jingle bell, and a small cart, drawn by a team of three exhausted horses, stopped before the front steps.

The new arrival leaped down from the cart and, after shouting, "Horses, and be lively about it!" entered the room. While he was listening with the usual amazement to the

stationmaster's answer that there weren't any horses avail-
able, I contrived, with all the eager inquisitiveness of a
bored man, to look my new companion over from head to
foot. He was under thirty, by the looks of him. Smallpox
had left indelible traces on his face, gaunt and yellowish,
with an unpleasant coppery tinge; his long hair, so black
that it had a bluish sheen, was coiling over the back of his
collar, and curled raffishly at the temples; his small, puffy
eyes were just for seeing with and nothing more; a few short
hairs bristled on his upper lip. His dress was that of an arrant squire, a frequenter of horse fairs: a loud, quite greasy
Caucasian overcoat, a faded silk cravat of lilac hue, a waistcoat with brass buttons, and gray, enormously belled trousers, from under which the tips of his unshined boots barely
peeped out. He emitted an overpowering reek of tobacco
and vodka; upon his red and thick fingers, almost hidden
by the sleeves of his overcoat, one could see rings of silver
and brummagem. Such figures are to be met with in our
Russia not by the dozen but in their hundreds; acquaintance
with them doesn't, one must truthfully say, afford any gratification whatsoever, but, despite the prejudice with which I
contemplated the newcomer, I could not help noticing the
lackadaisically kind and passionate expression of his face.

"There, this gentleman is also waiting here more than an
hour, sir," remarked the stationmaster, pointing me out.
More than an hour! The villain was deriding me.

"Yes, but perhaps he's not as hard-pressed as I am," retorted the new arrival.

"That, now, is something we have no means of knowing,
sir," the stationmaster said morosely.

"Is there absolutely no way you can manage it, then? Are
there no horses whatsoever?"

"There's no way, sir. Not a single horse to be had."

"Well, in that case, order a samovar for me. We'll wait a
while—there's no help for it." The newcomer seated himself
on a bench, tossed his cap on the table, and passed a hand
over his hair. "I say, have you already had tea?" he asked
me.

"I have."

"But would you care for some again, to keep me company?"

I agreed. The stout, ruddy samovar appeared on the table
for the fourth time. I got out a bottle of rum. I hadn't erred

in taking my companion for a backwoods squire. His name was Peter Petrovich Karataev.

We got to talking. Not even half an hour had passed since his arrival when, with the most kindhearted frankness, he was telling me the story of his life.

"I'm on my way to Moscow, now," he informed me as he was finishing his fourth glass. "There's no longer anything for me to do in the village."

"But why isn't there?"

"Well, there just isn't—nothing at all. The property has gone all to pieces; I've ruined the peasants, I must confess; we've had bad years lately—crop failures, all sorts of calamities, don't you know. . . . But then," he added, looking off to one side despondently, "what sort of a property owner am I!"

"But why not?"

"Come, now!" he cut me short. "Are property owners anything like me? You see, now," he went on, twisting his head to one side and assiduously sucking away at his pipe, "looking at me just so you might think that I really may be somebody—and yet, I must confess, I received but a middling education: hadn't means enough. You must forgive me; I'm a frank person and, after all—" he didn't finish his speech and gestured hopelessly with his hand. I fell to assuring him that he was mistaken, that I was very glad we had met and so on, after which I remarked that, apparently, one didn't need overmuch education to run an estate.

"I agree," he replied. "I agree with you. But still, one does need a special inclination of that sort. There are some who do God knows what and it doesn't matter! But I . . . Permit me to inquire: are you yourself from Peter's town, or from Moscow?"

"I am from Petersburg."

He let out a long stream of smoke through his nostrils:

"Well, I'm heading for Moscow to get into the civil service."

"What position have you got in mind?"

"I don't rightly know—whatever may turn up. I'm afraid of the service, I confess: like as not one may be held to account for something. I've been living in the village all the time, have gotten used to it, you know. But there's no help for it—need is driving me! Oh, what that need is doing to me!"

"You'll be living in the capital, at any rate."

"The capital . . . well, I don't know what's so good there, in the capital. We'll see; perhaps things are good there, actually. And yet it seems there really couldn't be anything better than living in the village."

"Really, is it impossible for you to live in the village any longer?"

He sighed. "It's impossible. It's not even mine by now, you might say."

"Why, how is that?"

"Well, there's a certain kind soul sprung up there, a neighbor. . . . Matter of a promissory note—" Poor Peter Petrovich passed a hand over his face, mused a while, and tossed his head. "Oh well, what's the use! And, I confess," he added after a brief silence, "I have nobody to blame—it's my own fault. I loved to put up a brave front. I do love putting up a brave front, the Devil take it!"

"Did you have a good time in the country?" I asked him.

"Sir," he replied, speaking deliberately and looking me straight in the eye, "I owned twelve leashes of coursing hounds, such hounds, I tell you, as there aren't many of." The last phrase he got out in singsong. "If it came to a gray hare they would run it down right off, and if it were a red deer they'd be as vicious as snakes—downright serpents, they were. And I could have boasted of my wolfhounds, too. It's all over and done with now. There's no reason for lying. I went gunning, as well. I had a clever bitch, Countess; she was extraordinary as a pointer, never failed when it came to scenting game, just tops. There were times I'd come to a bog and tell her 'Cherchez!' Well, if she didn't bother searching, were you to go through there with a dozen dogs you wouldn't flush a thing—you'd be just wasting your time. But if she did make a stand she'd gladly die without stirring from the spot, so she would! And ever so well-behaved in the house, she was. Offer her bread with your left hand and say: 'A Jew ate of it,' why, she wouldn't take it, mind you; but offer it to her with your right and say: 'A young lady ate of it,' she'd take the morsel right off and eat it up. I had one of her puppies and wanted to bring it along to Moscow, but a friend of mine begged me hard to give it to him, together with my gun. 'Brother,' said he, 'in Moscow you'll have other things on your mind; there an altogether different life will begin, brother.' And so I gave him the puppy, and the gun as well—all that sort of thing was left behind back there, you know."

"Why, you would have been able to hunt in Moscow as well."

"No, really, what's the use? I wasn't able to hold onto my place, so now I'll have to take whatever comes along. But there, it would be better if you'd be kind enough to inform me—does living come high in Moscow?"

"No, it's not too high."

"Not too high? But tell me, please—there are Gypsies living in Moscow, aren't there?"

"What Gypsies?"

"Why, those that go about the fairs."

"Yes, you'll find them in Moscow."

"Well, that's fine. I love the Gypsies, the Devil take it—I love them," and a sparkle of dashing gaiety appeared in Peter Petrovich's eyes. However, he suddenly took to fidgeting on his bench, then grew thoughtful, let his head sink, and held his empty tumbler out to me.

"Let's have some of your rum," said he.

"Why, there's no more tea."

"No matter; let me have it plain, without any tea. Eh!"

Karataev placed his arms on the table and laid his head on them. I gazed at him in silence and was, by now, expecting those sentimental exclamations—even, if you like, those tears—which a befuddled fellow is so generous with; but when he raised his head I was, I confess, struck by the profoundly sorrowful expression on his face.

"What's the matter with you?"

"Nothing, sir. Just happened to think of old times. An old story, sort of. I'd tell you, but then I feel ashamed about annoying you—"

"Not at all!"

"Yes," he went on with a sigh, "strange things do happen —take my own case, for instance. There, I'll tell it to you, if you like. However, I don't know—"

"Do tell it, my dear Peter Petrovich!"

"If you like, then. And so, in a manner of speaking, here's what happened to me. I was living in a village, sir. Then, quite unexpectedly, a certain girl took my eye—ah, and what a girl she was! A beauty, clever, and how kind, too! Matrena, they called her. However, she was just an ordinary wench—that is, you understand, a serf, a country girl. And

a wench that belonged not to me but to another owner—
that was just the rub. Well, then, I fell in love with her—
such an odd thing to happen, sir, really—and, of course,
she fell in love with me. And so Matrena began begging me
to buy her freedom. I was to buy her freedom from her mistress, now. Besides, I myself was turning the thing over in
my mind. And her mistress, now, was rich, a dreadful old
curmudgeon; she lived about ten miles away from me. Well
then, one fine day, as they put it, I up and gave orders to
harness a team of three to a droshky—for the shaft horse I
had a thorough-paced animal, an extraordinary brute, which
was just why he was called Lampurdos. I dressed myself in
my best and rode off to Matrena's mistress.

"I drove up—it was a great house, with wings and a garden. Matrena was waiting for me at a turn of the road; she
was about to say something to me, but merely kissed my
hand and stepped aside. Well, I came into the entry and
asked if the lady of the house was at home. And the flunky,
such a tall fellow he was, said: 'How shall I announce you?'
I said to him: 'You can announce, brother, that Karataev
the landowner, now, has come to talk over a business matter.' The flunky walked off; I waited there and kept thinking: 'What's going to happen? Guess she'll jack up the price
frightfully, the beast, for all that she's rich. She'll ask five
hundred rubles, like as not.' Well, the flunky came back at last
and said: 'This way, please.'

"I followed him into the reception room. There I saw a
tiny, yellow-skinned crone, sitting in an easy chair, blinking
her eyes.

" 'What is it you wish?'

"First off, you know, I considered it necessary to let her
know I was glad to make her acquaintance.

" 'You're in error—I'm not the lady of the house but a
relation of hers. What is it you wish?'

"Here I remarked that it was precisely with the mistress
that I had to talk matters over.

" 'Maria Iliyinichna is not receiving today; she's not feeling well. What is it you wish?'

"There was no help for it, said I to myself. I explained
to her the situation I was in. The old woman heard me out.

" 'Matrena? What Matrena?'

" 'Matrena Theodorova, Kulikov's daughter.'

" 'Theodore Kulik's daughter—why, how do you happen to know her?'

" 'Just by chance.'

" 'And is your intention known to her?'

" 'It is.'

"The old woman fell silent. Then:

" 'Why, I'll take that good-for-nothing and—'

"I confess I was astonished.

" 'But why, if you please? I'm ready to pay a sum for her—if you'll just be kind enough to state it.'

"The old shrew simply hissed at this.

" 'There, you've certainly struck on something to astonish us with. We have such great need of your money! But I'll certainly fix her—I certainly will! I'll knock the foolishness out of her.' The old woman went into a coughing spell from malice. 'Don't things suit her here, or what? Ah, but she's a she-devil, may the Lord forgive me for sinning with that name!'

"I flared up, I confess: 'Why do you threaten the poor wench? Really, just how is she at fault?'

"The old woman crossed herself: 'Ah, Thou my Lord, Jesus Christ! Why, am I not free to do what I will with my own serfs?'

" 'Why, she doesn't belong to you!'

" 'Well, now, that's something which is up to Maria Iliyi-nichna; it's none of your affair, father of mine. But as for this Matreshka, now, I'm going to show her whose serf she is.'

"I almost threw myself at the cursed old woman, I confess, but I bethought me of Matrena and my arms sagged. I can't tell you how frightened I became; I fell to persuading the old woman: she could take whatever she liked for the girl, now.

" 'But what do you want with her?'

" 'She's proven to my liking, mother; do consider my situation. . . . Permit me to kiss your hand,' and I actually did kiss the old wretch's hand!

" 'Well,' the witch mumbled toothlessly, 'I'll tell Maria Iliyinichna; it'll be as she wills. As for you, drop in in a couple of days.'

"I left in great disquiet. I was beginning to surmise that I had started off on the wrong foot, had uselessly let them perceive how I felt—but I had caught on too late.

"Two days later I set out to see the grand lady. I was

shown into her study. A profusion of flowers, excellent furnishings, and herself sitting in some sort of a fancy easy chair with her head thrown back and lolling against cushions. And the kinswoman I'd met before was also sitting right there, as well as some miss or other, almost an albino, in a green dress, with a crooked mouth—a companion, she must have been.

" 'Pray be seated,' said the old woman, sort of snuffling.

"I sat down. She began questioning me: How old was I, and where had I served, and what did I intend to do, and all this so high and mighty, with an important air. I answered in detail. The old woman picked up a handkerchief off a table and fanned herself with it, and then fanned herself some more.

" 'Katherina Karpovna has informed me of your intention,' said she. 'She has informed me; but,' she said, 'I've laid it down as a rule for myself not to release any people of mine for service. It is not only unseemly but impractical in a decent household: it's quite irregular. I've already issued instructions,' said she. 'It's no use your putting yourself out any further.'

" 'How would I be putting myself out, if you please? But, perhaps, you have need of Matrena Theodorovna?'

" 'No,' said she, 'I haven't.'

" 'Then why don't you want to let me have her?'

" 'Because it doesn't suit me to do so—it doesn't suit me, and that's all there is to it. I've already issued instructions: she's being sent to a village out on the steppe.'

"It was just as though a thunderbolt had struck me. The old woman said a couple of words in French to the young lady in green: the latter left the room.

" 'I,' she went on, 'am a woman of strict principles, and besides my health is weak. I can't bear any excitement. You're still a young man, whereas I am an old woman and have the right to give you advice. Wouldn't it be better for you to settle down, to marry—look around for a good match: rich brides are scarce, but one can find a girl who is poor yet of good morals.'

"You know, I stared at that old woman and couldn't make out a thing she was jabbering about. I heard her talking about getting married, but what she had said about a village out in the steppe kept ringing in my ears. Getting married! What the devil!"

At this point the narrator came to an abrupt stop and gave me a look: "You're not married, are you?"

"No."

"Well, of course, you know how things are. I couldn't hold myself in: 'Oh, if you please, mother of mine—what sort of bosh are you spouting? What's all this about getting married? I simply want to find out from you, are you willing to let your wench Matrena go or not?'

"The old woman started in oh'ing:

" 'Oh, he's upset me! Oh, order him to go away! Oh!'

"Her kinswoman jumped up and ran over to her and began yelling at me. And the old woman never left off moaning: 'What have I done to deserve this? This means, then, that I'm no longer mistress in my own house? Oh, oh!'

"I grabbed my hat and dashed out as if I were crazy.

"Perhaps," the narrator went on, "you may condemn me for having become so strongly attached to a girl of low estate, and really, I have no intention of justifying myself. That's the way things fell out. Would you believe it, I had no rest either day or night. . . . I was in torment! Why, I kept thinking, have I sent the poor wench to perdition? I would break into cold sweat every time I recalled that she was tending geese, going around in a peasant's overcoat, and that at her owner's orders life was made as wretched for her as possible, while the village elder, a lout in tarred boots, was cursing her out with the vilest curses. Well, I couldn't hold out: I found out what village she had been sent to, got on a horse, and rode there. Got there only the next day, toward evening. Evidently they hadn't expected any such low-down trick on my part and had issued no order concerning me. I went straight to the elder, as though I were just a neighbor. I stepped into the yard, and what do I see but Matrena, sitting on a porch, with her head sunk on her hand. She was just about to cry out but I shook my finger at her and pointed out of the gate, to a field beyond the yard. I entered the hut, gabbed a while with the elder, told him a devilish pack of lies, and then, biding the right moment, came out to where Matrena was waiting. She simply threw herself on my neck, the poor little thing. She, my little dove, had lost color, had grown thin.

"I told her, don't you know: 'It's nothing, Matrena; it's nothing, don't cry,' yet at the same time the tears kept running and running from my own eyes. Well, anyway, I myself became ashamed at last: 'Matrena,' I told her, 'tears won't help the fix we're in any, but here's what: we've got to act decisively, as they say. You'll have to run off with me—that's what we'll have to do.'

"Matrena was simply stunned: 'How can that be! Why, I'll be done for—why, they'll eat me up alive, for good and all!' — 'Foolish girl, who'll ever find you?' — 'They'll find me, they'll find me without fail. Thank you, Peter Petrovich. I'll never forget your kindness, but you'd better give me up now: that's my fate, it looks like.' — 'Eh, Matrena, Matrena, but I figured you were a wench of spirit.' And, true enough, spirit she had aplenty. She was a soul, a soul of gold! 'What's the use of your staying on here? It's all one—things can't be any worse. There, tell me, now: you've had a taste of the elder's fists, haven't you?'

"Matrena simply flared up, and her lips began to quiver: 'Why, because of me life will be made unbearable for my family.' — 'Oh, the deuce with your family! Are they going to put it out of the village, or what?' — 'They will put it out. My brother for one, sure enough.' — 'And your father?' — 'Well, they won't put my father out of the village; he's the only good tailor they've got.' — 'There, you see? As for your brother, he won't be ruined because of this.'

"Would you believe it, it was all I could do to talk her over; she also got the notion of arguing that I, now, would be held to answer for all this. 'Well,' I told her, 'that's something which really doesn't concern you.' In the end, however, I carried her off—not this time but another: I came with a cart, at night, and carried her off."

"You carried her off?"

"I did that. Well, then, she came to live at my place. My house wasn't large; there weren't many servants. My serfs, I must tell you without any ifs or buts, respected me; they wouldn't have betrayed me for any considerations. I began to lead a merry life. Matrenushka rested up, got her health back; well, then, I became attached to her. And what a wench she was! Where did she get all her cleverness from? Why, she knew how to sing, and dance, and play the guitar. I wouldn't let my neighbors see her: like as not they would have blabbed. But I did have one bosom friend, Gornostaev, Pantelei. Do you know him, by any chance? He simply lost his heart to her; really, he used to kiss her hands, just as if she were a highborn lady. And Gornostaev, let me tell you, was nothing like me: he was an educated man, had read all of Pushkin; when he'd get to talking with Matrena and me we'd listen with all our ears. He taught her to write. What a queer stick he was! And how I used to dress her up—far better than any governor's lady. I had a short coat made for her, of raspberry-hued velvet and hemmed with fur. And did that coat sit well on her! A high-class Moscow dressmaker made it, narrow at the waist, after a new fashion.

"And what an odd girl this Matrena was! Times were she'd get into a thoughtful mood and just sit there for hours on end, her eyes fixed on the floor, without as much as twitching an eyebrow; and I'd be sitting there, too, and would gaze at her, yet couldn't get my fill of gazing, just as though I'd never seen her before. She might smile—and at that my heart would simply quiver, as if someone had tickled it. Or else, all of a sudden she'd fall to laughing, joking, dancing; she'd take me around so warmly, so hard that my head would start spinning. There were times when I'd keep thinking, from morn till night, of but one thing: What else could I pleasure her with? And, would you believe it, I gave her things just to see how she, who was my soul, would be gladdened, turning all red for joy, how she would start trying on my gift, then walk up to me and kiss me.

"Nobody knows how Kulik, her father, got wind of the affair; the old man came to see us, and then up and burst into tears. . . . We lived like that for five months or so, and I wouldn't have minded living through all eternity with her like that, but then my fate is such an accursed one!"

Peter Petrovich paused.

"What happened?" I asked him with sympathy.

He made a gesture of hopelessness:

"Everything went to the Devil. And it was none other than I who brought about her ruination. My Matrenushka was passionately fond of sleigh riding, and used to drive the sleigh herself: she'd put on her short coat and her embroidered mittens from Torzhok and just keep on urging the team. We took our rides always in the evening, you know, so's not to meet up with anybody. But, as things fell out somehow, there turned up such a glorious day, you know: frosty out, clear, no wind . . . so we started off on a ride. Matrena took the reins. Well, then, I was keeping an eye on her. Where was she heading? Could it be for

Kukuevka, the village belonging to her mistress? Sure
enough, Kukuevka it was.

"So I said to her: 'Where are you driving to, you madwoman?' She looked at me over her shoulder and smiled a
little. As much as to say: Let's have us a real fling! 'Eh,'
thought I, 'let come what may!' For it would be grand to
dash past her mistress' manor house, wouldn't it? It would
have been grand—tell me yourself, now? Well, then, we
drove on. My thorough-paced shaft horse simply floated
along; my off horses, I must tell you, turned into perfect
whirlwinds. There, we could even see the Kukuevka church.
I gave a look—and there's a little old green sleigh-coach
crawling along the road and with a flunky clinging on the
footboard behind. Matrena's mistress—the mistress herself!
—out for a ride. I got scared, first off, but Matrena, now,
she just lashed the horses with the reins and rushed straight
at the sleigh-coach. The coachman, now, you understand,
he saw some sort of a fiery chariot swooping toward him;
he wanted to swerve, you know, but did it too sharply and
overturned the sleigh-coach, now, into a snowdrift. The
glass shattered; the grand lady screamed, *Ai, ai, ai! Ai, ai,
ai!* Her companion kept squeaking, 'Stop them! Stop them!'
but we passed them and got away from there as fast as
God would let us.

"We were going at a gallop, but I kept thinking there
was going to be trouble; I hadn't done right in letting her
drive to Kukuevka.

"Well, what do you think? Sure enough, the lady had
recognized Matrena, and she recognized me as well, the
old creature, and she up and lodged a complaint against
me: 'My runaway wench, now, is living at Squire Karataev's,'
and at the same time showed her gratitude in a fitting manner. Next thing I knew, there was the district inspector of
police driving over to my place. Now that inspector was a
man I knew, Stepan Sergheich Kuzovkin, a good fellow—
that is, properly speaking, not a good fellow at all. Well,
he drove over and said: 'Peter Petrovich, how come you to
do all this? Your culpability is serious, and the laws are
clear on this point.' — 'Well, naturally,' I told him, 'you
and I are going to have a little talk about this matter, but
wouldn't you like to have a bite after your ride?'

"As to having a bite, he consented readily enough, but
at the same time he said: 'Justice has its demands; judge

for yourself.' — 'Of course, there is such a thing as justice,'
I told him, 'there it is, of course. . . . By the way, I've
heard you own a little black horse. Well, wouldn't you like
to swap it for my Lamperdos? . . . But as for the wench,
Matrena Theodorova, she's not on my place.' — 'Well, Peter
Petrovich,' said he, 'the wench is on your place. After all,
we're not living in Switzerland. And as for swapping my
nag for Lamperdos, we might do that—and we might, like
as not, accept your horse just so.'

"This time, however, I managed to get rid of him somehow. But the old lady started raising more of a fuss than
ever: 'I don't care if it costs me ten thousand rubles,' said
she. You see, when she had laid her eyes on me, the notion
had popped into her head of marrying me to her green-
faced lady-companion. I found this out later on. That's just
why she'd gotten so wrought up against me. What won't
these highborn ladies think of! Out of boredom, it must be.

"I had a bad time of it: I spared no money, now, and
I also kept Matrena in hiding, but it was no go! They
got me so dizzy I didn't know whether I was coming or
going. I went deep into debt, I lost my health.

"Well, one night I was lying in bed and thinking: 'Lord
God, why do I have to endure all this? What am I to do,
when I can't get over loving her? There, I can't, and that's
all there is to it!'—when, all of a sudden, Matrena walked
into my room. At that time I had her in hiding at a farmstead of mine, a little more than a mile from my house.
I became frightened.

" 'What, can it be they found you even there?'

" 'No, Peter Petrovich,' said she, 'nobody's troubling me
at Bubnovo. But will that keep up for long? My heart,' said
she, 'is sore strained, Peter Petrovich; it's you, my darling,
that I feel sorry for. I'll not forget your kindness for all
eternity, Peter Petrovich, but now I've come to bid you
farewell.' — 'What are you saying, what are you saying,
you madwoman? Farewell? What do you mean by farewell?'
— 'Well, it's simple. . . . I'll just go and give myself up.'
— 'Why, you madwoman, I'll lock you up in the attic!
Or are you thinking of finishing me off entirely? Do you
want to be the death of me or what?' The wench said
nothing; just kept staring at the floor. 'There, now, speak
up, speak up!' — 'I don't want to be causing you any more
trouble, Peter Petrovich.' There, go and try reasoning with

her! 'Why, do you realize, you fool—do you realize, you . . . you madwoman—' "

Peter Petrovich broke into bitter sobs.

"And, what do you think?' he went on, smashing his fist against the table and trying to knit his eyebrows even as the tears were coursing down his flaming cheeks. "Sure enough, the wench gave herself up. She went and gave herself up—"

"The horses are ready, sirs!" the stationmaster announced pompously as he entered the room.

Both of us stood up.

"Well, whatever became of Matrena?" I asked.

Karataev made a gesture of hopelessness.

A year after my encounter with Karataev I had occasion to visit Moscow. One day, before dinner, I happened to drop in at a coffeehouse located behind Hunters' Row, the original Moscow Coffeehouse. In the billiard room, through the billows of tobacco smoke, I caught glimpses of flushed faces, mustaches, topknots, old-fashioned Hungarian jackets, and decidedly Slavophilic coats of the latest cut. Thin little ancients in unassuming surtouts were reading Russian newspapers. The help flitted by nimbly, carrying trays and stepping softly on the green runners. The merchants were drinking their tea in excruciating concentration.

Suddenly, from the billiard room, a man emerged, somewhat disheveled and not altogether steady on his legs. He shoved his hands in his pockets, let his head droop, and looked about him vacantly.

"There, there, there! Peter Petrovich! How are you getting on?"

Peter Petrovich almost threw himself on my neck and, swaying slightly, dragged me into a small private room.

"Here, now," said he as he solicitously seated me in an easy chair, "you'll be all right here. Waiter, beer! No, make it champagne, I mean! Well, I hadn't expected you, I confess. I hadn't expected you. Been here long? Staying long? There, God has brought this about, as they say, now—"

"Yes, do you remember—"

"Why shouldn't I remember—why shouldn't I?" he hurriedly broke in. "That's something from the past—something from the past—"

"Well, what are you doing here, my dear Peter Petrovich?"

"I am living, as you can see. Life is good here; the folks here are agreeable. I have quieted down here." And, with a sigh, he raised his eyes heavenward.

"Have you a post?"

"No, sir, I haven't as yet, but I think I'll find something definite soon. But what does a post matter? People—that's the main thing. What people I've come to know here!"

A lad entered with a bottle of champagne on a black tray.

"There, he's a fine fellow, too. . . . Isn't that so, Vassya —you are a fine fellow? Here's to your health!"

The lad stood there awhile, then tossed his small head in deference, smiled, and went out.

"Yes, the people here are fine," Peter Petrovich went on. "They have feelings, they have souls. . . . I'll introduce you. Would you like me to? Such splendid lads. They'll all be glad to know you. I'll tell them. . . . But Bobrov died, which is a pity."

"What Bobrov?"

"Serghei Bobrov. A splendid man; took me under his wing, ignoramus and yokel that I was. Gornostaev, Pantelei, also died. They've all died, all of them!"

"You've been living in Moscow all this while? Haven't visited your village?"

"The village . . . they've sold my village."

"They've sold it?"

"Auctioned it off. There, it's a pity—why didn't you buy it?"

"What will you live on, then, Peter Petrovich?"

"Why, I won't starve to death. God will provide! If there won't be any money, there will be friends. But what's money? Dross! Gold—nothing but dross!"

He puckered up his eyes, rummaged in one of his pockets, and held out his palm to me with two fifteen-kopeck coins and a ten-kopeck one.

"What's this? Dross, isn't it?"—and the money went flying to the floor. "But tell me, have you read Polezhaev?"

"I have."

"Have you seen Mochalov in *Hamlet?*"

"No, I haven't."

"You haven't, you haven't. . . ." And Karataev's face

264

paled, his eyes began to dart restlessly, while his lips twitched slightly. "Ah, Mochalov, Mochalov! 'To die, to sleep,' " he uttered in a stifled voice and went on:

> " 'No more, and by a sleep to say we end
> The heartache, and the thousand natural shocks
> That flesh is heir to; 'tis a consummation
> Devoutly to be wish'd. To die, to sleep . . .

"To sleep, to sleep!' " he muttered several times.
"Tell me, please—" I began, but he went on with fervor:

> " 'For who would bear the whips and scorns of time,
> The oppressor's wrong, the proud man's contumely,
> The pangs of despis'd love, the law's delay,
> The insolence of office, and the spurns
> That patient merit of the unworthy takes,
> When he himself might his quietus make
> With a bare bodkin? . . .
>   Nymph, in thy orisons
> Be all my sins remember'd.' "

And he let his head sink on the table. His speech was becoming stammering and thick.

" 'A little month!' " he uttered with new force:

> " 'A little month, or ere those shoes were old
> With which she follow'd my poor father's body,
> Like Niobe, all tears! . . .
> O God! A beast that wants discourse of reason
> Would have mourn'd longer—' "

He brought a goblet of champagne up to his lips, but did not drink any and went on:

> " 'For Hecuba!
> What's Hecuba to him, or he to Hecuba,
> That he should weep for her? . . .
> Yet I,
> A dull and muddy-mettled rascal, peak. . . .
>   Am I a coward?
> Who calls me villain? Breaks my pate across? . . .
> Gives me the lie i' the throat? . . .
> Ha!
> 'Swounds, I should take it! For it cannot be
> But I am pigeon-liver'd and lack gall
> To make oppression bitter—' "

Karataev dropped his glass and clutched his head. It seemed to me that I had come to understand him.

"Oh, well," he managed to say at last, "evil to him who recalls the past. Isn't that so?"—and he broke into laughter. "Here's to your health!"

"Are you going to remain in Moscow?" I asked him.

"I'll die in Moscow!"

"Karataev!" came a loud call from an adjoining room. "Karataev, where are you? Come here, dear fella!"

"They're calling me," he managed to say, rising heavily from his seat. "Goodbye; drop in on me if you can: I live at ————."

But the very next day, through unforeseen circumstances, I had to leave Moscow and saw no more of Peter Petrovich Karataev.

THE TRYST

I WAS RESTING in a birch grove; it was autumn, about the middle of September. From the very morning an intermittent drizzle had been falling, replaced at times by warm sunshine; the weather was unsettled. The sky would now be overcast with spongy white clouds, then suddenly clear for an instant in spots, whereupon from behind the parted clouds azure would appear, radiant and caressing, like some splendidly beautiful eye. I sat there, and looked about me, and listened. The leaves were making the faintest noise over my head; by their noise alone one could tell what time of year it was. It wasn't the gay, laughing tremor of spring, nor the whispering-in-the-very ear, the prolonged gossip, of summer, nor the timid and chill babbling of late autumn, but a barely audible, slumbrous chatter. A faint breeze was barely, barely creeping over the treetops.

The grove, rain-moistened, was ceaselessly changing within, depending on whether the sun was shining or drawing a cloud over itself; now the grove would be all illumined, as though everything within it had suddenly smiled: the slender trunks of the birches, which grew not too close to one another, would unexpectedly take on the tender sheen of white silk, the small leaves lying on the ground suddenly turned to motley and burst into the glow of ruddy gold, while the beautiful stalks of tall, curly lady ferns, already tinted with their autumnal hue, like the hue of overripe grapes, simply wove an open pattern, endlessly entangling and crisscrossing before one's eyes; then, just as suddenly, everything around would turn faintly bluish: the vivid pigments became momently extinguished, the birches stood all white, void of any sheen, white as freshly fallen snow yet untouched by the chill scintillation of a wintry sunbeam—and stealthily, slyly, the finest of drizzles would begin sowing itself and whispering through the woods.

The leafage of the birches was still almost entirely green, even though it had turned perceptibly paler; but here and there one came upon some rather young birch, standing all by itself, all in red or all in gold, and it was something not to be missed to see how vividly it flared up in the sun when its rays would suddenly break through, gliding and mottling, through the close network of slender branches freshly laved by the glittering rain. Not a single bird could one hear: all of them had snuggled down somewhere and fallen silent; only rarely did the jeering little voice of a tomtit ring out like a tiny steel bell.

Before I had made a halt in this small birch forest I and my dog had passed through a grove of towering aspens. I confess I have no great love for that tree, the aspen, with its trunk of pale lilac and its gray-green metallic leafage, which it rears as high as it can and spreads in a tremulous fan through the air; I have no love for the eternal swaying of its round, untidy leaves, clumsily hooked onto long stalks. An aspen can be fine only on certain summer evenings when, towering by itself amid low brushwood, it comes face to face with the smoldering rays of the setting sun, and glistens and quivers, bathed from summit to roots in a uniform glaze of yellow-purple, or when, on some clear windy day, the whole tree is noisily streaming and babbling against the blue sky, and its every leaf, caught up by an impetuous straining, seems to be longing to break loose, to fly off and rush away into the distance. But, as a general thing, I have no love for this tree and therefore, without stopping to rest in the aspen grove, I had managed to reach the little forest of birches, had nestled down under a small tree the branches of which began at no great distance from the ground and consequently could shield me from the rain, and, having had my fill of admiring the surrounding view, had fallen into that untroubled and gentle sleep which only hunters know.

I can't say how long I slept, but when I opened my eyes all the inner recesses of the woods were filled with the sun, and in all directions, through the joyously noisy leafage, one could catch glimpses of the vividly azure sky that seemed to sparkle; the clouds, scattered by the rampaging wind, had disappeared; the weather had cleared up, and in the air one could feel that peculiar, crisp freshness which, filling the heart with a certain sensation of vigor, almost always foretells a calm and clear evening after an inclement day.

I had just gotten ready to get up and try my luck anew, when my eyes were suddenly caught by a motionless human form. I looked more closely: it was that of a young peasant girl. She was sitting twenty paces away from me, with her head cast down in deep thought and her hands fallen in her lap; in one, half open, lay a thick nosegay of field flowers and, at her every breath, it slid down upon her checked skirt. Her fresh white blouse, buttoned at neck and wrists, lay in short soft folds about her waist; a double string of large yellow beads fell from her neck onto her breast. She was very far from bad-looking. Her thick, light hair of a beautiful ashen hue was parted into two painstakingly combed half-circles emerging from under a narrow scarlet band that came down almost on the forehead, a forehead as white as ivory; the rest of her face was barely sunburned to that aureate tan which only a fine skin can acquire.

Her eyes I could not see—she kept them lowered—but I did see her fine, arched brows, her long lashes: these were moist, and upon one of her cheeks was the dried trace, glistening in the sun, of a tear that had stopped at her very lips, which had turned a trifle white. Her small head, all of it, was most endearing: even the nose, slightly thick and round, did not spoil it. I liked particularly the expression of her face: so simple and meek was it, so sad and so full of a childlike bewilderment before her own sadness.

She was evidently waiting for someone; something crackled faintly in the woods: she immediately raised her head and looked over her shoulder: in the transparent shade I caught the quick gleam of her eyes, big, clear, and timorous as those of a doe. For a few moments she listened intently, without taking her wide-open eyes from the spot whence the faint sound had come; then she sighed, turned her head

269

ever so quietly, bent over still more, and began picking her
flowers over slowly. Her eyelids reddened, stirred in bitter
sorrow, and a fresh tear rolled from under the thick lashes,
coming to a rest on her cheek and sending forth sparkling rays.

A rather long time passed thus; the poor girl never moved,
save for a despondent gesture of her hands every now and
then, and kept listening, listening all the time. Anew something was noisy in the woods: she became alert. The noise
did not cease, it was becoming clearer, was nearing; at last
one could hear resolute, nimble footsteps. She straightened
up and seemed to turn timid; her intent gaze wavered—
from expectation, apparently. A man's figure flitted through
the thicket. She looked closely, all her face suddenly
flamed in a blush, she smiled joyously and happily, was
just about to stand up—and immediately drooped again,
paled, became confused; only then did she lift up her tremulous, almost imploring gaze to the newcomer, as he halted
beside her.

I eyed him from my ambush with curiosity. He did not,
I confess, create a pleasing impression upon me. He was, judging by all the signs, the spoiled valet of some young, rich
seigneur. His dress betrayed a pretension to taste and a
dandified negligence; he had on a quite abbreviated overcoat of a bronze shade, buttoned to the very collar, probably a hand-me-down of his master's, a pink little cravat
tipped with lilac, and a stiff cap of black velvet trimmed
with gold braid, pulled down over his very eyebrows. The
round collar of his white shirt mercilessly propped up his
ears and cut his cheeks, while the starched cuffs covered
his hands right down to the red and crooked fingers, adorned
with silver and gold rings set with forget-me-nots of tur-
quoise. His face, rosy, fresh, brazen, belonged to that category of faces which, insofar as I have been able to observe,
almost always move men to indignation and, regrettably,
are very often found pleasing by women. He was obviously
trying to bestow upon his rather coarse features a disdainful and bored expression; he was forever puckering
up his milky-gray eyes, which were diminutive enough even
without that, making wry faces, letting the corners of his
lips droop, affectedly yawning, and with a negligent although not quite adroit nonchalance, would now put up
his hand to fix the reddish, devilishly curled locks at his
temples, then to pluck at the short yellow hairs springing up

on his thick upper lip—in a word, he was posturing insufferably. He had started his posturing as soon as he had caught sight of the peasant girl awaiting him; with a slow, rolling step he walked up to her, stood there a while, shrugged, shoved his hands in the pockets of his overcoat, and having barely deigned to bestow a fleeting and apathetic glance at the girl, lowered himself to the ground.

"Well, now," he began, continuing to look somewhere off to one side, rocking one foot and yawning, "have you been here a long while?"

The girl was unable to answer him at once.

"Yes, sir, a long while, Victor Alexandrych," she managed to say at last in a barely audible voice.

"Ah!" He took off his cap, majestically passed a hand over his thick, tightly curled hair, which began almost at his eyebrows, and, having looked about him with dignity, carefully covered his precious head again. "Why, I'd actually forgotten about it entirely. Besides, look at that rain!" He yawned again. "There's no end of things to attend to; one can't see to everything, yet on top of that my gentleman has to be scolding. We're setting out tomorrow—"

"Tomorrow?" uttered the girl and fixed a frightened look upon him.

"Yes, tomorrow. There, there, there—please!" he anticipated her hurriedly and in vexation, on perceiving that she was now all aquiver and had let her head droop. "Please, Akulina, don't cry. You know I can't bear it." And he wrinkled up his blunt nose. "Otherwise I'm leaving right now. What sort of foolishness is this—sniveling!"

"There, I won't, I won't," Akulina hastened to say, making an effort and gulping down her tears. "So you're setting out tomorrow?" she added after a short silence. "When will God grant us to see each other again, Victor Alexandrych?"

"We'll see each other, we'll see each other yet. If not next year then later on. Master wants to enter civil service in Petersburg, it looks like," he went on, getting the words out negligently and somewhat through the nose. "And, maybe, we'll go abroad, too."

"You'll forget me, Victor Alexandrych," Akulina uttered sadly.

"No, why should I? I won't forget you; only you must be a sensible girl; don't act foolish; listen to your father.

But I won't forget you—oh, no." Unperturbed, he stretched himself and again yawned.

"Don't forget me, Victor Alexandrych," she continued in an imploring voice. "There, how I loved you, it seems—seems I've done everything for you. . . . You tell me to listen to my father, Victor Alexandrych. But then, how am I to listen to my father—"

"And why not?" He uttered these words as if they were coming from his stomach, as he lay on his back with his hands placed under his head.

"Why, how can that be, Victor Alexandrych—for you yourself know—"

She fell silent. Victor toyed a while with the steel chain of his watch.

"You, Akulina, aren't a foolish wench," he began at last, "so don't be talking nonsense. It's your own good I'm after. Do you understand me? Of course you aren't foolish; you aren't altogether a peasant, so to say, and your mother, too, wasn't always a peasant. But still, you got no education, so you must do as you're told."

"But it's frightening, Victor Alexandrych."

"Tut, tut—what nonsense, my dear girl: you sure have found something to be frightened of! What's that you got there?" he added, having moved closer to her. "Flowers?"

"Yes, flowers," Akulina answered despondently. "Here's some field tansy I plucked," she went on, livening up somewhat, "that's good for calves. And this, now, is bud marigold —that's against scrofula. There, just look at it—what a wonderful little flower; I've never seen such a wonderful little flower in all my born days. Here's forget-me-nots, and here's marjoram—mother's-darling, they call it. . . . And here's something I plucked just for you," she added, getting a posy of the bluest cornflowers out from under the yellow tansies, bound with the slenderest of grass blades. "Do you want them?"

Victor languidly put out his hand, accepted the offering, sniffed negligently at the flowers, and fell to twiddling them in his fingers, now and then turning his eyes upward in thoughtful dignity. Akulina was contemplating him. . . . There was in her melancholy gaze so much of tender devotion, of adoring submission and love. She loved him, and she dared not weep, and was saying farewell to him and admiring him for the last time; but he lay there, lolling like a sultan, and with magnanimous patience and condescension was tolerating her adoration. It was with indignation, I confess, that I studied his red face, through the affectedly disdainful indifference of which a satisfied, sated self-conceit was peering. Akulina was so splendid at that instant: all her soul was trustingly, passionately unfolding before him, was drawn to him, was yearning to caress and be caressed, but he . . . he let the cornflowers drop on the grass, pulled out of a side pocket of his overcoat a round bit of glass rimmed with bronze, and began trying to squeeze it in over his eye; however, no matter how he strove to retain it with the help of a frowning eyebrow, a pursed-up cheek, and even his nose, the monocle kept right on popping out and falling back into his hand.

"What may that be?" the wonder-struck Akulina asked at last.

"A monocle," he answered with an important air.

"What's it for?"

"Why, to see better with."

"Do let me have a look."

Victor made a wry face, but handed the bit of glass to her. "Watch out, don't break it."

"No fear, I won't break it." She timidly brought it up to her eye. "I can't see a thing," she remarked guilelessly.

"Why, you have to pucker up your eye, now," he retorted in the tone of a displeased instructor. She puckered up the eye in front of which she was holding the bit of glass. "Why, not that one, foolish! The other one!" Victor cried out and, without giving her a chance to correct her error, took the monocle away from her.

Akulina turned red, laughed ever so faintly, and turned away.

"Looks like it weren't for the likes of me," she remarked.

"I should say not!"

The poor thing was silent for a space and then sighed deeply.

"Ah, Victor Alexandrych, what will things be like for me without you?" said she suddenly.

Victor wiped the monocle with the skirt of his overcoat and placed it back in his pocket.

"Yes, yes," he spoke up at last, "you'll find it hard at first, sure enough." He patted her shoulder condescendingly; she reached for his hand, taking it down from her shoulder ever so gently, and kissed it timidly. "Yes, yes, now—you're a kindhearted wench, sure enough," he went on with a self-satisfied smirk, "but what can one do? Judge for yourself! After all, the master and I can't be staying on here; it'll be winter soon, and to be in a village in the winter— you know that yourself—is simply abominable. But it's altogether another matter in Petersburg! There's simply such wonders there as you, silly girl, couldn't picture to yourself even in a dream. What houses, what streets—and when it comes to sassiety, to culture, why, you'd simply be amazed!" Akulina was listening to him with devouring attention, her lips parted a little, like a small child's. "However," he added, having begun to turn restlessly on the ground, "what's the use of me telling you all this? For you couldn't understand it!"

"But why not, Victor Alexandrych? I've understood it; I've understood everything."

"My, what a girl!"

Akulina cast down her eyes.

"That's not the way you used to talk to me before, Victor Alexandrych," she managed to say without lifting her eyes.

"Before? . . . Before! Listen to that, will you? Before!" he commented as if in indignation.

They were both silent for a while.

"However, it's time for me to be going," Victor announced and propped himself on his elbow as a preliminary to rising.

"Do wait a little bit longer," Akulina uttered in an imploring voice.

"What's the use of waiting? For I've already said goodbye to you."

"Wait a little," Akulina repeated.

Victor again lay down comfortably and took to desultory whistling. Akulina would not take her eyes off him for a moment. I could notice that she was little by little becoming agitated; her lips twitched now and then, her pale cheeks had taken on a faint scarlet glow.

"Victor Alexandrych," she began speaking at last in a breaking voice, "it's a sin on your part . . . it's a sin on your part, Victor Alexandrych—by God, it is!"

"Just what is a sin?" he asked, his eyebrows frowning, as he raised his head slightly and turned it toward her.

"It's a sin, Victor Alexandrych. You might at least say one kind word in farewell; you might at least say one little word to me, miserable orphan that I am—"

"But what am I to say to you?"

"I don't know; you know that better than I, Victor Alexandrych. There, you're going away, and if you'd at least say one little word. . . . What have I done to deserve this?"

"What a queer girl you are! But what can I do?"

"One little word, at least—"

"There, she's started harping on that one string," he let drop with vexation and stood up.

"Don't be angry, Victor Alexandrych," she hastened to add, barely keeping her tears back.

"I'm not angry, but you're silly. . . . What is it you want? For I can't marry you, can I? I can't, can I? Well, what is it you want, then? What is it?" He thrust his face forward, as though awaiting an answer, and spread his fingers wide.

"I want nothing . . . nothing," she answered, stammering and hardly daring to hold out her quivering hands to him, "but still, if you'd just say one little word in farewell, at least—" and with that her tears streamed forth.

"There, that's the way of it—she's turned on the tears now," Victor let drop cold-bloodedly, tipping his cap from the back onto his eyes.

"I want nothing," she went on, strangling from her tears and covering her face with her hands, "but how will things be for me in my family—what will things be like for me? And what's going to happen to me, what will ever become of me, miserable creature that I am? They'll marry me off to someone I don't love, and me an orphan. . . . Such a sorrow to fall on my poor head!"

"Keep on with your song-and-dance, keep right on," Victor muttered in a low voice, shifting from foot to foot where he stood.

"And if he'd say but one little word at least, only one little word. . . . 'Akulina,' he might say, 'I, now—' "

Sudden sobs that racked her breast would not let her finish; she slumped to the grass and, burying her face in it, broke into bitter, bitter weeping. . . . All her body was convulsively agitated; the nape of her neck simply heaved. Her long-restrained grief had, at last, spurted forth in a torrent. Victor stood over her for a while; he stood there, shrugged, turned about, and went off with great strides.

A few instants passed. . . . She quieted down, lifted her head, leaped up, looked about her, and wrung her hands; she was about to run after him but her legs gave in—she fell to her knees. I could not restrain myself and darted toward her, but she had hardly seen me clearly than, gathering strength from some unknown source, she got up with a faint cry and vanished behind the trees, leaving her scattered flowers on the ground.

I stood there a while, picked up the posy of cornflowers, and came out of the grove into the open. The sun was low in the bleak, clear sky; its rays, too, seemed somehow to have turned wan and chill: they did not shine—they flowed widely as an even, almost watery light. No more than half an hour remained till evening, yet the sunset glow was barely, barely catching on fire. A gusty wind was rushing toward me over the yellow, dried stubble; small shriveled leaves, hurriedly swirling up before it, raced past me, across the road, along the edge of the copse; that side of it which faced the field like a wall was all aquiver and sparkling distinctly yet not vividly with tiny sparks; upon the reddish grass, upon dead grass blades, upon straws—everywhere—countless strands of autumn gossamer glistened and uneasily stirred. I halted. . . . A melancholy mood came over me; a dismal fear of winter none too far off was, it seemed, stealing through the cheerful yet chilling smile of withering nature. High overhead, cleaving the air heavily and sharply with its wings, a circumspect raven flew by; it turned its head, eyed me askance, soared up, and, with staccato cawing, disappeared beyond the forest; a great flock of pigeons swept by, wheeling, on their way from some threshing floor, and, after suddenly swirling up in a pillar, fussily settled over a field—a sign of autumn, that! Someone rode by beyond a denuded knoll, his empty cart clattering loudly. . . .

I came home; but for a long time the image of poor Akulina would not leave my mind, and her cornflowers, withered long since, are still treasured by me. . . .

A PRINCE HAMLET
OF THE SHCHIGROV DISTRICT

DURING ONE OF my trips I received an invitation to dine at
the house of Alexander Michailych G——, a rich landowner and a Nimrod. His settlement was some three miles
from the tiny village where I was staying at the time. I put
on my frock coat (a thing I would not advise anybody to
leave home without, even when going hunting), and started
out for Alexander Michailych's place. The dinner was set
for six o'clock; I arrived at five and found a great multitude
of gentlefolk already there, in various uniforms, in civilian
dress and other, less definable garments. The host met me
amiably but immediately dashed off to the pantry. He was
expecting an important dignitary and was experiencing a
certain excitement, not at all in keeping with his position in
the world and his wealth. Alexander Michailych had never
been married and had no liking for women; the company at
his gatherings consisted of bachelors and unattached men.
He lived on a grand footing and had enlarged and deco-
rated his ancestral chambers magnificently; he used to import fifteen thousand rubles' worth of wine from Moscow
yearly and, in general, was held in great esteem. Alexander
Michailych had, ever so long ago, resigned from civil service and was not striving for honors of any sort. What, then,

was compelling him to be so importunate about having a grand personage visit him and to be agitated, since the very morning, on the day of this ceremonial dinner? That is something which remains clothed in the obscurity of the unknown, as a certain pettifogger of my acquaintance used to say whenever he was asked whether he took bribes from willing contributors.

Having parted from my host, I began walking about the rooms. Almost all the guests were utter strangers to me; a score or so were already seated at the card tables. Among these devotees of preference whist were two military men with noble but slightly shopworn faces, several civilians in tight high collars and with drooping, dyed mustaches, such as you will find only among determined but well-intentioned people (these well-intentioned ones were sorting their cards with an important air, and, without turning their heads, raised their eyes in a sidelong look whenever anybody came near them), five or six provincial minor officials with round little bellies, chubby and perspiring little hands, and demurely immobile little feet (these gentlemen spoke in a soft voice, smiled meekly in all directions, held the hands dealt them very close to their dickies and, whenever they played trumps, did not tap on the table but, on the contrary, let their cards drop undulatingly on the green cloth, and, as they stacked their winnings, made a light creaking noise, quite deferential and decorous).

The other gentry were sitting on divans or huddling in knots close to the doors and about the windows; one, a landowner, no longer young but womanish in his looks, was standing in a corner, becoming startled from time to time, turning red and twiddling the watch seal on his abdomen in embarrassment, even though no one was paying any attention to him; some of the gentlemen, in rounded frock coats and checked pantaloons turned out by Fierz Kliuhin of Moscow, perpetual master of the tailors' guild, were carrying on a discussion with unusual ease and liveliness, turning the fat and clean-shaven napes of their necks with great ease; a young man of twenty-five, shortsighted and fair, dressed in black from head to toe, was obviously timid yet smiling caustically.

Just as I was beginning to feel somewhat bored, however, I was suddenly joined by a certain Voinitzin, a young man who had never finished his higher education, and now was

living in Alexander Michailych's house in the capacity of
. . . one would be hard put to it to say in just what capacity. He was an excellent shot and knew how to train dogs.
I had known him as far back as my Moscow days. He belonged to the category of those young people who, in the
old days, used to "play the cataleptic" at every oral examination—that is, they would not answer a word to the examining professor's questions. These gentlemen were also
called, in fancy language, side-whiskerists. (These are matters of auld lang syne, you will kindly note.) The thing
would go like this: they would call out a name—Voinitzin's,
for example. Voinitzin, who up to that point had been sitting stiff and upright on his bench, drenched in hot sweat
and slowly but senselessly rolling his eyes every which way,
would stand up, hurriedly button his uniform to the very
collar, and sidle up to the examiner's desk.

"Please take one of the tickets," the professor would tell
him amiably. Voinitzin would stretch out his hand and tremulously finger the stack of tickets.

"Yes, but no choosing, if you please," some outside but
cantankerous little ancient, a professor from some other department, who had become inspired with sudden hatred for
the hapless side-whiskerist, was sure to remark. Voinitzin
submitted to his fate, took a ticket, showed its number, and
went off to sit by a window while the man ahead of him was
answering the question put to him. As he sat by the window
Voinitzin never took his eyes off his ticket, save, perhaps, to
look about him slowly, as before; on the whole, however, he
did not stir hand or foot.

But now his predecessor had finished, had been told "Very
well, you may go," or even "Very well, sir—very well, indeed, sir," depending upon his abilities. Then Voinitzin's
name was called out; Voinitzin stood up and with a firm
step approached the desk.

"Read the question on your ticket," he was told. Voinitzin,
using both hands, brought the ticket up to his very nose,
read it out slowly, and slowly lowered his hands. "Well,
sir, answer, if you please," the same professor drawled out,
throwing his torso back and crossing his arms on his breast.
A silence as of the grave ensued. "Well, now, sir!" Voinitzin
remained silent. The little ancient from another department
was working himself into a conniption fit: "Do say something!" My Voinitzin said never a word, as though in a coma.

The closely cropped nape of his neck jutted out sharply and immovably to meet the curious glances of his fellow students. The eyes of the little ancient from another department were on the verge of popping out: he was definitely hating Voinitzin.

"This is odd, I must say," remarked another examiner. "Why are you standing there like a deaf-mute? There, don't you know the answer? Is that it? In that case just say so."

"Let me take another ticket," the unfortunate fellow uttered in a stifled voice. The professors exchanged glances.

"Very well, if you like," answered the chief examiner with a hopeless gesture. Voinitzin took a new ticket, went off to his window again, again returned to the desk, and again kept as mum as if his throat had been slit. The little ancient from another department was by then quite capable of devouring him alive. Finally they shooed him away and gave him a zero. Do you think that at that point, at least, he would leave? You've got another guess coming! He went back to his place, sat there just as immovably as before until the examination was all over, and, as he left, called out: "Well, I sure am in hot water! What a fix!" And all that day he traipsed about Moscow, clutching his head every now and then and bitterly cursing his hapless lot. He would not, of course, buckle down to his books, and the next morning the same story was repeated all over again.

It was this very Voinitzin, then, who sat down next to me. He and I talked about Moscow, about hunting.

"If you like," he whispered to me suddenly, "I'll introduce you to the leading wit here—"

"If you'll be so obliging."

Voinitzin led me up to a man of very short stature, mustachioed and with a topknot combed high, wearing a brown frock coat and a vivid cravat. His jaundiced, mobile features really did exude intellect and malice. A fleeting, caustic smile was incessantly distorting his lips; his dark, puckered-up little eyes peered out provocatively from under uneven lashes. Standing near him was a certain landowner, broad, soft, sweet—a downright Sugar Honeyevich—and one-eyed. He laughed beforehand at the witticisms of the little man and seemed, for all the world, to be dissolving from delight. Voinitzin presented me to the wit, whose name was Peter Petrovich Lupihin. After the introduction we exchanged the usual preliminary greetings.

"Oh, allow me to present my best friend," Lupihin suddenly began in a sharp-edged voice, seizing the saccharine landowner by the hand. "There, don't be hanging back, Kirilla Seliphanych," he added, "nobody's going to bite you. Here, sir," he went on, as the embarrassed Kirilla Seliphanych kept bowing and scraping as awkwardly as if his abdomen were falling away, "here, sir, I commend him to you as the finest of gently born gentlemen. He enjoyed excellent health up to the age of fifty, but all of a sudden got the notion of doctoring his eyes, in consequence of which he has become one-eyed. Since then he has been doctoring his peasants with the same success. Well, they in their turn, with that same sort of loyalty—"

"My, what a man this is—" Kirilla Seliphanych managed to mutter—and broke out laughing.

"Finish what you wanted to say, my friend. Eh, do finish it," Lupihin chimed in. "For, like as not, they may elect you judge, and elect you they will, see if they don't. Well, of course, the assessors will do your thinking for you, we'll suppose; but then one must, in any event, be able to express an idea, even though it may be not your own. The governor of the province may, as ill luck will have it, pay you a visit and ask: 'Why is the judge stammering?' Well, now, suppose they say: 'He's had a stroke of paralysis, poor fellow.' — 'In that case,' he'll say, 'you must let his blood.' And that, in your position, you will yourself agree, is unseemly."

The saccharine landowner was simply bowled over by laughter.

"My, just see how he laughs," Lupihin went on, maliciously eyeing Kirilla Seliphanych's rocking abdomen. "And why shouldn't he be laughing?" he added, turning to me. "He's well fed, healthy, has no children, his muzhiks aren't mortgaged—for he's doctoring them; his wife is somewhat daft." Kirilla Seliphanych turned away a little, as though he hadn't caught this clearly, and kept on laughing all the while. "There, I too am laughing, and yet my wife has run off with a surveyor." He bared his teeth. "Why, didn't you know that? Of course she did! After all was said and done she up and ran off and left me a letter: 'My dear Peter Petrovich, forgive me, now: carried away by passion, I am going far away with the friend of my heart. . . .' And the surveyor captured her by wearing skintight pantaloons and not trimming his nails. You are astonished? 'There's a frank fellow, now!' And, my God, we steppe squires are forthright in telling the truth and shaming the Devil. However, let's go off to one side. What's the use of our sticking so close to the future judge, now—"

He took me by the arm and we walked over to one of the windows.

"I have the reputation hereabouts of a wit," he told me during the course of our talk. "Don't you believe it. I am simply an embittered fellow and wrangle out loud: that's just why I'm so free and easy. And really, why should I be standing on ceremony? I don't value anyone's opinion a copper's worth, and I'm not out for anything; I am malicious— well, what of it? At least a malicious man has no need of intellect. And you wouldn't believe how refreshing it is to be like that. There, now, just take a look at our host, for example! Come, what's he dashing about like that for, if you please? He's forever glancing at his watch, smiling, sweating, putting on an air of importance, making us famish. What a rare sight, to be sure—a person of rank! There, there —he's dashed off again; he's actually hobbling along. Just look at him!"

And Lupihin broke into squealing laughter.

"Only trouble is, there are no ladies here," he went on with a deep sigh. "It's a stag affair; if it weren't, this is the sort of thing that offers fine opportunities for the likes of us. Look, look," he cried out suddenly, "here comes Grand Duke Kozelsky—there, that tall fellow with the beard, sporting yellow gloves. You can see right off he's been abroad. And he always arrives as late as this. He is, I must tell you, as stupid all by himself as any two horses in a merchant's turnout—and yet you ought to see how condescendingly he launches into conversation with the likes of us, how magnanimously he deigns to smile in response to the pleasantries of our ravenous mammas and their daughters! And even he himself lets off witticisms now and then, even though he is only a transient here—but then, what witticisms they are, to be sure! For all the world as if he were sawing away at a stout cord with a dull knife. He just can't stand me. . . . I'm going over and bow to him."

And Lupihin ran off toward the Grand Duke.

"And there's my personal enemy coming," he let drop, having suddenly come back to me. "Do you see that stout man, with the dark-brown face and bristles on his head—

there, the one who has raked off his cap and is clutching it, making his way along the wall and looking about him on all sides like a wolf? I sold him a horse that cost a thousand for four hundred rubles, and this dumb creature now has the full right to despise me—and yet, for all that, he himself is so devoid of any comprehension, especially in the morning, before he has had his tea, or right after dinner, that, if you say to him: 'How are you?' why, he'll answer with: 'What is it, sir?' And there's a general coming," Lupihin continued. "A civilian general, retired—a bankrupt general. He has a daughter made of beet sugar, and a refinery suffering from scrofula. . . . I beg your pardon: I didn't say that just right, but no matter—you understand. Ah, an architect, too, has found his way here! A German, and yet—wonderful to relate!—he sports a mustache and doesn't know his work. Oh, well, what need has he of knowing his work, as long as he can take bribes and put up as many columns —or pillars, rather—as possible, for our pillars of society!"

Lupihin again went off into peals of laughter. But suddenly an uneasy excitement spread through the whole house. The grand dignitary had arrived. The host simply surged into the anteroom. A few devoted members of his household and some zealous guests streamed after him. The noisy talk became transformed into a gentle, pleasing hum, like unto the buzzing of bees in their native hives at springtime. Only one irrepressible wasp, Lupihin, and that magnificent drone, Kozelsky, did not lower their voices. . . . And lo, at last, entered the queen bee: the grandee entered. All hearts darted off to meet him; the torsos of those sitting raised themselves somewhat; even the landowner who had bought the horse so cheap from Lupihin—even that landowner let his chin rest on his bosom. The grandee maintained his dignity in a way that could not have been bettered. Nodding, his head held far back, as though he were bowing, he uttered a few words of approval, each of them beginning with the letter *a*, pronounced drawlingly and through the nose; he glanced, with an indignation bordering on bloodthirstiness, at the beard of Grand Duke Kozelsky, and tendered to the bankrupt civilian general with a refinery and a daughter the index finger of his left hand.

After a few minutes, in the course of which the grandee had had time to remark twice that he was ever so glad he had not come too late for dinner, the whole gathering bent its steps to the dining hall, with the aces leading.

Is there any need of telling the reader how the grandee was enthroned in the place of honor, between the civilian general and the marshal of the nobility for the province, a man with freedom and dignity all over his face, utterly in keeping with his starched dickey, unencompassable vest, and round snuffbox (the snuff was French)? How the host saw to things, dashed about, bustled, encouraged his guests to eat and drink, smiled, in passing, at the grandee's back, and, standing in a corner like a schoolboy, hastily stayed his hunger with a small plate of soup or a bit of beef; how the major-domo brought in a fish well over a yard in length and with a posy stuck in its snout; how the servants, all in livery, all of austere appearance, morosely pressed now Malaga, now dry Madeira upon each highborn gentleman, and how almost all the highly born gentlemen, especially those well along in years, as though submitting unwillingly to a sense of duty, put away glass after glass; how, finally, the champagne corks began to pop and the stentorian proposals of healths commenced: all this, probably, is only too well known to the reader. But what struck me as most remarkable was the anecdote told by the grandee himself, amid an all-prevailing, joyous hush. Someone—apparently the bankrupt general, a man acquainted with the latest literature—mentioned the influence of women on all men, but particularly upon the young ones.

"Yes, yes," the grandee chimed in, "that's true enough; young people ought to be kept in submission or, like as not, they'll lose their heads over every skirt." A smile as merry as a child's flitted over the faces of all the guests; in the eyes of one of the landowners there was a sparkle of gratitude, actually. "For young people are foolish." The grandee, probably for the sake of impressiveness, would now and then change the generally accepted accenting of words. "There, you might take my son Ivan, for example," he went on. "The fool is just going on twenty, and yet he ups and says to me: 'Let me have your consent to marry, Father.' So I say to him: 'Serve a while first, you fool.' Well, there were tears, and despair; but then, you know the way I am. . . ." The grandee uttered "the way" from his belly rather than with his lips; he kept silent a while and looked majestically at his neighbor the general, at the same time elevating his eyebrows far more than one might have expected. The civilian general inclined his head pleasingly, somewhat favoring one shoulder, and took to blinking with exceeding rapidity the eye turned upon the grandee. "And what do you think?" the grandee began speaking again. "Now he himself writes me: 'Thanks, Father,' he says, 'for having knocked some sense into my fool head.' There, now, that's the way to act."

All the guests, naturally, fully agreed with the raconteur, and somehow seemed to grow animated from the pleasure and instruction they had derived.

After dinner the entire company got up and moved on to the drawing room with considerable noise—yet a noise nonetheless decorous and apparently permitted on this occasion. They sat down to cards.

Somehow or other I got through the time till evening came and, having given my coachman instructions to have my carriage ready for five o'clock in the morning, retired for the night. However, that day I was still fated to make the acquaintance of a certain remarkable person.

Owing to the great influx of guests no one had sleeping accommodations all by himself. In the small, greenish-tinted, and rather damp room to which Alexander Michailych's major-domo brought me there was already another guest, completely undressed. On seeing me he nimbly dived under his blanket, covered himself with it to his very nose, turned and tossed a little on his shifty featherbed and fell quiet, peeping out keenly every now and then from under his cotton nightcap. I approached a second bed (there were only two in the room), undressed, and lay down between the damp sheets. My roommate began to toss and turn in his bed. I wished him good night.

Half an hour passed. Despite all my efforts I could not fall asleep; unwanted and vague thoughts straggled one after the other in an endless file, stubbornly and monotonously, just like the buckets of a water-raising machine.

"Ah, you aren't sleeping, apparently?" my roommate remarked.

"As you can see," I answered. "Why, are you also unable to sleep?"

"I never feel like sleeping."

"How is that?"

"Why, just so. I fall asleep without myself knowing what made me do so; I lie and lie there, and then fall asleep."

"Why do you go to bed, then, before you feel sleepy?"

"But what would you have me do?"

I made no reply to my roommate's question.

"What makes me wonder," he went on after a brief silence, "is why there are no fleas here. What likelier spot could there be for them?"

"It sounds as if you were regretting their absence," I remarked.

"No, I'm not regretting it; but I do love consistency in all things."

"My," I reflected, "what words he uses!"

My roommate was again silent for some time.

"Would you like to make a bet with me?" he suddenly began, rather loudly.

"What about?"

"Hm . . . what about? Why, this: I feel certain that you're taking me for a fool."

"Really, now!" I murmured with amazement.

"For a country bumpkin, an ignoramus. Confess it—"

"I haven't the pleasure of knowing you," I countered. "What reasons have you for concluding—"

"What reasons? Why, the mere sound of your voice is one: you reply to me so negligently. Yet I am not at all what you think—"

"Allow me—"

"No, *you* must allow *me* to speak. In the first place, I speak French no worse than you do, and as for German, I speak it actually better; in the second place, I spent three years abroad, living eight months in Berlin alone. I have mastered Hegel, my dear sir; I know Goethe by heart; over and above that, I was in love for a long while with the daughter of a German professor—and when I got home I married a consumptive young lady, bald-headed yet quite a remarkable person. Therefore I'm one of your sort; I am no country bumpkin, as you suppose. I, too, am corroded by introspection, and there's nothing of the forthright about me."

I raised my head and looked with redoubled attention at this odd person. In the dim light of the night candle I could barely make out his features.

"There, you're looking at me right now," he went on after adjusting his nightcap, "and in all probability are asking yourself: 'How is it I hadn't noticed him today?' I'll tell you why—because I do not raise my voice, because I hide myself behind others, behind doors, avoid conversing with anybody; because the major-domo, as he carries a tray past me, raises his elbow beforehand to the level of my chest. . . . And whence come all these things? From two causes: in the first place I'm poor and, in the second, I've become resigned. Tell the truth: you never noticed me, did you?"

"I actually hadn't the pleasure—"

"There, now," he interrupted me, "there, now, I knew it."

He raised himself a little and crossed his arms; the long shadow of his nightcap on the wall bent and fell on the ceiling. "But do confess, now," he added, giving me a sudden sidelong look, "I must seem very much of an odd person to you, an original, as they say, or, like as not, something rather worse: are you, by any chance, thinking that I'm putting on the role of an odd person?"

"I must again repeat to you that I don't know you—"

He cast down his eyes for a moment.

"Why have I so suddenly become talkative with you, an utter stranger? The Lord—the Lord alone knows!" He sighed. "It isn't owing to the kinship of our souls, after all! Both you and I are decent people, that is to say, egoists: you haven't anything in the least to do with me, nor I with you—isn't that so? But both of us can't sleep. Why not chat a little, then? For I am at my best, and that's something which happens but rarely with me. I'm timid, you see, and timid not on account of my being a provincial, a fellow of no rank, a poor man, but on account of my being a frightfully selfish person. But there are times, under the influence of favorable circumstances, of chance occurrences—which, however, I am unable either to determine or foresee—when my timidity vanishes entirely: as right now, for instance. Were you now to confront me even with the Dalai Lama himself, why, I'd ask him for a pinch of snuff. But, perhaps, you feel sleepy?"

"By no means," I hastened to assure him. "I find it very pleasant to talk with you."

"That is, I am amusing you, you mean to say. So much the better. And so, sir, I will inform you that they call me an original here—that is, I am called so by those on whose tongues my name may pop up, among other nonsensical things. 'None o'er my fate is much concerned. . . .' Their idea is to needle me. Oh, my God! If they but knew. . . . Why, the very reason I am perishing is because there's absolutely nothing original about me, except for such stunts as, for instance, my present conversation with you; but then such stunts aren't worth a bent pin. That's the cheapest and lowliest sort of originality."

He turned his face toward me and flung up his arms.

"My dear sir!" he exclaimed. "I am of the opinion that, as a general thing, it is the originals alone who live well on this earth; they alone have the right to live. As someone has said, *mon verre n'est pas grand, mais je bois dans mon verre*— my glass isn't anything great, but it's my own glass I'm drinking out of. You see," he added in a low voice, "how pure my French pronunciation is. What matters it to me if your head is great and capacious, and that you understand everything, that you know a great deal, that you keep an eye on the times—yet have nothing of your very own, peculiarly yours, belonging entirely to you! Just one more dumping ground of commonplaces in this world, but what pleasure can anyone derive from that? No, go ahead and be foolish, actually, but let it be after your own fashion! Have your own bouquet, a bouquet all your own—there, that's the thing! And don't think that my demands as to that bouquet are excessive. God forfend! Of such originals there is no end; no matter where you look, there's your original; every living person is an original, but then *I* have failed to be of their number!

"Yet at the same time," he went on after a short silence, "what expectations I aroused in my youth! What a high opinion I myself nurtured about my person before my departure abroad, as well as shortly after my return! Naturally, while I was abroad I kept my ears cocked, I tried to get by all on my own, even as befits my sort, those who grasp everything for themselves in their minds, who grasp everything, yet in the end, look and behold you, they haven't grasped even their A B C's!

"An original, an original!" he harked back to the phrase, shaking his head reproachfully. "They call me an original, but in reality it turns out that there isn't a person in the world less original than your most obedient servant. Really, I must have been born, even, in imitation of someone else— yes, by God! I live, too, just as if I were imitating sundry literary confectioners whom I have studied thoroughly. I live thus in the sweat of my brow; and I studied, and fell in love and, at last, married, just as though through no wish of

288

my own but as if fulfilling something that was either a duty or a task—who can make out what it was!"

He snatched off his nightcap and threw it on the bed.

"I'll tell you my life. Would you like me to?" he asked me in a jerky voice. "Or, rather, a few features of my life?"

"You would oblige me."

"On second thought, no; I'd better tell you how I came to marry. For marriage is an important matter, the touchstone of the whole man; he is reflected in his marriage as in a mirror. But then that comparison is far too hackneyed. . . . Excuse me, I'm going to have a pinch of snuff."

He got a snuffbox out from under his pillow, opened the lid, and resumed speaking, flourishing the open snuffbox.

"Put yourself in my place, my dear sir. Judge for yourself what benefit—just what benefit, if you'll be kind enough to tell me—I could derive from the encyclopedia of Hegel? What is there in common, tell me, between this encyclopedia and Russian life? And how would you have applied it to our way of life—and not this encyclopedia alone, mind you, but German philosophy in general? I'll go further: how would you apply science?"

He bounded up a little on his bed and began apostrophizing, muttering in a low voice, clenching his teeth in rancor:

"Ah, so that's it, that's it! If that's the case, why did you go traipsing abroad? Why didn't you stick at home and study the life about you on the spot? You would then have learned its needs as well as its future, and would also have come to a clear understanding of your calling, so to say. . . . But, if you'll be so kind," he went on, having again changed his voice, as though justifying himself and growing timid, "how in the world is my sort to make a study of that which not a single clever person has yet written down in a book? I would even rejoice to take lessons from it—from Russian life, that is—but then it just keeps silent, the darling. 'You've got to understand without any explanations, now.' But then that's beyond my strength; you must give me an inference, place a conclusion before me. A conclusion? 'Very well,' they tell me, 'here's a conclusion for you: just listen to our Moscow sages—aren't they veritable nightingales, now?' But that's just the trouble, that they trill like Kursk nightingales, but don't speak like human beings. There, I kept thinking and thinking: science, you might imagine, is all the same everywhere, and so is truth—so I up and set out, with God's help, for a strange region, to the pagans. Well, what would you: youth overcame me, and pride. I didn't feel like becoming bloated with fat before my time, you know—even though it's actually a healthy thing, they say. But then, incidentally, he to whom nature hasn't given flesh isn't likely to see fat on his body, either!

"However," he added after a little reflection, "I believe I promised to tell you how I came to get married. Listen, then. In the first place, I must inform you that my wife is no longer in this world; in the second place—well, in the second place, I see that I'll have to tell you of my youth, for otherwise you won't understand anything. For you don't feel like sleeping, do you?"

"No, I don't."

"Well, that's fine. Just listen, now, to M'sieu' Kantagriuhin snoring away in the next room—not at all genteel! . . . The parents I was born to weren't at all rich—I say 'parents' because, according to tradition, I had a father as well as a mother. I don't remember him; they say he wasn't any too bright, that he had a big nose and a lot of freckles and was red-headed, and also had a way of taking snuff up one nostril only; his portrait hung in mother's bedroom, showing him in a red uniform with a black collar reaching right up to his ears—an exceedingly hideous portrait. They used to lead me past it whenever I was headed for a whipping, and on such occasions my mother would always point it out to me, adding: 'He would have given you a still worse hiding.' You can imagine how that encouraged me. I had neither brother nor sister; that is, to be truthful, there had been some sort of a little brother, always bedridden; he had the English disease—rachitis, you know—in the back of his neck; but then he died, somehow all too quickly. And why, come to think of it, should the English disease make its way not only into the Kursk province but the district of Shchigrov itself? But that's not the main thing! Mother busied herself with my education, with all the impetuous zeal of a steppe landowner: she busied herself therewith right from the splendiferous day of my birth until such time as I reached sixteen. Are you following the course of my story?"

"Of course; do go on."

"Very well, then. And so, as soon as I reached sixteen my mother, without the least delay, up and kicked out my

French tutor—who was a German by the name of Philipovich and hailed from the Greeks of the Nezhin district—entered me at a university, and then gave up her soul to the Almighty, leaving me to a dear uncle of mine, a pettifogger by the name of Koltun-Babura, a character known even outside of the Shchigrov district. This dear uncle of mine, the pettifogger Koltun-Babura, robbed me, in the usual order of things, as clean as a whistle. But, again, that's not the main thing. I entered the university quite well prepared—I must be quite just to my mother on that point; but my lack of originality could be noted even then. My childhood had been in no way distinguished from the childhood of other young men: I had kept growing just as stupidly and listlessly, as if under a featherbed, had taken just as early to getting poems down by heart, and to turning wishy-washy under the pretext of being pensively inclined . . . what was I leading up to with that, now? Oh, yes: being pensively inclined toward the Beautiful, and so on. At the university I did not strike out upon any different path: I immediately found myself in a Little Circle. Times were different then. But, perhaps, you don't happen to know just what sort of a thing a Little Circle is? If I remember rightly, Schiller has said somewhere:

> *Gefährlich ist's, den Leu zu wecken,*
> *Und schrecklich ist des Tigers Zahn,*
> *Doch das schrecklichste der Schrecken—*
> *Das ist der Mensch in seinem Wahn!* [1]

That, I assure you, wasn't what he wanted to say; what he wanted to say is: *Das ist ein* Little Circle *in der Stadt Moscau!*"

"But just what do you find terrible about a little circle?" I asked.

My roommate grabbed his nightcap and shoved it down over his nose.

"What do I find so terrible about it?" he cried out. "Why, just this: a Little Circle is . . . why, it's the perdition of any independent development; a Little Circle is a hideous sur-

[1] Dreadful it is to rouse the lion,
And terrible the tiger's tooth—
Yet the most terrible of terrors
Is man deep sunk in his untruth.

rogatum for society, for woman, for life; a Little Circle . . . oh, wait a minute—I'll tell you what a Little Circle is! A Little Circle—that's a lazy and listless way of living together, side by side, with something which is given the significance and form of sensible work; a Little Circle replaces conversation with disquisitions, habituates you to sterile chatter, draws you away from doing any really beneficial work all by your lonesome, vaccinates you with the literary itch—deprives you, finally, of the freshness and virginal fortitude of soul. A Little Circle—why, it's just vulgarity and boredom under the name of fraternity and friendship, a coupling of misunderstandings and pretenses under the pretext of frankness and sympathy; in a Little Circle, thanks to the right of each friend to shove his unwashed fingers right into the vitals of a comrade at any time and at any hour, no one has a clean, untouched spot in his soul; in a Little Circle they bow down in worship before the empty-headed spellbinder, the self-conceited smart aleck, the premature ancient; they dandle the versifier without any gifts but with 'cryptic' thoughts; in a Little Circle seventeen-year-old lads deliver cunning and finicky discourses on women and love, while in the presence of women they are dumb or talk with them as if a woman were a book—and the things they talk about! Crafty eloquence flourishes in the Little Circle; in the Little Circle they watch one another every bit as expertly as police agents! Oh, you Little Circle! You are no Little Circle—you are a bewitched circle, in which more than one decent fellow has perished!"

"Really, permit me to remark that you're exaggerating," I interrupted him. My roommate looked at me in silence.

"Perhaps. The Lord knows how I am; perhaps I am exaggerating. But then, there's only one pleasure left for the likes of me—that of exaggerating. There, sir, that's how I spent four years in Moscow. I am unable to describe to you, my dear sir, how fast, how frightfully fast this time passed; that's something actually sad and vexatious to recall. I'd get up in the morning, I remember, and then start off, just as if I were tobogganing downhill. First thing I knew I'd already hit bottom; there, it was evening already; there, the sleepy servant was encasing me in a frock coat; I'd dress up and toddle off to some friend's place and light up my little pipe, drinking tumbler after tumbler of weak tea and discoursing on German philosophy, love, the eternal sun of the spirit, and other such transcendental subjects. But even there I met original, individual persons; now and then one of these, no matter how he strove to break himself, to bend himself double, had nevertheless to let nature have her way with him; I alone, miserable creature that I was, kept molding myself as if I were soft wax, and my sorry nature did not evince the least resistance!

"In the meantime I had turned twenty-one. I came into possession of my inheritance—or, more correctly, that part of my inheritance which my guardian had thought it most prudent to leave me; I gave power of attorney for the management of all my hereditary lands to Vassilii Kudriashov, a house serf who had been granted his freedom, and went off abroad, to Berlin. I stayed abroad, as I've already had the pleasure of informing you, for three years. Well, and what was the upshot? Even there, abroad, I remained the same unoriginal being.

"First of all, it goes without saying that I didn't gain even a smidgeon of knowledge of the real Europe, of the European way of life; I listened to German philosophers and read German books in the very place of their origin . . . that's all the difference between myself and other tourists consisted of. The life I led was a cloistered one, just as if I were a monk of some sort; I became chummy with retired lieutenants, hagridden, just as I was, by a thirst for knowledge—all, however, quite slow of understanding and not gifted with the gift of words; I became exceedingly friendly with dull-witted families from Penza and other grain-yielding provinces; I traipsed from coffeehouse to coffeehouse, read periodicals, went to the theater of evenings. With the natives I had but little to do, conversing with them in a manner that was somehow strained, and never saw any of them at my place, with the exception of two or three tenacious young fellows of Jewish origin, who were forever dropping in on me and borrowing money—a good thing *der Russe* trusted them.

"A strange freak of chance tossed me, at last, into the home of one of my professors. Here's just how it happened: I'd come to him to enroll in a course, but he suddenly up and invited me to an evening at his home. This professor had two daughters, twenty-seven or thereabouts, such squat things—God be with them!—with such splendiferous noses, their curls all primped and their eyes pale blue, but their hands red, with white nails. One was called Linchen, the other Minchen. I took to calling at the professor's. I must tell you that this professor was—well, not exactly stupid, but sort of dazed: when on the platform he spoke quite coherently, but at home he lisped and kept his spectacles up on his forehead all the time; he was, for all that, the most learned of men. Well, what do you think? It suddenly seemed to me that I'd fallen in love with Linchen—yes, that's how it seemed to me, for all of six months.

"I spoke with her but little, it's true—for the most part I merely contemplated her; but I did read all sorts of touching pieces to her, squeezed her hand on the sly and, of evenings, indulged in reveries with her at my side, looking stubbornly up at the moon—or else simply looking up. Besides that, she could brew coffee so excellently! What more could one wish for, you might think? Only one thing embarrassed me: at those very moments of, as they say, ineffable beatitude I, for some reason, had a gnawing feeling at the pit of my stomach and a depressing, cold shiver would dart through my belly.

"At last I could no longer stand such happiness and ran away. After that I passed all of two years abroad: I was in Italy, stood dutifully before the Transfiguration in Rome, and I stood dutifully before the Venus in Florence as well; I would be plunged into sudden and exaggerated rapture, as if I were overcome by rage; of evenings I scribbled versicles, or would start keeping a diary; in short, here too my behavior was like that of everybody else. I don't understand a thing about painting and sculpture, for instance. Were I simply to come right out with it . . . but no, how could I! You must hire a cicerone, dash off to look at frescoes—"

He again cast down his eyes and again threw off his nightcap.

"Well, I came back to my native land at last," he went on in a tired voice. "I arrived in Moscow. In Moscow an astonishing change took place in me. Abroad I'd kept silent, for the most part, but here I suddenly began talking with unexpected liveliness and, at the same time, conceived God alone knows what dreams concerning myself. I came upon some accommodating persons to whom I seemed all but a genius; the ladies listened to my perorations with sympathy; I, however, wasn't able to keep my footing at the height of my fame. One fine morning saw the birth of a bit of gossip concerning me (whoever brought it forth into God's world I know not: it must have been some old maid of the male sex—there's no end of such old maids in Moscow); it was born and started letting shoots and tendrils, just as strawberries do. I became all tangled up in them, wanted to leap free, to tear these viscous filaments—but it was no use at all. I went away. Well, even here I turned out to be a flibbertigibbet: I should have marked time, ever so calmly, till this mishap was over—there, the way people wait to get over nettle rash—and those same accommodating people would again have met me with open arms, the same ladies would again have smiled at my discourses. . . .

"But that's just the trouble: I'm not an original person. Conscientiousness suddenly awakened within me, you see: I became ashamed, somehow, of chattering, chattering without ever shutting up, yesterday at a house on the Arbat, today at one on the Truba, tomorrow at Sitzevo-Vrazhok, and always about the one and the same thing. Yes, but what if that's the thing they demand? Take a look at the real combatants in this field: chattering doesn't mean a thing to them; on the contrary, that's all they really need: here and there you'll find a fellow among them who's been working his tongue for the twentieth year by now, and always heading in the same direction. What a lot do self-assurance and ambition mean! And I did have it—ambition, I mean—and even now it hasn't quieted down altogether. But then here's the bad feature, I'm telling you again: I'm not an original fellow; I have stopped halfway: nature should have issued considerably greater ambition to me, or else given me none at all.

"But at first I really did have a trying time of it; besides that, the trip abroad had definitely exhausted my resources; but as for marrying some merchant miss, with a young but already flabby body, I didn't want to do it—and I withdrew to my village. I think," my roommate added, after giving me another sidelong look, "that I can pass over in silence my first impressions of village life, all hints as to the beauty of nature, the tranquil charm of solitude, and so forth—"

"You may, you may," I hastened to respond.

"All the more so," the narrator went on, "since all that is bosh—at least as far as I am concerned. I was as bored in the village as a puppy when you lock it up—although I confess that, as I was passing a familiar birch grove on my way back, for the first time in spring, my head began to swim and my heart palpitated from a vague, delectable expectancy. But these dim expectations, as you yourself know, never materialize; on the contrary, it is other things which come to pass, things which one doesn't at all expect: murrains, arrears, being sold under the hammer, and so on, and so on. Getting along somehow from day to day, with the assistance of Yakov the steward—who had taken the place of the previous manager and who subsequently turned out to be as great a robber, if not a greater one, and who on top of that poisoned my existence with the odor of his tarred boots —I one day recalled a certain family I knew in the vicinity, consisting of an ex-colonel's widow and her two daughters; I had my droshky harnessed and drove off to see my neighbors. That day must remain memorable to me forever; six months later I married the widow's younger daughter!"

The narrator let his head sink and lifted his hands heavenward.

"Yet at the same time," he went on with vehemence, "I wouldn't wish to inspire you with a bad opinion of my late wife. God preserve me from that! This was the noblest, the kindliest of beings, a being that loved and was capable of all sacrifices, although I must confess, just between us, that if I hadn't had the misfortune of losing her I'd probably be in no state to be talking with you right now, since there still is, to this very day, a certain stout wooden beam in my concrete barn on which I had been about to hang myself, many's the time!

"Certain pears," he resumed after a short silence, "have to lie a certain time in earth, in a cellar, in order to come into their proper flavor, as they say; my late lamented, evidently, also belonged with such products of nature. Only now am I rendering full justice to her. For instance, only now do the recollections of certain evenings I spent with her before marriage not only fail to arouse the least bitterness in me but, on the contrary, move me almost to tears. Her people weren't rich; their house, quite old-fashioned, built of wood but comfortable, stood on a hill between a garden that had turned into a wilderness and a courtyard grown over with grass and weeds. A river flowed by at the foot of the hill, and one could barely see it through the dense leafage. A big terrace led from the house into the garden; an elongated flower bed, covered with roses, flaunted itself before the terrace; growing at each end of this flower bed were two acacias, which the late colonel had twisted together into the form of a screw when they had been mere saplings. A little farther on, in the very thick of the raspberry beds, neglected and run wild, stood an arbor, most quaintly painted within but so very ancient and decrepit on the outside that, looking at it, one felt uncanny.

"French doors led from the terrace into the drawing room, and this is what met the curious gaze of the observant visitor: stoves of figured tiles in the corners; a pianoforte, that sounded rather sour, to the right, piled up with manuscript music; a divan upholstered in faded, light-blue stuff with off-white stripes; a round table; two whatnots holding porcelain and beadwork knickknacks going back to the days of Catherine the Great; on one of the walls the familiar portrait of a flaxen-haired maiden with a dove nestling on her bosom and with her eyes rolled up; on the table, a vase of fresh-cut roses. . . .

"You see in what detail I describe everything. It was in that very drawing room, on that very terrace, that the entire tragicomedy of my love was played out. My neighbor, the colonel's widow herself, was a vile-tempered female, with the perpetual hoarseness of rancor in her throat, a tyrannous and snarling creature; of her daughters one, Vera, was in no way distinguishable from the run of young ladies in the backwoods; the other was called Sophia—it was Sophia I had fallen in love with. The two sisters had still another room, a tiny one, which they shared as a bedroom, with two little virginal beds of wood, yellowish little albums, little pots of mignonette, the walls hung with portraits of their friends, male and female, done in pencil and done rather poorly (standing out among these was that of a certain gentle-man with an unusually energetic expression on his face and a still more energetic signature, who in his youth had aroused inordinate expectations and who, like all of us, had wound up nowhere), with busts of Goethe and Schiller, German books, withered wreaths, and other objects left as mementoes.

"However, I entered this room infrequently and unwill-ingly: for some reason I found myself gasping for breath there. Also—an odd thing!—I liked Sophia best of all when I sat with my back to her, or else, if you like, when I was thinking—or rather dreaming—of her, especially of an eve-ning, out on the terrace. At such a time I gazed at the evening glow, at the trees, at the small green leaves, already turned darker but still standing out against the roseate sky; within the drawing room Sophia would be seated at the pianoforte and incessantly picking out some favorite, passionately pensive phrase from Beethoven; her vile-tempered crone of a mother was peacefully and intermittently snoring as she sat on the divan; in the dining room, flooded with a torrent of ruby-tinted light, Vera was bustlingly getting tea ready; the samovar was doing an intricate hissing solo, just as though it were rejoicing over something; the little pretzels broke with gay crackling, the spoons rang as they tapped against the cups; the canary, which had been mercilessly clattering all through the day, would suddenly fall quiet and merely chirp every now and then, as though it were asking about something; a transparent, light little cloud shed a few drops in passing. . . . But me, I sat and sat there, I listened and listened; I gazed, my heart expanding, and once more it seemed to me that I was in love.

"And so, under the influence of just such an evening, I once asked the crone for her daughter's hand, and two months or so later I was married. It seemed to me that I loved her. . . . And surely it's high time I knew, and yet, calling God to witness, I don't know even now whether I loved Sophia or not. She was a kind, intelligent, taciturn being with a warm heart; but God knows why, whether from having lived so long in a village, or for some other reasons, she had at the bottom of her soul (provided the soul has such a thing as a bottom) a hidden wound or, to put it better, a small oozing wound, which could not be healed in any way, and besides she could not even give it a name, nor could I. About the existence of this wound I surmised, naturally, only after marriage. No one could say I didn't struggle with her over it—nothing helped, however! When I was a child I had a greenfinch which our cat had once chanced to get into its paws for a while; it had been rescued and nursed back to health, but my poor greenfinch never did recover fully; it sulked, pined away, ceased to sing. The thing wound up with a rat getting into the bird's open cage one night and biting off his beak, in consequence of which the greenfinch at last made up its mind to die. What cat had gotten my wife in its paws I do not know, but she sulked and pined away in the same way as my unfortunate greenfinch. Now and then it seemed as if she herself wanted to perk up, to flutter playfully out in the fresh air, out in the sun and in freedom; she'd try it—and then curl up into a little ball. And yet, how she loved me, how many times did she assure me that she had nothing more left to wish for— oh, the Devil take it!" He spat aside. "Yet her eyes were at the same time simply dimming. Hadn't there been something in her past, I wondered. I made inquiries: there proved to be nothing. Well, and now judge for yourself: an original person would have shrugged, sighed a couple of times, perhaps, and then taken to living after his own fashion. But I, being an unoriginal being, began eyeing rafters, longingly and long. All the habits of an old maid—Beethoven, night strolls, mignonette, correspondence with friends, albums, and all the rest—had corroded her to such an extent that she just couldn't become habituated to any other way of life, especially to the life of a mistress of a household; and yet at the same time it is, after all, mirth-provoking for a married woman to languish from a nameless yearning and to sing, of evenings, 'Wake her not when the dawn cometh!'

"And so, sir, that's how we dwelt in bliss for three years; on the fourth Sophia died in giving birth to our first child and—a strange thing!—it was just as though I had felt beforehand that she would never be able to present me with a son or daughter, and the land with a new dweller. I remember how they buried her. In the spring, it was. Our parish church isn't big, and it's old; the iconostasis has turned black, the walls are bare, the brick floor is broken in places; there is a big, antiquated holy image on each choir stall. They carried in the coffin, placed it in the very middle before the altar rails, put a faded pall over it, placed three candles about it. The service began. A decrepit little sacristan, girded low with a broad green belt and with his hair tied into a tiny queue, was sadly mumbling in front of the pulpit; the priest, who was also an old man, with a kindly and near-sighted little face, in a lilac cassock damasked with yellow, was officiating both for himself and for the sacristan. The fresh leaves of young birches, taking up the entire breadth of the open windows, were stirring and murmuring; the odor of grasses drifted in from the churchyard; the red flames of the wax candles grew wan in the joyous light of the spring day; the sparrows simply filled the whole church with their chirping and, at infrequent intervals, the ringing call of a swallow that had flown in resounded under the cupola.

"Amid the aureate dust of a sunbeam the flaxen heads of the muzhiks—there weren't too many of them—bobbed nimbly as they prayed for the departed; incense smoke escaped in a thin, light-bluish stream from the vents of the censer.

"I gazed upon the dead face of my wife. My God! Even death, death itself, had not set her free, had not healed her wound: there was still that hurt, timid, mute expression—just as if, even in the coffin, she felt embarrassed. The blood within me stirred in bitterness. A kindly being had she been, a kindly being—yet she had done best even for herself by dying!"

The speaker's cheeks had turned red and his eyes had dimmed.

"Having at last gotten rid of the heavy despondence which had taken possession of me after my wife's death," he began speaking again, "I had an idea of buckling down, as they say, to work. I entered the civil service in the provincial capital; but in the great chambers of the official building I used to get severe headaches—my eyes, too, functioned badly; other reasons, also, came aptly. I retired. I had wanted to take a trip to Moscow but, in the first place, I hadn't enough money and, in the second . . . well, I've already told you that I had become resigned to my lot. This resignation had come upon me suddenly—and, at the same time, not at all suddenly. In spirit, now, I had become resigned long before, but then my head still did not feel like bowing itself. I ascribed the diffident state of my feelings and thoughts to the influence of country life, of misfortune. On the other hand, I had by now been long noticing that almost all my neighbors, both the young and the old, who had at first been abashed by my learning, by my trip abroad and the other advantages of my education, not only had had time to get perfectly used to me but had even begun to treat me with a blend of rudeness and the sort of condescension one shows to a simpleton, without bothering to hear my comments to the end and no longer bothering to use 'sir' in addressing me. I've also forgotten to tell you that during the first year of my marriage I had, out of boredom, made an attempt to embark on literature and had even sent something to a certain periodical—a novelette, if I'm not mistaken—but after some time I received a respectful letter from the editor, which said, among other things, that my intellect could not be denied but that my talent could, whereas in literature the prime requisite was, precisely, talent.

"In addition to that it had come to my ears that a certain transient from Moscow—the kindest of young men, by the bye—had let drop his casual opinion of me, during an evening party at the governor's, to the effect that I was a vapid fellow and that there was nothing to me. But my semivoluntary bedazzlement still continued; I didn't feel like batting my own ears down, you know; finally, one fine morning, my eyes were opened. Here's how it came about. The police inspector for the district had driven over to my place, to call my attention to a fallen bridge on my land-holdings, which bridge I had absolutely no money to repair. As he was having a bit of salted sturgeon after his glass of vodka, this condescending guardian of law and order chided me in a fatherly way about my carelessness; he entered into my position, however, and advised me all I had to do was to order my muzhiks to fill up the stream with manure, lit his stubby pipe, and began to talk of the forthcoming elections.

"The man who was at that time contending for the honorary title of marshal of the nobility was a certain Orbassanov, an empty-headed blowhard, and a grafter to boot. Besides, he was distinguished neither for wealth nor a good social position. I expressed my opinion concerning him, and quite offhandedly, at that: I was rather looking down my nose at Orbassanov, I confess. The inspector patted my shoulder kindly and good-naturedly let drop: 'Eh, Vassilii Vassilievich, it's not for the likes of you and me to be discussing such people. Where do we get off to do so? The shoemaker ought to stick to his last.' — 'Oh, please!' I retorted in vexation. 'Really, what's the difference between this Orbassanov and myself?' The police inspector took the pipe out of his mouth, popped out his eyes—and then simply exploded in laughter. 'Well, what a funny fellow, I must say!' he managed to get out at last, laughing so hard that tears came to his eyes. 'Just think of him springing a thing like that, eh? What do you think of him?' And right up to his departure he did not stop jeering at me, now and then giving me a dig in the ribs with his elbow, and by this time talking to me with the utmost familiarity.

"He left, finally. That was the last drop; my cup overflowed. I paced up and down the room several times, stopped in front of a mirror, and, after contemplating my confused face a long, long time, I slowly thrust out my tongue and shook my head with a smile of bitter mockery. The veil had fallen from before my eyes; I saw clearly, clearer than I saw my face in the mirror, what a fatuous, insignificant, and unnecessary man I was, and what an unoriginal one!"

The narrator kept silent for some time.

"In one of Voltaire's tragedies," he resumed despondently, "some seigneur or other rejoices because he has reached the ultimate limit of misfortune. Even though there's nothing tragic in my fate, yet I confess that I've had a taste of something of that sort. I have come to know the venomous raptures of icy despair; I have experienced how delectable it is, throughout a whole morning, taking one's time and lying in bed, to curse the day and hour one was born—yet I could not become resigned right off. And really, judge for yourself: lack of money kept me fettered to my hated village; neither running an estate, nor civil service, nor literature, nothing had proven suitable to me; I kept aloof from other landowners, books had become detestable to me; to the dropsically plump and unwholesomely sensitive misses who tossed their locks and feverishly parroted the word 'life' I did not represent anything engrossing ever since I had ceased to chatter and go off into raptures; neither did I know how to withdraw into utter solitude, nor could I do so.

"I took to—what do you think of that?—I took to traipsing around from neighbor to neighbor. As though intoxicated by contempt for my own self, I purposely subjected myself to all sorts of petty humiliations. The servants passed me by at table; I was met coldly and haughtily; at last they took no notice of me at all; they wouldn't even give me a chance to put in my oar in the general conversation, and there were times when I myself would, from around a corner, play yes man to some chatterbox, a most stupid one, who in times past, in Moscow, would have been enraptured to kiss the hem of my overcoat, the dust of my feet. . . . I would not even permit myself to think that I was indulging in the wormwood gratification of irony. What sort of irony is it, if you please, when you're all by your lonesome! There, sir, that's how I acted for several years in a row, and how I am still acting, right up to now—"

"What sort of disgraceful conduct is that, now?" the sleepy voice of Kantagriuhin grumbled in the next room. "What fool has gotten the notion of talking in the middle of the night?"

The man who had been telling the story dived nimbly under his blanket and, peering out timidly, shook a warning finger at me:

"Sh . . . sh. . . ." he got out in a whisper and, as though apologizing and bowing in the direction of the Kantagriuhian voice, uttered with deference: "I obey you, sir, I obey—excuse me, sir. . . . It is right and proper for him to sleep," he went on anew in a whisper. "He has to replenish his forces—well, now, if only to be able to eat on the morrow with the same undeviating gusto. We have no right to disturb him. Besides, it would seem I've already told you everything I wanted to tell; probably you, too, want to sleep. I wish you good night."

The storyteller turned away with feverish rapidity and buried his head in the pillows.

"Permit me, at least," I asked, "to learn with whom I have had the pleasure of conversing—"

He raised his head briskly:

"No, for God's sake," he broke in on me, "don't ask my name, either from me or from others. Let me remain an unknown being to you; a Vassilii Vassilievich whom fate has winged. Besides that I, as an unoriginal fellow, actually don't rate any specific name. But if you're absolutely bound to give me some tag, why, you might call me . . . you might call me Prince Hamlet of the Shchigrov District. Of such Hamlets there is a slew in every district but, perhaps, you haven't come up against others. . . . So fare you well."

He again burrowed into his featherbed and, next morning, when they came to wake me, he was no longer in the room. He had gone away before dawn.

CHERTOPKHANOV AND NEDOPIUSKIN

On a certain hot day in summer I was driving back in a cart after hunting; Ermolai was dozing and nodding as he sat beside me; the dogs, which had fallen asleep, were bouncing at our feet as if they were dead. The driver was constantly flicking the gadflies off the horses with his whip. The white dust was racing in a light cloud after our cart. We entered a thicket of brushwood. The road turned out to have even more ruts than the stretch before; the wheels began to catch against branches. Ermolai started awake and looked about him.

"Eh!" he spoke up. "Why, there must be grouse hereabouts. Let's get down."

We stopped and went into the woods. My dog chanced upon a covey. I fired, and was about to reload when suddenly loud crackling arose behind me and, parting the bushes, a man on horseback rode up to me.

"May I, er, be permitted to learn," he began in an arrogant voice, "by what right you are, er, hunting here, m'dear sir?"

The unknown was speaking with unusual rapidity, disjointedly and through his nose. I looked at his face: never, in all my born days, had I seen his like. Imagine, amiable readers, a bit of a man, fair-haired, with a red, upturned little nose and the longest of rusty-hued mustachios. A Persian cap, coming to a sharp point and topped with raspberry-colored broadcloth, covered his forehead right down to the eyebrows. He was dressed in a yellow, bedraggled Caucasian overcoat with cartridge loops of black plush across the chest and tarnished silver braid along every seam. Dangling over his shoulder was a hunting horn, sticking in his belt was a dagger. A skin-and-bones, hump-nosed, rusty-colored horse was swaying under him as if it were dazed from charcoal fumes; two wolfhounds, gaunt and crook-pawed, were also right there, milling about under the horse's legs.

The stranger's face, his gaze, his voice, his every motion, his whole being, breathed of harebrained derring-do and inordinate, unheard-of pride; his pale-blue, glassy eyes were diverging and crossing, like a drunkard's; he kept tossing his head far back, puffing out his cheeks, snorting, and shuddering with all his body, just as though from an excess of dignity, for all the world like a turkey cock. He repeated his question.

"I didn't know that shooting was prohibited here," I answered.

"My dear sir," he resumed, "you're on my land here."

"I'll go, if you like."

"May I, er, be permitted to learn," he retorted, "if I have the honor of conversing with one of the nobility?"

I gave him my name.

"In that case please go right ahead and hunt. I am of the nobility myself, and am very glad to be of service to another nobleman. As for my name, it's Chertop-khanov—Pantelei Chertopkhanov."

He bent forward, let out a whoop, drew his horse's neck into an arch; the horse took to tossing its head, reared up on its hind legs, dashed to one side, and crushed a dog's paw. The dog started yelping, piercingly. Chertopkhanov seethed, began hissing, whacked his fist over the horse's head right between its ears, leaped to the ground faster than any lightning, inspected the dog's paw, spat on the wound a few times, kicked the dog in the ribs to make it stop yelping, grabbed the horse's withers, and set his foot in the stirrup. The horse threw up its muzzle, hoisted its tail, and dashed sideways into the bushes; Chertopkhanov started hopping on his one free leg—however, he finally did manage, somehow, to land in the saddle; he started whirling his quirt as if he were out of his senses, blew blast after blast on his horn, and galloped off.

I hadn't had time to recover fully from the unexpected appearance of Chertopkhanov when suddenly, almost without any noise, a rather stout little man of forty came riding out of the bushes on a diminutive, blackish jade. He halted, took off his brimmed cap of green leather, and in a voice soft and ever so high, asked me whether I hadn't seen a man on a rusty-colored horse. I answered that I had.

"In what direction did he deign to go?" he went on in the same voice and without putting on his cap.

"That way, sir."

"Thank you most humbly, sir."

He made a clucking noise with his lips, threshed his legs over his diminutive jade's ribs, and went off at a jog trot—*clippety-clop, clippety-clop*—in the indicated direction. I kept looking after him until his cap, the points of which looked like horns, disappeared behind the branches. This new stranger did not, in his appearance, resemble his predecessor in the least. His face, plump and as round as a globe, expressed shyness, kindheartedness, and meek resignation; his nose, likewise plump and round, mottled with tiny blue veins, revealed him as a voluptuary. Not a hair, even the smallest, remained on the forepart of his head; at the back of it his hair stuck out in blondish, rather scanty tufts like tiny queues; his little eyes, which looked just as if their slits had been cut through with a blade of reed grass, blinked in a kindly sort of way; sweetly smiling were his red and succulent lips. He had on a surtout, quite worn but neat, with a standing collar and brass buttons; his small trousers, of broadcloth, had crept high—over the yellow tops of his boots one could see his fat little calves.

"Who's that?" I asked Ermolai.

"That? That's Nedopiuskin, Tihon Ivanych. Lives at Chertopkhanov's."

"What is he, a poor man?"

"He isn't rich; but then Chertopkhanov hasn't a copper, either."

"Then why has this fellow come to live with him?"

"Why, you see, they've become fast friends. The one never goes anywhere without the other. There, it sure holds true: where the steed goes with his hoof, the crayfish goes with its claw."

We came out of the bushes. Suddenly two coursing hounds started yapping close to us and a full-grown white hare dashed off through the oats, which were quite high by now. Right after him the dogs, the coursing hounds as well as the wolfhounds, jumped out at the edge of the woods, and right after the dogs Chertopkhanov himself came flying. He wasn't shouting, wasn't setting the dogs on, wasn't doing any hallooing: he was gasping, gulping—disjointed, senseless sounds escaped now and then from his gaping mouth; he was dashing along with his eyes goggling and was frenziedly lashing his unfortunate horse with his quirt. The wolfhounds came up; the white hare squatted, doubled back sharply, and dived, past Ermolai, into the bushes. The wolfhounds sped by.

"Ru-u-un, ru-u-un!" the swooning hunter began to babble with an effort, just as if he were tongue-tied. "Watch out, dear man!"

Ermolai fired. The wounded white hare rolled head over heels along the smooth and dry grass, gave one upward leap, and let out a piteous cry as he felt the teeth of a hunt-crazed hound. The coursing dogs immediately came up, tumbling over themselves in their haste.

Chertopkhanov flew down off his horse like a tumbling pigeon, snatched out his dagger, ran up to the dogs, spreading his legs wide as he ran, with ferocious adjurations snatched the mangled hare away from them, and with his whole face distorted, plunged his dagger into its throat up to the very hilt—plunged it in and went off into gabbling laughter. Tihon Ivanych appeared at the edge of the woods.

"Ho-ho-ho-ho-ho-ho-ho-ho!" Chertopkhanov began to clamor again.

"Ho-ho-ho-ho," his comrade echoed him calmly.

"However, one really ought not to hunt in summer," I remarked, pointing the trampled oats out to Chertopkhanov.

"It's my own field," Chertopkhanov answered, barely able to breathe.

He dressed the hare, fastened it to his saddle, and distributed the paws among the dogs.

"I owe you for the shot, my good man," he remarked, in keeping with hunting usage, as he turned to Ermolai. "As for you, dear sir," he added in the same disjointed and grating voice, "I thank you."

He got up on his horse.

"May I, er, be permitted to learn your name . . . I've forgotten it."

I again gave him my name.

"Very glad to make your acquaintance. Should the occasion arise, I beg of you to drop in on me—you'll be welcome. . . . But where is that Thomka, Tihon Ivanych?" he went on, heartily vexed. "We hunted the hare down without him."

"Why, his horse foundered under him," Tihon Ivanych answered with a smile.

"Foundered? What do you mean? Orbassan foundered? Pshaw! Pfut! Where is he—where?"

"There, beyond the woods."

Chertopkhanov brought his quirt down on the horse's muzzle and was off at a breakneck gallop. Tihon Ivanych bowed to me twice—once for himself and once for his comrade—and again went off into the bushes at a jog trot.

These two gentlemen had greatly aroused my curiosity. What could have bound with ties of inseverable friendship two beings so unlike in their natures? I began making inquiries. Here is what I found out.

Chertopkhanov, Pantelei Eremeich, had throughout the district the reputation of a dangerous and harebrained fellow, a proud stick, and a fire-eater of the first order. He had served in the army for a short while and had resigned "over an unpleasantness" as an ensign—that rank concerning which an opinion has spread that it is no rank, just as a hen is considered no bird. He came from an ancient, once wealthy line; his grandsires had lived on a magnificent scale, the way the steppe squires do—which is to say that they kept open house for those who were invited as well as those who weren't, feeding these guests as if they were fattening them for slaughter, issuing eight bushels of oats at a time to strange coachmen for each troika, keeping musicians, singers, jesters, and dogs; on high holidays they made the common folk drunk on wine and mead; in winter they drove all the way to Moscow on their own horses, in ponderous, old-fashioned coaches, while at other times, for months at a stretch, they would vegetate without a copper and subsist on poultry and whatever victuals might be around the house.

When Pantelei Eremeich's father had come into the estate it was already ruined; he in his turn also had a mighty good time out of it and, dying, left to Pantelei, his sole heir, the tiny mortgaged village of Bezsonovo,[1] with thirty-five souls of the male sex and seventy-six of the female, as well as thirty-eight acres and a bit over (all of it hard to work) in the wasteland of Kolobrodova—for which, however, no deeds of any sort were found among the papers of the departed.

The departed had, it must be confessed, bankrupted himself in the oddest fashion: it was "economic considerations" which had proven his undoing. According to his understanding of things it did not behoove a nobleman to be dependent on merchants, city slickers, and other such "cutthroats," as he put it: he started on his place all possible sorts of crafts and workshops. "That's both more seemly and cheaper," he used to say. "Economic considerations!"

He never forsook this pernicious idea until the end of his life; it was precisely this which ruined him. But then, he surely had his fill of fun! There was never a whim which he denied himself. Among his other fancies he thought of constructing, in accordance with his own notions, a family coach so enormous that, despite the strenuous teamwork of all the peasants' horses (which, together with their owners, had been rounded up throughout the village), the vehicle rolled over and went all to pieces on the slope of the first hill it came to. Eremei Lukich (that's what they called Pantelei's father) ordered a monument to be put up on that hill slope but, on the whole, wasn't in the least put out.

He also got the notion of putting up a church—all by himself, of course, without the aid of any of your architects. He burned a whole forest to fire the bricks, laid a foundation so enormous that it would have done even for a cathedral in the provincial capital, raised the walls, and began putting up the cupola. The cupola collapsed. He tried it again—the cupola again fell down; he tried it a third time—the cupola crashed down for the third time. It was then that my Eremei Lukich became downright thoughtful: things weren't at all right, he reflected—there must be some accursed witchcraft mixed up in all this—and suddenly he up and ordered all the old women in the village to be soundly flogged. Soundly flogged they were, each and every one—but, just the same, he never did put up that cupola.

1 "Sleepless."—*Trans.*

He went in for rebuilding the peasants' huts according to a new plan—and all out of economic considerations: he'd put three farmyards together in a triangle and, right in the middle of that triangle, he'd raise a pole with a gaily painted birdhouse for starlings and a flag on top of it.

Every day he used to get some new maggot into his head: now he'd take to cooking soup out of burdocks, then to shearing all the hair off the horses' tails to weave into caps for his house serfs, or he'd be getting all set to sow nettles in place of flax, or to feed the pigs on mushrooms. One day he happened to read a little piece by a Harkov landowner, one Hriak-Hrupersky, in the *Moscow Intelligencer,* about the benefits of morality in the life of the peasants, and the very next day he issued an order to all the peasants to get the Harkov landowner's piece by heart. Get the piece by heart the peasants did; the master asked them, had they understood what it was about? The head clerk answered that, now, how could they help understanding it?

About the same time he decreed, for the sake of system and out of economic considerations, that all his subjects were to be renumbered, and that each was to have his number embroidered on his collar. No sooner did each one come across his master than he'd already be calling out: "Number Such-and-Such coming!"—while the master would answer him kindly: "Go, and God be with you!"

However, despite all system and economic considerations, Eremei Lukich little by little came to a quite embarrassing pass: he started off by mortgaging his little villages, and after that he took to selling them; it was the Treasury Department itself which sold the last nest of his grandsires (the settlement with the unfinished church); fortunately, this didn't happen while Eremei Lukich was still alive—he would never have been able to bear this blow—but two weeks after his demise. He had succeeded in dying in his own house, in his own bed, surrounded by people whom he owned and tended by a physician whom he also owned. Just the same, Bezsonovo was all the estate that came down to Pantelei.

Pentelei learned of his father's illness when he was already in the army, while the unpleasantness already mentioned was at its most vehement stage. He had just reached his nineteenth year. From his very childhood he had never left the parental home and, under the guidance of his mother, Vassilissa Vassilievna, the kindest-hearted of women but utterly dull-witted, he had grown up a petted darling and a young master. She had attended to his education all by herself. Eremei Lukich, up to his neck in economic considerations, had other things on his mind. True, he had once chastised his son with his own hands, because the boy had pronounced *Rtzy* [2] as *a-Rtzy;* on that day, however, Eremei Lukich had been sorrowing with a deep and secret sorrow: his best hound had killed itself by dashing against a tree.

Vassilissa Vassilievna's cares concerning Pantiusha's education had, however, been confined to a single excruciating effort; in the sweat of her brow she had hired as his tutor a superannuated soldier, a certain Bierkopf, by origin an Alsatian, and to the very day of her death she trembled like an aspen leaf before him: "Well, now," she kept thinking, "if he should throw up his place I would be done for! Where could I turn? Where could I find another teacher? Why, it was just about all I could do to lure this fellow away from a neighboring lady!" And Bierkopf, being a man of penetration, at once took advantage of the exceptional nature of his position: he used to get dead drunk and sleep from morning till night. On finishing his "course of learning" Pantelei had entered the army. Vassilissa Vassilievna was no longer among the living. She had passed away half a year before this important event, from fright: she had seen, in a dream, a man all in white, mounted on a bear. Eremei Lukich had followed his better half shortly afterward.

Pantelei, at the first news of his illness, had come galloping home at breakneck speed; however, he did not find his parent alive. But what was the astonishment of the dutiful son when, utterly unexpectedly, he was transformed from a rich heir into a pauper! There are few who can bear up under such a sharp break. Pantelei became a savage; he turned ferocious. From a man who, although a harum-scarum sort, had been honest, generous, and kind, he became transformed into a proud stick and a fire-eater, ceased having anything to do with his neighbors—before the rich ones he felt ashamed, the poor ones he looked down upon—and treated everybody, even those established in authority, with un-

2 The Slavonic name of the letter R.—*Trans.*

heard-of impudence: "I, now, am a nobleman enrolled in the columns of the Book of the Nobility." On one occasion he had all but shot the commissioner of rural police, who had walked into his room without removing his cap. Naturally the authorities, for their part, also would not let him get away with anything and, whenever they got the chance, threw their weight around, but just the same, people were rather afraid of him, because he was a dreadful pepper pot and, with hardly a preliminary word, would propose fighting with dirks. At the least contradiction Chertopkhanov's eyes diverged, his voice broke. "Ah, *va-va-va-va-va*," he babbled, "damn my body and soul!"—and he was fit to be tied. But, all else aside, his hands were clean, he had never been mixed up in anything.

No one, naturally, ever called on him. Yet, for all that, the soul within him was a kind, even a great soul, after its fashion: he could not abide injustice and oppression, even when the victim was neither a kinsman nor a friend of his; he stood up for his muzhiks like a rocky fortress.

"What!" he would say, frenziedly pounding his own head. "You're going to touch my people, *my* people? May my name not be Chertopkhanov, then—"

Tihon Ivanych Nedopiuskin, unlike Pantelei Eremeich, could not take pride in his origin. His sire had sprung from the class of freeholders, those who own no more than a patch of land, and only after forty years in the civil service had he gained a footing among the gentry. Nedopiuskin, *père*, belonged to the number of those people whom fate persecutes with a ferocity that seems like personal hatred. During the entire course of threescore years, from his very birth to his very demise, the poor man struggled against all those privations, ailments, and adversities that are the lot of little people; he was as hard put to it as a fish beating its head against the ice; he did not eat enough, did not sleep enough; he had to kowtow, he hustled and bustled, he grew despondent and was racked by anxiety, shivered over every copper, had been wronged in the service actually "through no fault of his own," and when at last he had come to die he had done so either in a garret or a cellar, without having contrived to earn a crust of daily bread either for himself or his children. Fate had harried him to the last, as a rabbit is harried in the chase. A kindly man had he been, and an honest, yet he had taken bribes—from a ten-kopeck piece to all of two rubles, inclusively.

Nedopiuskin, *père,* had a wife, gaunt and consumptive. He had children, too: fortunately they had all died off young, with the exception of Tihon—yes, and a daughter, Mitrodora, who had been nicknamed "the shopkeepers' fashion plate" and who, after many lugubrious and mirth-provoking adventures, had married a retired pettifogger.

But the father had, after all, managed during his lifetime to place Tihon in a chancellery as an ungraded clerk; however, immediately after the death of his sire, Tihon had resigned. The eternal alarms, the excruciating struggle against cold and hunger, the distressing despondence of his mother, the bustling despair of his father, the coarse oppressions of landlord and shopkeeper—all this daily, never-ceasing woe had developed in Tihon a timidity beyond all reason: at the mere sight of one of his superiors he would quiver and become deadly still, like some small captured bird. He abandoned civil service.

Nature, indifferent and, perhaps, mocking as well, puts different abilities and inclinations into men, without at all taking into consideration their position in society and their means; nature, with that solicitude and love so peculiar to it, had molded out of Tihon, the son of a poor petty official, a being sensitive, indolent, soft, susceptible—a being drawn to enjoyment, gifted with extraordinarily fine senses of smell and taste—nature had molded him, had meticulously put in the finishing touches and then . . . had left it up to this handiwork of hers to grow up on sauerkraut and stinking fish, And lo, it had grown up, this handiwork of nature's, had started, as they say, "to lead its life." And then the fun began.

Fate, which with never a letup had been tearing with its fangs Nedopiuskin the father, now tackled the son as well: evidently it had acquired a taste for Nedopiuskins. With Tihon, however, it acted differently: it did not torture him —it amused itself with him. Not once did fate bring him to desperation, it did not compel him to undergo the shameful torments of hunger, but it did toss him from pillar to post over all of Russia, from Great-Ustiug into Czarevo-Kokshaisk, from one degrading and mirth-provoking position to another: now it would graciously make him a "major-domo" to a snarling and jaundiced Lady Bountiful, now place him

313

as a hanger-on to a rich skinflint of a merchant, or appoint him head of some domestic chancellery in the house of a popeyed seigneur who had his hair clipped after the British style; next it would make of him a half steward, half jester to a squire who hunted with hounds.

In a word, fate compelled poor Tihon to drink, drop by drop and down to the last drop, all the bitter and venomous potion of a servile existence. He had, in his time, served for the heavy-handed capriciousness, the sleep-laden and vicious ennui, of idle seigneurs. How many times, all by himself in his room, dismissed at last with "Godspeed" by the horde of guests who had had their sweet fill of fun, would he vow, all ablaze with shame, with icy tears of despair welling in his eyes, to sneak away the very next day, to try his luck in the city, to find himself a place, no matter how wretched, as a clerk—or else, while he was at it, to die of hunger in the street. But, in the first place, God had not endowed him with any strength; secondly, he was harried by timidity and, thirdly and lastly, how was he to solicit a place for himself, whom was he to turn to?

"They won't give me a chance," the unfortunate fellow used to whisper, tossing despondently in his bed. "They won't!"

And the next day he would again get back into harness.

His situation was all the more excruciating in that nature, even though so solicitous, had not apportioned to him even a moiety of those abilities and gifts without which the trade of an entertainer is all but impossible. He could not, for instance, either dance in a bearskin overcoat, turned with the fur lining out, until he fell down in exhaustion, or play the merry-andrew and indulge in pleasantries in the immediate proximity of freely swinging dog whips; if he was put out of doors, mother-naked, in a twenty-degree frost, he would now and then catch cold; his stomach could digest neither wine mixed with ink and other vile stuff, nor chopped-up agarics and toadstools, served in vinegar.

The Lord alone knows what would ever have become of Tihon, if the last of his benefactors, a tax farmer who had grown very rich, hadn't gotten the whim, in a merry hour, of adding a codicil to his will: "As for Zezya (the same being Tihon) Nedopiuskin, I leave and bequeath to him, in perpetual and hereditary possession, my honorably acquired village of Bezselendeievka, with all the appurtenances thereto." A few days later the benefactor, as he was sitting over a sterlet chowder, got his quietus from a stroke of paralysis. A great to-do was raised; the legal authorities swooped down and put seals on all the property, all in due form. The relatives gathered from far and near; the last will and testament was unsealed; it was read—Nedopiuskin's presence was called for. Nedopiuskin put in his appearance. Those gathered knew, for the most part, what sort of position Tihon Ivanych had held under his benefactor; deafening outcries, mocking congratulations poured forth in greeting to him.

"The landowner—there he is, the new landowner!" the other heirs kept shouting.

"Well, now, really," chimed in one of them, well known as a wag and a wit, "well, now, sure enough, we have here, one may say . . . well, now, actually . . . as it were . . . what they call, now . . . an heir!" And all those there simply split their sides laughing.

Nedopiuskin for a long while would not believe his good fortune. They showed him the will: he turned red, shut his eyes hard, started waving the others away and, sobbing, burst into torrents of tears. The laughter of those gathered there turned into a deep and unbroken roar. The village of Bezselendeievka consisted of two and twenty serf souls, all in all; no one greatly regretted not having gotten it: why, then, when one had the chance, shouldn't one have a bit of fun? Only one heir, Rostislav Adamych Schtoppel, who came from St. Petersburg, a man of imposing appearance with a Greek nose and the noblest of expressions on his face, could not restrain himself; he edged up to Nedopiuskin and gave him a haughty look over his shoulder.

"You, as far as I have been able to notice, my dear sir," he began with disdainful negligence, "were attached to the estimable Theodore Theodorovich in the capacity of a retainer whose duty it was to—amuse, shall we say?"

The gentleman from St. Petersburg expressed himself in unbearably pure, lively, and correct language. The distraught and agitated Nedopiuskin hadn't caught clearly the words of this gentleman whom he did not know. All the others, however, immediately fell silent; the wit smiled condescendingly. Monsieur Schtoppel rubbed his hands and repeated his question. Nedopiuskin looked up in amazement and opened his mouth. Rostislav Adamych narrowed his eyes caustically.

"I felicitate you, my dear sir," he went on. "True, it isn't every man, we may say, who would consent to earrrrn his daily bread in such a manner, but—*de gustibus non est disputandum;* that is, every man to his taste. . . . Isn't that so?"

Someone in the back rows let out a squeal of amazement and delight, a squeal abrupt yet decorous.

"Tell me," Monsieur Schtoppel quickly resumed, encouraged very much by the smiles of the entire assembly, "to what talent in particular do you owe your good fortune? No, don't be ashamed—*do* tell us: all of us here are, so to say, our own people, *en famille*. Isn't that so, gentlemen—all of us here are *en famille?*"

The heir to whom Rostislav Adamych had chanced to turn with this question did not, unfortunately, know French, and therefore confined himself merely to a grunt of approval. Another heir, however, a young man with yellowish blotches on his forehead, hurriedly chimed in with some phrase in broken French and concluded with "of course!"

"Perhaps," Monsieur Schtoppel began again, "you know how to walk on your hands, with your legs up in the air, so to say?"

Nedopiuskin looked about him despondently: all the faces wore malevolent sneers, all eyes were misted over with pleasure.

"Or, perhaps, you know how to crow like a rooster?"

An explosion of laughter burst all around Nedopiuskin, and immediately subsided, stifled by expectation.

"Or can you, perhaps, balance things on your nose—"

"Stop that!" a harsh and loud voice suddenly broke in on Rostislav Adamych. "How is it you're not ashamed to torture the poor man?"

They all looked over their shoulders. Standing in the doorway was Chertopkhanov. As a nephew, four times removed, of the late tax farmer, he too had received a letter inviting him to attend the family conclave. Throughout the reading of the will he had, as always, kept himself proudly aloof from the others.

"Stop it," he repeated, with his head proudly thrown back.

Monsieur Schtoppel quickly turned around and, catching sight of somebody poorly dressed, unimpressive, in a low voice asked a man standing next to himself (it never does any harm to be cautious):

"Who's that?"

"Chertopkhanov—he's no eagle," the other answered in his ear.

Rostislav Adamych assumed a haughty air.

"And who are you to be issuing orders?" he said through his nose. "What sort of fine-feathered bird may you be, permit me to ask?"

Chertopkhanov flared up like gunpowder from a spark. Fury cut off his breath.

"*Dz-dz-dz-dz,*" he began hissing, just as if he had been strangled, and suddenly thundered: "Who am I? Who am I? I am Pantelei Chertopkhanov, a nobleman enrolled in the Book of Nobility; my great-great-grandsire's grandsire served the czar—but who may *you* be?"

Rostislav Adamych turned pale and took a step backward. He had not expected such a repulse.

"I am a fine-feathered bird, I! I am a fine-feathered bird. . . . *O, o, o!*"

Chertopkhanov lunged forward; Schtoppel leaped back in great agitation—the guests rushed to head off the aroused squire.

"Pistols, pistols, pistols at once—at the drop of a handkerchief!" Pantelei, now infuriated to the utmost, kept shouting. "Either that or you'll apologize to me, and to him, too."

"Apologize, apologize!" the alarmed heirs surrounding Schtoppel were muttering. "Why, he's such a madman, he's all set to slit your throat."

"Pardon me, pardon me, I didn't know," Schtoppel began babbling. "I didn't know—"

"Apologize to him, too!" vociferated Pantelei, who would not abate.

"I ask your pardon also," added Rostislav Adamych, turning to Nedopiuskin who, in his turn, was shaking as if he had the ague.

Chertopkhanov calmed down, walked up to Tihon Ivanych, took him by the arm, looked about him challengingly, and without encountering a single glance, triumphantly, amid profound silence, walked out of the room together with the new owner of the honorably acquired village of Bezselendeievka.

They never parted from that day on. (The village of Bezselendeievka was only a little over five miles from Bezsonovo.) Nedopiuskin's unbounded gratitude soon passed

317

into abject veneration. The soft, weak, and not altogether pure Tihon bowed down to the very dust before the fearless and disinterested Pantelei.

"It's no trifling matter, is it?" he reflected now and then. "Why, he talks to the governor—and looks him right in the eye. So help me Christ—he just looks right at him!"

His wonder at Chertopkhanov brought him to the verge of bewilderment, of a prostration of his spiritual powers; he considered him an extraordinary man, clever, learned. And it must be said that, no matter how poor Chertopkhanov's education had been, by comparison with Tihon's it nevertheless might have seemed brilliant. Chertopkhanov, it is true, read but little in Russian, and understood French poorly—so very poorly that once, to the question of a tutor who was a Swiss: *"Vous parlez français, Monsieur?"* he had answered: *"Je ne* understand—" and, after a little reflection, added: *"—pas."* But, just the same, he remembered that there had been a Voltaire in this world, a writer ever so pungent, and that Frederick the Great, King of the Prussians, was another distinguished person, in military matters. Of the Russian writers he esteemed Derzhavin, but it was Marlinsky, the historical novelist, whom he loved, and he had bestowed the name of Ammalat-Bey on his best hound.

A few days after my first meeting with these two friends I set out for the village of Bezsonovo to see Pantelei Eremeich. His little house could be seen from afar; it was stuck on a bare spot, a third of a mile from the village—all out in the open, as they say, just like a hawk over a plowed field. Chertopkhanov's entire manorial seat consisted of four ancient log structures, each of a different size: to wit, a small house, a stable, a barn, and a bathhouse. Each building squatted by itself: one couldn't notice any all-enclosing fence or any gate.

My driver drew up in perplexity near a well that was half rotted and clogged up with rubbish. Close to the barn several gaunt and bristling wolfhound pups were tearing a dead horse to pieces—Orbassans, probably: one of them raised its bloodied muzzle at first, let out a few hurried yaps, and fell anew to gnawing at the exposed ribs. Standing by the horse was a lad of seventeen with a face yellow and puffy; he was dressed like a Cossack but was barefooted; he kept glancing with an important air at the dogs entrusted to his care, and every now and then would lash out with his whip at the bloodthirstiest ones.

"Is the master at home?" I asked.

"Why, the Lord knows where he is!" answered the lad. "You might knock."

I jumped down from the droshky and approached the front entrance of the main building.

Squire Chertopkhanov's dwelling presented a quite melancholy appearance: the logs of which it was built had turned dark with time and had bellied out; the chimney had tumbled down; the corners were rotted from the damp and had sagged; the small windows, their panes a dull dove gray, peeped out with an inexpressibly dour air from under the shaggy thatching, drawn down like a cap: certain ancient trollops have eyes like that.

I knocked; no one responded. However, I could hear, on the other side of the door, someone sharply enunciating the Slavonic names of the first letters of the Russian alphabet:

"*Az, Buki, Vedi!* Come, now, you fool," a husky voice was saying, "*Az, Buki, Vedi, Glagol* . . . no, not now! *Glagol, Dobro—Yest, Yest!* [3] Come, now, you fool!"

I knocked once more.

The same voice called out:

"Come in, whoever it is—"

I stepped into a small, empty entry and through an open door caught sight of Chertopkhanov himself. He was sitting on a chair in a greasy Bukhara dressing gown, ballooning Ukrainian trousers, and a red skullcap; with one hand he was squeezing the muzzle of a young poodle and, in the other, holding a bit of bread over its very nose.

"Ah!" he uttered with dignity and without making a move to get up. "I am very glad you have called. Sit down, I beg you. I am fussing with this poodle Vensor. . . . Tihon Ivanych," he added, raising his voice, "please come here. We have a guest."

"Right away, right away," Tihon Ivanych answered from an adjoining room. "Masha, hand me my cravat."

Chertopkhanov turned anew to Vensor and placed the bit of bread on the poodle's nose. I looked about me. There was no furniture whatsoever in the room, save for a warped extension table on thirteen legs of unequal lengths and four

3 "Eat! Eat!"—*Trans.*

319

chairs with their straw bottoms sagging; the walls, which ever so long ago had been whitewashed, with blue spots that looked like stars, had peeled in many places; hanging between the windows was a small mirror, broken and tarnished, in an enormous frame of would-be mahogany. Standing in the corners were guns and long-stemmed tobacco pipes; cobwebs dangled from the ceiling in thick and black threads.

"*Az, Buki, Vedi, Glagol, Dobro,*" Chertopkhanov was slowly enunciating, and then suddenly cried out in a frenzy: "*Yest! Yest! Yest!* What a stupid animal. . . . *Yest!*"

But the ill-starred poodle merely shuddered from time to time and could not bring himself to open its mouth; he kept on squatting there, with his tail tucked in under him in a pained sort of way and, with his muzzle all twisted, was despondently blinking and puckering his eyes, as though he were saying to himself: "You know how it is, your will be done, my master!"

"Go ahead and eat—there! Take it!" the indefatigable squire kept repeating.

"You have frightened him completely," I remarked.

"Well, in that case, out with him!"

He shoved the dog away with his foot. The poor fellow got up quietly, let the bread fall off his nose, and went off, as though on tiptoe, into the entry, deeply offended. And, truly: here was a stranger, who had come for the first time, yet look at the way they were treating him.

The door of the adjoining room gave a cautious creak and Nedopiuskin entered, amiably bowing and smiling. I got up and also bowed.

"Don't disturb yourself, don't disturb yourself," he began to babble.

We made ourselves comfortable in our chairs. Chertopkhanov went into the next room.

"Is it long since you have favored our native region with your presence?" Nedopiuskin began in a soft voice, coughing carefully into his fist and, out of decorum, keeping his fingers before his mouth for a little while.

"Going on the second month now."

"As long as all that, sir?"

We kept silent for a while.

"Pleasant weather we're having now," Nedopiuskin resumed and gave me a grateful look, as though the weather were in my keeping. "Grain doing remarkably well, one may say."

I inclined my head as a mark of agreement. We kept silent for another while.

"Pantelei Eremeich hunted down two gray hares yesterday," Nedopiuskin began again, not without an effort, evidently desirous of enlivening the conversation. "Yes, sir—ever so big, sir—the hares I mean, sir."

"Has your friend Chertopkhanov good dogs?"

"Most amazing ones, sir!" Nedopiuskin responded with gratification. "The first throughout the province, one may say." He moved closer to me. "But that's nothing, sir. What a man Pantelei Eremeich is! Whatever his wish, no sooner does the notion strike him than, look and behold you, everything's all done, everything's already simply seething, sir. Pantelei Eremeich, I must tell you—"

Chertopkhanov came into the room. Nedopiuskin smiled slightly, fell silent, and indicated him with his eyes, as though he would say: "There, you will surely see for yourself." We began to talk about hunting.

"Would you like me to show you my pack?" Chertopkhanov asked and, without having waited for my answer, called out for Karp.

A husky fellow in a nankeen caftan of green, with a collar of blue and buttons such as are used on liveries, entered the room.

"You tell Thomka," Chertopkhanov let drop jerkily, "to bring Ammalat and Gazelle here—and everything is to be just right: you understand?"

Karp distended his whole mouth in a grin, emitted an indeterminate sound, and went out. Thoma appeared, his hair neatly combed, his belt tightly drawn, in boots and with the dogs. I, out of politeness, admired the stupid animals (all borzois are inordinately stupid). Chertopkhanov spat right up Ammalat's nostrils—which, however, apparently afforded that hound not the least pleasure. Nedopiuskin in his turn patted Ammalat, on the rear end.

We again fell to chatting. Chertopkhanov little by little relaxed completely, stopped ruffling up like a fighting cock and snorting; the expression on his face changed. He looked at Nedopiuskin and at me.

"Eh!" he exclaimed suddenly. "Why should she be sitting

321

there all by her lonesome? Masha! I say, Masha! Do come here!"

Someone stirred in the next room, but there was no response.

"Ma-a-sha," Chertopkhanov called again in a caressing voice, "come here. There's nothing to be afraid of."

The door opened, ever so quietly, and I beheld a woman of twenty, tall and graceful, with a swarthy Gypsy face, yellow-into-hazel eyes, and a braid as black as pitch; her large white teeth simply sparkled from between her full and red lips. She had on a white dress; a light-blue shawl, fastened at her very throat with a gold pin, covered her thin, thoroughbred arms halfway. She took a couple of steps with the timid awkwardness of a savage, halted, and fixed her eyes on the floor.

"Here, let me introduce you," said Pantelei Eremeich. "Not my wife, exactly, but the same as my wife, you might say."

Masha colored a little and smiled in confusion. I made her quite a low bow. She was very much to my liking. Her aquiline nose, ever so thin, with distended, half-transparent nostrils, the bold outline of her arched eyebrows, her pale cheeks, just a trifle sunken—all the features of her face expressed a self-willed passion and an insouciant audacity. From under a tight braid two rows of short, glossy hairs went down the broad back of her neck—a sign, these, of good blood and strength.

She walked over to the window and sat down. I did not want to increase her embarrassment and started a conversation with Chertopkhanov. Masha turned her head ever so slightly and began darting looks at me from under her brows, stealthily, quickly, like a wild creature. Her glance actually seemed to flicker, just like a snake's forked tongue. Nedopiuskin took a seat near her and whispered something in her ear. She smiled again. When she smiled she puckered her nose slightly and lifted her upper lip a little, which gave her face a look that was a cross between the feline and the leonine.

"Ah, you touch-me-not!" I reflected, in my turn glancing stealthily at her sinuous waist, her sunken chest, and angular, sharp movements.

"What do you say, Masha," Chertopkhanov asked her, "wouldn't it be a good idea to treat our guest to something?"

"We have some jam," she answered.

322

"Well, bring us the jam—and some vodka, while you're at it. And listen, Masha," he called after her, "bring your guitar, too."

"What for? I'm not going to sing."

"Why not?"

"I don't feel like it."

"Eh, nonsense! You'll feel like it, if—"

"If what?" asked Masha, quickly contracting her eyebrows.

"If you're asked," Chertopkhanov concluded, not without embarrassment.

"Ah!"

She went out, returning shortly with jam and vodka, and again sat down by the window. One could still see a little wrinkle on her forehead; her brows kept rising and falling, like the feelers of a wasp. . . . Have you ever noticed what a vile-tempered face a wasp has? "Well," I reflected, "there's bound to be a thunderstorm." The conversation did not catch on. Nedopiuskin had become altogether quiet, and was smiling in a strained way; Chertopkhanov was puffing, turning red, and goggling his eyes; I was just getting ready to leave!

Masha suddenly stood up, opened a window abruptly, and heartily vexed, shouted "Axinia!" to a village woman passing by. The woman, startled, was about to turn, but slipped and plopped heavily to the ground. Masha threw herself back and burst into ringing laughter: Chertopkhanov also began laughing; Nedopiuskin squeaked in delight. We all perked up. The storm had broken with but a single lightning flash . . . the air cleared.

Half an hour later no one would have recognized us: we were chattering and romping like children. Masha was livelier than all of us; Chertopkhanov was simply devouring her with his eyes. Her face had paled, her nostrils were distended, her eyes were ablaze and, at the same time, dimming. The savage had let herself out to the full. Nedopiuskin hobbled after her on fat and stubby little legs, like a drake after a duck. Even Vensor had crept out from under a built-in bench in the entry, had stood at the threshold and contemplated us for a while, and suddenly taken to leaping and barking.

Masha fluttered out into the next room, brought her guitar, threw the shawl off her shoulders, perched on a chair, lifted her head, and launched into a Gypsy song. Her voice rang and quavered like a small cracked bell of glass, flaring up and dying away. One's heart felt gladsome—and scary. . . . "*Ai, zhghi, govori!*—ah, sear, let me hear! . . ." Chertopkhanov launched into a lively dance. Nedopiuskin started stamping and shuffling. Masha's whole body was twisting and squirming, like birch bark on a fire; her thin fingers scampered over the guitar; her swarthy throat rose slowly under a double string of amber beads. Now she would suddenly fall silent, sink in exhaustion, pluck the strings with apparent unwillingness, and Chertopkhanov would stop, merely jerking one shoulder and shuffling on one spot, while Nedopiuskin kept nodding his head like a toy porcelain mandarin; then she would be trilling anew, like a madwoman, would straighten her torso and thrust out her chest, and Chertopkhanov danced again, squatting down to the floor, leaping up to the very ceiling, spinning like a humming top, calling out "Lively, now!"

"Lively, lively, lively, lively, now!" Nedopiuskin chimed in in a patter.

I rode away from Bezsonovo late in the evening.

THE END OF CHERTOPKHANOV

A COUPLE OF years after my visit to his place Pantelei
Eremeich's calamities began—calamities, precisely. Mishaps,
troubles, and misfortunes had befallen him even before, but
he had paid no attention to them and gone on "reigning"
as usual. The first calamity that overtook him was the most
poignant: Masha parted with him.

It is difficult to say what had impelled her to leave his
roof, to which, apparently, she had become thoroughly accustomed. Chertopkhanov to the end of his days clung to the
conviction that the cause of Masha's perfidy was a certain
young neighbor, a retired captain of uhlans, by the nickname of Jaff, who according to Pantelei Eremeich captivated
women solely because he was forever twirling his mustache,
used an extraordinary amount of pomade, and could "Hm!"
significantly; however, it must be supposed that in this instance it was rather the wanderlust of the gypsy blood flowing
in her veins which had worked upon her. Whatever it was,
the fact remains that one beautiful summer evening Masha,
after tying certain of her rags together in a small bundle,
went away from Chertopkhanov's house.

She had spent the three days before that sitting in a nook,
all hunched up and hugging the wall, like a wounded vixen—
and if she would but utter a word! For all she did was to

let her eyes dart about, and kept falling into deep thought, and twitching her eyebrows, and baring her teeth a little, and fidgeting with her hands as though she were trying to muffle herself. "Spells" such as that used to come over her before, too, but none had ever lasted long. Chertopkhanov knew this and therefore was not troubled himself and did not trouble her. But when, upon returning from the kennels where his last two coursing hounds had "pegged out" (as his whipper-in put it), he was met by a maidservant who in a quavering voice informed him that Maria Akinthievna, now, had bidden her to give him her regards, that she had bidden her to tell him that she wished him well, but that she would nevermore return to him—Chertopkhanov, after circling a couple of times on one spot and letting out a hoarse growl, at once dashed off after the runaway (taking his pistol along, just in case).

He overtook her a little over a mile from his house, near a small birch grove on the highway to the district capital. The sun was low over the horizon—and all things around them momentarily took on a purple tinge: trees, and grasses, and the earth.

"You're going to Jaff, to Jaff!" Chertopkhanov got out in a moan as soon as he had caught sight of Masha. "To Jaff!" he repeated, running up to her and all but stumbling at every step.

Masha stopped and turned around to face him. She was standing with her back to the light—and seemed all black, just as if she were carved out of ebony. The whites of her eyes alone stood out like silvery almonds, while the eyes themselves—the pupils—had grown still darker.

She tossed her little bundle aside and crossed her arms.

"You're going off to Jaff, you worthless creature!" Chertopkhanov reiterated, and was about to seize her by the shoulder but, meeting her gaze, became abashed and began to shuffle where he stood.

"It isn't to Jaff I was going, Pantelei Eremeich," Masha answered evenly and quietly. "The whole thing is, I can't go on living with you."

"What do you mean, you can't? How come? Why, have I wronged you in any way?"

Masha shook her head:

"You haven't wronged me in any way, Pantelei Eremeich. The only thing is, I've grown wearisome at your place.

Thanks for all that's past, but as for staying on—no, I can't do it!"

Chertopkhanov was amazed; he actually slapped his thighs and bounded up a little.

"Why, how has all this come about? You lived on and on, never knowing anything but pleasure and peace and, all of a sudden, 'I've grown wearisome! There, now, I'll up and leave him!' And she takes a kerchief, and throws it over her head, and off she goes. And yet she's been getting every mark of respect, no worse than any lady—"

"That's something I really have no need of," Masha interrupted him.

"What do you mean, you have no need of it? From a fly-by-night Gypsy you get right in amongst the ladies—and you have no need of it? What do you mean, you have no need of it, you lowborn creature? Why, would anybody believe a thing like that? There's hidden perfidy here—perfidy!"

He began hissing again.

"I have no perfidy whatsoever in my thoughts, and never did have," Masha uttered in her canorous and distinct voice. "But I've already told you: wearisomeness overcame me."

"Masha!" Chertopkhanov called out and thumped his chest with his fist. "There, stop this, that'll do you; you've tortured me a while—well, enough is enough! By God, now! Only think of what Tisha will say—you might take pity on him, at least!"

"You give my regards to Tihon Ivanovich, and tell him—"

Chertopkhanov flailed his arms: "Oh, no, you don't—you're not getting away! Your Jaff will wait till Doomsday!"

"Mister Jaff—" Masha began.

"What sort of *Mees-ter* Jaff is he?" Chertopkhanov mimicked her. "He's nothing but a low-down knave and an out-and-out swindler—and he's got a face on him like an ape's."

For all of half an hour did Chertopkhanov contend with Masha. Now he would draw closer to her, now leap away from her; now he would swing back his arm as if to strike her, now bow low before her, and weep, and upbraid.

"It's beyond me," Masha persisted. "I feel so downhearted. This wearisomeness will be the end of me."

Little by little her face took on such an apathetic, almost somnolent expression that Chertopkhanov asked her if, by some chance, she hadn't been given some nightshade to drink.

"It's the wearisomeness," she repeated for the tenth time.

"Well, now, what if I were to kill you?" he cried out suddenly and snatched the pistol out of his pocket.

Masha smiled; her face became animated.

"Well, why not? Kill me, Pantelei Eremeich. It's all up to you. But as for going back, go back I won't."

"You won't?" Chertopkhanov cocked the hammer of his pistol.

"I won't, dearest dear. I won't, not as long as I live. My word is steadfast."

Chertopkhanov unexpectedly thrust the pistol into her hand and squatted on the ground:

"Well, in that case *you* kill me! I have no desire to live without you. I have become unbearable to you, and everything has become unbearable to me."

Masha stooped, picked up her bundle, laid the pistol on the grass (with its muzzle away from Chertopkhanov), and moved closer to him.

"Eh, dearest dear, what are you killing yourself with grief over? Or don't you know what we Gypsy girls are like? That's our nature, our way. Once wearisomeness comes it makes us part with our men, it calls one's soul to strange and far-off parts—how is one to remain then? Keep your Masha in remembrance. Such another mate you will never find; nor will I ever forget you, my falcon. But as to our life together, that's all over and done with!"

"I loved you, Masha," Chertopkhanov muttered through the fingers clutching his face.

"And I loved you, too, Pantelei Eremeich, dearest friend of mine!"

"I loved you; I love you now, madly, unreasoningly, and when I now think how you are forsaking me, for no reason on earth without as much as a by-your-leave, and will go wandering the world over—well, it does seem to me that if I weren't such a hapless wretch and on my uppers you wouldn't have forsaken me!"

Masha merely smiled wryly in answer to his words.

"And yet you always said I didn't care for money at all," said she and, with a full swing, struck Chertopkhanov on the shoulder. He leaped to his feet:

"Well, you might at least take some money from me—for how can you go like that, without a copper? But, best of all, kill me! I'm talking sense to you—kill me while you're at it!"

Masha again shook her head: "Kill you? And what sort of

thing do they send people to Siberia for, my dearest dear?"

Chertopkhanov shuddered: "So it's only the fear of a sentence to hard labor that's holding you back—"

He slumped on the grass again.

Masha stood over him for some time in silence.

"I feel sorry for you, Pantelei Eremeich," said she with a sigh, "for you're a fine fellow, yet there's no help for it. Farewell!"

She turned away and took a couple of steps. By now night had fallen and dim shadows came floating from everywhere. Chertopkhanov scrambled up and seized Masha from behind by her elbows.

"So you're going away, you snake? Going to Jaff!"

"Farewell," Masha repeated significantly and sharply, wrenched herself free, and went on.

Chertopkhanov followed her with his eyes, ran to the spot where the pistol was lying, seized it, took aim, fired. . . . But, just before squeezing the trigger, he jerked his hand upward: the bullet, humming, sped over Masha's head. She gave him a look over her shoulder—and kept on going, with never a pause, swinging along just a trifle, as though she were taunting him.

He covered his face and started running.

But he had not run fifty paces off when he suddenly halted, as though rooted to the spot. A familiar, all too familiar voice came floating to his ears. Masha was singing. " 'Time of youth, of splendid beauty,' " sang she; every sound seemed to spread through the evening air, plaintively and sultrily. Chertopkhanov cocked his ears. The voice kept receding, ever receding; now it died away, now it again came streaming back, barely audibly, yet still searingly.

"She's doing it to spite me," Chertopkhanov thought, but immediately got out in a groan: "Oh, no! That's her way of bidding me farewell forever,"—and he burst into torrential tears.

The following day he showed up at the rooms of Mr. Jaff; Mr. Jaff, since he was a true man of the world, did not favor rustic solitude, and had settled in the district capital, to be "nearer to the young ladies," as he put it. Chertopkhanov did not find Jaff; according to his valet he had left for Moscow the evening before.

"There, it's just as I thought!" Chertopkhanov cried out

ferociously. "They had it all made up between them; she ran off with him—but you just wait!"

He burst into the young cavalry captain's study, despite the valet's resistance. In this study, hanging over a divan, was an oil painting of the master of the house in his uhlan's uniform.

"Ah, so there you are, you tailless ape!" thundered Chertopkhanov, leaped up on the divan, and sending his fist through the taut canvas, smashed a great hole therein. "Tell your worthless master," he turned to the valet, "that for lack of his own vile phiz, Squire Chertopkhanov has disfigured his painted one; and should he crave any satisfaction from me, he knows where to find Squire Chertopkhanov. Otherwise I'll find him out myself! I'll seek out the low-down ape if he is at the bottom of the sea!"

Having uttered these words Chertopkhanov jumped down off the divan and withdrew in triumph.

But Cavalry Captain Jaff did not demand any satisfaction whatsoever from him—he did not even come across him anywhere; as to Chertopkhanov, he thought no more of seeking out his enemy, and no set-to of any sort materialized between them. Masha herself disappeared shortly thereafter, and nothing more was heard concerning her.

Chertopkhanov had a spell of hard drinking, but he "came to." However, at this point a second calamity overtook him.

II

To be precise, his bosom friend, Tihon Ivanovich Nedopiuskin, departed this life.

Two years before his death his health had started to go back on him: he began to suffer from asthma, was forever dozing off and, on awaking, could not come to himself quickly: the country doctor asserted that he was undergoing "little strokes." During the three days preceding the departure of Masha, those three days when she had "grown wearisome," Nedopiuskin had kept to his bed in his tiny village of Bezselendeievka: he had caught a severe cold. Masha's action had therefore overwhelmed him all the more unexpectedly; it overwhelmed him in all likelihood even more than it had Chertopkhanov himself. Owing to the meekness and timorousness of his nature he did not evince anything but the tenderest commiseration for his friend, as well as a hypersensitive bewilderment. Yet everything within him had burst asunder and sagged.

"She has taken my soul out of me," he whispered to himself, perching on his favorite little leatherette-upholstered divan and twiddling his thumbs. Even when Chertopkhanov had gotten over it he, Nedopiuskin, did not, and kept on feeling that there was "a void within him." "Right here," he would say, indicating the center of his chest, a little above his stomach.

Thus did he drag on until winter. The first frosts relieved his asthma somewhat, yet on the other hand he was visited not by any "little stroke" but by a real one. He did not lose his memory at once; he could still recognize Chertopkhanov and, in answer to the despairing outcry of his friend: "Come, now, Tisha—how can you leave me without my permission; you're acting every bit as badly as Masha," he even answered with a tongue that was growing numb: "Why, P. . . a . . . sei E . . . e . . . ich, I wo' be g'ad to . . . bey you 'ight now—" This, however, did not hinder him from dying that same day, after waiting in vain for the coming of the country doctor, for whom, at the sight of the hardly cold body, there remained nothing to do save to ask, with a sad awareness of the transitoriness of all things on earth, for "a nip of vodka and a bit of salted sturgeon."

His estate Tihon Ivanych willed, as might have been expected, to his most esteemed benefactor and magnanimous protector, Pantelei Eremeich Chertopkhanov; yet it brought no great benefit to the esteemed benefactor, inasmuch as it had to be sold shortly under the hammer—partly to defray the expenses of a monumental statue over the testator's grave, which Chertopkhanov (evidently a quirk of his father's had found an echo in him!) had gotten it into his head to erect over the dust of his friend. This statue, which was to represent a praying angel, he had ordered by mail from Moscow; but the broker to whom he had been recommended, surmising that connoisseurs of sculpture are but rarely to be met with in the provinces, sent him, instead of an angel, the goddess Flora, inasmuch as the broker, through a stroke of luck, had come by her statue for nothing; it had for many years adorned one of the neglected gardens going back to the times of Catherine the Great in suburban Moscow. It was a rather elegant, rococo thing, however, with plump little hands, puffy ringlets, a garland of roses on its bared bosom, and a sinuous waist. And so, to this very time, the mythological goddess stands thus, one tiny foot lifted gracefully over the grave of Tihon Ivanych, and regards with a truly Pompadourish simper the browsing calves and moping sheep around her—those never-failing visitors of our village cemeteries.

III

Having lost his faithful friend, Chertopkhanov had another spell of hard drinking, and this time a far more serious one. His affairs went downhill altogether. There was nothing to hunt with; his last coppers went, his last few miserable serfs ran off every which way. The solitude that now came for Pantelei Eremeich was absolute: there wasn't a person for him to exchange a word with, to say nothing of easing his soul. Only the pride within him did not diminish. On the contrary, the worse his circumstances became, the more supercilious and arrogant and inaccessible did he himself become. Toward the last he became a complete savage. One consolation, one joy remained to him: an amazing saddle horse, a gray stallion of the Don breed whom he had dubbed Malek Adel—a truly remarkable animal.

And the manner of his coming by it was as follows.

As he happened to be riding on horseback through a neighboring village, Chertopkhanov caught the hubbub of muzhiks gathered in a shouting mob around a pothouse. In the midst of this mob stalwart arms were flailing away at one unvarying spot, with never a stop.

"What's going on there?" he asked in his usual authoritative tone from an old country wife standing near the threshold of her hut. Leaning against the lintel and apparently drowsing, she kept glancing in the direction of the pothouse. A towheaded little boy in a calico shirt, with a tiny cross of cypress wood on his bare little chest, his small legs spread out, and his tiny fists clenched, was sitting between her bast sandals; a chick was also right there, pecking away at a petrified crust of rye bread.

"Why, the Lord knows, father of mine," answered the crone and, leaning over, placed her wrinkled dark hand on the little boy's head. "Sounds like our lads was killin' a Jew."

"What do you mean? What's all this about a Jew? What Jew?"

"Why, the Lord knows who he is, father of mine. There's some Jew or other turned up in our midst; but as from where the wind has blown him this way—who can tell? Come to your mamma, Vassya, my little gentleman. Shoo, shoo, you vile critter!" the crone drove off the chick, while Vassya clutched at her wraparound skirt. "Well, so they're killin' him, my dear sir."

"What do you mean, they're killing him? What for?"

"Why, I don't rightly know, father of mine. Must be for something, if they are. And why shouldn't they kill him? For sure, father of mine, he crucified Christ!"

Chertopkhanov let out a whoop, laid the quirt hard on his horse's neck, dashed straight at the crowd, and having ridden right into it, began drubbing the muzhiks right and left with that selfsame quirt, indiscriminately, accompanying the blows with his choppy voice:

"Take the law—into your own hands—will you? Take the law—into your own hands? It's up to the law—to punish—and not up to—private individuals! It's up to—the law! The law! The law!"

It did not take even two minutes for the mob to ebb away in all directions—and a small, gaunt, swarthy being in a nankeen caftan, a being all tattered and disfigured, was revealed lying on the ground before the pothouse. Face pale, eyes rolled up, mouth gaping. . . . What was this—the petrifaction of terror, or already death itself?

"What did you kill the Jew for?" Chertopkhanov asked in a thundering voice, shaking his quirt ominously.

The crowd hummed faintly in answer. One muzhik was nursing his shoulder, another his side, a third his nose.

"He's handy when it comes to fighting!" came from the rear ranks.

"He is—with a quirt! Anybody could fight that way!" another voice spoke up.

"Why did you kill the Jew, I'm asking you, you confounded barbarians!" Chertopkhanov repeated.

But at this point the being on the ground nimbly leaped to his feet and, having run behind Chertopkhanov, quickly seized the side of his saddle.

Unanimous laughter broke out in the crowd.

"Plenty of life in him!" again came from the rear ranks. "Same as a cat!"

"You' Highness, defend me, save me!" the unfortunate Jew

was babbling in the meanwhile, hugging Chertopkhanov's leg to his breast, "Fo' they will kill me, they will kill me, You' Highness!"

"Why are they doing this to you?" Chertopkhanov asked him.

"I swea' befo' God I can't say! Their cattle has sta'ted dying—so they suspect I'm to blame. But how could I—"

"Well, we'll get to the bottom of it later!" Chertopkhanov cut him short. "Now you just hold on to my saddle and follow me. As for you," he turned to the crowd, "do you know who I am? I am Pantelei Chertopkhanov, and I live in the hamlet of Bezsonovo; well, you just go ahead and lodge a complaint against me, whenever you think it best—and against the Jew, too, while you're at it!"

"Why should we complain?" A gray-bearded, staid muzhik spoke up with a low bow; he looked for all the world like a patriarch of old (however, he had not been at all behind the others in sailing into the Jew). "We know Your Grace, Pantelei Eremeich, father of mine; we are most grateful because Your Grace has taught us a lesson!"

"Why should we complain?" others chimed in. "But as for that unbaptized one, we'll have our way with him! He won't get away from us!"—"We'll get him, now, same's a hare out in the field—"

Chertopkhanov twitched his mustachios, snorted, and rode off at a walk to his village, accompanied by the Jew whom he had delivered from his oppressors, even as once he had delivered Tihon Nedopiuskin from his.

IV

A few days later a Cossack lad, the only serf still remaining to Chertopkhanov informed him that some man had arrived on horseback and wanted to speak to him. Chertopkhanov came out on the front steps and saw the little Jew whom he had rescued, mounted on a magnificent Don steed standing immovably and proudly in the middle of the yard. The Jew was not wearing his cap but holding it under his arm; his feet were not in the stirrups but in the stirrup straps; the torn skirts of his caftan hung down on both sides of the saddle. On catching sight of Chertopkhanov he smacked his lips, and jerked his elbows, and jiggled his legs. But Chertopkhanov not only made no answer to his greetings but actually became angry; he actually flared up all of a sudden: a mangy Jew daring to sit on such a splendid horse—what an indecency!

"Hey you, you Ethiopian phiz!" he shouted. "Climb down right away, if you don't want to be dragged off into the mud!"

The Jew submitted without any delay, tumbling like a sack off the saddle—and, holding the bridle with one hand, smiling and bowing, drew nearer to Chertopkhanov.

"What do you want?" Pantelei Eremeich asked him with dignity.

"Your Highness, may it please you to take a look—what do you think of this little steed?"

"Mm, yes. . . . A good horse. Where did you get it from? Stole it, most likely."

"How could anybody do a thing like that, You' Highness? I'm an honest Jew; I didn't steal it. But that I did get it for You' Highness, that's so. And how ha'd I twied—how ha'd! But then, what a steed it is! It's absolutely impossible to find such another anywhe' on the Don! Just see, You' Highness, what a steed it is! Please come over this way, do. Whoa, whoa—now, toin 'ound, stand sideways! And let's take the saddle off him. Well, what think you of him, You' Highness?"

"A good horse," Chertopkhanov repeated with assumed indifference—and at the same time his heart was simply pounding against his ribs. For he was far too passionate a lover of horseflesh and was a good judge thereof.

"Go ahead, just pat him, You' Highness! Pat his little neck!" And the Jew snickered. "That's it."

Chertopkhanov, as though unwillingly, put his hand on the steed's neck, patted it a couple of times, then ran his fingers from the withers down the back and, having reached a certain little spot over the kidneys, pressed upon it slightly, like a true expert. The steed immediately stretched out his backbone and, after turning his head for a sidelong look at Chertopkhanov out of one haughty dark eye, blew out his breath hard and shifted his forelegs.

The Jew began laughing and clapped his hands a little. "He acknowledges his maste'—his maste', You' Highness!"

"There, stop your lying." Chertopkhanov cut him short in irritation. "If it comes to buying the horse . . . I haven't the wherewithal, and as to presents, well, so far I've never accepted any—not only from a Jew, but even the Lord God Himself!"

"If you will be so kind—how could I eve' be so bold as to make you a pwesent of anything!" exclaimed the Jew. "You buy it, You' Highness—and as fo' the bit of money, why, I'll wait."

Chertopkhanov became thoughtful.

"What will you take?" he finally got out through his teeth.

The Jew shrugged: "Why, the same as I paid for him. Two hund'ed 'ubles."

The horse was worth twice—and, if you like, even thrice— this sum. Chertopkhanov turned away to hide a feverish yawn.

"And the money—when?" he asked, forcing himself to knit his brows and without looking at the Jew.

"Why, wheneve' You' Highness likes."

Chertopkhanov threw his head back, but did not look up.

"That's no answer. You talk sense, you of the tribe of Herod! Am I to be indebted to you, or what?"

"Well," the Jew spoke hastily, "in six months, let's say. Is that agweeable to you?"

Chertopkhanov made no answer. The Jew was trying to look into his eyes:

"Is that agweeable to you? Will you have it put in the stable?"

"I don't need the saddle," Chertopkhanov got out jerkily. "Take the saddle—you hear?"

"Of course, of course—I'll take it, I'll take it!" the over-joyed Jew began to babble and tossed the saddle up on his shoulder.

"As to the money," Chertopkhanov went on, "you'll get it in six months. And not two hundred but two hundred and fifty. Silence! Two hundred and fifty, I tell you! That's what I owe you."

Chertopkhanov still could not bring himself to look up. Never yet had the pride within him suffered so much. "It's a gift, plain as plain," the thought persisted. "He's offering it to me out of gratitude, the devil!" And he felt both like embracing the Jew and giving him a beating. . . .

"You' Highness," the Jew began, plucking up heart and grinning, "the bwidle ought to be handed ove' fwom the skoit of my coat to the skoit of yours, after the Wussian custom—"

"There, now, what will he think of next! A Jew—and Russian customs! Hey, who's there? Take the horse and lead it to the stable. And pour out some oats for him. I'll come there myself right away and have a look. And know this: his name is Malek Adel!"

Chertopkhanov had already gotten to the top of the front steps, but he turned sharply on his heels, descended, and, having run up to the Jew, squeezed his hand hard. The other bent over and had already stretched out his lips to kiss the other's hand—but Chertopkhanov leaped back and, having uttered in a low voice, "Not a word of this to anybody!" vanished through the door.

V

From that day on Malek [1] Adel became the chief care, the chief joy in the life of Chertopkhanov. He came to love him as he had never loved Masha herself; he became more closely attached to him than to Nedopiuskin. But then, what a steed Malek Adel was! Fire, veritable fire; plain gunpowder, he was—yet he had the staid dignity of a lord! Endowed with great endurance, knowing no fatigue, offering no resistance no matter which way you turned him, and as for his feed— why, it didn't come to anything. If there was nothing else, he'd gnaw the earth under him. If he went at a walk, it was like being borne along in somebody's arms; if at a trot, it was like being rocked in a cradle; but if he started to gallop —then even the wind couldn't catch up with him! He'd never get winded, now: that was because he had so many air vents. Of steel his legs were, and as for stumbling—never did such a mishap befall him! Jumping over a ditch or a stake fence didn't mean a thing to him—and what a clever beast he was! He'd just run when you called him, with his head way up: if you bade him stand still and walked off yourself, he wouldn't as much as budge, but the moment you started coming back, he'd whinny ever so slightly, as if to say: "Here I am!" And there wasn't a thing he was scared of: in the darkest of night, in a blizzard itself, he'd hit on the right road. As to letting any stranger lay a hand on him—why, he'd just chew him to pieces! And no dog had better come nigh him: he'd let it have it with a foreleg over its forehead

[1] "King."—*Trans.*

—bang!—and that was the last of *that* dog. A steed with self-respect; you might wave a whipstock over him, just for the looks of the thing—but the Lord keep you from touching him! But what's the use of talking—it wasn't just a horse, but a downright treasure!

When Chertopkhanov would start in singing the glories of his Malek Adel—why, you'd wonder where he got all his eloquence from. Then, too, how he groomed him and how he cherished him! The hair upon him had the sheen of silver —not old silver, but new, the kind with a dark tinge to it. Run your hand over it, and you couldn't tell it from velvet! The saddle, the dainty saddlecloth, the snaffle bridle—every bit of the harness was so well made, so well kept, so well cleaned that you could just pick up a pencil and make a picture of it. Chertopkhanov himself (what more could one ask for?), with his own hands, plaited both the forelock and the mane of his favorite, and washed his tail with beer, and even, more than once, anointed his hooves with a special salve.

He used to mount Malek Adel and be off—not to call on his neighbors (even as before he didn't want to have any truck with them), but to ride across their fields, past their manor houses: "Admire my horse from afar, now, you fools!" Or else he'd happen to hear of some hunt some·where—some rich squire was setting out for some remote field; so he'd head that way right off, and be caracoling in the distance, against the horizon, astonishing all the beholders by the beauty and fleetness of his steed, but without letting anybody come near him. On one occasion some hunter actually started after him with all his retinue; seeing that Chertopkhanov was getting away from him, he began yelling after him with all his might, the while his horse galloped along at full speed:

"Hey, you! Listen! Take anything you like for your horse! I won't begrudge even a thousand! I'll give you my wife, my children! Take everything I own, to the last stitch!"

Chertopkhanov suddenly threw Malek Adel back on his haunches. The hunter flew up to him:

"Father of mine!" he shouted. "Tell me, what do you want? My own father!"

"Wert thou czar," Chertopkhanov uttered, articulating every syllable (and, mind you, he hadn't so much as heard of Shakespeare in all his born days), "and wert thou to

338

give me thy kingdom for my horse, I would not take even that!" He said this, burst into peals of laughter, made Malek Adel rear up, turned him around in midair on his hind legs, as if he were a humming top or a whirligig—and was off, just like a flash, across the stubble. As for the hunter (a count, they say he was, and of the richest), he dashed his cap against the ground, and then threw himself down and buried his face in the cap! Half an hour did he lie thus. . . .

And what else should Chertopkhanov do save treasure his steed? For was it not through his favor that Chertopkhanov turned out to have anew an indubitable point of superiority, the last one, over all his neighbors?

VI

In the meanwhile time was passing, the day of payment was nearing, yet Chertopkhanov not only did not have the two hundred and fifty—he hadn't even fifty. What was he to do, how could he mend matters?

"Well, if it comes to that," he decided at last, "if the Jew won't be moved, won't want to wait a while longer, I'll give him house and land, and I myself will get up on my steed and go wherever my eyes may lead me! I'll die of hunger—but I won't give up Malek Adel!"

He was very much disturbed, and even had thoughtful spells—but at this point fate (for the first time and the last) took pity on him and smiled upon him: some distant aunt, whose very name was unknown to him, left him in her last will and testament a sum that, in his eyes, was enormous: all of two thousand rubles! And this money he got, so to say, in the very nick of time: one day before the coming of the Jew. Chertopkhanov all but went mad for joy—yet he did not so much as think of vodka: from the very day that Malek Adel had come to him he wouldn't take a drop in his mouth. He ran off to the stable and kissed his friend on either side of his muzzle, over the nostrils—on the spot where the hide of horses is so sensitive.

"Now we'll never part!" he kept exclaiming as he patted Malek Adel's neck under his well-combed mane.

On coming back to the house, he counted off and sealed in a packet two hundred and fifty rubles. Then he day-dreamed a while, lying on his back and puffing away at a short pipe, of what he would do with the rest of the money,

339

to wit—of what dogs he would acquire: the real Kostroma breed, and red ones, at that, spotted all over, without fail! He even had a chat with Perfishka, his Cossack lad, to whom he promised a new cossackeen, with yellow galloons at all the seams—and then laid him down to sleep with his spirits in a most beatific state. He had a bad dream: he had apparently gone to a hunt, only not on Malek Adel but on some odd beast, something like a camel; a vixen, ever so white, white as snow, was running toward him. He wanted to raise his dog whip, he wanted to set the dogs on her—but instead of a whip he was holding a bundle of bast wisps, and the vixen was running before him and mocking him by putting out her tongue. He leaped off his camel, stumbled, fell . . . and that right into the hands of a gendarme, who summoned him to the governor general—in whom he recognized Jaff!

Chertopkhanov awoke. It was dark in the room; the roosters had just chanted their second song.

Somewhere far, far off, a horse whinnied.

Chertopkhanov raised his head. Once more he heard whinnying—high whinnying, ever so high.

"That's Malek Adel whinnying," it occurred to him. "That's his whinny! But why is it so far off? Holy Fathers! It can't be—"

Chertopkhanov suddenly turned cold all over; he instantly sprang out of bed, groped until he found his boots and clothing, dressed, and taking the stable key from under his pillow, leaped out into the yard.

VII

The stable was situated at the very end of the yard; one of its walls faced an open field. Chertopkhanov could not insert the key in the lock at first, his hands were trembling so, nor could he turn the key at once. He stood stock-still for a while, holding his breath: if only he might hear something stirring on the other side of the door!

"Little Malek! My Malek!" he called out in a low voice. There was dead silence. Chertopkhanov involuntarily tugged at the key; the door creaked and opened. It was unlocked, then. He stepped over the threshold—and called to his steed anew, this time using his full name: "Malek Adel!" But his faithful comrade did not respond: only a mouse ran rustling

340

through the straw.

Thereupon Chertopkhanov darted to that one of the three stalls which had been Malek Adel's. He went straight into the stall, although the darkness all around was such that you might as well have been blinded. It was empty! Chertopkhanov's head began to spin; he felt as if a church bell had begun reverberating inside his skull. He wanted to say something, but all he did was to hiss. And, groping with his hands at top and bottom of the partitions, gasping for breath, with his knees buckling, he made his way from stall to stall. In the third, filled almost to the top with hay, he collided against one wall, then the other, fell, rolled head over heels, scrambled to his feet, and suddenly ran headlong through the half-open door out into the yard.

"They've stolen him! Perfishka! Perfishka! They've stolen him!" he began bawling for all he was worth.

Perfishka, the Cossack lad, in nothing but his shirt, came bouncing out of the cubbyhole in which he slept.

They collided like two drunkards, the master and his sole servant, in the middle of the yard; as if they were stupefied by charcoal fumes they began circling around each other. The master could not make clear what had happened, nor could the servant make out what was being demanded of him.

"Trouble! Trouble!" babbled Chertopkhanov. "Trouble! Trouble!" the Cossack lad kept repeating after him.

"A lantern! Bring a lantern and light it! A light! A light!" escaped at last from Chertopkhanov's swooning breast. Perfishka dashed into the house.

But to light the lantern, to strike a light, was no easy matter: sulphur matches were considered a rarity at that time in Russia, the last embers had long since gone out in the kitchen, it took some time to find a tinderbox, and when found it worked but poorly. Gnashing his teeth, Chertopkhanov tore it out of the hand of the bewildered Perfishka and began striking the flint himself: the flow of sparks was copious but the curses (and even groans) flew still more copiously; the wick, however, either would not catch fire, or went out, despite the teamwork of four straining cheeks and lips! Finally, after five minutes or so (no sooner), a tallow candle end broke into a warm little glow at the bottom of the broken lantern and Chertopkhanov, accompanied by Perfishka, rushed into the stable, raised the lantern over his head, and looked about him.

The place was absolutely empty.

He leaped out into the yard and ran through it in every direction, but the steed was nowhere there. The wattle fence surrounding the estate of Pantelei Eremeich had long since fallen into decrepitude and in many places leaned over close to the ground. Alongside the stable it had fallen down altogether, for about a yard in width. Perfishka pointed out this spot to Chertopkhanov.

"Take a look at this, sir! That hole weren't there in the daytime. There, even the stakes are sticking up out of the ground—somebody must have pulled 'em up, for sure."

Chertopkhanov rushed over with the lantern and swung it close to the ground.

"Hoofs, hoofs, tracks of horseshoes, tracks, fresh tracks!" he fell to muttering in a patter. "Here's where they led him across—here, here!"

He instantly sprang over the wattle fence and, shouting: "Malek Adel! Malek Adel!" ran right out into the field.

Perfishka remained in bewilderment near the wattle fence. The circle of light from the lantern soon vanished, swallowed up by the murk of a starless and moonless night.

Ever fainter, fainter sounded the despairing outcries of Chertopkhanov.

VIII

The dawn glow had already begun when he came back home. He no longer looked like a human being; there was mud all over his clothes, his face had taken on a wild and frightful appearance, his eyes had a morose and dull look. In a hoarse whisper he drove Perfishka from him and locked himself up in his room. He could hardly keep on his feet from fatigue—yet he did not lie down on his bed, but sank on a chair near the door and clutched his head.

"They've stolen him! They've stolen him!"

Yet in what manner had the thief contrived to steal Malek Adel, who even in the daytime would let no stranger come near him? And steal him without noise, without a sound? And how explain the fact that not a single yard dog had let out a bark? True, there were but two of them, two young pups, and those two, because of cold and hunger, used to dig themselves into the ground. But still—

"And what am I going to do now without Malek Adel?"

342

the thought haunted Chertopkhanov. "I have now been deprived of my last joy; the time has come to die. Buy another horse—since by luck I'm in the money now? But where is one to find another such horse?"

"Pantelei Eremeich! Pantelei Eremeich!" a timid call sounded on the other side of the door.

Chertopkhanov leaped to his feet:

"Who's there?" he shouted in a voice that sounded like a stranger's.

"It's me, Perfishka—your servant."

"What do you want? Or has he been found—has he come running home?"

"By no means, Pantelei Eremeich; but that Jew fellow that sold him to you—"

"Well?"

"He's come."

"Ho-ho-ho-ho-ho!" Chertopkhanov began to bray—and suddenly flung the door open. "Drag him in, drag him in! Drag him in here!"

At the sudden sight of the disheveled, wild figure of his benefactor, the Jew, standing behind Perfishka's back, was about to show a clean pair of heels—but Chertopkhanov overtook him in two bounds and, like a tiger, pounced at his throat.

"Ah! So you've come for the money! For the money!" he began to rattle in his throat, as though it were not *he* who was doing the choking, but as if somebody were choking *him*. "You steal him in the night, but in the daytime you come for the money?"

"Have mercy, You' . . . High . . . ness!" the Jew attempted to moan.

"Tell me, where's my horse? Where did you hide him? Whom did you pass it on to? Tell me, tell me—go ahead and tell me!"

By this time the Jew was past even moaning; even the expression of fright had vanished from his now livid face. His arms were sagging, dangling; his whole body, furiously shaken by Chertopkhanov, was swaying to and fro like a reed.

"I'll pay you your money, I'll pay you in full, to the last copper," Chertopkhanov kept shouting. "But I'll strangle you like the commonest chick if you won't tell me everything, at once—"

343

"Why, you've already strangled him, master," the Cossack lad Perfishka remarked humbly.

It was only then that Chertopkhanov came to his senses. He released the neck of the Jew; the latter simply crashed flat on the floor. Chertopkhanov caught him up, seated him on a bench, poured a tumbler of vodka down his throat, and brought him to. And, having brought him to, he entered into talk with him.

It turned out that the Jew hadn't the slightest notion of the theft of Malek Adel. And besides, why on earth would he be stealing the horse which he himself had obtained for the "most estimable Pantelei E'emeich"?

Thereupon Chertopkhanov led him to the stable. Together they looked over the stalls, mangers, the lock on the door; they rummaged through the hay and straw, after which they passed on to the yard; Chertopkhanov pointed out to the Jew the hoofprints near the wattle fence—and suddenly smote his thighs:

"Hold on!" he cried out. "Where was it you bought the horse?"

"In the Maloa'changelsk distwict, at the Ve'hosensk fair," the Jew answered.

"From whom?"

"A Cossack."

"Hold on! Was this Cossack young or old?"

"Middle-aged; settled in his ways."

"And what did he look like? What's his description? Must have been an out-and-out knave, never fear?"

"He must have been a knave, You' Highness."

"What did he tell you, then, this knave—had he owned the horse long?"

"Fa' as I wemembe', he said it was a long time."

"Well, then, there's nobody else would steal the horse but he. He and none other! Just judge for yourself; listen to me —stand over here . . . what do they call you?"

The Jew became flutteringly alert and darted a look out of his dark, small eyes at Chertopkhanov:

"What do they call *me*?"

"Well, yes—what's your nickname?"

"Moshel Leiba."

"Well, judge for yourself, Leiba, my friend—you're an intelligent man: whom, except his old master, would Malek Adel allow to lay a hand on him? Why, the fellow both saddled and bridled him, and took the horse blanket off him—there it is, lying on the hay! He made himself right at home! For Malek Adel would have kneaded anybody else but his former master into a ball with his hoofs! He'd have raised such a rumpus as would have roused the whole village. Do you agree with me?"

"Well, yes, I do agwee with you, You' Highness—"

"That means, then, that the first thing we must do is to find that Cossack!"

"Yes, but how is one to find him, You' Highness? I saw him just that once—and whe' may he be now, and what's his name? *Ai, vai, vai!*" added the Jew, woefully shaking his scanty ritual side locks.

"Leiba!" Chertopkhanov shouted suddenly. "Look at me, Leiba! For I've lost my reason, I'm not my own self! I'll kill myself with my own hands if you don't help me!"

"Yes, but how can I—"

"Come along with me—and we'll start looking for that thief!"

"But whe' will we go?"

"To the fairs, along the highways, along the byways, among horse thieves, through towns, through villages, through crofts—everywhere, everywhere! And as for money, don't you worry—I've come into an inheritance, brother! I'll blow in my last copper, but I will get back my friend. And the Cossack that did us evil won't get away from us! Wherever he goes, there go we! If under the ground—we go under the ground too! If he goes to the Devil—why, we'll go to Satan himself!"

"Well, now, why go to Satan?" the Jew remarked. "We can do even without him."

"Leiba!" Chertopkhanov chimed in. "Leiba, even though you're a Jew, and your faith is a vile one, yet the soul in you is better than some Christian ones! Take pity on me! There's no use of my going off alone; alone I won't be able to bring this thing off. I'm just a pepper pot, but you have a head on your shoulders—a head of gold! That's the way your tribe is—it has attained to everything without being instructed! Maybe you have your doubts: Where would I ever get any money, now! Come to my room, and I'll show you all the money. Take it, take the cross from around my neck—only give me back Malek Adel, give him back to me, give him back to me!"

345

Chertopkhanov was shivering as if in a fit of ague, the sweat was pouring down his face and, mingling with tears, became lost in his mustachios. He was squeezing Leiba's hands, he implored him, he all but kissed him. He was in a frenzy. The Jew at first attempted to object, to assure the other that it was utterly impossible for him to absent himself, that he had business matters to attend to—but what was the use! Chertopkhanov would not even listen to anything. There was no help for it: poor Leiba consented.

The next day Chertopkhanov, together with Leiba, rode out of Bezsonovo in a peasant cart. The Jew had a somewhat confused air; he was bouncing with all his wizened body in his shaky seat and hanging onto the dashboard with one hand; the other he held pressed to the bosom of his coat, where a packet of banknotes wrapped up in a piece of newspaper was lying. Chertopkhanov sat like a carven image of wood, merely letting his eyes rove all around and breathing deeply; he had a dagger stuck in his belt.

"There, thou evildoer who has parted us, beware now!" he muttered as they came out on the highway.

His house he had entrusted to his Cossack lad, Perfishka, and the country wife who cooked for him, a deaf and ancient creature whom he had given shelter to out of compassion.

"I shall come back to you on Malek Adel!" he had shouted to them in farewell. "Or else I shall not return at all!"

"You might marry me at least, or something!" Perfishka waxed witty, nudging the cook's ribs with his elbow. "We'll never see the master again anyway, no matter how long we wait—but we're likely to die of boredom if we don't do something!"

IX

A year went by—a whole year—no tidings whatsoever of Pantelei Eremeich reached them. The cook died; Perfishka himself was already preparing to abandon the house and set out for town, whither he was being lured by a cousin of his, who was living at a wigmaker's as an apprentice, when suddenly the rumor spread that his master was returning. The parish deacon had received a letter from Pantelei Eremeich himself, in which the latter informed him of his intended arrival in Bezsonovo, and requested that his servants be informed in good time—so that they might arrange a suitable welcome for him. The way Perfishka understood these words was that he ought to get rid of some of the dust, at least; however, he did not put too much belief in the authenticity of the tidings. But conviction concerning what the deacon had said was forced upon him a few days later, when Pantelei Eremeich himself, *in propria persona*, appeared in the court-yard of the estate, mounted on Malek Adel.

Perfishka darted toward his master and, holding one of the stirrups, was about to help him to dismount, but the other jumped down by himself and, throwing a glance of triumph all around him, declaimed loudly:

"I said I would search out Malek Adel, and search him out I did, despite all enemies and fate itself!"

Perfishka walked up to him to kiss his hand, but Cher-topkhanov paid no attention to the zeal of his servant. Lead-ing Malek Adel after him on a halter, he set off with great strides toward the stable. Perfishka took a closer look at his master—and felt uneasy. "Oh, how much thinner he has be-come and how he has aged during the year—and his face has become so stern and hard!"

Pantelei Eremeich ought to be rejoicing, it seemed, because he had attained what he had been after; and rejoice he did, sure enough—and yet, for all that, Perfishka felt uneasy; he was even frightened.

Chertopkhanov placed the steed in his former stall, slapped him lightly on the croup, and said, "There, now you're home again! Watch out, then!"

That same day he hired a reliable watchman, a fellow without home or kin, took up his quarters again, and began living as of old. . . .

Not altogether as of old, though. But more of this later.

On the next day after his return Pantelei Eremeich called Perfishka to him and, for lack of any other auditor, began telling him (without losing awareness of his own dignity, naturally, and in a bass) how he had succeeded in recovering Malek Adel. During the narrative Chertopkhanov sat with his face to the window and smoked a long-stemmed pipe, while Perfishka stood on the threshold, with his hands be-hind his back and, gazing respectfully at the nape of his lord and master's neck, listened to the tale of how, after many vain attempts and journeyings, Pantelei Eremeich had at last found himself at the fair in the Romnas, by this time alone, without the Jew Leiba who, owing to the weakness of his character, had been unable to hold out and had run away from him; how, on the fifth day at the fair, as he was already preparing to depart, he for the last time had taken a walk along the rows of carts and had suddenly caught sight, tied to a wagon pole, among three other horses, of none other than Malek Adel! How he had recognized him immediately—and how Malek Adel had recognized him, had begun to whinny, and to tug, and paw the earth.

"And he wasn't with the Cossack that had sold him," Chertopkhanov went on, still without turning his head and in the same bass, "but with a Gypsy trader; I, naturally, laid my hands on my horse and wanted to get it back by force, but that beast of a Gypsy started yelling as if someone had thrown scalding water over him; he began calling God to witness before the whole market place that he'd bought the horse from another Gypsy—and wanted to produce witnesses. I spat in disgust—and paid the money over: the Devil and all with him! The main thing that matters to me is that I have sought out my friend and have found peace for my soul.

"Then there was the time in the Karachev district when, taking the Jew Leiba's word, I sailed into a Cossack; I took him for my thief and beat his whole face into a pulp; however, that Cossack turned out to be a priest's son—and he got damages for defamation from me: a hundred and twenty rubles. Well, money comes and goes, but the main thing is that Malek Adel is again with me! I'm happy now; I'm going to enjoy some peace. As for you, Porphyry, I have but one instruction for you: soon as you see a Cossack anywheres in the neighborhood—which God forfend!—why, that very second, without saying a word, you just run and fetch me my gun, and you can bet I'll know what I've got to do!"

Thus did Pantelei Eremeich speak to Perfishka; that was what his lips uttered—but at heart he was not as calm as he claimed to be.

Alas! Deep down in his soul he was not altogether certain that the steed he had brought home was actually Malek Adel.

X

A difficult period ensued for Pantelei Eremeich. It was precisely peace of mind he enjoyed least of all. True, good days did occur; the doubt that had arisen within him seemed nonsense; he drove the absurd notion away from him, like a persistently annoying fly, and even laughed at his own self. But there also occurred bad days; the unrelenting notion would begin to gnaw and scrape at his heart anew, like a mouse under the floor—and he was beset with torments, corroding and secret. During the memorable day when he had recovered Malek Adel, Chertopkhanov had felt nothing but beatific joy. But the next morning, when under the low shed of his inn he had begun saddling his find, near whom he had passed the whole night, something pricked him for the first time. He had merely tossed his head; nevertheless the seed had been dropped. During his homeward journey (it had taken a week) the doubts had not risen within him often; they had grown stronger and clearer only when he had come back to his Bezsonovo, only when he had found himself in the place where the former, indubitable Malek Adel had lived.

On the way home he had ridden for the most part at a walk, rocking along, looking to this side of him and that, puffing away at a stubby pipe and not cogitating on anything in particular, unless it were that he'd up and say to himself: "Whatever the Chertopkhanovs set their heart on, they'll attain! You can't fool with 'em," and would smile a little. But upon his homecoming an altogether different state of affairs began. All this, of course, he kept to himself; his self-esteem, if nothing else, would not have permitted him to evince his inner alarm. He would have "torn in two" anyone who would have hinted even remotely that, apparently, the new Malek wasn't the old one, he accepted congratulations on his "fortunate find" from the few persons whom he had to come in contact with, but he did not seek these congratulations, he avoided contact with people more than ever—a bad sign! He was almost constantly examining (if one may use the expression) Malek Adel; he would ride off on him somewhere as far as possible to some field and put him to the test, or would go off stealthily into the stable, lock the door after him, and taking a stand before the steed's very head, would look into his eyes and ask him in a whisper: "Is it thou? Is it? Is it?" Or else he would look him over in silence, and that ever so intently, for hours on end, by turns rejoicing and muttering: "Yes. It is he! Of course it is!" But then he would be racked anew by perplexity and even confusion.

And it was not so much the physical dissimilarities of *this* Malek Adel as against *the other* which confused

Chertopkhanov. However, they were not great in number: *the other's* tail and mane had been somehow not so thick, and his ears were more pointed, and his pasterns shorter, and his eyes lighter in hue—but all these things may have merely seemed so: it was the moral discrepancies, so to say, which confused Chertopkhanov. *The other's* habits had been different, all his ways were unlike *this* Malek's. For instance: *that* Malek Adel looked around and whinnied, ever so lightly, as soon as Chertopkhanov set foot in the stable, while *this* fellow kept right on champing his hay as though nothing at all were happening, or else he dozed, with head lowered. Neither animal would stir when the master was jumping out of the saddle; but *that* one, when they called him, would immediately come in answer to the voice, whereas *this* one remained rooted to the spot like a tree stump. *That* one galloped just as fast as *this* one, but could leap higher and further; *this* one went more freely at a walk, but was more shaky at a trot, and at times "dipped," or "interfered," with his shoes: that is, he struck the rear ones against the front ones—*the other*, God save us, was free of any such shameful failing. *This* fellow, (so thought Chertopkhanov) was forever twitching his ears, in such a foolish way, whereas *that* one was just the other way: he'd lay one ear back and keep it that way as he eyed his master! *The other*, as soon as he saw that things weren't clean near him, used to kick out with one of his hind hoofs against the partition of his stall, but to *this* fellow it made no difference: you could pile up the manure to his very belly, for all he cared. *The other*, for instance, if you made him stand facing the wind, would breathe in at once with his full lungs, and shake himself, whereas all *this* fellow did was to keep on snorting; rain dampness used to upset *the other*, but *this* one didn't think anything of it. . . . Coarser, this fellow was—coarser! And there was nothing pleasant about him, as there was with the other, and he drew tight on the rein. . . . Oh, what was the use of talking! *The other* had been a horse dear to one's heart, but *this*—!

That is what Chertopkhanov thought now and then, and these thoughts brought up a bitter taste within him. But then, at other times, he would let his steed go at full speed over a field that had just been plowed, or would compel him to jump down to the very bottom of a washed-out ravine and then jump out again at its steepest place, and the heart within him would swoon from rapture, loud whoops would escape his lips, and he knew, *knew* of a certainty, that it was the authentic, the indubitable Malek Adel under him, for what other horse was capable of doing what this horse did?

However, here too things were not without mishap and trouble. The protracted search for Malek Adel had cost Chertopkhanov a great deal of money; he no longer thought of dogs of the Kostroma breed, and rode about the neighborhood all by himself, just as he had done before.

And so one morning Chertopkhanov, a little over three miles from Bezsonovo, came across a hunting party of that same count before whom he had pranced so dashingly a year and a half before. And the same situation was simply bound to occur; even as on that day, so now a winter hare upped and jumped before the hounds from under a hedgerow dividing two fields on the slope of a hill! After him—after him! The whole hunt simply flew off, and Chertopkhanov flew off likewise, only not together with the others, but two hundred paces or so off to one side of them—exactly as he had done that other time. An enormous washout had cut crookedly across the hillside and, traversing Chertopkhanov's path, grew gradually narrower as it went higher and higher; nevertheless, at the point where he had to jump across it—and where a year and a half ago he actually had jumped across it—it still had a width of eight paces, and a depth of fourteen feet. In anticipation of triumph, a triumph he would repeat in so miraculous a manner, Chertopkhanov let out victorious whoops and shook his quirt (the hunters, despite all their galloping, never took their eyes off the fiery horseman); his steed was flying like an arrow; there, the washout was before his very nose—there, there, take it at one stride, as thou didst at that time!

But Malek Adel stopped short, wavered to the left, and galloped off *along* the precipice, no matter how hard Chertopkhanov jerked his head to one side, toward the washout. . . .

He'd turned yellow, then; had shown a lack of faith in himself!

Thereupon Chertopkhanov, all ablaze with shame and wrath, almost weeping, let the reins drop and drove the steed straight ahead, up the hill, away, away from those hunters, only that he might not hear them jeering at him, only that he might vanish as soon as possible from their accursed eyes!

With flanks crisscrossed by lash marks, all in a lather,

351

Malek Adel came galloping home, and Chertopkhanov immediately locked himself in his room.

"No, this is not he—this is not my friend. The other might have broken his neck but would never have failed me!"

XI

It was the following incident, however, that definitely "did" for Chertopkhanov, as the saying goes. He was once making his way on Malek Adel through the back lots of the priest's tract surrounding the church in whose parish the tiny hamlet of Bezsonovo lay. With his Cossack shako pulled low over his forehead, hunched up and with hands drooping on the pommel of his saddle, he was plodding on; his soul was uneasy and far from joyous. Suddenly someone called out after him.

He halted his steed, looked up, and saw his correspondent, the deacon. In a brownish cap with three flaps atop his tawny hair, which he wore in a queue, clad in a yellowish nankeen caftan, girdled well south of his midriff by some baby-blue oddment, the servitor of the altar had gone forth to inspect his scrap of a diocese and, having espied Pantelei Eremeich, had deemed it his duty to pay him his respects— and, while he was at it, to wheedle something, anything at all, out of him. Without that sort of hind thought clerical persons, as we all know, do not enter into conversation with laymen.

But Chertopkhanov was in no mood for the deacon; he barely acknowledged his bow and, having mumbled out something through his teeth, had already lifted up his quirt.

"Ay, what a most magnificent steed yours is!" the deacon hastened to add. "Of a certainty, one may say it does you honor. Verily, you are a man of wondrous mind—even like unto a lion!" Father Deacon was noted for his eloquence— whereby he irked Father Priest vastly, inasmuch as the latter had not the gift of the word: even vodka did not loosen his tongue. "Of one goodly creature, through the work of evil men, you were bereft," the deacon went on, "yet, without despairing in the least but, on the contrary, placing still greater trust in Divine Providence, you have acquired another unto yourself, in no way inferior, but, probably, superior to the other, inasmuch as—"

"What are you batting about?" Chertopkhanov sullenly

352

cut him short. "What other steed, now? This is the very same animal—this is Malek Adel. I recovered him. Listen to the man, blabbing just to hear himself talk—"

"Eh, eh, eh, eh!" articulated the deacon, seeming to drawl, actually, his fingers toying with his beard, and his light, avid eyes straying over Chertopkhanov. "How could that be, my dear sir? Your steed—may God help my memory—was stolen during the past year, a fortnight or so after the Feast of the Intercession, and now we're at the tag end of November—"

"Well, and what of that?"

The deacon's fingers still kept toying with his beard:

"That means a year and a bit over has gone by since then, and the steed you had then was a dappled gray, even as the one you have now—except that he has actually grown darker, if anything. But how could that be? For gray horses, now, grow a great deal lighter in the space of a year!"

Chertopkhanov shuddered—as though someone had prodded his chest with a boar spear next his heart. And, truly: horses of a gray color *do* change! How was it a thought as simple as that had never entered his head up to now?

"Thou bundle of anathemas! Get away from me!" he barked out suddenly, his eyes flashing madly, and on the instant disappeared from the sight of the astounded deacon.

There! Everything was at an end!

This time everything actually was at an end, everything had burst into smithereens, his last card had been beaten! Everything had come crashing down together from that one word "lighter."

Gray horses grow lighter!

Gallop, gallop, thou accursed! Thou wilt not escape that word by galloping!

Chertopkhanov flew home and again locked himself in.

XII

That this wretched crowbait wasn't Malek Adel, that between him and Malek Adel there did not exist the least similarity; that any man at all endowed with horse-sense should have seen this from the very first; that he, Pantelei Chertopkhanov, had been deceived in the most vulgar manner—no, that he had purposely, premeditatedly taken in his

353

own self, that he himself had loosed this fog to becloud his own eyes—there now remained not the least doubt of all this!

Chertopkhanov paced up and down his room, invariably turning on his heels when he reached each wall, like a beast in a cage. His vanity was suffering unbearably, but it was not the pain of wounded vanity alone that was torturing him: despair, too, had taken possession of him, malice was strangling him, the thirst for revenge was flaring up within him. But revenge against whom? Whom was he to revenge himself upon? The Jew, Jaff, Masha, the deacon, the horse-thieving Cossack, all his neighbors, the whole world—his own self, finally? His mind was becoming muddled. His last card had been beaten! (This simile was to his liking.) And he was again the most insignificant, the most disdained of men, a laughingstock for all, a merry-andrew grinning through a horse collar, a hopelessly beaten loser in the childish card game of "booby," a butt of a sneer—to a deacon! He imagined, he pictured clearly to himself how this abominable windbag would start telling the story of the gray horse, of the foolish squire. Oh, curses!

In vain did Chertopkhanov try to abate his spreading spleen; in vain did he attempt to assure himself that this . . . horse, even though it was no Malek Adel was, after all . . . a good one, and could serve him for many a year; he would immediately spurn this thought as though there were contained therein a new affront to that *other* Malek Adel, before whom he considered himself at fault even without this. Naturally! This knacker's hide, this nag, he, like a blind man, like a blockhead, had compared to him, to Malek Adel! And as to that service which this nag might yet perform for its master—why, would he ever honor it by mounting it? Not for anything! Never! Give it away to a knacker (a Tatar knacker, at that), give it to dogs to feed on—it wasn't worthy of anything else! Yes! That would be best of all!

For over two hours did Chertopkhanov tramp about his room.

"Perfishka!" he suddenly issued his command. "Go to the pothouse this minute; fetch six quarts of vodka here! Do you hear? Six quarts, and be quick about it! I want that vodka to be standing on that table this second!"

The vodka did not delay its appearance on Pantelei Eremeich's table, and he settled down to his drinking.

XIII

Whoever would have had a glimpse of Chertopkhanov then, whoever could have been a witness of that sullen resentment with which he drained tumbler after tumbler, that person would have experienced inexplicable fear. Night had fallen; a tallow candle was burning dimly on the table. Chertopkhanov had ceased tramping from corner to corner. He was sitting, all flushed, with glazed eyes which alternately looked at the floor or stared fixedly through the dark window; he would get up, pour out vodka for himself, drain it off, sit down again, again fix his eyes on one point, and sit without stirring—his breathing would merely quicken and his face turn a darker red. Some resolve was, apparently, ripening within him, a resolve which even he himself found confusing, yet to which he was gradually becoming accustomed; one unvarying thought was importunately and unremittingly bearing down upon him; one unvarying image was being limned ever more clearly before him, while within his heart, under the incandescent pressure of deep intoxication, the irritation of malice was by now being replaced by a feeling of brutality, and an ill-boding sneer was appearing on his lips.

"Come, it's time!" he uttered in some sort of a business-like, almost wearisome voice. "Enough of hanging around!"

He drank off a final tumbler of vodka, took down the pistol hanging over the bed . . . loaded it, put a few percussion caps into his pocket, "just in case," and set out for the stable.

The watchman ran toward him as he was about to open the door, but Chertopkhanov yelled at him: "It's me! Or are you blind? Get along with you!"—and the watchman stepped a little to one side. "Get along to bed!" Chertopkhanov yelled at him again. "There's nothing here for you to watch! What a rare sight! What a treasure, to be sure!"

He entered the stable. Malek Adel—the spurious Malek Adel—was lying on a bed of straw. Chertopkhanov gave him a kick, saying: "Get up, you crowbait!" He next untied the halter from the manger, took off the horse blanket and threw it on the ground, and, roughtly turning the obedient horse around in the stall, led it out into the yard, and from the yard into a field, to the extreme astonishment of the watchman, who just couldn't understand where his master was setting out to in the nighttime, leading an unbridled horse

355

on a halter. He naturally felt afraid to ask him, merely following him with his eyes, until he vanished at the turn of the
road leading to a forest nearby.

XIV

Chertopkhanov walked along with great strides, without
stopping and without turning around; Malek Adel (let us
call him by that name to the last) submissively paced along
after him. The night was rather light; Chertopkhanov could
make out the serrated outline of the forest, showing as a
solid black splotch ahead. Gripped by the night cold, he
would most probably have become tipsy from the vodka he
had drunk if not . . . if not for another, a stronger tipsiness,
which took violent possession of his whole being. His head
had grown heavy; the blood was reverberatingly pounding in
his throat and ears, but he went on firmly, and knew where
he was going.

He had resolved to kill Malek Adel; all day long he had
been thinking of nothing else. Now he was resolved to do it.

One could not say he was embarking on this deed with imperturbability, but with self-assurance, rather, and irrevo-
cability, without turning back, as man embarks on something
in submission to a sense of duty. To him this *thing* seemed
very *simple:* having annihilated the self-styled pretender,
he would at one stroke become quits with *everything:*
punish himself for his folly, and vindicate himself before his
real friend, and would prove to all the world (Chertopkhanov
was very much concerned about all the world) that you
couldn't play tricks on him. But, chiefest of all: he would
annihilate himself along with this impostor—for what had
he, Chertopkhanov, to live for?

How all this found stowage in his head, and why it
seemed to him so simple, is not easy, even though not altogether impossible, to explain. Wronged, lonely, without a
kindred human soul near him, without a copper, and also
with his blood fired by liquor, he was in a state bordering
on insanity, and there is no doubt that in the most absurd
freaks of insane persons there is, in their eyes, a certain logic,
and even a rightness. At any rate, Chertopkhanov felt fully
assured of his rightness; he did not waver, he was hastening
to carry out the verdict upon the culprit without, however,
giving any clear account to himself just whom, precisely, he

356

was designating thus. To tell the truth, he was thinking but little of that which he was preparing to do. "Things must, *must* be brought to an end!"—that was what he kept repeating to himself, dully and sternly. "An end must be put to things!"

As for the inculpable culprit, he kept on jogging along submissively behind his master's back. . . . But in the heart of Chertopkhanov there was no pity.

XV

Not far from the edge of the forest whither he had brought his horse, there stretched a small gully, half grown over with young oaks. As Chertopkhanov was descending into it Malek Adel stumbled and all but fell on him.

"What are you after, accursed one—crushing me?" Chertopkhanov shouted and, just as if he were defending himself, snatched the pistol out of his pocket. By this time it was not cold fury he felt but that especial numbness of sensibility which, so they say, takes possession of a man about to commit a crime. But his own voice frightened him—so wild a sound it had under the overhanging dark branches, amid the rotten and musty dampness of the forest gully! In addition to that, in answer to his outcry, some large bird suddenly fluttered in a treetop over his head. Chertopkhanov shuddered. It was as though he had roused up a witness to his deed—and where, of all places? In this godforsaken spot, where he should not have met a single living creature.

"Go, you devil, to all the ends of the earth!" he got out through his teeth and, releasing Malek Adel's halter, with a full swing struck him on the shoulder with the pistol grip. Malek Adel lost no time in turning around, scrambled out of the gully and . . . broke into a run. But the clatter of his hoofs did not break the silence very long; the wind that had sprung up confused and muffled all sounds.

Chertopkhanov in his turn slowly made his way out of the gully, reached the edge of the forest, and plodded off for home. He was dissatisfied with himself; the heaviness which he felt in his head, in his heart, was spreading through all his limbs; he walked along angry, glowering, unsatisfied, hungry, as though someone had wronged him, had taken from him his prey, his food—such sensations as the suicide knows who has been foiled from fulfilling his intention.

357

Suddenly something nudged him from behind, between his shoulders. He looked around: Malek Adel was standing in the middle of the road. He had followed his master, had nudged him with his muzzle—had made his presence known.

"Ah!" Chertopkhanov yelled. "It's you, you yourself, who have come to meet your death! Very well, then!"

Quick as a wink he had snatched out his pistol, pulled back the trigger, put the muzzle to Malek Adel's forehead, fired. . . .

The poor animal shied to one side, reared up, leaped back ten paces or so, and suddenly crashed ponderously and began breathing hard, sprawling convulsively on the ground.

Chertopkhanov pressed his palms to his ears and started running. His knees were buckling under him. And his tipsiness, and malice, and stolid self-assurance all fled from him at once. There remained only an emotion of shame and hideousness—and the realization, the indubitable realization, that this time he had put an end to himself as well.

XVI

Six weeks later the Cossack lad Perfishka deemed it his duty to stop a commissioner of rural police who happened to be riding past the Bezsonovo estate.

"What do you want?" asked the keeper of law and order.

"If you please to step into the house, Your Honor," the lad answered with a low bow. "Pantelei Eremeich is about to die, it looks like; well, naturally, I'm scared."

"What? About to die?" the commissioner questioned him.

"Just so. At first he kept on stowing away vodka, day after day, but now he's took to his bed, and he's gotten much too thin. The way I figure, he don't even understand anything rightly. Lost his tongue altogether."

The commissioner clambered down off his cart.

"Well, did you go after the priest, at least? Has your master confessed? Has he received the last sacrament?"

"By no means, sir."

"How's that, brother?" the official frowned. "How can anybody act like that—eh? Or don't you know that there's a big penalty for that sort of neglect—eh?"

"Why, I asked him even as far back as three days ago, and yesterday, too," the abashed lad said eagerly. " 'Won't you order me to run for the priest, Pantelei Eremeich?' — 'Keep

358

still, you fool,' said he. 'Don't be shoving your nose in what's none of your business.' And today, soon as I started telling him what was going on, he just looked at me, and his mustache bristled."

"And did he drink much?" asked the commissioner.

"Ever so much! But you just do us a favor, Your Honor—please come into his room."

"Very well—show me the way!" growled the official, and followed Perfishka.

An astonishing sight awaited him.

In a rear room of the house, dank and dark, on a humble cot, covered over with a horse blanket, with a shaggy Cossack felt cloak for a pillow, lay Chertopkhanov, by now no longer pale but yellowish-green, the hue of the dead, with eyes sunken in under glazed lids, with a nose grown sharply pointed (but still reddish) jutting over rumpled mustachios. He was lying dressed in his invariable Caucasian overcoat with cartridges across the chest, and in blue ballooning Circassian trousers. A shako with a raspberry-hued crown covered his forehead to the very brows. In one hand he was holding his hunting quirt; in the other, an embroidered tobacco pouch—Masha's last gift. A big empty square bottle stood on the table near the bed, while at the head of the bed, fastened with pins to the wall, one could see two watercolors: one, as far as one could make it out, represented a stout man with a guitar in his hands—probably Nedopiuskin; the other depicted a galloping horseman. The horse resembled one of those fabulous animals which children draw upon walls and fences, but the painstakingly shaded dapplings on its gray coat and the cartridges across the chest of the horseman, the pointed tips of his boots and his enormous mustachios, left no room for doubt that this drawing was meant to represent Pantelei Eremeich mounted on Malek Adel.

The bewildered commissioner of rural police did not know what to do. Dead silence reigned in the room.

"Why, he must have died already," he reflected and, raising his voice, called out: "Pantelei Eremeich! Oh, Pantelei Eremeich!"

Thereupon something extraordinary took place. Chertopkhanov's eyes slowly opened, the extinguished pupils moved at first from right to left, then from left to right, rested upon the visitor, saw him. Something began to flicker amid their

359

dim blankness, a similitude of a look appeared within them; the lips, turned livid, slowly became unstuck and a hoarse voice, now verily a voice from the grave, was heard:

"Pantelei Chertopkhanov, a nobleman of an ancient line, is dying; who can hinder him? He is indebted to no one; he demands nothing. Let him be, men! Get ye hence!"

The hand holding the quirt made an attempt to lift itself a little. In vain! The lips again became stuck together, the eyes closed—and, as before, Chertopkhanov was lying on his hard cot, stretched out flat and with his heels together.

"Let me know when he dies," the official, going out of the room, whispered to Perfishka. "As for the priest, I think somebody could go after him even now. After all, things ought to be done properly; he ought to receive the last rites."

That same day Perfishka went after the priest; and on the following morning he had to inform the commissioner of rural police that Pantelei Eremeich had died the same night.

When he was being buried, two people followed his coffin: Perfishka, his Cossack lad, and Moshel Leiba. Word of Chertopkhanov's demise had in some way or other reached the Jew, and he did not fail to pay the last devoirs to his benefactor.

LIVING RELICS

> Land long-suffering, my own—
> Land of all the Russian people!
> —F. Tiutchev

"A bone-dry fisherman," proclaims a French proverb, "and a sopping-wet hunter offer a sorry sight." Never having been addicted to the piscatorial sport, I'm no judge of a fisherman's mood in fine, clear weather, and to what extent a good catch during an inclement spell outweighs the discomfort of a soaking. To a hunter, though, rain is a downright calamity. It was to precisely such a calamity that Ermolai and I were subjected during one of our excursions after grouse into the Belevsky district.

The rain hadn't let up from the very dawning. And what hadn't we done to escape it! We had put rubber capes over our heads, and we had stopped under trees, to avoid the raindrops as much as possible. But the waterproof capes (to say nothing of their interfering with our shooting) let the water through in the most shameless manner; as for the trees, it certainly did seem, at first, as if there was no dripping under them—but then the moisture that accumulated on the leaves would suddenly break through: each bough would drench us as if out of a rainspout; a tiny rivulet would make its way underneath the neckband and course down the spine. . . . And that (as Ermolai put it) was the limit and all!

"No, Peter Petrovich!" he cried out at last. "Things can't go on like this! We can't do any hunting today. The dogs' scent is gettin' drownded out; the guns are missing fire—" and he spat in disgust. "Sure is a problem!"

"What are we to do, then?"

"Why, here's what we'll do. Let's drive over to Alexeievka. Maybe you don't know the place—it's a sort of a small farmstead belonging to your mother; a little over five miles from here. We'll spend the night there, and on the morrow—"

"We'll come back here?"

"No, not here. I know some spots beyond Alexeievka. Lots better for grouse than the ones over here!"

I didn't bother questioning my faithful companion as to why he hadn't brought me to those other spots in the first place, and that same day we managed to reach this small farmstead of my mother's, the existence of which, I confess, I hadn't even suspected up to then. This farmstead proved to have a small lodge, most decrepit but unoccupied and, for that reason, clean; I passed a restful enough night in it.

The next day I awoke quite, quite early. The sun had just risen; there wasn't as much as a cloudlet in the sky; everything around me gleamed with a double gleam: the gleam of the newly born morning rays and that of yesterday's downpour. While they were harnessing a two-wheeled cart for me I went for a stroll through what had once been an orchard but by now had run wild, having advanced upon the small lodge on all sides with its fragrant, sap-filled wildwood. Ah, how fine it was out in the open air, under the clear sky wherein the larks were fluttering, whence the silver beads of their ringing voices came pouring down! They must have borne away drops of dew on their wings, and their songs, too, seemed bedewed. I even doffed my cap and breathed joyously, to the fullest. On the slope of a not very deep ravine, right next to the paling, one could glimpse beehives; a narrow little path led to them, winding like a snake between the unbroken walls of high steppe grass and nettles, over which reared the spiky stalks of dark-green hemp, wind-sown there from God knows whence.

I set out along this path and reached the beehives. Standing alongside was a small wattled shed, such as is used for storing the beehives away for the winter. I looked in at the half-open door: it was dark, dry, quiet within, smelling of mint, of melissa. A sort of platform had been put up in a corner and lying upon it, covered with a blanket, was some tiny figure or other. I turned to leave.

"Master, oh, master! Peter Petrovich!" I caught a voice—faint, slow, soughing, like the rustle of swamp sedge.

I stopped.

"Peter Petrovich!" the voice repeated. "Come nearer, please!" It was coming from the corner, from the platform I had noticed.

I approached, and was petrified in astonishment. Lying before me was a living human being—yet just what was it?

The head was utterly withered, all of one hue, the hue of bronze, for all the world like an icon limned in the ancient style; the nose was narrow, like a knife blade; the lips were hardly to be seen: one could catch only the white gleam of teeth and eyes and, escaping from under a headkerchief onto the forehead, scanty wisps of yellow hair. Near the chin, where the blanket folded over, two diminutive hands, of the same bronze hue as the face, were stirring, fidgeting with fingers that were like tiny sticks. I looked closely: the face was not only not hideous but actually beautiful, yet frightening, extraordinary. And all the more frightening did this face seem to me because I saw upon it, upon its cheeks of metallic hue, a smile struggling . . . struggling, yet unable to expand.

"You don't recognize me, master?" the voice fell to whispering again; it was as though it were evaporating from the barely moving lips. "Yes, and how should you! I'm Lukeria. . . . Remember? The girl who used to lead the round dances at your mother's, in Spasskoe. . . . I used to lead off the chorus, too. Remember?"

"Lukeria?" I cried out. "Is it really you? How can that be?"

"Yes, it's me, master, me. I'm Lukeria."

I didn't know what to say and, as if I had been stunned, kept staring at this dark, immobile face, with its radiant and deathlike eyes fixed upon me. How could it be? This mummy —Lukeria, the foremost beauty among all our house serfs, tall, plump, with a peaches-and-cream complexion, always laughing, always dancing, always singing. Lukeria, that clever girl Lukeria, whom all the young lads used to court, after whom I myself—a boy of sixteen—used to sigh in secret.

"Good heavens, Lukeria," I managed to say at last, "whatever happened to you?"

"Why, this is the sort of calamity that's befallen me! Come, don't you be squeamish, master—don't look down on my misfortune, sit you down on that little tub, for otherwise you won't be able to hear me. You can tell what fine voice I'm in now! My, but I'm glad I saw you! How come you to be in Alexeievka?"

Lukeria was speaking very softly and faintly, yet not haltingly.

"Ermolai, the hunter, drove me over here. But do tell me everything—"

"Tell you about my calamity, now? If you like, master. This happened to me a long while ago by now, six or seven years back. At that time they'd just betrothed me to Vassilii Polyakov. Remember him? Well-built fellow, he was curly-headed—he worked as a butler for your mother at the time. Why, you weren't in the village by then—you'd gone off to Moscow to study. This Vassilii and I were very much in love; I couldn't get him out of my head—and, too, this whole thing happened in the spring. Well, then, one night . . . it was getting close to daybreak . . . yet I couldn't fall asleep; a nightingale was singing so wonderfully sweet out in the garden! I couldn't help it—I got up and came out on the porch to listen. He was going off into such trills, such trills. Suddenly I thought I heard someone calling me, ever so softly. The voice sounded like Vassya's: 'Lusha!' I looked off to one side, and, owing to my being only half awake, I guess, I missed my footing and flew right off the top step and fell *smash!* against the ground. And it seemed like I hadn't banged myself up badly, for I got up quickly enough and went back to my room. Only thing was, it was just like something in my innards, inside my belly, had torn loose. . . . Let me catch my breath, just one minute, master—"

Lukeria fell silent, while I kept staring at her in amazement. The thing which really amazed me was that she was telling her story almost gaily, without any oh'ing or sighing, not complaining in the least and without making a play for sympathy.

"Since that same accident," Lukeria went on, "I began to wither, to pine away; my skin turned dark; it became hard for me to walk, and later on I hadn't any control over my legs; I couldn't either stand or sit, felt like lying down all the time. And I didn't want to eat or drink; I got worse and worse all the time. Your mother, through the goodness of her heart, had the doctors in to see me, and she sent me to a hospital, too. However, there was no relief for me. And there wasn't even one medical man could as much as tell what sort of ailment it was I had. And what didn't they do to me: they seared my back with red-hot irons, they made me sit in chopped ice—and nothing came of it all. Toward the end I got to be nothing but a bag of bones. And so the masters decided at last it wasn't any use treating me any more; yet it's kind of awkward to be keeping any cripples at the manor house . . . well, then, they shifted me to this village, seeing as how I've got relatives here. And that's how I live, as you can see."

Lukeria fell silent again and again forced herself to smile.

"However, this is dreadful, the situation you're in!" I exclaimed, and not knowing what more to say, asked: "But what about Polyakov, this Vassilii?" An exceedingly stupid question, that.

Lukeria turned her eyes away a little.

"What about Polyakov? He grieved and he grieved—and in the end married another, a girl from Glinnoye. Do you know Glinnoye? It's not far from us. Agraphena, they called her. He was very much in love with me—but he's a young man, now; you couldn't expect him to stay single. And what sort of a mate would I have been to him? And the wife he found was fine, kindhearted, and they've got little ones. He's living close by, as a clerk for a squire in the neighborhood; your mother gave him leave, with a passport, and—glory be to God—he's getting along fine."

"And that's how you go on, lying here all the time?" I resumed my questioning.

"Yes, that's just the way I lie here, master. Going on the seventh year now. In the summertime, you see, I lie here in this wattled shed, but when it gets to be cold they'll carry me over into the bathhouse entry. That's where I lie."

"But who tends to you? Is there anybody looking after you?"

"Why, there's kindhearted folks here as well as elsewhere. They don't neglect me. And, besides, I don't need much tending. As to eating, I guess I eat almost nothing, and as for water—well, there it is, in that mug: there's always a supply of clear spring water handy. I can stretch enough to reach that mug by myself; I still have the use of one arm. Yes, and there's a girl here, a little orphan—every so often she's bound to look in, for which I am grateful. She was here just now; you didn't happen to meet her? A pretty, fair little thing. She brings me flowers; I'm ever so fond of them—of flowers, that is. We haven't any garden flowers now. There were, but they're all gone. But then field flowers are beautiful, too; they have an even finer smell than garden ones. There, you take lilies of the valley, now; the wild ones are ever so much more appealing!"

"And don't you feel bored, or uneasy, my poor Lukeria?"

"Well, what can a body do? I wouldn't want to lie to you: at first it was most wearisome, but later on I got used to it, got so I could endure it—and it didn't matter so much; there's others still worse off."

"In just what way, now?"

"Why, there's some haven't any shelter at all! And there's some that are blind or deaf! But I, glory be to God, can see splendidly, and can hear everything, everything! A mole may be burrowing underground—well, I can hear even that. And I can catch every scent, even though it be ever so faint. When the buckwheat comes into blossom out in the field, or a linden in the garden, why, there's no need of telling me, even: I'll be the first to catch the scent right off. Just as long as there's a breeze blowing from there. No, what's the use of angering God? There's many in worse fixes than mine. Take even this, for example: there's them among the hale who might fall into sin ever so easily; but me—why, sin itself has departed from me. Just the other day Father Alexis, our priest, now, was about to give me the sacrament, and so he says: 'You, now, haven't a thing to confess—for how could you, in your condition, commit any sin?' But I answered him: 'And what of sinning in thought, Father?' — 'Well,' said he, and he laughed to himself, 'that's no great sin.'

"Well now, I suppose, I'm not so powerful sinful as far as that same sinning in thought goes," Lukeria went on, "for I've taught myself not to think, and, even more strictly, not to recollect anything. Makes the time pass quicker."

I was surprised, I must confess.

"You're all, all alone, Lukeria; how, then, can you prevent thoughts from coming into your head? Or do you sleep all the time?"

"Oh, no, master! It isn't always I can sleep, now. Even

366

though I have no great pains, yet there's something nagging in me there, in my very innards, and in my bones as well; it won't let me sleep as I ought. No . . . I keep lying, just so; I just keep lying still all by myself, simply lying still and not thinking; I feel that I'm alive, that I breathe—and that's all there is to me. I look, I listen. The bees out amongst the beehives buzz and hum; a dove will perch on a roof and start in to coo; a little setting hen will wander in with her chicks to peck at crumbs, or else a sparrow flutters in, or a butterfly—it's all a great pleasure to me. Why, year before last some swallows actually wove a nest for themselves over there, in that corner, and reared their little ones. My, how interesting that was! One of the birds would fly in and head for the little nest, hang over it, feed the brood, and then fly off. Then you'd look again; there would be another swallow coming to take the other's place. Sometimes it wouldn't fly in, but just dart by the open door—but the babies would start right off cheeping and opening their beaks wide. I was expecting them to come the next year, too, but they say that a certain hunter hereabouts shot them down. And whatever could it have profited him? A swallow—why, all of it is no bigger than a beetle. What wicked creatures all of you hunters are!"

"I don't shoot swallows," I hastened to remark.

"And then there was one time," Lukeria resumed, "well, there was plenty to laugh at! A rabbit ran right in here, for a fact! The hounds were chasing him, or something like that; anyway, what did he do but barge right in through the door! He sat up, ever so close to me, and sat that way for a long time, I must say, his nose sniffing all the time and his whiskers twitching, like a sure-enough army officer! And he kept looking at me. Must have grasped, that is, that he had nothing to fear from me. At last he reared up, went hippety-hop to the door, looked back when he got to the threshold, and that was the last you saw of him! What a funny fellow!"

Lukeria glanced at me, as if to say: "Wasn't that funny, now?" I laughed a little, to humor her. She bit her parched lips.

"Well, in the wintertime, of course, things are somewhat worse for me, since it's dark; it would be a pity to light a candle—and besides, what would be the use? Even though I do know my A B C's, and was always much given to reading, yet what is there to read? There are no books whatsoever here, and even if there were, how am I to hold one—how am I to hold a book, now? Father Alexis, to divert me, brought me an almanac once, but he saw it weren't any use and took it back again. However, even though it's dark, there's still things to listen to: a cricket will start in with its chirping, or a mouse take to scratching away somewheres. That, now, is when it's a fine thing . . . to keep from thinking!

"Or else I repeat prayers," Lukeria went on after a brief rest. "Only thing is, I don't know so many of them—of these same prayers, now. And besides, what's the use of me wearying the Lord God? What can I implore Him for? He knows what I need better than I do. He has sent me this cross to bear; that means He loves me. That's how we're bidden to think. I'll repeat the Lord's Prayer, the Hymn to the Virgin, the Acathyst for All that Sorrow, and then lie here all by myself, without thinking any thoughts, not even the least. And things aren't so bad!"

A minute or two went by. I did not break the silence and did not stir on the narrow little tub that served me for a seat. The cruel, stony immobility of the living, unhappy being lying before me was communicated to me as well: I, too, seemed to be in a catalepsy.

"Listen, Lukeria," I began at last. "Listen to what I'm going to suggest to you. If you want me to, I'll make the arrangements: they'll move you to a hospital, a good hospital in the city. Who knows, maybe they can cure you, after all. In any case, you won't be all by yourself."

Lukeria's eyebrows stirred, ever so slightly; she sighed. "Oh, no, master," she got out in a troubled whisper. "Don't move me to a hospital. Leave me be. I'll have to bear only greater torments there. What manner of use is there in trying to cure me? There, one time a doctor happened to come here; he wanted to examine me. 'Don't trouble me, for Christ's sake,' I begged him. No use! He started in turning me over, he tried to limber up my arms, my legs, bending and unbending them: 'I'm doing this for science,' said he; 'that's what I'm working for, that's why I'm a man of science! And you,' said he, 'have no call to oppose me, for they've put a decoration about my neck because of my labors, and it's none other than you simpletons that I'm trying to do my best for!' He mauled me and he mauled me, gave my affliction a name —a long, highfalutin name, it was—and with that he went away. But me, all my bones, down to the smallest, ached naggingly for all of a week. I'm all by myself, you say—all by myself, all the time. No, not all the time. People do come to visit me. I'm quiet and peaceful; I don't bother anybody. Country girls drop in on me and chatter about this and that; a pilgrim woman may wander in and get to telling me about Jerusalem, about Kiev, about the holy towns. And besides, I'm not afraid of being by myself. It's even better so—by God, it is! Leave me be, master. Don't take me to any hospital. I feel grateful; you're kindhearted. Only leave me be, darling."

"Well, just as you wish; just as you wish, Lukeria. I supposed it would be only for you own good—"

"I know, master, that it was for my own good. But, master, my dear one: what human being can help another? Who can enter into another's soul? A human being must help his or her own self! There, now, you mayn't believe it, but there's times when I'm lying all alone like this . . . and it's just as though there was no one in all the world save myself. As if I were the only one alive! And it seems to me as if something was going to come over me. . . . I get to thinking such deep thoughts, it's downright amazing!"

"And what are your deep thoughts about at such times, Lukeria?"

"That, too, is something a body simply can't tell, master; there's no making it clear. And besides, one forgets it later on. It's just as though a little cloud were to come, were to shed its moisture; it gets so fresh then, so fine—but there's no grasping just what it was that happened. Only thing is, I keep thinking: had there been any people about me, nothing of this sort would happen and I wouldn't be conscious of anything save my affliction."

Lukeria sighed painfully. Her breast, just like her limbs, was not under her control.

"When I look at you, master," she resumed, "I feel that you're ever so sorry for me. But don't you feel sorry for me, really now! For instance, here's something I'm going to tell you; at times, even now. . . . Surely, you remember what a merry creature I was in my time? A tomboy! Well, do you know what? Even now I sing songs."

"Songs? You?"

"Yes, songs, old songs, choral songs, songs for feasts, carols, all sorts of songs! For I know a lot of them, now, and I haven't forgotten them. Only thing is, now, I don't sing

369

any songs for dancing. The state I'm in now, they aren't just the thing."

"How do you sing them, then, to yourself?"

"To myself, and aloud. Can't sing them very loud, now, but just the same you could make them out. There, as I was telling you, a little girl comes to see me. A little orphan, you know, a bright thing. So I've taught her: she's already taken over four songs of mine. Or don't you believe me? Hold on; I'll show you right away—"

Lukeria plucked up her courage. The thought that this half-dead being was getting ready to sing aroused an involuntary horror in me. But before I could utter a word a long-drawn-out, barely audible yet pure and true sound began quivering in my ears . . . a second followed, and a third. "In the Low Meadows" was what Lukeria was singing. She was singing with the expression on her petrified face unchanged, with even her eyes fixed on one point. Yet how touchingly did this poor, strained little voice ring, wavering like a wisp of smoke, how she longed to pour out all her soul! It was no longer horror I felt: it was unutterable pity that was squeezing my heart as in a vise.

"Oh, I can't go on!" she got out suddenly with something like a moan. "Haven't strength enough. . . . For I've been overjoyed at seeing you."

She closed her eyes.

I laid my hand on her tiny, chill fingers. She glanced up at me, and her dark lids, fringed with aureate lashes like those of ancient statues, closed anew. An instant later they began to gleam in the half murk. They were moist with tears.

I still did not stir.

"What a woman I am!" Lukeria got out suddenly with unexpected force, and having opened her eyes wide, tried to blink the tears from them. "Isn't it a shame? Why am I carrying on like this? This hasn't happened to me in a long while . . . since that very day when Polyakov—Vassya—came to see me, last spring. Whilst he was sitting with me and talking—well, it didn't matter; but when he left I cried plenty, all alone here! Where did I ever get all those tears from? But then, we women don't have to go shopping for tears. Master," added Lukeria, "maybe you've got a spare handkerchief on you. . . . Don't be squeamish, wipe my eyes—"

I hastened to do as she wished, and made her keep the

handkerchief. She refused it at first: "What do I need such a present for, now?" The handkerchief was a very plain one, but fresh and white. Then she clutched it in her feeble fingers and did not unclench them again. Having gotten used to the darkness in which both of us were, I could make out her features clearly, could even notice the slight flush that had come through the bronze of her face, could discover in this face (so, at least, it seemed to me) traces of its erstwhile beauty.

"There, master, you were asking me," Lukeria began speaking again, "whether I sleep. I sleep rarely, true enough, but each time I do I have dreams, fine dreams! In my dreams I never see myself ill. I'm always so well, and young. . . . There's only one thing to make me grieve: when I awaken, I want to have a really good stretch, but there I am, as though I were forged in chains. Once I dreamed such a wonderful dream! Would you like me to tell it to you? Well, listen. I saw myself standing in a field, like, and all around me was rye—such tall rye, so ripe, as if it were of gold! And there was a rusty-colored little dog with me, it seems—vicious as can be, aiming to bite me all the time. And, it seems, there was a sickle in my hand—and no common sickle, either, but the crescent moon itself; you know, when it looks like a sickle. And with that same sickle moon I had to reap that same rye clean. Only thing was, I was all tuckered out from the heat, and the moon was blinding me, and a lazy streak had come over me, and there were cornflowers growing all around me—and what huge ones! And all of them had turned their little heads toward me. And I was thinking: 'There, I'll pluck me a lot of these cornflowers; Vassya has promised to come, so I'll weave a wreath for myself first; I'll still have time to do my reaping. I started plucking the cornflowers, but they kept melting, simply melting away in my fingers, no matter what I did! I just couldn't weave a wreath for myself. Yet at the same time I already heard somebody coming toward me; he was ever so near, now, and calling 'Lusha, Lusha!' — 'My,' I was thinking, 'that's bad; I haven't had time to weave the wreath! Well, no matter, I'll put this crescent moon on my head in place of the cornflowers.'

"So I put the moon on, just as if it were one of those high headdresses, and at once I myself burst into such radiance that I lit up all the field around me. I looked: there was

371

someone gliding toward me, over the very tips of the ears of grain, ever so fast—only it wasn't Vassya but Christ Himself! And how I come to know it was Christ I couldn't tell you; He weren't the way He's shown on holy images; but He it was, sure enough! Beardless, tall, young, all in white—save that His belt was of gold—and He held out His hand to me.

" 'Fear not,' said He, 'My bride, my adorned, follow thou after Me; thou wilt lead the choral dances in My Kingdom of Heaven and play the songs of Paradise.' And then I simply clung with my lips to His hand! My little dog at once snapped at my legs, but just then we soared up and up! With Him ahead . . . His wings unfurled until they took up all the sky—long, they were, like the wings of a gull— and I flew after Him. And that little dog had to fall back. Only then did I grasp that this little dog was my affliction, and that there would no longer be any place for it in the Kingdom of Heaven."

Lukeria fell silent for a few moments.

"And I had another dream as well," she began anew. "Or, maybe, it was a vision I had; I don't rightly know which. Seemed to me as if I were lying in this very shed, and my late parents, my father and my mother, had come to see me, and they bowed low before me, but they themselves weren't saying anything. And I asked them: 'What for are you bowing to me, my father and my mother?' — 'Why,' said they, 'because you're going through such a martyrdom here on earth that you have thereby eased not only your soul, but have taken a great burden off us as well. And things have become ever so much better in the other world for us, too. You're done with all your sins; now you're overcoming ours.' And, having said this, my parents bowed to me again, and I couldn't see them any more; all I could see was the walls. Later on I was beset with very many doubts as to just what it was that had happened to me. I even told it to Father Alexis at confession. But he thinks it weren't any vision, because visions can come only to one of the spiritual calling.

"Or here's still another dream I had," Lukeria went on. "I dreamed I was sitting by the side of a highway, like, under a willow; I was holding a peeled staff, there was a sack slung over my shoulders, and my head was bound with a kerchief —an out-and-out pilgrim woman! I had to go far, far away somewheres, on a pilgrimage. And there were lots of pilgrims going past me all the time; they trudged along quietly, as though unwillingly, all of them heading the same way; all their faces were dismal, and they all looked very much like one another. And what did I see but a woman winding in and out amongst them and darting about; she was all of a head taller than the others, and the clothes on her were kind of odd, just as though they weren't like ours—not at all Russian. And her face, too, was odd: the face of one much given to fasts, and stern. And it looked as if all the others were steering clear of her, but she suddenly wheeled about and headed straight for me. She halted and stared: and her eyes were like a falcon's, yellow, big, and clear— ever so clear. And she said to me: 'I am your death.' I ought to have gotten scared, by rights; but, on the contrary, I was glad as glad can be; I was crossing myself! And that woman, that death of mine, she said to me: 'I feel sorry for you, Lukeria, yet take you with me I cannot. Farewell!' Lord! How sad I became then! 'Take me,' I told her, 'mother of mine, my dearest one, take me!' And my death turned around to me and began telling me things. . . . I grasped that she was appointing me my hour, but in such a way that I couldn't grasp her meaning, not at all clearly. 'After Saint Peter's day,' it sounded like. With that I awoke. That's the sort of amazing dreams I have, now."

Lukeria lifted up her eyes . . . and fell into deep thought.

"But here's my trouble: there's times a whole week may go by, yet I may not fall asleep even once. Last year a certain great lady was passing through here; she saw me and gave me a small vial with a medicine against sleeplessness: bade me take it ten drops at a time. It helped me ever so much, and I used to sleep, only I've used up that vial long since. Do you happen to know what medicine that was, and how could one get it?"

The great lady who had been passing through had evidently given Lukeria opium. I promised to get her a small vial like that, and once more could not but wonder aloud at her fortitude.

"Eh, master!" she retorted. "Why do you say that? What sort of fortitude is there about me? There, Simeon Stylites had plenty of it, right enough: he spent thirty years in standing on a pillar! And then there was another saint who was out to please God: he ordered himself to be buried in the ground, right up to his breast, and the ants were eating his face away. . . . Or here's something else that one lay reader told me: there was a certain land, and the Hagarenes had overcome that land in war, and they tortured and killed all the dwellers therein, and no matter what the latter did they just couldn't free themselves. And there appeared in their midst a sainted virgin; she took a great sword, put on armor weighing two and seventy pounds, went forth against the Hagarenes, and drove them all beyond the sea. But, having driven them forth, she said to them: 'Now go ahead and burn me at the stake, for such was the vow I had taken, that I was to die a fiery death for my people.' And the Hagarenes took her and burned her at the stake, and her people were thenceforth freed for all time! There, that was a great deed! But me, what do I amount to?"

I wondered to myself at this point how far and in what guise the legend of Joan of Arc had come in its wanderings and, after a short silence, asked Lukeria how old she was.

"Twenty-eight . . . or nine. Haven't reached thirty yet. But what's the use of numbering them—numbering the years, that is? Here's something else I'll tell you—"

Lukeria suddenly coughed in an oddly stifled way and let out a slight moan.

"You're talking a great deal," I remarked to her. "It may do you harm."

"That's true enough," she got out in a barely audible whisper. "Our talk is at an end, but let come what will! Now, when you'll drive off, I'll have my fill of silence for as long as I want. At least I have eased my soul—"

I began bidding her goodbye, repeated my promise of sending her the medicine, begged her once more to think hard and tell me whether there was anything else she needed.

"I've no need of anything; I'm satisfied with everything, praise be to God," she uttered with the greatest effort, yet much moved. "May God grant health to all! However, master, you might talk your mother into—the peasants hereabouts are poor—into abating their quitrent, even if only a little! They haven't land enough, they have no advantages. They would pray to God for you. . . . But as to me, I've no need of anything; I'm satisfied with everything."

I gave Lukeria my word to fulfill her request, and was already nearing the door when she called me over to her again.

"Do you remember, master," said she—and something wonderful flickered within her eyes and over her lips— "what a braid I used to have—do you remember? It reached to my very knees. For a long while I couldn't find the heart to cut it, to cut hair like that! But how could I comb it, the state I'm in now? So in the end I cut it off. Yes . . . well, forgive me, master, I can't talk any more."

That same day, before setting out to hunt, I had a talk about Lukeria with the village constable. I found out from him that they had given her the name "Living Relics" in the village; that, on the whole, there was no bother because of her; you never heard a murmur from her nor any complaints. "She herself never demands anything but, on the contrary, is thankful for everything; a quiet little body for fair, I must say. She has been stricken down by God"—that was how the constable concluded—"it must have been for her sins, then; however, we won't go into that. But as for condemning her, let's say—no, condemn her we do not. Let her be!"

Several weeks later I found out that Lukeria had died. Death had come for her, after all . . . and "after Saint Peter's day," at that. They said that on the very day of her death she had kept hearing the pealing of bells all the time, even though the distance from Alexeievka to the church is reckoned at over three miles—and it had been on a weekday. Lukeria had been saying, however, that the pealing was coming not from the church, but "from above." Probably she had not dared to say: from Heaven.

RATTLING WHEELS

"TELL YOU WHAT," announced Ermolai, coming into the hut where I was staying (as for me, I had just dined and had lain down on a camp cot to rest up a little after a rather successful but tiring hunt for grouse; this was around the tenth of July and the hot spells were persistent and frightful), "tell you what: we're all out of bird shot."

I leaped off the cot.

"We're all out of bird shot? Why, I figure we took well over twenty pounds with us from the village—a whole bag of it!"

"That's true enough, and it was a big bag, at that: should have lasted a couple of weeks. But who knows what happened! A hole must have worn through or something like that, but there it is, for a fact: there's no bird shot. Ten loads or so left."

"What are we to do, then? The best spots are ahead—we've been promised half a dozen bevies for tomorrow."

"Why, send me to Tula. It's not far from here: only thirty-five miles. I'll get there in a jiffy and will bring back bird shot, all of thirty pounds, if you order me to."

"But when would you start out?"

"Why, right away, if you like. What's the use of delaying? There's only one hitch: we'll have to hire horses."

"What do you mean, we'll have to hire horses? And what have we got our own horses for?"

"Can't go on our own. The shaft horse has gone lame, mighty bad!"

"Since when is that?"

"Why, not so long ago; the coachman took it to be shod. Well, he sure shod it! Must have run up against a poor smith. Now the horse can't even step on that leg. A foreleg, it is. Even carries it raised, the way a dog would."

"Well, now, was the shoe taken off at least?"

"No, it weren't, yet taken off it should be. Must have drove a nail right into the quick, like as not."

I ordered the coachman to be called. It turned out that Ermolai hadn't lied: the shaft horse really couldn't put its injured hoof down. I at once gave instructions to have the offending shoe taken off and to place the animal on damp clay.

"Well, now, what are your orders? Should I hire horses to go to Tula?" Ermolai would give me no peace.

"Why, is it possible to find any horses in this backwoods?" I raised my voice in involuntary vexation. The village we found ourselves in was not on the map, godforsaken; all its inhabitants apparently hadn't a whole rag to their backs; we had encountered difficulty in finding a hut, nothing as palatial as one with a chimney but just something halfway roomy.

"It's possible," Ermolai answered with his usual imperturbability. "What you said about this village is true enough; however, there was a certain peasant that used to live in this very place—and he was ever so smart! And rich! Had nine horses. He died, and his oldest son runs everything now. A fellow who's a fool amongst fools, but for all that, he hasn't managed to waste all of his father's property. We'll get the horses from him. Give me the word and I'll fetch him. His brothers, I've heard, are keen lads, but just the same, he's the head of the family."

"But how is that?"

"Why, here's how—he's the oldest! Which means the younger ones must knuckle under." Here Ermolai voiced his opinion of younger brothers in general, using strong (and unprintable) terms. "I'll bring him here. He's a simple man. A fellow like that—shouldn't be much trouble to come to terms with him!"

While Ermolai was going after the "simple" man it occurred to me: wouldn't it be better if I went to Tula myself?

377

In the first place, having been taught by experience, I had but poor confidence in Ermolai: I had once sent him to town to make some purchases; he had promised to carry out all my commissions in a single day, and had disappeared for all of a week; he had spent all the money on drink and came home on foot, although he had started out in a racing droshky. Secondly, there was a horse trader I knew in Tula—I might buy a horse from him to replace the lamed shaft horse.

"The matter is settled!" I reflected. "I'll make the trip myself; as for sleeping, I can do it as we ride along; fortunately the tarantass is a comfortable one."

"I've brought him!" Ermolai exclaimed, barging into the hut a quarter of an hour later. His entrance was followed by that of a well-grown muzhik in a white shirt, blue breeches, and bast sandals, almost an albino, shortsighted, with a small wedge-shaped red beard, a long puffy nose, and a gaping mouth. He really did look like a simple soul.

"Here you are, if you please," Ermolai announced. "He's got the horses, and he's agreeable."

"That is, I mean to say—" the muzhik began in a husky voice and haltingly, tossing his wispy hair and fiddling with the hat he was holding. "I, I mean to say—"

"What do they call you?" I asked.

The muzhik fixed his eyes on the floor, as though he had fallen into thought. "What do they call me, you mean?"

"Yes; what's your name?"

"Why, my name would be . . . Philothei."

"Well, here's what, brother Philothei: you, I've heard tell, own some horses. Bring over a team of three: we'll hitch them to my tarantass—I've got a light one—and you can drive me to Tula. There'll be a moon out tonight; it won't be dark, and we'll have a cool night for driving. What's the road like hereabouts?"

"The road? The road's not so bad. It'll be fourteen mile or so to the main highway, all in all. There's one spot . . . that's not so good; but otherwise it's not so bad."

"Just what is the spot like that's not so good?"

"Well, we'll have to ford a river."

"Why, are you going to Tula yourself?" Ermolai asked me.

"Yes, I'm going myself."

"Well!" remarked my faithful servant and shook his head. "Well, well, well!" he repeated, spat in disgust, and went out. The trip to Tula evidently no longer held any attraction for him; it had turned into a trifling and uninteresting matter.

"Do you know the road well?" I turned to Philothei.

"How could I help knowing the road! Only thing is, I mean to say, you may do as you like, but I can't go . . . on account of how could a body up and go, all of a sudden, like—"

It turned out that Ermolai in hiring Philothei had declared that he wasn't to worry his fool head about getting paid— and that was all he had told him! Philothei, even though a fool (according to Ermolai), had not been satisfied with this mere declaration. He began by asking fifty rubles, an enormous sum; I offered him ten rubles, a low sum. We got down to dickering; Philothei held out at first, then began to give in, but none too easily. Ermolai, who had dropped in for a moment, fell to assuring me that "This fool" — "My, but he's taken a liking to that word!" Philothei remarked in a low voice—"this fool don't know how to reckon at all," and, while he was at it, reminded me that some twenty years back a wayside inn which my mother had put up at a well-frequented spot, at the crossing of two main highways, had failed utterly because the old house serf who had been placed there as host really did not know how to reckon moneys but appraised them solely by quantity: thus, to give an instance, he would let a silver twenty-five-kopeck coin go for six big copper five-kopeck coins—not without doing some powerful swearing, however, while he was at it. "Oh, you Philothei— you're a Philothei, sure enough!" Ermolai exclaimed at last and, sorely vexed, slammed the door as he was leaving. Philothei had made no retort to him, as though realizing that to bear the name of Philothei really was somewhat awkward, and that it was actually permissible to reproach a man for such a name, even though, properly speaking, the one to blame was really the priest who hadn't been fittingly recompensed at his, Philothei's, christening.

However, get together we did, at last, on the sum of twenty rubles. Philothei went off after the horses and an hour later brought no less than five of them for me to choose from. The horses turned out to be fair, although their manes and tails were all in elflocks and their bellies big, as taut as drumheads. Two of his brothers, who did not resemble him at all, had come along with Philothei. Small, dark-eyed, pointy-nosed, they truly created the impression of "keen" lads; they talked much and fast—they "jabbered," as Ermolai put it; however, they submitted to the oldest brother.

They dragged the tarantass out from under an overhang, fussed with it and with the horses for an hour and a half, now loosening the rope traces, then pulling them tight as tight! Both of the younger brothers were absolutely set on harnessing a dappled gray as the shaft horse, " 'Cause he's the beatingest hoss goin' downhill," but it was the shaggy horse that Philothei decided on—and the shaggy horse it was that they put between the shafts!

They stuffed the tarantass with hay and shoved the lamed shaft horse's collar under the driver's seat—against the event of having to fit it to a new horse, if one were bought in Tula. Philothei, who had had time to run home and come back in his father's long white duster, tarred boots, and a towering cap that looked like a conic cake, the kind usually baked from buckwheat flour, now solemnly clambered up on the box. I took my seat and looked at my watch: it was a quarter to eleven. Ermolai did not as much as say goodbye to me but took to beating his dog Valetka; Philothei began tugging at the reins and called out "Hey, there, my little ones!" in the highest of falsettos; his brothers, one on each side, sprang forward, lashing the off horses under their bellies, and the tarantass started off, turned out of the gate into the street (the shaggy horse had been about to make a dash for its own stable but Philothei had knocked some sense into it with a few strokes of his whip), and then we popped out of the village and went tooling over a quite level road between unbroken rows of hazel bushes.

The night was a calm one and glorious, the most suitable of nights for traveling. The wind would now rustle in the bushes, making their branches sway, then it would die down, but the silvery little clouds one could see dotting the sky here and there remained motionless; the crescent moon rode high and shed a clear light all around. I stretched out on the hay and had already dozed off—but then I happened to remind myself of the spot that wasn't "so good" and became alert.

"Well now, Philothei, is it far to the ford?"

"The ford, you mean? A little over five mile, that'll be."

"A little over five miles," I reflected. "We won't get there in less than an hour. One can take a nap in the meanwhile. . . . Do you know the road well, Philothei?" I questioned him again.

"Why, how can one help knowing it—the road, that is! This isn't the first time I'm driving over it."

He added something else, but by that time I no longer heard him clearly. I was asleep.

I was aroused not by my own intention to wake up exactly an hour later (such awakenings are of frequent enough occurrence) but by some strange, even though faint, plashing and gurgling under my very ear. I raised my head.

What wonders were these? There I was, lying in the tarantass as before, while all around the tarantass, a foot below its edge, no more, a moonlit expanse of water was tremulously breaking into small distinct eddies. I looked ahead: sitting up on the box like an idol, head downcast, back bent, was Philothei, while still further ahead, just above the murmurous water, were the arc of the shaft bow and the heads and backs of the horses. And everything was so motionless, so noiseless, just as if all this were happening in some ensorcelled realm: in a dream, in a fairy-tale dream. What was going on here? I looked back from under the hood of the tarantass. . . . Why, we were in the very middle of the river; its bank was thirty paces away.

"Philothei!" I called out.

"What is it?" he responded.

"How can you ask 'What'? Be reasonable! Where in the world are we?"

"In the river."

"I see that we're in the river! Why, at that rate we'll soon drown. Is that the way you cross a ford? Eh? Why, you're asleep, Philothei! I wish you'd answer."

"I've slipped up a mite," responded my charioteer. "I guess I took and swerved aside, for my sins, and now we've got to wait a bit."

"What do you mean, we've *got* to? Whatever are we going to wait for?"

"Why, now, let Shaggy get his bearings; whichever way he turns, now, that's the way we've got to go."

I moved up a little higher in the hay. The shaft horse's head did not as much as stir above the water. The only thing that could be seen in the clear moonlight was one of its ears barely, barely moving, now backward, now forward.

"Why, he's asleep, too, that shaggy horse of yours!"

"No," answered Philothei. "He's sniffing the water now."

And again everything fell quiet, save for the water plashing as faintly as before. I, too, became comatose.

Moonlight, and night, and river, and we in the midst of that river. . . .

"What's that hissing noise?" I asked Philothei.

"That? Them's ducklings amongst the reeds . . . and then, again, it might be snakes."

Suddenly the head of the shaft horse began to toss, its ears pricked up, it snorted, stirred. "Gid-gid-gid-gidddap!" Philothei suddenly started yelling at the top of his voice and, rising in his seat, took to brandishing his whip. The tarantass instantly budged with a jerk; it plunged ahead against the river waves and started off, lurching and rocking. At first it seemed to me that we were going under, sinking into the depths; however, after two or three jolts and dips the expanse of water seemed, somehow, to have lowered abruptly. It kept getting lower and lower, the tarantass seemed to spring out of it—there, the wheels had already appeared, and the tails of the horses—and now, raising mighty and great showers of drops that scattered in the nacreous light of the moon into sheaves of diamonds—no, not diamonds but sapphires—the horses blithely and all together drew us up on the sandy bank and came out on the road, going uphill and vying with one another as they stepped out with their glisteningly wet legs.

"Well," the notion popped into my head, "will Philothei say now: 'I was right after all,' or something of that sort?" Philothei, however, did not say a word. Consequently I in my turn did not deem it necessary to upbraid him for his carelessness and, settling down in the hay, made another try at falling asleep.

However, fall asleep I could not, not because I wasn't tired after the day's hunting and not because the alarm I had just experienced had driven off sleep, but because we now happened to be passing through stretches that were far too beautiful to miss. There were far-spreading, wide-open, grassy water-meadows with a host of small glades, little lakes, rills, creeks overgrown at each end with osiers and willow bushes: forthrightly Russian stretches, beloved of the Russian folk, like those to which the legendary Men of Might of our ancient tales-of-things-that-were would betake themselves to hunt for white swans and gray wild ducks with bow and arrow. The well-beaten road wound along in a yellowish ribbon, the horses ran lightly—and I could not close my eyes for admiring the scene! And all this was flowing by so gently and smoothly under the friendly moon. Take Philothei—well, even he was profoundly stirred.

"Those go by the name of Saint Egor's meadows amongst us," he turned around to me. "And after them, now, will come the Grand Duke's meadows; there's no other such meadows in all Russia. My, but how beautiful they are!" The shaft horse snorted and shook itself. "The Lord be with thee!" Philothei addressed it staidly and in a low voice. "How beautiful they are!" he repeated and sighed, and then let out a prolonged grunt. "There, the haymowing will start soon, and what a world of that hay they'll rake in—something awful! Then, too, there's shoals of fish in them creeks. Bream *that* big!" he added in singsong. "In short, there's no need of dying." He suddenly lifted his head: "Eh, look at that, will you! Over that lake, now—is that a crane standing there? Can it be catching fish even at night? Eh, drat it! That's a broken-off branch and no crane. Sure went wide of the mark. And it's the moon that's misleading you all the while."

Thus did we ride on and on. . . . But then the meadows came to an end at last, patches of woodland appeared and plowed fields; a hamlet off to one side winked with two or three lights; only a couple of miles remained to the main highway. I fell asleep.

When I woke up anew it was not of my own volition. This time it was Philothei's voice that roused me.

"Master, oh master!"

I sat up. The tarantass was halted on a level spot, in the very middle of the main highway; turned around on his box to face me, with his eyes distended (I was actually astonished: I hadn't imagined that his eyes were so big), Philothei was significantly and mysteriously whispering: "Wheels rattling! Wheels rattling!"

"What are you saying?"

"I'm saying, there's wheels rattling. Bend down, now, and listen. Hear them?"

I put my head out of the tarantass, held my breath—and actually caught, somewhere far, far behind us, a faint intermittent rattling, apparently that of rolling wheels.

"Hear them?" Philothei repeated.

"Well, yes," I answered. "There's a carriage of some sort coming."

"No, you don't hear right—listen! There! Jingle bells . . . and whistling, too. Hear it? Take your cap off, now—you'll hear better."

I didn't take my cap off but did cup my ear. "Why, yes— could be. What of it?"

Philothei turned around to his horses. "That's a cart rolling along. Unloaded; the wheels are rimmed with iron," he remarked and picked up his reins. "There's a bad lot riding in it, for there's many of them that's up to mischief hereabouts, close to Tula."

"What bosh! What makes you suppose that they're simply bound to be a bad lot?"

"It's the truth I'm telling you. With jingle bells . . . and in an unloaded cart—what else should they be?"

"Well, now, is it still very far to Tula?"

"Why, there's still ten mile to go, and there's never a dwelling hereabouts."

"Well, in that case drive livelier; no use hanging around here."

Philothei brandished his whip, and the tarantass again rolled on.

Although I hadn't placed any faith in what Philothei had said, I nevertheless could no longer fall asleep. What if all this were really so? An unpleasant feeling stirred in me. I sat up in the tarantass (I had been lying down until then) and began looking to this side and that. While I had been asleep a light mist had come up—not over the earth, however, but up in the sky; it hovered high above: the crescent moon hung in it like a whitish blotch, as if amid smoke. Everything had dimmed, become confused, though lower down things could be seen more clearly. Flat, desolate stretches all around us: fields, everywhere fields; here and there low bushes, ravines—and again fields, for the most part fallow, grown over with wretched weeds. Deserted . . . dead! If only a quail would call somewhere, at least!

We rode along for half an hour or so. Philothei kept swinging his whip and clucking encouragingly, but neither he nor I spoke as much as a word. There, we'd made our way to the top of a hillock. Philothei halted the troika and immediately declared:

"Wheels rattling . . . wheels ra-attling, master!"

I again leaned out of the tarantass but I might as well have remained under its hood, so plainly, even though from afar, did the rattling of cartwheels, the sound of men shrilly whistling, the jingle of little bells and even the beat of horses' hoofs reach my ears; I thought I heard even singing and laughter. The wind was, it is true, coming from that direction, but there was no doubt that the unknown wayfarers had drawn nearer to us by a mile—or even two, perhaps.

Philothei and I exchanged glances; he merely shoved his hat from the nape of his neck down over his forehead and at once, bending over his reins, started lashing the horses. They dashed off at a gallop, but gallop for long they could not and fell into a trot again. Philothei kept on lashing them: we simply had to get away!

I could not account to myself why I, who at first had not shared Philothei's suspicions, should now suddenly arrive at the conviction that the men riding behind us were, sure enough, a bad lot. I had heard nothing new; there were still the same jingle bells, the same rattling of an unloaded cart, the same intermittent whistling, the same vague hubbub. . . . But now I no longer had any doubts—Philothei could not have been mistaken!

And now another twenty minutes went by. During the last few of these twenty minutes, through the rattling and rumbling of my own vehicle, we could already catch a different rattling and a different rumbling.

"Stop, Philothei," said I. "It won't matter—it'll be all the same in the end!"

Philothei whoa'd in a scared way. The horses instantaneously came to a stop, as though rejoicing at the chance of a rest.

Holy fathers! The jingle bells were simply roaring at our very backs, the cart was thundering (and a jarring thunder it was), the men were whistling, shouting, and sing-

ing, the horses snorting and drumming on the ground with
their hoofs. . . .

They had caught up with us!

"Tro-o-ouble!" Philothei drawled in an undertone, and,
with an irresolute cluck, fell to urging on the horses. But at
that same instant something dashed forward, yelped, boomed
—and the most tremendous of rattletrap carts, harnessed
with a troika of lean horses, made a sharp turn and, like a
whirlwind, drove around us, galloped ahead, and at once
fell into a walk, blocking the road.

"That's a highwaymen's trick, if there ever was one,"
Philothei commented in a whisper.

I must confess I felt a chill go through my heart. I began
straining my eyes, peering into the semidarkness of moonlight veiled over with vapors. Half a dozen men in shirts,
their peasant overcoats unbuttoned, were half sitting, half
lying in the cart ahead of us; two of them were bareheaded;
their big booted feet hung dangling over the tailboard, their
arms were jiggling up and down aimlessly, their bodies were
bouncing. . . . A drunken lot, it was plain to see. Some of
them were bawling at the top of their lungs—just so, whatever happened to pop into their heads; one was whistling
very shrilly and in perfect tune, another was cursing; seated
on the box and driving was some giant or other in a sheepskin jacket. They were going at a walk, as if they were
paying no attention to us. What could we do? We went in
their wake, likewise at a walk, willy-nilly.

For a quarter of a mile or so did we move along in such
fashion. The suspense was excruciating. As for escaping, defending ourselves—there was no use in even thinking of
anything of that sort. There were six of them, and what
wouldn't I have given for just a stick! Turn around? Why,
they would immediately catch up with us. I recalled a line
of Zhukovsky's (in a passage where he speaks of the
murder of Field Marshal Kamensky):

The brigand's ax, a scurvy weapon . . .

Or else they would tighten a filthy rope about your windpipe, and into a ditch with you! Lie there, rattling in your
throat and threshing about like a rabbit in a twitch-up
noose. . . .

Eh, things were in a bad way!

But there they were, going at the same walk and paying no attention to us.

"Philothei!" I whispered. "Make a try for it—go more to the right, as if you meant to pass them."

Philothei made a try, going to the right—but the others immediately went to the right as well. Passing them was out of the question.

Philothei made another attempt: he went to the left. But they would not let him get past their cart this time either. They even burst out laughing. Which meant that they were deliberately blocking us.

"Highway robbers, sure as sure," Philothei whispered to me over his shoulder.

"But what are they waiting for?" I asked, likewise in a whisper.

"Well, up there ahead, in the hollow, there's a little bridge over a stream—that's where they'll finish us off. That's how they always work it—near bridges. Our goose is cooked, master!" he added with a sigh. "It's hardly likely they'll let us off alive, because their main concern is to hide all traces. There's one thing I feel sorry about, master: there go my three horses—my brothers, now, will never get them!"

I should have wondered at this point how Philothei could possibly be worrying about his horses at such a moment but, I confess, I myself had other things on my mind besides him. "Will they really kill us?" I kept repeating to myself. "For what reason? I'll give them everything I've got anyway—"

But the little bridge was getting ever nearer, was becoming more and more clearly visible.

Suddenly raucous whoops broke out, the troika ahead of us seemed to swirl up—it dashed away and, having reached the little bridge, halted in mid-career as if it were rooted to the spot, a trifle to one side of the road. My heart simply sank within me.

"Oh, brother Philothei," said I, "it's our death we're driving to. Forgive me if I have brought your death upon you."

"What fault is it of yours, master! There's no getting around one's fate. There, Shaggy, my faithful little horse," Philothei apostrophized the shaft horse, "get going, brother, go on! Serve out your last service! It's all one. . . .

387

God's blessing be upon us!" And he let his troika out in a trot.

We began nearing that little bridge, nearing that sinister cart, which was standing stock-still. Everything had fallen quiet within it, as if deliberately. Not a peep out of them! It was the stillness of a pike, or a hawk, or any feral beast as its prey draws near. There, we came abreast of the cart . . . when suddenly the giant in the sheepskin jacket leaped out of it—and headed straight for us.

Never a word did he say to Philothei, yet the latter immediately drew his reins tight of his own accord. The tarantass came to a stop.

The giant placed both hands on the carriage door and, inclining his shaggy head forward and baring his teeth in a grin, speaking in a quiet, even voice, delivered the following in a factory hand's patter:

"Honored sir, it's from an honest feast we're coming, from a wedding; it's one of our fine fellows that went and got wed and, all fitting and proper, we put him to bed. All of us lads are young and devil-may-care; we sure drank a lot at that there affair, but now we have nothing to sober up on. So won't your gracious self be so kind and favor us with some small change—oh, ever so trifling a sum, enough for a pint or so for each man jack of us, shall we say? We would drink to your health, we would toast your honor; but if you shouldn't do us that favor—well, we beg you not to be vexed at us!"

"What is this?" the thought came to me. "Mockery? Derision?"

The giant was still standing there, with his head down. At that same instant the crescent moon crept out of the mist and shed its light on his face. It was smiling fatuously, was that face, smiling with eyes and with lips. Yet there was no threat to be seen there . . . but it did seem to be all on the alert . . . and the teeth were so white and big. . . .

"It'll be a pleasure . . . here you are," I hastened to say and, getting the purse out of my pocket, I took two silver rubles out of it (at that time silver coin was still current in Russia). "There, if that will do."

"Many thanks!" the giant rapped out in soldierly fashion, and his thick fingers made an instant snatch—no, not at the purse and everything in it, but only at those two rubles. "Many thanks!" He tossed back his hair and ran over to the

388

cart. "Lads!" he shouted. "The traveling gentleman has been
kind enough to give us two silver rubles." The others suddenly broke into terrific gabbling. The giant piled up on the
box.

"May good luck stay with you!"

And that was the last we saw of them. The horses started
off, and the cart went thundering uphill—there, one more
fleeting glimpse of it against the streak of darkness that divided earth from sky, and it dropped out of sight as it
topped the rise.

There, neither the rattling of wheels, nor the shouting,
nor the jingle of bells was any longer to be heard.

A dead hush fell over everything.

Philothei and I didn't recover any too quickly.

"Ah, you, what a tomfool!" he got out at last and, taking
off his hat, fell to crossing himself. "A tomfool for sure,"
he added and turned around to face me, rejoicing all over.
"And yet he must be a good man, for sure! Now, now, now,
my little ones! Shake a leg! You'll come through safe and
sound! All of us will! It was him that wouldn't let us
drive past—it was him, now, that was driving the horses.
What a tomfool, that lad. Gid-gid-gid-gidddap—God be with
you!"

I, too, kept silent, but I felt fine at heart. "We'll come
through safe and sound!" I repeated to myself and sprawled
out in the hay. "We got off cheap!" I even felt somewhat
ashamed—why had I ever recalled that line of Zhukovsky's?
Suddenly an idea came into my head.

"Philothei?"

"What is it?"

"Are you married?"

"I am that."

"And have you any children?"

"Yes, I have children, too."

"How is it you didn't call them to mind, then? You felt
sorry about the horses, but what about your wife, your children?"

"But why should I feel sorry about them? For it weren't
they who were about to fall into the hands of thieves. Still,
I did have them in mind all the while. And I have them in
mind right now, ever so much." Philothei was silent for a

space. "Maybe it was . . . on account of them that God spared you and me."

"But come, weren't they really highwaymen, by chance?"

"Why, how can one tell? Can one get inside another man's soul? Another man's soul is a darksome thing, we all know that. Still, it's always best to have God on your side. No, I always keep my family in mind. Gid-gid-gidddap, my little ones, get going, and God be with you!"

It was almost daylight when we were driving up to Tula. I was lying in the unconscious state of half-sleep.

"Master," Philothei suddenly spoke to me, "do take a look: there they are, standing near the pothouse. That's their cart."

I raised my head: there they were, true enough, and their cart was there, and so were their horses. The familiar giant in the short coat suddenly appeared on the threshold of the drinking establishment. "It's your money we're drinking up, sir!" he called out, waving his cap. "Well, now, coachman," he added, with a wag of his head in Philothei's direction, "I guess you got a good scare that time, eh?"

"Merry as can be, that man," Philothei commented after driving a hundred and fifty feet from the pothouse.

We arrived in Tula at last; I bought bird shot and, while I was at it, tea and spirits, and even got a horse from the dealer I knew. At noon we set out on our return trip. As we were driving by the spot where we had first heard the rattling of the cartwheels behind us, Philothei—who, having had a drop or two in Tula, turned out to be quite a talkative fellow (he even told me fairy tales!)—as we were driving by the spot, Philothei suddenly broke into laughter.

"But do you remember, master, how I kept saying to you all the time: 'Wheels rattling . . . rattling, now, rattling!' " He swept his arm wide several times. The verb struck him as most amusing, somehow.

That same evening we came back to his village.

I told Ermolai of the incident we had been through. Since he happened to be sober he expressed no sympathy whatsoever and merely hm'd, whether in approval or reproach was something which he himself, I suppose, could not have told. But two days later he informed me with satisfaction that on that very night when Philothei and I had been on our way to Tula, and on that very same road, some merchant or other had been robbed and murdered. I at first did not believe this news, but later on was compelled to do so: its authenticity was confirmed for me by the commissary of rural police, who had come galloping to the inquest. Hadn't it been from this very "wedding" that our devil-may-care fellows were returning, and wasn't the merchant the "fine lad" whom they had, in the words of the waggish giant, "put to bed"?

I stayed on for five days more in Philothei's village. Each time I met him I would say to him:

"Well, are the wheels rattling?"

"A merry fellow, that was," he would answer me each time, and start laughing in his turn.

EPILOGUE:
FOREST AND STEPPE

. . . And, by degrees, he felt that he was drawn
Back to the land, the garden's shaded lawn,
Where age-old lindens their giant shadows spread,
And lilies of the valley their virgin fragrance shed;
Where weeping willows, in a straggling row,
Over the dam their rounded heads bend low;
Where fair oaks guard rich fields of cornstalks fair,
And nettles and wild hemp make pungent the spring
    air. . . .
There, there to go; there the free meadows seek,
Where earth like velvet lies, as black and rich
    and sleek;
Where, like a sea, where'er the eye may turn,
Billow on billow the stalks of ripe rye churn;
Where sunlight streams, gold-heavy to the sight,
From out the rounded clouds that float translucent,
    white—
There all is fine. . . .

*   —From a poem consigned to the flames*

It may well be that the reader has by now become somewhat wearied of my sketches; I hasten to reassure him by
promising to limit myself to those fragments already in
print; yet, in parting from him, I cannot refrain from saying
a few words about hunting.

Hunting with gun and dog is splendid in itself, *für sich,*

as they used to say in the old days; however, even if we suppose that you are not a hunter born, you, nonetheless, love nature; you cannot, therefore, help envying us of the hunting fraternity. . . . Hearken, then.

Do you know, for instance, what a delight it is to venture forth in the spring, before the dawn glow? You come out on the front porch. Stars are blinking here and there in the dark-gray sky; a humid breeze comes surging in a light wave from time to time; you can catch the restrained, indistinct whispering of night; the trees, drenched in shadow, are faintly murmurous. There, a carpet is spread on the cart, the chest with the samovar is put at your feet. The off horses are shrinking from the chill, snorting, and shifting their legs daintily; a brace of white geese, who have awakened just now, makes its way silently and leisurely across the road. Beyond the wattle fence, in the garden, the watchman is peacefully snoring; every sound seems to remain fixed in the still air, seems to remain fixed and does not pass on.

There, you are seated; the horses spring forward as one, the cart has started with a great clatter. You are off, off past the church, going downhill to the right, crossing the dam. The vapor is barely beginning to swirl up like smoke from the pond. Feeling a trifle chill, you muffle your face in the collar of your overcoat; you feel like dozing. The horses splash their hoofs noisily through puddles, the driver is whistling softly and intermittently.

But now you have covered about three miles . . . the rim of the sky is glowing crimsonly; the jackdaws in the birches are awakening, flitting ungainly from branch to branch; the cock sparrows are chirking near the weather-beaten hayricks. The air grows light, the road is plainer, the sky becomes clear, the small clouds show white, the fields green. Rushlights burn red within huts; voices, still sleep-laden, are heard outside the gates. And in the meanwhile the dawn glow is bursting into flame: there, bands of gold have already stretched themselves across the sky, steaming mist is swirling in the ravines, skylarks are sonorously singing, the predawn wind has started to blow, and gently the purple sun floats to the surface. Light will burst forth in a very torrent; your heart will flutter into alertness, like a bird. What freshness, lightness, loveliness! You can see far all around you. There, beyond that copse, lies the village; there, somewhat farther off, is another, with a white church; over there is a small grove of birches on a hill; beyond it lies the swamp for which you are heading. Go faster, you horses, faster! Onward, at a full trot!

Only a couple of miles left, no more. The sun is rising fast; the sky is clear. The weather will be glorious. A herd of cows has started from the village, ambling toward you. By now you have gotten up on the hill. What a view! The river winds along for six miles or so, gleaming dully blue through the mist; beyond it lie meadows of a watery green, beyond the meadows are gently sloping knolls; lapwings, calling, are soaring over the swamp; through the moist glitter suffusing the air the far-off vista is clearly emerging—not at all the way it does in summer. How freely the breast breathes, how quickly the limbs move, how much stronger man grows when enveloped by the fresh breath of spring!

And what about a summer morning in July? Who, save a hunter, has experienced what a joy it is to roam at dawn through the bushes? The tracks of your feet fall in a green line on the dewy, whitened grass. You part a dripping bush—and the accumulated warm night smell breathes full upon you; the air is all saturated with the fresh bitterness of wormwood, the honey of buckwheat and clover; in the distance, like a wall, stands an oak forest, and it glistens and glows crimson in the sun; the air is still fresh, yet one already feels that sultriness is not far off. Your head spins languidly from the excess of sweet smells. There is no end to the brushwood—save that, here and there, the ripening rye shows yellow and the buckwheat reddens in short narrow streaks.

And now you catch the creaking of a cart; the muzhik drives at a walk and makes sure to put his horse in the shade beforehand. You exchange greetings with him and go on—the clanking of a scythe rings behind you. The sun is climbing higher, ever higher. The grass has dried quickly. There, the day has already become sultry. An hour passes, then another. The sky darkens at the edges; the motionless air breathes forth prickly sultriness.

"Where could a body get a drink of water here?" you ask a reaper.

"Why, you'll find a wellspring down there, in the ravine."

You make your way down, through thick hazelnut bushes entangled with clinging grass, to the bottom of the ravine. Sure enough, right by the steep side, a spring lurks; a scrub oak has greedily thrown its pawlike branches over the water; from the bottom, covered with fine, velvety moss, great silvery bubbles rise, swaying. You throw yourself on the ground; you drink your fill at last, yet you feel too lazy to stir. You are in the shade, breathing in the fragrant dampness, you feel fine, but across from you the bushes are becoming incandescent and seem to be turning yellow.

But what was that, just now? The wind has made a sudden swoop and sped by; the air has shuddered all about you: is it going to thunder, by any chance? You come out of the ravine: what's that leaden streak on the horizon? Is it the sultriness intensifying? Or a cloud drawing nearer? But there —a lightning flash shows faintly. Eh, but that's a thunderstorm coming up! The sun is still shining brightly all around: it's still possible to hunt. The cloud grows, however; its foremost edge balloons like a sleeve, bends over in an arc. The grass, the bushes, everything has suddenly darkened. Hurry! There, that looks like a hay barn—hurry! You've managed to reach it by running, have gone in. What a rain, eh? And those lightnings? Here and there, through the straw thatch, water drips on the fragrant hay.

However, the sun has begun to shine again blithely. The storm has passed; you step outside. My God, how gaily everything sparkles all around, how fresh the air is and how rarefied, what a smell there is of strawberries and mushrooms!

But now evening comes on. The evening glow has flamed into a conflagration and encompassed half the sky. The sun is setting. The air is, at close range, somehow especially transparent, just as though of glass; in the distance a soft glow, warming the eye, is nestling down; a crimson sheen is falling with the dew upon the meadows that so recently were drenched by torrents of liquid gold; from the trees, from the bushes, from the tall hayricks, long shadows have begun to scamper.

The sun has set; a star has kindled, and is quivering in the fiery sea of the sunset. There, it pales; the sky turns indigo; individual shadows disappear; the air becomes swollen with murk. Time to be heading home, to the village, to the hut where you are to pass the night. Throwing the gun over your shoulder you walk rapidly, disregarding your fatigue. And in the meanwhile night is coming on; by now you can't see a thing twenty paces off; the dogs are barely perceptible white blotches in the gloaming ahead. Over there, above the black bushes, the rim of the sky grows vaguely brighter. What can it be? A house burning? No; it is the moon rising. And over there, below, to the right, the little lights in the village are already aglimmer. And here, at last, is your hut. Through the small window you see the table, covered with a white cloth, a candle burning, the supper waiting. . . .

Or else you order the racing droshky to be harnessed and set out for the forest, after woodcock. It is a blithe thing to be making your way over a narrow path, between two walls of tall rye. The ears of grain flick your face gently; the corn-flowers catch at the horse's legs, the quail are calling all around you; your horse is going at a lazy trot. And here is the forest. Shade and silence. The graceful aspens babble high above you; the long, drooping branches of the birches barely stir; a mighty oak stands, like some warrior, close to a beautiful linden. You are driving over a green path mottled with shadows; great yellow flies hang motionless in the aureate air and then suddenly fly off; the midges whirl in a pillar, growing lighter in the shade, darkening in the sunlight; the birds are singing peacefully. The golden little voice of the hedgesparrows sounds with innocent, garrulous joy: that voice is in keeping with the fragrance of the lilies of the valley. On, on, deeper into the forest. It becomes thicker. An inexplicable quietude falls upon your soul—and all around you, too, everything is so slumbrous and still. But now a wind has sprung up, and the treetops have turned noisy, and their noise is as of waves subsiding. Tall grasses grow here and there through last year's dark-brown leaves; there are mushrooms, standing aloof under their small caps. A white hare may leap out unexpectedly—your dog, barking resoundingly, will dash off after it. . . .

And how fine this very same forest is late in autumn, when the snipe come winging! They do not keep to the very heart of the forest; they must be sought along its edges. There is no wind, nor is there any sun, or light, or shade, or movement; an autumnal bouquet, like the bouquet of wine, is diffused through the air; a fine haze hangs in the distance over the yellow fields. Through the denuded, dark-brown boughs the still sky is serenely bleak; the last golden leaves dangle here and there upon the lindens. The dank earth is springy underfoot; the high dry stalks of grass never stir; long threads of caught gossamer shimmer on the blanched grass. The breast breathes tranquilly, yet a strange disquiet comes over your soul. You are walking along the skirt of the forest, keeping an eye on your dog, yet at the same time beloved images, beloved faces, those of the dead and the living, come to memory; long-slumbering impressions unexpectedly awaken; the imagination soars and sweeps along like some bird, and everything moves and stands so clearly before your eyes. The heart either suddenly quivers and pounds, passionately plunging ahead, or becomes irretrievably sunk in recollections. All your life unrolls before you lightly and quickly, like a scroll; a man is master of all his past, of all his senses, of all his forces, of all his soul. And nothing around him hinders him—there is no sun, nor wind, nor noise. . . .

And what of the autumnal day, clear, a trifle chill (actually frosty in the morning), when some birch, as though it were a tree out of a fairy tale, all of gold, stands out like a beautiful painting against the pale-blue sky; when the low sun no longer warms yet shines brighter than the sun of summer, while the small grove of aspens is shot through and through with glitter, as though it were a lissome and light thing for it to be standing there denuded; when the hoarfrost is still showing white at the bottom of the dales, while the fresh breeze stirs, ever so quietly, the fallen, mummified leaves and drives them along; when blue waves race joyously along the river, making the geese and ducks scattered over it bob rhythmically, and a mill, half-screened by osiers, is clattering away in the distance, with pigeons rapidly circling over it, turning the radiant air to motley. . . .

Fine, also, are the misty days of summer, even though hunters have no great love for them. On such days you can't shoot: a bird, fluttering out from under your very feet, vanishes instantly in the whitish murk of the unmoving fog. But how still, how inexpressibly still, everything around you is! Everything has awakened, and everything is keeping silent. You walk past a tree—it will not stir: it is blissfully slothful. Through the fine haze evenly diffused in the air a long furrow shows black before you. You take it for a forest close by; you approach: the forest transforms itself into a high hedge of wormwood growing on the boundary of a field. Above you, around you—everywhere—is the fog. But now the breeze stirs slightly: a tatter of pale-blue sky emerges dimly through the thinning haze, now seemingly beginning to swirl like smoke; an aureately yellow ray will suddenly burst through, streaming in a lengthy torrent, lashing down on the fields, then coming to rest against a grove—and lo, everything is veiled over again. For a long time does this struggle go on, but how unutterably magnificent and clear the day becomes when the light finally triumphs and the last billows of the warmed fog at first roll together and spread like table covers, then coil and vanish in the profound, gently shining height. . . .

But now you've gotten ready to ride off into the far-off plain, into the steppe. For some seven miles you have been making your way over crossroads—and here is the highway, at last. You ride a long, long while past never-ending cart trains, past little wayside inns, each with a samovar hissing under an overhang, each with wide-open gates and its well, through fields the eye cannot take in, along green hemp fields. The crows flit from willow to willow; country wives, with long rakes in their hands, are wandering off into the fields; a wayfarer, in a worn caftan of nankeen, with a beggar's wallet over his shoulder, plods along with a weary step; a landowner's ponderous carriage, harnessed with six big and broken-down horses, is floating toward you. A corner of a pillow sticks out of the carriage window, while on the backboard, sitting sideways on a mat sack and holding onto a bit of rope, is an overcoated footman, spattered with mud to his very eyebrows.

And here is the little town that is the capital of the district, with its wretched, lopsided little houses of wood, it's never-ending fences, stone structures belonging to the merchantry and uninhabited, an ancient bridge over a deep gully. . . . On, on!

Now the steppe regions have begun. When you look down from a hill, what a view! Round, low knolls, plowed and sown to their very tops, surge out in broad waves; ravines grown over with bushes wind among them; small groves are scattered about like elongated islands; narrow paths run from village to village, and churches gleam whitely; between the willow bushes one glimpses the sparkle of a small river, girded in four places by dams; far off on the plain there is a single file of bustards that seem to be sticking out of the ground; a little old manor house, with its outbuildings, its orchard and threshing floor, has nestled up cozily to a small pond.

But you ride on and on. The knolls become smaller and smaller; there is almost no timber to be seen. Here it is at last—the steppe, illimitable, unencompassable to the eye!

And what about a day in winter, when you go after rabbits, wading through snowdrifts, breathing the frosty, nipping air, puckering your eyes involuntarily from the blinding, fine sparkle of the soft snow, admiring the green color of the sky over a reddish forest! . . . And what of the first days in spring, when everything around and about gleams and comes crashing down, when through the heavy vapor steaming up from thawed snow you can already scent the warmed earth; when above the thawed patches of earth, under the oblique rays of the sun, the skylarks are trustfully singing and, with blithe bluster and roar, torrents go swirling from one ravine into another. . . .

However, it is time to be done. Quite apropos, I have mentioned the spring: in the spring parting comes easy; in the spring even those who are happy are drawn to far-off vistas. . . . Farewell, reader; I wish that all things may go steadfastly well with you.

This book, designed by
William B. Taylor
is a production of
Edito-Service S.A., Geneva

Printed in Switzerland